A Season in Picardy

Sam Lutton

BookLocker
Saint Petersburg, Florida

Published by BookLocker.com, Inc., St. Petersburg, Florida.

Printed on acid-free paper.

BookLocker.com, Inc.
2021

First Edition

By the same author

The Gamov Incident

Acknowledgements

The medical practices described in this novel came from numerous sources, notably *War Surgery* (1915) by Doctor Edmond Delorme (translated into English by Doctor H. Meric); and *Stretchers* (1929), Professor Frederick A. Pottle's account of his service with an American hospital unit during World War I. Other notable memoirs include those of Doctor Eric Payten Dark, Royal Australian Military Corps, and Doctor Harry L. Smith, United States Army Medical Corps.

One can find the exploits of volunteer ambulance drivers prior to America's entry into World War I in *Friends of France—The Field Service of the American Ambulance Described by its Members*; Houghton Mifflin Company (1916).

In his 1914 article *Paris at Bay*, war correspondent Arthur Ruhl described the shooting of an Alsatian boy who playfully brandished a toy gun at German soldiers. That story provided the basis for an entry in Michael Jerome's fictional journal.

The lyrics for *Over There*, *Pack Up Your Troubles in Your Old Kit Bag*, and *Send Me Away With a Smile* came from World War I songs written by George M. Cohan, George Henry Powell, and Louis Weslyn/Al Piantadosi, respectively.

In the Epilogue, Isaac Watts penned Robert Butler's "nearly forgotten stanza" in a 1719 book of hymns entitled *The Psalms of David*.

Other authors, historians, and writings I have no doubt forgotten or misremembered also provided valuable insights into the lives, moods, and attitudes of that vanished generation who experienced "the war to end all wars."

Have you forgotten yet?...

Do you remember the stretcher-cases lurching back
With dying eyes and lolling heads—those ashen-grey
Masks of the lads who once were keen and kind and gay?
Have you forgotten yet?...

Look up, and swear by the green of the spring that you'll never
forget.

Siegfried Sassoon; *Aftermath* (1919)

Prologue

- 1 -

Arrondissement de Passy
Paris, France
April 1918

Police Superintendent Fernand Raux opened the dog-eared case file and slowly thumbed his way through a half-dozen crime scene photographs of the dead soldier.

Unsolved homicides were a sour reality of his profession, but the murder of a decorated military officer during wartime was uniquely repugnant, ultimate proof of man's bewildering ability to worsen a catastrophe. A soldier might die on a battlefield, one more among the multitudes already lost, but even the most jaded combat veteran would not expect death while enjoying leave at home, and certainly not at the hands of someone other than the enemy.

Yet, such was the situation here.

With so many foreign troops blundering about these days, identifying murder suspects was doubly difficult. Still, those sometimes-troublesome allied soldiers—British, American, and dark-skinned French colonials from North Africa—were preferable to the hated *Boche*, an impious race whose minions occupied trenches a mere seventy-five kilometers from his beloved city.

However, neither jurisdictional challenges from military authorities nor the proximity of Germany's black-helmeted legions discouraged the police officer. Instead, unsolved homicides intensified his determination; a condition, his wife once remarked, that frustrated her persistent dietary ministrations to ease the worsening discomfort of his stomach ulcer.

Spousal concerns notwithstanding, Fernand Raux had few illusions. Human existence was an imperfect enterprise. Justice did not always prevail over iniquity. Despite persistent efforts, a small number of killings invariably went unsolved. In those instances Raux took solace from his belief in a Final Reckoning. Individuals who committed murder would eventually pay for their crime, if not here on Earth then certainly in the eternal fires of Hell after God passed judgment on their wretched souls.

He turned toward the rain-spattered window, his mood no less dreary than the weather. From a crumpled package he extracted a cigarette, placed the tube between his lips, and fired the tip with a silver lighter. Then his eyes returned to the file before him.

The scene documented in this manila folder was unlike the violent disorder he and his detectives typically found at a murder site. The crisp photographs suggested a peculiar neatness: an eerie staging more considerate than callous.

Nearly two months had passed since discovery of the French artillery officer's body on the Quai de Passy. Lieutenant Guy Jean Aubray, his wallet and money untouched, had suffered a single gunshot wound to the heart, no doubt fired from a pistol at close range, facts evidenced by the recovered bullet and powder burns on the soldier's blue tunic.

What piqued Raux's curiosity was the unusual positioning of Aubray's corpse. The murderer had arranged the Lieutenant's body neatly, as a mortician might for viewing: legs straight, ankles together, hands crossed at the chest. Pinned to dead soldier's tunic was the *Croix de Guerre,* France's newest decoration for gallantry in wartime. Centered on the ribbon was a red enameled star, an award reserved for those wounded in battle. A few blood specks marred the red and green-striped ribbon attached to the medal.

The obvious signs of respect led Raux to suppose the officer's death might have been unintentional. Was the killer another soldier, perhaps an acquaintance? Was this crime the appalling result of a drink-induced argument? The bullet—an 8mm round presumably fired from a standard-issue French military revolver—bolstered his 'comrade in arms' theory.

He took a deep drag on his cigarette, blew a shivering blue plume towards the high-coffered ceiling of his office, and continued to study photographs.

Aubray's uniform was unkempt—not what one might expect of a decorated officer. The soldier had also skipped a shave and his mustaches needed fresh wax; evidence of a man who no longer cared about his appearance.

The proximity of the Lieutenant's body to the American Ambulance Field Service headquarters on Rue Raynouard made the Hottinguer mansion a logical starting point for this investigation. Unfortunately, exhaustive interviews with three-dozen American officers and enlisted men yielded no viable suspects.

The dead soldier's widow however, had appeared apprehensive—perhaps even a little guilty—as though she understood the motive behind her husband's premature demise. Further investigation into Madame Lizette Aubray's social life revealed transient affairs with several men—illicit liaisons conducted while her husband was away at the front. Discovery of her marital deceits did not surprise Raux. In addition to obvious signs of discomfiture during that first interview, Madam Aubray exuded a slightly tainted demeanor; a sly amorality not wholly concealed by fine clothes.

Did Lieutenant Aubray's shabbiness indicate that he'd discovered his wife's infidelities? Did he become despondent and indifferent regarding his personal appearance? Perhaps he met death while confronting his wife's latest lover—possibly another soldier. It was a promising hypothesis but nothing substantial came of it. Predictably, his re-reading of the old file uncovered nothing new.

Raux took a final puff from his Gauloises Caporal and then snubbed out the half-smoked cigarette in the heavy glass bowl of his ashtray: a monstrosity created from the hollowed out and preserved three-toed hind foot of an African elephant. The grotesque but functional artifact—a bizarre fiftieth birthday gift from his otherwise discerning wife—held a dozen or more crushed cigarette butts.

He raked his tongue with front teeth but an acrid, tarry residue persisted. His doctor had told him nicotine could have a calming effect on the nerves, but forty cigarettes a day might be overdoing it.

Raux unclasped pince-nez and gently rubbed the bridge of his nose with thumb and forefinger. He tucked glasses into a vest pocket, closed the folder and returned it to the desk drawer. The clock mounted on the wall to his left emitted eight soft chimes; time to go home. He stood and stretched, grimacing as blood tingled through stiff muscles.

If his visceral hunch was correct and Aubray's killer was indeed another soldier, one who had not already met death in a filthy, vermin-infested trench, then something might yet develop. Unfortunately, solving murder cases became less of a possibility with each passing week.

Still, one must always hope for the best.

- 2 -

Michael Jerome slithered his way through the bone-chilling mud of a once-fertile wheat field.

High overhead a German flare suddenly hissed and sputtered beneath a tiny white parachute. He lay still and sucked in air through clenched teeth. The aromas of death, burnt sulfur and wet, freshly churned earth seeped into his nostrils.

The flare's slowly rotating incandescence revealed a shattered landscape trembling with shadows. Loose strands of barbed wire dangled from canted wooden posts. His eyes followed the rusted skeins as they uncoiled across a pockmarked countryside littered with abandoned weaponry, broken equipment, and fallen soldiers.

From a low hill four hundred yards from where he lay came the hollow *tap-tap-tap* of an enemy machine gun. He held his breath for a long moment while the deadly clatter echoed once more.

Cowering in the darkness of No Man's Land was not where he was supposed to be. Despite the grim military situation, nobody expected ambulance drivers to leave their vehicles and remove wounded men from a still-contested battlefield; stretcher-bearers had that dangerous but necessary responsibility. Even so, there were too many casualties for the unarmed and overworked *brancardiers* to handle. Jerome could not sit dry and comfortable inside his ambulance while soldiers lay injured and waiting for medical attention.

Hours ago, this ruined farmland had clamored with ear-shattering gunfire, artillery explosions, and the screams of wounded and dying men. Nightfall had ushered in exhausted silence, an unsettled quiet broken only by intermittent shots as edgy sentries fired at shadows, real or imagined.

The flare's white-hot glow flickered several times and then winked out. A velvet gloom settled over him once more. He raised his head and then eased forward again, pushing himself through slick ooze.

The rain had passed and a pale half-moon, its milky glow filtered now and then by swiftly passing clouds, allowed Jerome to navigate the sodden field. He paused when he recognized the dull glint of a discarded French helmet, its curved metal crest reminiscent of plumed knights from a bygone era. A bareheaded man—thick black hair plastered against his skull—lay on his back and grimaced into the night sky. The bearded soldier clutched a Lebel, the durable French infantry rifle dating from the late 1880s. He turned his head as Jerome approached, and then smiled in recognition. The Frenchman's voice was no more than a hoarse whisper.

"Ce que vous apporte ici, mon ami?"

What brought me here? Jerome thought. Good question.

"The weather," he replied in French. "I came here to enjoy your fine spring sunshine."

The soldier chuckled softly.

Jerome felt a bloom of warmth inside his chest, a brotherly affection born of shared danger and unspeakable hardship. Despite fear and physical discomfort, he did not feel out of place. Strange as it may have seemed to those back home in St. Louis—especially Margaret, his quick-witted fraternal twin—here was where he belonged. Memories of his pleasant life in America were more like the recollections of a simpleton rather than what he now felt. Witnessing the daily ration of obscenities had fashioned him into something studier, adding an impermeable starch to the soft pliancy of his former being.

The war had clearly changed him, but tatters and patches of who he once was remained embedded within the fabric of his strange new self: a contrary quilting marred by the soiled threads of a haunting, dishonorable act. Jerome knew he could never dissemble those tainted strands of disrepute without unraveling the others…

With effort, he refocused attention on the Frenchman, *"Etes-vous blessé?"* Are you wounded?

"Oui, mes jambes."

He examined the soldier's legs. Hardened clots of coagulated blood had pasted trousers to wounds on both legs but there was no indication of persistent bleeding. Still, he had seen enough shattered limbs to realize the *poilu* could not move without assistance. He would have to drag the soldier to the dressing station near to where he had parked his ambulance.

Another flare popped and glittered to life, this one much closer. Both men froze.

The Maxim's hollow echoes reached his ears a split second after bullets spattered into thick mud five yards ahead of where they lay. Teeth clamped shut, Jerome held his breath and waited. An agonizing moment passed: then another row of muddy fountains erupted, not quite as close.

"L'idiot doit être aveugle," the Frenchman hissed.

Jerome tried to ignore icy fingers clawing at his insides. He said, "The idiot might be blind, my friend, but he has an excellent machine gun."

"D'accord!" the soldier whispered.

The flare fizzled and died.

"Time to go," Jerome murmured.

He grasped the Frenchman's collar and pulled him toward a blasted out section of barbed wire fence and the friendly troops beyond, an effort made easier by slippery mud. The *poilu* uttered a soft moan between clenched teeth and then became quiet. They stopped twice more on their way to the dressing station, shivering under spiraling flares as the German gunner fired random bursts.

Once inside the dressing station, Jerome watched as a weary-eyed ambulance surgeon exposed the soldier's wounds by scissoring away muddy, blood-stained trousers. The doctor gently probed both legs with black rubber-gloved fingers. "A severe injury," he told the gasping *poilu*, "but you will live to tell grandchildren how you protected France from Hun barbarians." A brief time later, Jerome helped load the bandaged and sedated soldier plus three others into his ambulance, sliding the stretchers into two-above-two racks.

Finally, an hour or so before dawn, Jerome stumbled inside makeshift quarters built of logs and sandbags. He removed his helmet and filthy trench coat and then eased himself onto an empty ammunition box. Fumbling with the sticky laces of mud-encrusted boots added to his exhaustion. Tempted by the marginal comfort of his lumpy pallet, he instead took a wash in cold water, retrieved pen and a brown leather journal from his kit bag, and began to write.

March 26, 1918 – Tuesday

Another long day... actually nearer two.

My ambulance section labored forty hours without pause or letup, driving wounded men from the dressing station west of Roye to the field hospital at Montdidier—a five-mile trip I repeated many times, bouncing and sliding over a narrow dirt road pulverized by artillery and soaked to a pudding by autumn rains.

Their suffering is a constant reminder of the cruel and contrary nature of this war and how a solitary secret can deform the normal pattern of one's life. I despair the condition in which I find myself, yet no resolution is possible without worsening an already tragic situation.

Something must change.

-3-

The soft tone of the front door chime interrupted Margaret Jerome's reading of *My Antonia*, the final volume of Willa Cather's Great Plains trilogy. She set the book aside, rose, and then strode toward the high-ceilinged foyer. Margaret swung open the massive, custom-crafted front door and stared into the troubled eyes of the uniformed Western Union delivery boy. One hand found her stomach as nausea rippled through her insides. With the other, she grasped the door's edge for support."

"I have a telegram for Mr. and Mrs. Jerome," he announced, reaching into his messenger bag. "It's from the Secretary of War," he added quietly.

Her knees quivered as the boy extended a hideous yellow envelope.

The echo of approaching footsteps on parquet worsened the hollow rush of air surging against her eardrums.

"Who is it, Margaret?" her mother called.

Please God, no… not Michael…

1

"Isn't this exciting," Beatrice Jerome said. "Sailing off to France with so many handsome young men."

Margaret met the blue eyes of her twenty-year-old sibling: a younger version of herself, trim frame made even slimmer by the tightly laced corset hidden beneath summer traveling clothes.

They stood on the promenade deck with others similarly dressed, a civilian minority scattered among increasing numbers of chattering soldiers, an ebullient chorus adding to the humdrum arising from hundreds of dockside well-wishers.

"Everyone seems so happy. There's even a brass band," Beatrice added.

Margaret gently fingered the small black rosette pinned to the material above her left breast. "Perhaps they haven't lost anyone, yet," she suggested.

Beatrice returned her attention to the long ranks of soldiers entering the ship two decks below. "Yes, that's probably it."

Margaret followed her sister's gaze as more troops dismounted Army trucks, formed in columns along Pier 2, and then boarded the USS *Mongolia*; a passenger liner turned U.S. Navy troopship moored at the Port of Hoboken.

The brown queue shuffled up the aft gangway. Each man shouldered a lumpy duffle bag and a slung rifle while grasping the gang rope with his free hand. One by one they ducked through the rectangular hatch and disappeared into the ship's interior. Most had smiles on their faces; white teeth gleaming beneath wide-brimmed campaign hats.

She turned her eyes to the crowded wharf.

A brass band played 'Yankee Doodle' from a raised platform, its high sides draped in colorful bunting—red, white, and blue folds rippling in fresh morning sunlight. Hordes of spectators and well-wishers, many waving tiny U.S. flags, sang in tune with the melody or cheered from the quay: a swirl of upturned faces and bobbing heads topped by caps, straw boaters, and a dozen styles worn by ladies plain and grand.

Policemen stood at measured intervals; their casual presence sufficient to hold the crowd behind a low barricade. Other policemen straddled well-groomed chestnut mounts and kept order along a narrow driveway clogged with a stuttering line of automobiles, Army trucks, and horse drawn carriages, each stopping to disgorge passengers before moving on. A disharmony of laughter, music, and light-hearted banter rose in soft waves, a pleasant clamor frayed and fluttered by desultory breezes chuffing up the Hudson River.

Margaret felt a cold shiver, there and gone in an instant, that left her with a sense of melancholy bewilderment. *They've forgotten the Lusitania. They don't understand what might happen to us. I pray God it never does.*

Five years earlier the Jerome family had sailed to Europe on Cunard's luxurious ocean liner RMS *Lusitania*. That delightful summer vacation was now an errant memory from another life. The *Lusitania* now lay beneath three hundred feet of water a dozen miles off the Irish coast, victim of a German submarine—a barbarous act that had claimed twelve hundred unfortunate souls.

A similar fate might await those now boarding *Mongolia*. Many of these soldiers—perhaps Beatrice and herself—might find themselves dumped into the middle of the cold North Atlantic or drowned while trapped inside the shrieking darkness of a doomed ship.

If newspaper reports were accurate, the Kaiser's U-boats roamed the sea at will, an unseen menace capable of attacking any allied vessel within range. Given the brutal nature of this latest European conflict, sailing to France aboard a vulnerable steamship was not an event one should celebrate with unrestrained enthusiasm.

Yet here she was, about to sail to war-ravaged France, plodding through a nightmare spawned by the unexpected arrival of a Western Union telegram. Barely able to stand on watery knees, she had watched her mother's trembling fingers tear open the sickly yellow envelope. That devastating missive had announced the death of Lieutenant Michael P. Jerome, only son of Emily and Big Mike; fraternal twin of Margaret; big brother to Beatrice.

Margaret refused to accept it.

In the first place, Michael wasn't a lieutenant; he was a civilian working with the American Field Service. In the second, how could such an awful thing happen? Her brother was an ambulance driver, not a front-line soldier constantly at risk. Motoring around in a rescue vehicle was not supposed to be any more hazardous than operating an automobile. He might suffer injury in an accident, but *killed* in action? That didn't seem possible.

Finally, and most compelling, Margaret believed she and her brother shared a third consciousness, a mutual awareness of extraordinary experiences felt by one or the other. That sense of psychic unity arose from several incidents in their past, events that validated and strengthened her conviction. It was something they both accepted, even without the telling.

Given her strong belief in a fraternal connection, Margaret found it impossible to accept the reality of her brother's death. If anything terrible had happened to him, then she would have sensed his distress: that shared cognizance would have signaled what Michael had felt.

But she had experienced no insight, no sudden awareness of his fate. If what the Army said was true, then Michael had suffered a violent death and Margaret had perceived nothing. How could she have been so oblivious to such a catastrophic event? Had that shared consciousness failed at a critical moment, or was their psychological kinship nothing more than comforting delusion?

The ship's horn sounded, a shuddering basso that interrupted her reverie and overwhelmed all conversation. As the deep echo faded and dock sounds returned, Margaret's eyes followed a bright yellow taxi as it eased to a stop just below where she stood.

A tall young man wearing an Army officer's uniform—riding boots, flared breeches, high-collared tunic, and visor cap—opened the rear door and stepped onto the quay. He paid the driver and chatted for a moment while a porter removed luggage from the taxi's trunk.

As he led the porter up the forward gangway—an entry reserved for passengers berthed in the upper decks—the soldier looked up, his eyes scanning the crowded rails. The gesture afforded Margaret a clear view of his face.

"There's another nice-looking man," Beatrice observed wistfully. "Not exactly handsome, but still rather pleasant to look at."

"I wonder if he truly understands what he's in for," Margaret replied.

"Do *we*?" Beatrice asked.

Margaret studied her sister's furrowed brow and slight frown.

"Do you regret leaving Mother and Father as we did?"

"A little. Do you suppose they'll ever forgive us?"

"We had no choice, you *know* that. They were on the mend, but still too sick to travel. Had we not taken their place, these tickets would have gone to waste. Besides, it took all Father's influence to secure even a single stateroom like the one we share. Given the war, it might have taken months to find another passenger ship not commandeered by the government. Meanwhile, we would have done nothing regarding Michael."

"I suppose you're right," Beatrice said. But then her lips turned slightly upward, forming a half-smile. "But Father was right about not being properly chaperoned. Do you suppose we might become the source of scandalous gossip?"

"I believe he was less concerned about the chaperone and more worried about the two of us on the same ship, travelling through dangerous waters."

Her tiny smile eased to an expression of mild concern. "Yes, of course."

The ship's horn bellowed again, an obvious signal to a waiting dock crew who manhandled fore and aft gangways, sliding them back onto the pier before taking in thick mooring ropes. A tugboat edged alongside. As the big ship eased away, dozens of additional soldiers joined Margaret and Beatrice on deck. They pressed against the rail—sometimes two and three deep—shouting and waving to the crowd. The dockside gathering became louder and more animated, their cheers unrestrained and vigorous.

The tug nudged the larger vessel farther into the Hudson River. As the space between the wharf and the troopship grew more distant, the cheering became subdued, a fading hubbub replaced by the persistent chug of the tugboat. Once clear of the dock, the tug pushed the *Mongolia's* stern upstream, a maneuver that slowly brought the Woolworth Building into view. Soaring sixty stories high—New York's tallest structure—the white Gothic tower loomed over lesser companions.

A second tug joined the first and both eased the bigger ship downstream toward Ellis Island. Soon they glided past the Statue of Liberty and then into New York's Upper Bay. Once through the narrows and down the far end of Ambrose Channel, the tugs blew their horns and turned away. The big ship answered with a double blast, gathered steam, and headed out to sea under her own power.

Rather than disperse, the passengers remained close to the rails, savoring one last look at the country they called home. Margaret watched the land slowly diminish to a thin gray hump in the distance. With her gaze fixed on the receding mainland, she thought again of the terrible sequence of events that had led her to this place. She also felt a looming sense of finality: the end of a life familiar and the beginning of one yet unknown.

As the *Mongolia* steamed eastward, trailing a curved pale wake that blended into the darker sea, the reliability of Michael's companionship, a closeness she had known since sharing their mother's womb, likewise receded from her future. The gentle roll of the ship reminded her that the once-solid ground upon which she had confidently trod for her entire life no longer existed. Absent the constancy of her brother's presence, Margaret felt herself unmoored from the life she had known for as long as she could remember.

The deepening sense of isolation increased as the sea edged skyward and swallowed the land.

2

"Good afternoon, gentlemen," the colonel said.

Subdued conversations faded to an expectant hush.

First Lieutenant Robert Myles Butler and fifteen other U.S. Army medical doctors occupied individual oak seats with attached writing tables. The matched unit reminded Butler of the vanished life of a schoolboy who once believed in magic and fairytales and honorable knights in gleaming armor; memories of a pleasant, too-brief childhood.

The inside compartment, about eighteen feet square, served as a gathering room suitable for briefings or, as it now appeared, formal presentations. Compared to the light June air on deck, the atmosphere inside the room was stale and gamey. An oscillating fan mounted on a front corner wall near the ceiling swept the compartment at regular intervals, its undulating whine reminiscent of mosquitoes on the prowl.

"For those of you whom I have not had the pleasure of meeting, I am Colonel Dawes, your commanding officer for the duration of this crossing. Welcome aboard the *Mongolia*."

The Colonel, a graying, round-faced man with liquid blue eyes, paused before continuing. His erect posture complimented an immaculate woolen uniform: high-collared tunic, Sam Browne belt, and flared breeches tapering to gleaming brown riding boots.

"I trust you found lunch in the dining room?" His question

produced nods and a few low mumbles from the assemblage. "In any case," he continued, "you are new to the Army and presumably unfamiliar with injuries incurred during wartime. This is the first of several daily gatherings, the purpose of which is to introduce you to the unique nature of battlefield wounds and their treatment. To that end, I shall begin by issuing a text which you will find invaluable."

Colonel Dawes reached for a triple stack of books resting on a nearby desktop and gave an appropriate number of copies to the first man in each of four rows. "Please be good enough to pass one to the man behind you."

Butler took his copy, a blue volume about an inch thick, and read the title stamped into the front cover:

War Surgery
Dr. Edmond Delorme
Translated to English by Dr. H. de Meric

"What I have just handed out is, for all intents and purposes, your surgical bible for the duration. Here you will discover much about the nature and treatment of war injuries. Doctor Delorme is a distinguished French military surgeon; one who has a great deal of experience in these matters."

Butler looked up and met the Colonel's watery gaze.

"Most, if not all of you," the Colonel continued, his eyes moving across the group, "have practiced surgery in civilian hospitals, in some cases for many years. You will find those technical skills invaluable. However, let me assure you that removing gall bladders and distended appendices from otherwise healthy individuals has little relevance to what you will encounter in France."

He placed both hands behind his back, one hand holding the wrist of the other, and began to pace.

"For example: A surgical procedure one might normally complete in four hours must be done in one or two, often under less-than-ideal sanitary conditions." The Colonel paused and his gaze moved from man to man. "And those of you not familiar with large scale calamities will experience first-hand—and no doubt come to despise—the true meaning of the word *triage*."

Butler removed a fountain pen and leather-covered notebook from the breast pocket of his tunic. He flipped the notebook open, unscrewed the pen's cap, and thumbed to a clean page. He wrote and then underlined the word.

The Colonel stopped pacing. "Which of you comprehend the French language sufficient to decipher what is meant by *triage*?"

The term was familiar—having to do with arranging things in order—however, Butler could not recall the exact medical context.

A red-haired captain who looked to be in his mid-thirties raised a hand and received the Colonel's quick nod in return.

"Sir, I believe the literal translation means 'sorting', does it not?"

"You are lexically correct, Captain O'Mara; but, as in most things, there is also a less obvious facet to the definition."

Butler found himself leaning forward, pen poised.

"The Latin root word is *tria*, meaning 'three'. Thus, *triage* is a three-tupled sorting procedure, one devised and first used by Doctor Dominique Larrey, a military surgeon in Napoleon's army. During a particularly bloody engagement Doctor Larrey found it necessary to categorize the vast numbers of incoming wounded. This he did, regardless of rank or noble standing, by placing them into three groups."

The Colonel stopped pacing, faced the class and extended his thumb from a closed fist raised just above his belt. "First came the walking wounded: ambulatory cases, men whose wounds posed little danger of becoming fatal." His index finger joined the thumb.

"Second were those who required immediate assistance; that is, instantly or within the hour." His middle finger popped out. "And third came the mortally wounded; soldiers beyond the help of medical expertise. The latter unfortunates were carried into death tents or placed out-of-the-way where they were left to expire from their wounds."

He lowered his hand and paused, allowing time for his students to absorb the implications.

Captain O'Mara was quick to respond. "You mean they were left to die without medical attention of any kind? But that's horrible… and unethical!" O'Mara's jaw tightened and a blush rose from beneath his stiff collar, blending with close-cropped red hair.

Colonel Dawes smiled—a sad, humorless thinning of his lips. "It is one of many silent atrocities that arise from modern warfare. A reality, I pray, to which you will never become accustomed."

Silent atrocities? It was a phrase Butler found both confounding and outrageously callous. How could an atrocity remain silent? How could a life-ending judgment, coolly imposed by one human being upon another, remain voiceless and absent of compassion or consequence?

"But Colonel," Captain O'Mara persisted, "what about our obligation to act in the best interest of the patient?"

"I presume you're referring to *Salus aegroti suprema lex*," the Colonel intoned.

"Exactly, sir."

"I fear the Latin phrases you memorized in medical school may not always apply to battlefield situations. The well-being of the patient is certainly important; however, your primary obligation as a military surgeon is unambiguous. You must always focus your efforts on those who have the best chance of survival. *That* is your duty. *That* must be your primary concern. It would be foolish, criminally so, to waste precious time on those whom fate has already condemned."

"But Colonel, suppose they are suffering and in great pain? Do we just let them be and go about our business?" the Captain asked.

"No, of course not. In those particular cases, a vascular injection containing three grains of morphine sulphate in solution will ease their transition." The Colonel turned his attention to the others. "Each of you must learn to accept that cruel reality. In the desperate circumstances you will certainly encounter—situations which no words can accurately describe—you must commend the mortally wounded to God's care."

The Captain said nothing more. However, the look in his eyes and rigid facial expression told Butler that Captain O'Mara remained unconvinced.

As did Butler. He shared the Captain's skepticism, but hesitated to agree. 'Lieutenants,' he'd been told during his Army training, 'are the lowest, saddest face on the commissioned officer totem pole. A colonel who challenges the strategy of a general might be deemed courageous; however, a lieutenant who challenges the word of a colonel is a moron.'

Nevertheless...

What Colonel Dawes had defined as a third option of battlefield *triage* was contrary to everything Butler had learned regarding patient treatment and care. Formal education notwithstanding, a shattering childhood event—the simultaneous disappearance of both parents—stood out above all others.

That singular experience had seared an indelible truth into his adolescent mind: Each human life is precious and irreplaceable. While the comforting companionship of others might partially fill the void, the sense of loss would remain forever; a diminishing but never forgotten memory of a unique presence.

Despite stern words, Butler was positive the Colonel's odious recommendation to 'ease their transition' was not a proposition he should take seriously. Rather, he believed Colonel Dawes's objective was to shock the group; to wean them from certain attitudes held by newly commissioned surgeons like those in this room. No doubt the Colonel's suggestion was part of a focused effort to acclimate civilians to the rigors of military life. What other purpose might it have? Butler could imagine no circumstance that would compel him to administer a lethal dose of morphine to a patient under his care.

But the Colonel's grim, unyielding demeanor wove a thread of uncertainty into that assumption. Butler had experienced a similar feeling at age fourteen, on the day he arrived at St. George's Academy, an event signaling the end of a long, desperate summer.

Back then another truth had etched itself into the gray folds of his youthful brain: A human life is crisscrossed with the lives of others. His path had taken him to the present—a winding avenue filled with people and events and travels that had led him first to St. George's Academy, then college, medical school, and Mount Sinai Hospital.

Now, sailing aboard this vessel bound for France, the old perception returned. Another curve along the path in his life lay before him, beyond which lay an unknown destination. As was the case a dozen years ago, he had no choice but to continue toward whatever fate God had in store for him.

He stared at his notebook.

Underneath the word *Triage,* he wrote *Silent Atrocity.*

Next to that last phrase, contained within parenthesis, he wrote: *Not possible.*

3

Margaret awoke from an afternoon nap, her body sensing the ship's movement through calm seas. She had dreamed about Michael again, a regular occurrence since learning of his death. Almost without exception the dreams were like a series of linked photographs—brief, animated images from their shared past. Most were pleasant, forcing a smile as she recalled half-forgotten events.

Others, like this one, were less like photos and more like one of those moving picture shows, but more lifelike and realistic. Staring at the ceiling, Margaret recalled the actual event that had triggered her dream.

As was customary back then, Mike and Emily Jerome fled the heat and humidity so prevalent in St. Louis during summertime, escaping to cooler weather farther north. In 1908 they, their fourteen-year-old twins, and ten-year-old Beatrice occupied adjoining suites at the Grand Hotel on Mackinac Island, a popular vacation retreat located just beyond the tip of Michigan's Upper Peninsula.

On the third or fourth day, Margaret and some new-found friends were swimming in the lake, fooling around really; splashing and dunking each other, their playful jousts taking her farther and farther from shore.

Stopping to rest, Margaret misjudged the water's depth. She stood, expecting her feet to touch bottom that wasn't there. Sinking a few inches beneath the surface, she inhaled just enough water to choke. Unable to speak or breathe, toes bouncing against the sandy bottom, water-filled eyes glimpsing flashes of unaware playmates, the voice in her mind shrieked in silent panic. In those long, terrifying seconds while she flailed and sputtered, her lungs convulsing, Margaret knew she was drowning.

At that moment she felt a strong tug on her French braid. Seconds later her feet touched sand. Michael, grasping the long rope of floating auburn hair, had towed her into shallow water. "You're okay now, Mags," he told her as she coughed sprays of water and gasped fresh air. "You're back on solid ground."

Michael had sensed her peril and saved her life.

In the quiet, semi-darkness of her shared stateroom, Margaret again felt as she had during those long breathless moments of terror: the bottom had disappeared from beneath her feet. There was no firm ground upon which to stand, but this time Michael was not here to rescue her.

As her eyes grew moist, Margaret's faith in the presumed closeness shared by twins began to waver. For some reason, she had not perceived her brother's passing. Why had his sudden death escaped her notice?

Beatrice spoke, interrupting Margaret's inner turmoil. "Are you awake?"

"Yes, I am." The tone of her voice sounded near to normal.

"We're in the first seating," Beatrice said rising from her narrow bed, "but it's not quite time for dinner. Why don't we take a little stroll around the deck?"

"All right," Margaret replied, swinging her stockinged feet to the carpeted deck. "I could do with some exercise."

"Do you suppose we'll be separated from the others?" Beatrice asked, slipping into her shoes.

"What do you mean?"

"Will we civilians be dining on decks away from the soldiers?"

"I have no idea. Why do you ask?"

Beatrice shrugged, a bit too casually. "No reason."

Margaret allowed a tiny smile to touch her lips. "Oh? Does that mean you have no interest in meeting a few of those 'handsome young men' you mentioned earlier?"

"Whatever gave you that idea?" Beatrice replied. She stood and turned her back towards Margaret. "Now, please tuck me up."

A few minutes later—corsets re-laced, dresses neatly buttoned, faces washed and makeup modestly applied—they left the stateroom and made their way to the Promenade Deck.

*

According to the mimeographed information sheet located inside their stateroom, she and Beatrice would take their meals in the Officer's Dining Room, located one deck below from where they had taken a leisurely, late afternoon stroll.

The room was larger than Margaret expected, a space filled with eight long tables arranged to seat ten diners at each. As they stood waiting for a steward, Margaret noticed the presence of two-dozen or so other women, the majority wearing nurse's garb, casually scattered among mostly uniformed men. To her mild surprise the U.S. Navy did not segregate women to an out-of-the-way corner. Stewards, it seemed, filled tables on a first-come basis, probably to expedite meal service.

"Well," Beatrice whispered. "That answers my question."

A white-vested older man approached, greeted them politely, and then escorted them to a table having two vacant seats at one end. There were no 'head' or 'foot' settings; rather, five diners sat on either side of the table facing each other. Eight soldiers rose to their feet as she and her sister approached.

"Ladies," a thin, middle-aged officer said. "Welcome. Please allow me to begin introductions."

Margaret, seated at one end of the table, knew she would not remember the names of each man so she focused on the two closest to her and Beatrice. Major Gregory, the graying officer who had provided introductions, sat directly across from her. First Lieutenant Robert Butler—the pleasant-looking young soldier from the taxi—sat beside the Major and opposite Beatrice. As Margaret unfolded her napkin, she couldn't help but wonder about the apparent coincidence of their seating arrangement.

As their steward poured water and coffee, she recognized a familiar device worn by Major Gregory and the young Lieutenant. Each had a gold-colored caduceus—a winged staff entwined with facing serpents—pinned to the high collars of their brown tunics.

"Are you a medical doctor?" Margaret asked the Major.

"Yes I am, Miss Jerome. A Regular Army surgeon no less; have been for nine years. On the other hand, Lieutenant Butler is new to the Medical Corps. What is it now, Robert? Four months?"

"Yes, just about." His voice was soft and deeply resonant.

"Doctor Butler is one of our newest surgeons. He just completed officer training at Camp Gordon."

"Where did you practice medicine before joining up?" Margaret asked the Lieutenant."

"I was a third-year surgical resident at Mount Sinai Hospital in New York." He offered a sheepish half smile.

"And now you're an Army surgeon off to war. You must be proud and excited," Beatrice said.

The tiny smile faded as he stirred cream into his coffee. "One might think that, I suppose."

Margaret found his response perplexing. The Lieutenant's voice sounded cordial but his gray eyes revealed traces of skepticism.

Major Gregory said to Beatrice, "Miss Jerome, Lieutenant

Butler—a volunteer I might add—has nonetheless expressed grave doubts about America's involvement in a European conflict."

Margaret leaned back from the table. "Doubts...?"

Her brother Michael and several of his fraternity brothers had joined the American Field Service in 1916, long before the United States officially declared war on Germany; eager young men determined to help America's oldest ally. Other young men, for religious reasons or merely less inclined to risk their lives, became conscientious objectors, some even carrying signs and marching in 'No European War' parades. Was Lieutenant Butler a sympathizer, one of those so-called 'Conchies'? If so, then why had he volunteered?

"I don't think I understand," Beatrice said to the Lieutenant.

"Nor do I," Margaret added. "You volunteered, yet you just expressed doubts about the war. That's confusing."

Butler's voice remained pleasantly calm. "Really? In what way?"

"Well," she said, "France is an ally; a dear friend who needs our help to repel an invader; a barbaric neighbor whose U-boat sank the *Lusitania*. Hundreds of innocent women and children, including more than one hundred Americans, drowned. Aren't those reasons enough for us to become involved?"

He nodded—a slight movement of his head. "I understand how the premeditated taking of innocent lives can lead to war. Such conduct by one nation toward another is often sufficient cause for a declaration."

The Lieutenant's quiet demeanor and subdued tone of voice did little to soften the now-strained atmosphere. Did he not understand what was so obvious? Kaiser Wilhelm had condoned the killing of innocent Americans. Was this young doctor blind to reality or merely deceitful? "Lieutenant Butler, I'm not sure I understand your attitude."

Butler's cloud-gray eyes reflected discomfort and a hint of awkwardness. He set the cup on its saucer and then met her stare. "I'm sorry if I have offended you, Miss Jerome. That was not my intent." His eyes moved from hers and focused on the black rosette pinned to her lapel.

Margaret could detect no deceit in his voice or facial expression. The silence now hovering over their table, plus Beatrice's under-the-table knee nudge, tempted her to accept his word and move on to a less contentious subject. She opened her mouth, but other words spilled out. "Intended or not, what's done is done. It would help if you explained your position."

Lieutenant Butler's demeanor was unmistakable. Margaret waited while the Lieutenant carefully checked the level of coffee in his cup. It was nearly full so there was no need to summon the waiter, thus offering an opportunity for a change of topic. Finally he looked into her eyes, resigned to continue a topic he obviously did not want to discuss.

"Well," he began, "this all started when a Serbian zealot murdered Archduke Ferdinand in Sarajevo."

"Yes, I know about that," Margaret replied.

"Indeed. But the question I have is this: If Austria's Emperor Franz Josef was truly outraged over the murder of his nephew—infuriated enough to start a war in which America is now involved—then why was he absent from the state funeral?"

"The same question occurred to me as well," she admitted. "Why do you suppose that was?"

"I suspect the late Archduke was somewhat of an embarrassment to his uncle. That's probably why neither Franz Josef nor Kaiser Wilhelm saw fit to attend the funeral service for the Archduke and his wife Sophie, also killed by the attacker."

"You mean because the Archduke married beneath his station—

chose a woman of unequal social and noble rank?" Margaret suggested.

Butler nodded. "Yes, and I find that particular example of royal snobbery more pathetic than offensive. It reflects an attitude of entitlement; of privileges inherited rather than earned. In any case, I believe the Archduke's assassination provided a convenient excuse for Austria to punish Serbia."

"Punish an entire country because of one man? That doesn't seem reason enough."

"Miss Jerome, Russia and Serbia have been close allies since the Middle Ages. The average Serb likes and respects Tsar Nicholas. I believe their growing admiration for the Tsar—Kaiser Wilhelm's Russian cousin—threatened to undermine Austria's hold on its Balkan subjects."

"If your theory is correct, then this terrible war is nothing more than a family squabble over feudal possessions. Are you suggesting that all those soldiers died, and continue to die, for an unworthy cause?"

The young surgeon picked up his coffee cup and his mouth drooped in a slight frown. "Unfortunately, that might indeed be the case."

Margaret felt her ears growing warm, a rising flush she found difficult to keep under control. "I refuse to believe that five million young men have lost their lives because of a jealous feud between royal cousins."

"The number is closer to seven million, Miss Jerome."

She started to respond but instead remained silent. Five million, seven million; the numbers were beyond understanding. She could not comprehend the horror of such anonymous magnitudes. However, individual deaths were another matter. Individuals had faces and family and unique identities; individuals left behind memories of happiness and heartache—a haunting presence that would survive the solemn echoes of a funeral mass.

Margaret took several deep breaths trying to overcome the emotions swirling through her mind.

Beatrice finally spoke. "Lieutenant Butler, if you honestly believe this war is unnecessary, then how can you possibly serve a cause you don't believe in? That seems hypocritical."

He shrugged. "Perhaps it is, but the situation in France is more compelling than my personal opinion. Now that we're finally in it, a substantial number of American boys will become casualties—many more than anyone realizes. The Army will need surgeons. It seems the right thing to do."

He paused and Margaret sensed that he might add something more, but stewards arrived and served the first course—beef bouillon. Butler leaned back in his chair and remained silent.

Major Gregory smiled. "A well-timed interruption."

As she spooned rich broth into her mouth, Margaret attempted to quell the mixed feelings she felt toward the young surgeon. He was polite, well informed, and intelligent enough to earn a medical degree; but she found his attitude toward the war offensive. In light of Michael's death, how could she feel any different? Nevertheless, Lieutenant Butler had volunteered to serve in a conflict he did not support—to put himself in harm's way in service to others. His behavior was a contradiction, one she found difficult to resolve.

"If I may ask," Major Gregory said, pausing between polite slurps of bouillon. "What compels two proper young ladies to suffer the rigors of a troopship bound for war-torn Europe?"

It was a topic she had hoped to avoid, but their presence aboard this ship—two unchaperoned female civilians among so many in the military—was bound to pique the interest of the curious, the inquisitive, or the casually bored. She had been foolish to believe otherwise.

Margaret set her spoon aside while her mind attempted to fashion a straightforward reply; words that might explain the strange circumstances that had led her to this place.

4

The tersely worded telegram from the Secretary of War had not only destroyed their assumptions regarding the future, but it also created doubt regarding Michael's death. A series of telegrams between Margaret's father and someone named Weeks at the American Ambulance Field Service in Paris confirmed the unthinkable: Michael was indeed dead.

"What about the 'Lieutenant' title?" Margaret asked. "He wasn't in the Army, was he?"

"I'm not sure about that," her father answered absently. "There were certain organizational adjustments when America entered the war. But the Army became involved, so there's worse news."

"What could be worse?" Emily Jerome asked.

Mike Jerome frowned. "Nothing could be worse," he admitted. "But the Army has decided that remains won't be returned to America until after the war. In some cases, perhaps not even then."

"That is not acceptable!" Emily Jerome fumed.

Mike Jerome gently placed a brawny arm around his wife's shoulders. "Indeed it is not. That's why I sent a cable to Michael's superior. I told him we were on our way there to bring Michael home."

"They'd allow that?" Emily asked.

"Yes, but at our expense."

"Then we will see to it," Emily declared.

On a rainy afternoon a week following her father's announcement, Margaret sat alone in the study, attempting to concentrate on Edith Wharton's novel about the struggles of Charity Royall. It was difficult to keep focused and she kept losing track of the narrative. A haunting familiarity tugged at her consciousness, urging to... what?

She set the book aside while an idea took form.

Although he'd managed to secure but a single stateroom aboard a converted civilian ocean liner, the untimely arrival of influenza made a hash of Mike and Emily Jerome's travel plans. The difficult-to-obtain steamship tickets would go to waste—or so it seemed. Providence had spared her and Beatrice from illness. The more she thought about it, the more firmly an idea embedded itself in her mind.

Driven by a newfound sense of purpose, Margaret confronted her father and announced her intention to go in his place, making use of one of the two steamship tickets already purchased.

His reaction was not unexpected.

"Absolutely not!" he croaked, rising to an elbow from his sickbed in one of the guest bedrooms. Mike and Emily now occupied separate bedrooms per the doctor's instructions.

The obvious danger notwithstanding, he went on to say, a respectable young woman did not travel abroad without a suitable companion, and certainly not on a troopship crammed with rowdy soldiers.

Beatrice, probably hearing her father's irritated tone of voice, had slipped quietly into the room.

Mike Jerome's argument was sound; one Margaret could not easily counter. As she stood before him, trying to think of a way to explain her bone-deep sense of purpose, Beatrice spoke up.

"I agree with father," she said. "We have two tickets, and you simply cannot travel abroad without a chaperone. Both of us should go." Then she smiled. "We could chaperone each other."

On its own, the idea made sense. However, the oddity of a much younger sibling acting as moral guardian to an older sister seemed to have escaped Beatrice's notice. Nevertheless, seeing a way to soften her father's objection, Margaret agreed to the suggestion.

"But that makes it worse!" he retorted.

Margaret, truly unhappy about adding to her parent's misery, understood his reasoning. One young woman at risk was bad enough; *two* young women facing the same peril was not a remedy.

Her parents, bedridden and recuperating from a milder version of the deadly influenza now sweeping the Continent, became exhausted from the constant bickering. They had never given consent, had never stopped objecting even as Margaret and Beatrice packed their trunks, left the house, and took a taxi to Union Station.

As they settled themselves aboard the train, Margaret suspected that neither Emily nor Mike Jerome would ever forgive her impertinence. Nor could she blame them. She had taken advantage of a tragic situation to satisfy a compulsion she could not explain.

*

Beatrice's voice brought Margaret back to the present.

"I'll let you answer that question," she said.

Margaret blinked several times to settle her thoughts. Then she looked first at the young Lieutenant and then to Major Gregory. Both had paused, spoons poised just above the rim of their tureens, their eyes locked on hers.

"Beatrice and I are going to France for our brother, Michael."

The two medical officers exchanged quizzical expressions.

Lieutenant Butler raised an eyebrow. He looked first at Beatrice and then addressed Margaret. "Visiting your brother overseas during wartime? On a U.S. Navy troopship? How on earth did you manage that?"

Margaret shook her head. "No, not for a visit. We're going to Paris to claim his remains. Our brother was a volunteer ambulance driver. We intend to return his body to America. Our family doesn't want Michael buried so far from home."

Lieutenant Butler's eyes once again fixed on the black rosette attached to her dress, his expression one of uneasy comprehension.

Major Gregory said to Margaret, "Paris? Is that wise considering the bombardment?"

Beatrice jerked in her seat. "Bombardment?" The word fluttered from her mouth. "What on earth are you talking about? Has Paris been captured?"

The Major shook his head. "Not that I know of, but the German army is very close, fifty or so miles from the city."

"I don't understand," Margaret said.

"They have a siege gun," the Major told her. "A monstrous cannon capable of launching a two-hundred-pound explosive shell more than fifty miles. From what I've been told, dozens of those shells have struck all over the city."

Butler leaned toward the two sisters, a stern expression shadowing his face. "About two months ago," he began, "on Good Friday, one of those artillery shells struck a church near the Hotel de Ville. The explosion caused the roof to collapse killing nearly a hundred parishioners."

Beatrice gasped. "A *church?* They're blowing up *churches?* Why… that's *immoral!*"

Butler shrugged. "Perhaps it wasn't intentional. The cannon is indeed huge, but not very accurate. The shells can land anywhere. Perhaps you should reconsider your plans."

5

When Butler first stepped aboard the USS *Mongolia*, it never occurred to him that his first dinner conversation in mixed company would offend a young lady. His opinion regarding the war had clearly upset Miss Margaret Jerome, a woman whose sole reason for sailing to France was to retrieve the body of her dead brother, killed in a conflict Butler had sanctimoniously declared as unnecessary.

She must think me an opinionated fool... or worse.

He and Major Gregory had offered condolences. Butler had also attempted to smooth their rough beginning via inquiries about her interests and hobbies. She had provided brief, polite answers; however, Miss Jerome seemed immune to his peacemaking efforts.

After several unsuccessful attempts, Butler found himself reverting to form. As was his habit during most social gatherings, he retreated into the shelter of attentive silence. Why he'd chosen to voice his opinion regarding the war still baffled him. He was not prone to sharing his thoughts with strangers.

Later, in a private discussion, neither he nor the Major could fathom why Margaret Jerome had chosen to place both herself and her sister in danger. After all, their brother was dead; there was no need for haste. The task of retrieving his remains could surely wait until the war ended. Rushing off to France at this moment was not only dangerous, but foolhardy as well. Was she merely responding to her family's wishes or acting on impulse, a headstrong woman who insisted on having her way regardless of risk? Or might there be other reasons?

The inimitable complexities of the female mind continued to mystify him. Nevertheless, Butler was surprised to discover a growing desire to learn all he could about Miss Margaret Jerome.

He had intended to meet her at the entrance to the Officers' Dining Room, hoping that Miss Jerome would allow him to begin with a new slate, one unsullied by remarks she found offensive. She might even consent to sitting at the same table.

However, he was twenty-minutes late.

Colonel Dawes had dismissed them at four in the afternoon with instructions to read chapters three and four of Delorme's *War Surgery*. In his cabin, shared with another surgeon named Depuy who was always elsewhere, Butler had become so engrossed that he'd lost track of time.

At six-twenty he entered the dining room and eyed the seated diners. Margaret and Beatrice Jerome sat at a full table, facing away from him, their interest captured by the vigorous attentions of several young officers. He felt an unpleasant pang; a sour mixture of envy and disappointment. Yet, the cause was of his own making. Tardiness had prevented an opportunity to improve his situation with the elder Miss Jerome.

Major Gregory, seated across from Beatrice, caught his eye and offered a barely perceptible shrug.

"Please come this way, sir," a steward said.

Butler hesitated while he mulled another option.

The American convoy would zigzag its way across the North Atlantic, a course designed to thwart German U-boats who might be tracking them; a time-wasting maneuver Butler thought. In his mind there was an equal chance they would zig *towards* a waiting submarine as they were to zag *away* from one.

In any event, the voyage to Le Havre would last ten days—thirty meals. Before dismissing them Colonel Dawes had made it clear he expected each of his surgeons to dine no less than three times in the enlisted mess. 'Make yourself visible to the troops,' he had directed. 'You might learn something useful. Besides, it's good for morale.' It occurred to Butler that now was a good opportunity to do as the Colonel desired.

"Thank you, but I've changed my mind," he told the steward.

*

Compared to the subdued atmosphere of the Officers' Dining Room, the cavernous enlisted galley reeked with the steamy odors of warm food and echoed with the tinny clatter of pans and utensils and the banter of two hundred soldiers having as many conversations, each speaker seeming to vie for supremacy over others.

Several men eyed his uniform, pausing at the Sam Browne belt, a leather accoutrement worn by Army officers. Their looks reminded Butler that he was in *their* territory, an interloper encroaching into an unfamiliar realm. On the other hand, if he did not make a big issue of his presence—which was indeed his intention—the vast majority would probably ignore him.

Tucking the flat overseas cap under his belt, Butler tried his best to look unofficial. He joined one of four serving lines and edged toward steam tables manned by perspiring stewards. There, he made his first discovery.

Instead of china, enlisted men ate from rectangular steel trays: thin metal stamped into five compartments of varying dimensions, each about two inches deep. Taking his cue from those ahead of him, Butler lifted a damp tray from a stack and picked silverware from side-by-side containers.

Unlike a hospital cafeteria, Butler could not detect specific food aromas. Instead, here was a steamy mélange of not-unpleasant boarding house fare.

In turn, he accepted a fried patty made from chopped meat, mashed potatoes topped with thick brown gravy, and creamed corn; each deposited or ladled into various compartments with the practiced boredom of institutionalized routine. The line ended with bread and butter and frosted white cake on a huge baking sheet, pre-portioned into neat squares. From an urn he filled a thick porcelain mug with coffee and added cream from a glass pitcher beaded with condensation. Then he made his way toward the rows of occupied tables, looking for a place to sit.

"There's an empty spot over here, Lieutenant."

Butler turned toward the unfamiliar voice.

A soldier wearing a single chevron on his sleeve placed his tray on a nearby table and stood waiting, his expression a mixture of mild interest and casual indifference.

"Thank you," Butler said. He approached the soldier, a dark-haired young man who looked to be about twenty or so. Butler set his tray opposite the soldier's, pulled away a chair and sat. The private remained standing.

"Take a seat," Butler said. "Relax. Enjoy your dinner. This is not an inquisition."

The soldier smiled. "You mean like those conducted by Grand Inquisitor Torquemada, presumably at God's command?"

"Exactly," Butler replied, surprised and delighted with the private's wry sarcasm and knowledge of history. "This evening you will not be racked or flayed—at least not on an empty stomach." Then, obeying an impulse, Butler extended his hand.

Fraternization with enlisted men is not conducive to good military order. Such practices are strongly discouraged.

The stern admonition, uttered with such cold formality during his training at Camp Gordon, a huge Army cantonment northeast of

Atlanta, came immediately to mind. There, Butler had also suffered through numerous gas drills, learned to shoot a pistol, and studied field sanitation procedures. He also took time to polish his knowledge of the French language, attending evening classes taught by one Eva Woodbury and a select group of attractive Georgia belles.

"I'm Lieutenant Butler, Medical Corps," he said.

"Private First Class Mayo, Sir. Likewise in the Medical Corps," he replied, taking Butler's offered hand.

Butler eyed the metallic caduceus pinned to Mayo's collar. "So I noticed. Is that why you invited me to your table?"

Mayo shrugged and took up his knife and fork. "Yeah, I guess so... sir."

"That was considerate," Butler said, wanting to put Mayo at ease. "I mean, taking pity on an officer wandering around the enlisted mess."

"Think nothing of it, Lieutenant. My mother always said I had a soft spot for strays, but I don't think she meant people."

A soft chuckle erupted from Butler's throat. "Nevertheless, I think it's a fair analogy."

Using knife and fork, Butler cut into the fried patty and chewed a small portion. The meat had an unusual, rather unpleasant flavor: a distasteful mixture vaguely reminiscent of pork, beef, and some manner of fowl. Butler wondered if the odd taste was due to fillings and exotic spices or the bizarre result of reluctant couplings between unrelated domestic animals.

"Pretty good, huh?" Mayo said. "I could eat like this every day." He cut a chunk from his meat patty, swiped it lightly through brown gravy and popped the wet morsel into his mouth, chewing with obvious pleasure.

Butler did likewise with a second piece of meat, dipping it into gravy before taking another bite. Except for a slight taste of overcooked flour, the combination was better than he expected. In fact, the gravy had a dampening effect on the meat's sharp flavor.

"I take it you think the food on board the *Mongolia* is okay," he said, smoothing butter on a piece of bread.

Mayo nodded. "A lot better than Army chow. By a long shot."

That answered one question Colonel Dawes had put to them: *Are the men well fed?* Obviously, Private First Class Mayo thought so. On the other hand, the young soldier might be having great fun, secretly enjoying himself by pulling the leg of a witless and immensely gullible medical officer.

"Where's home?" Butler asked.

Mayo shrugged. "Different places. Texas, mostly. You?"

"New York... mostly."

"A city boy?"

"No. Upstate. Rochester."

"A city boy..." Mayo repeated, a statement rather than a question.

"I suppose that's true," Butler admitted. "Are you originally from Texas?"

Mayo shook his head while he chewed. Butler waited.

"Washington, Pennsylvania. It's a borough about thirty miles southwest of Pittsburgh."

"Texas is a long way from Pittsburgh's steel mills."

"That it is, Lieutenant. Out west, one can breathe actual air."

Over the course of a meal Butler intentionally lingered over—thus prolonging the conversation—Jack Mayo revealed segments of his life much as Butler might have done under similar circumstances: a grudging miser doling out pennies at Christmastime.

With gentle prodding Mayo's story became clearer. His father was a successful construction engineer, one who followed the work, moving his family from job to job every two or three years. However, nomadic wanderings had not deprived Jack of education.

High school diploma in hand, he had entered Texas A&M. Three years later, when it looked like America would enter the war in Europe, he and a dozen other returning seniors had postponed their fourth year and joined the Army.

"Did you volunteer for the Medical Corps?" Butler asked.

"Yes, sir. Because of my college background, the Army offered me a wartime commission—said I would make a good administrator, even a signal officer—but I declined the commission and became a medical orderly instead."

"May I ask why?"

"Well, before I enlisted I was thinking about leaving A&M for Baylor's new medical school. Becoming an admin officer didn't seem like a step in that direction."

"Do you still plan on attending Baylor after the war?"

Mayo shrugged. "I'd like to, but let's see what happens."

Butler was pleased with the conversation. There was a quality to the young soldier he found interesting: a mixture of intelligence, curiosity and a disinclination to share too many of his personal experiences. Butler seldom talked about himself and he tended to distrust those who did. A chatty woman could be charming at times; however, a person who constantly blathered about everything and nothing was merely filling silence with empty words.

He also believed Mayo's inconsistent use of "sir" and "lieutenant" was not disrespect for military rank, but rather from a growing sense of camaraderie between two men who found themselves in similar but unfamiliar surroundings.

"What happens when you arrive at Le Havre?" Butler asked.

"I won't know until I get to the replacement depot. Hopefully, they'll assign me to one of the American Expeditionary divisions and not shunt me off to a French or British outfit."

"I understand. It seems General Foch planned to use American troops piecemeal, blending them into front line units under the command of French officers."

"Yeah, I heard that," Mayo said, his voice on edge. "Our boys would be used like conscripts from one of their colonies."

"More or less. But I was told General Pershing graciously declined the offer."

"Black Jack should have told Foch to bugger off."

Mayo looked at his plate, then at Butler. "Sorry," he muttered. "That may have crossed the line."

Of course it had.

Casual conversation with a newly commissioned lieutenant was one thing—but openly voicing disrespect toward a high-ranking French military leader in the presence of an American Army officer was much different. The Army could prosecute an enlisted man for uttering such remarks. As a matter of fact, authorities could court martial an enlisted man for looking askance at a superior officer. It was one of the more intriguing things Butler had learned during his indoctrination at Camp Gordon. Under the Articles of War, 'silent insolence' was a chargeable offence.

"I believe your version is closer to the truth," Butler said. "But I'd be careful about expressing that opinion in mixed company."

Mayo's relief was evident. "I understand, Lieutenant."

The loudspeaker crackled: "Now hear this: The galley will close in five minutes."

Mayo placed his cutlery and empty mug on his tray and rose. "It was nice talking to you, Lieutenant."

"Likewise, Mayo," Butler said, getting to his feet. "We should do this again."

"Yes, sir."

Butler recognized the young man's tone. It was the unenthusiastic voice of a soldier responding to a not-to-be-taken-seriously invitation

51

from an officer. Mayo's response reminded Butler of his own attitude once, that of a new intern fresh out of medical school who acknowledged but did not really believe the suggestion from a celebrated and widely respected surgeon to 'get together sometime'. Both the intern and the surgeon understood that 'getting together' socially was not going to happen anytime soon.

Butler said, "I'm planning to take several meals in the enlisted mess before we get to France. Which would you suggest?"

"It doesn't matter to me, Lieutenant. Your choice."

He followed Mayo to where soldiers were noisily stacking used trays and placing cutlery and mugs into deep metal bins. On their way out Butler said, "How about breakfast, the day after tomorrow?"

"My section takes morning chow at 0600, Lieutenant—six o'clock."

"See you then, Mayo."

As they parted, Butler checked his pocket watch: a 14-carat gold Waltham Riverside once owned by his father. Time had once again escaped his notice. Even if he hurried, he would not be able to meet Margaret Jerome before 'lights out', a mandatory darkening of the ship, and the signal indicating passengers must retire to their shuttered cabins for the evening.

Yet, despite her cool attitude toward him, Butler wanted to see her again, to convince the young lady that he harbored no ill-will or disrespect toward her brother, or any soldier for that matter. It was the *war* he opposed, not those who felt compelled to serve what they believed was a just cause.

But, he admitted, that wasn't quite all of it. There was something else about being with her; a comforting attraction he'd felt when they'd first made eye contact. If he wished to explore a closer relationship with her—and he did—then he must find a way to overcome her displeasure.

Meeting her this evening however, was unlikely. Tomorrow he would attempt an earlier arrival—breakfast, this time—and wait for her to appear: A Stage Door Johnny hoping for a rare glimpse of a beautiful actress. With luck and more than a little presumption on his part, he might ameliorate the effect of his earlier blunder.

Thinking about their next meeting caused his ears to become unnaturally warm.

The Atlantic crossing would take nearly two weeks. Anything could happen between now and then.

6

Without warning, the loudspeaker interrupted their breakfast, emitting a burst of ear-shattering clangs followed by a commanding voice: "General Quarters! General Quarters!"

Margaret froze in her seat, startled by the unexpected announcement. Earlier drills had always been pre-announced. Could this be real? She met the eyes of Lieutenant Butler, who merely raised an eyebrow.

His mild reaction did not prevent the *Lusitania's* grim reality from intruding into her consciousness. *Have we been torpedoed? Are we going to sink?*

Margaret's childhood memory of unexpectedly deep water sent a quiver through her stomach. She was an excellent swimmer but had remained wary of unknown depths, a caution taken root during that long-ago summer on Mackinac Island.

The depths of Lake Huron were legendary, but the endless black fathoms beneath this ship conjured a special sense of dread. No matter how long she treaded water, the Atlantic would prevail, dragging her exhausted body into its cold, airless depths. Now, because of a compulsion she could not explain, the sea would claim Beatrice as well, leaving their parents childless. How could she have been so wrongheaded?

She felt Lieutenant Butler's hand on her forearm.

"Look at me," he said in a firm voice.

His gray eyes reflected calm confidence, a feeling she did not share.

"We're going to put on life jackets," he told her. "Then you and Beatrice will go to your muster station. Do you remember where that is?"

The answer came automatically. "Yes, it's station number six."

"And where exactly is that?" he asked as they rose and made for the open hatch. Beatrice and Major Gregory followed close behind.

The dining room was clearing but there were no signs of panic or confusion. A few mutters, murmurs and fragmentary phrases reached her ears. She said: "Station six is on this deck, near the middle of the ship, left side." Margaret pictured the spot in her mind, knowing where it was and how to get there.

"Please call it the *port* side, Miss Jerome. Now is not a good time to offend our seagoing hosts."

The mock serious look in his eyes and corresponding tone of voice drained tension from her body. She nodded. "I'll try to remember that."

Outside, they took life jackets from a steward.

"Keep moving, please. Go quickly to your muster station." he said, repeating the litany every few seconds or so.

They slipped life jackets over their heads and Lieutenant Butler helped her snug up the straps. Major Gregory did likewise with Beatrice.

"There you go, Miss Jerome," the Major said. "Try not to get your feet wet."

"That is *not* funny," Beatrice replied.

Major Gregory smiled. "This is probably another drill. German submarines rarely venture this far from the European mainland."

"But there is always a first time, isn't there?" Margaret said.

She and Beatrice soon joined three-dozen other passengers—half of them officers, the other half a mix of civilians, nurses, and enlisted soldiers—and took their places standing beneath Lifeboat No. 6 which hung suspended above them. A crewman then informed the group that passengers would not board lifeboats unless or until the captain declared an emergency.

Nobody appeared distraught or out of sorts. Margaret could not help but notice how orderly the process had unfolded, exactly like previous drills. Major Gregory could be right, after all.

"Look there!" a voice cried.

Margaret turned just as a warship approached from behind and passed alongside, slicing through the calm sea, trailing furious billows of smoke from four stacks—sooty plumes that merged and twisted away to a woolen smudge far astern.

"It looks so...*serious*," Beatrice murmured.

Indeed it did.

From her position in the front row, Margaret saw two more gray ships in the distance. They sailed behind and parallel to the *Mongolia's* course, side by side but separated by several hundred yards. A series of equally spaced geysers erupted from the sea behind each of the warships, followed by a dull explosion.

"Depth bombs," someone said. "There must be a U-boat out there."

An icy cold rivulet wormed through her empty stomach.

*

Butler was thinking about Margaret again. Aside from physical beauty, she exuded an aura; a magnetism that drew him closer. Yet, she had never flirted with him—had never exhibited that coy demeanor so common among unattached young women. Not that he expected it—not after his pious soliloquy about the wrongness of this war.

It had taken two days but today, with Major Gregory's affable demeanor smoothing the way, he had managed to seat himself across from the young lady at breakfast. But, as luck would have it, the alarm sounded moments after they sat, thwarting his attempt to make amends. He wondered when and where another opportunity might present itself. Fate had again intruded into his life as it had so many times before.

The morning sun lay well above the horizon, its yellow-orange glow filtered by a fat cumulus cloud whose edges quivered in hot-orange hues. The sunburst reminded Butler of a period he now considered his 'first life', a time of crystal interludes with his parents on Seneca Lake—sailing and fishing or just lazing in a cushioned chair on their cabin's flagstone verandah, enjoying the delicious idleness of summer vacation. It was a secret balm he hoarded, unwilling to dilute its soothing effect by sharing with another.

His legs tensed, keeping his body erect, as the *Mongolia* swerved to a different heading. As they steadied on their new course Butler had a clear view of a nearby American troopship. It lay dead in the water, its deck tilted portside toward the sea, the obvious victim of a German torpedo. When did this happen? Butler did not recall hearing an explosion during his aborted breakfast with Margaret.

Lifeboats swung outward from the stricken transport, descended from davits, and then slapped onto the sea's surface. Most appeared filled and disciplined crewmen worked oars, rhythmically pulling away from the sinking vessel.

Several dozen horses were visible on the main deck, confined to temporary canvas-roofed, wooden-sided pens. As the ship settled lower, cold seawater doused hot boilers located in the engine room. Steam jetted from several hatches blistering everything in its path. The already-skittish horses panicked in their stalls and kicked wooden slats into kindling. Once free however, their shod hooves found no traction on the wet, sloping deck. The terrified animals thrashed, skidded, and then tumbled over the rail. Bright sunlight glistened from sleek chestnut backs and quivering flanks. By ones and twos, the doomed creatures plunged into the sea.

As he watched, unable to avert his eyes from the unfolding tragedy, the term *horse latitudes* came to mind.

Conquistadors aboard Spanish Galleons—motionless on a dead-calm sea and running out of fresh water—had faced a cruel choice: risk dying of thirst while waiting for a wind to fill their sails, or sacrifice their equally water-starved horses. Forced overboard by desperate men, the pitiful screams from those drowning animals had given rise to a haunting term. Butler was not sure if the phrase had its origin in fact or sea lore, but it made no difference. This ship was far from the often-deadly calms of Capricorn and Cancer; nevertheless, the fate of these unfortunate creatures was no different from what might have occurred two hundred years ago.

He studied the commotion-filled deck and realized the torpedoed ship was settling at an alarming rate. There would not be sufficient time to fill, lower, and launch every lifeboat. The troopship would sink long before everyone was safely aboard one of the smaller boats. Rescuing men in the water while avoiding panic-stricken horses would take time. The sea's current would separate life-jacketed men and many might drift away and be lost.

By design or circumstance, the German U-boat commander had selected that one particular transport over the other five. As the doomed vessel slipped deeper into the sea, Butler wondered again if human existence was mere chance or part of God's Destiny for Mankind. If the Creator had a plan, then what Great Destiny required the lives of these unfortunate soldiers; or, for that matter, the seven million already lost in a great war? Wouldn't four million do? Or three million? What divine number would satisfy the cosmic levy of an unfathomable God?

Butler understood the notion of free will but he also wondered about its unrestrained nature. If God genuinely cared about His children, shouldn't there be some sort of Parental limit? Why wasn't there a rule or guideline regarding acceptable conduct—an involuntary reflex that would restrain mankind from slaughtering each other on such a massive scale? Free will was indeed a precious gift, but perhaps one too fragile for such careless children.

The *Mongolia* changed course and the scene shifted.

In the distance two warships sailing parallel to each other turned in opposite directions and reversed course. Foamy geysers erupted and trailed behind each ship, followed by dull explosions. The destroyers continued their methodical attack pattern over an ever-lengthening area. For a brief moment Butler wondered about the U-boat crew—frightened, desperate men attempting to evade their pursuers; to escape with their lives intact. But then he remembered the unlucky troopship: those already dead or dying and those destined for long immersion in a cold sea.

Despite his physician's oath—*Primum non nocere... First do no harm*—Butler hoped the German sailors would not live to sink other American troopships. The realization that he wished death upon his fellow human beings surprised and bothered him. As a medical doctor his sole interest was the well-being of those entrusted to his care. But what about personal survival? Did self-preservation trump his obligations as a surgeon?

The *Mongolia* plowed forward on its new course, leaving the American warships far behind. The muffled thud from depth bombs faded but their muted echoes lingered.

Where had he heard it before—that familiar soft booming, a sound like intermittent thunder from a distant summer storm? The memory arose, floating to the surface of his consciousness like a cork released from the bottom of a deep lake.

Yes, of course. The lake. How could he forget?

Long ago under cloudless skies he had heard similar booms echoing from the sloping banks of Seneca Lake, the largest and deepest of New York's Finger Lakes. Butler's father had called those sounds Guns of the Seneca. He'd also told young Butler of the many native legends associated with the phenomena. Among them, the Seneca tribe believed it was the sound of Manitou, the Great Spirit, still at work forming the earth.

Remembering a happier time brought a smile to his face. The past and present intermingled, one losing itself in the other, the sharp line between then and now softening to an amorphous tinge.

7

They went everywhere together: to recitals and plays and band concerts in Chestnut Park; to traveling circuses sprawled across Miller's Fairgrounds; to Eastern League baseball games at Culver Field, home of the Rochester Bronchos; to the annual State Fair in Syracuse, a summer event rich with the pleasant but contradictory aromas of still-warm fruit pies and barnyard animals.

Among all those pleasant recollections, the moments Butler cherished most were those at the lake, sitting outside their cabin on cushions attached to those big wooden chairs; his father standing at the wood-fired grill tending silvery filets of fresh-caught trout sizzling in a cast-iron skillet, his mother's special batter turning crusty and golden brown while hot lard bubbled and spat like a thousand miniature firecrackers on an endless Fourth of July. His mother lounged in an adjacent chair smiling at a secret joke, her dark hair tied in a long, single braid. In those idyllic moments he knew she loved both him and his father, each in her own special way and each without qualm or hesitation.

He was an integral part of their shared lives, the three of them seldom apart except for one weekend each month. His parents reserved that time for each other. Sometimes they drove to New York City for theatre or a musical show; at other times they sailed by themselves on the big lake during summer months. On those occasions they would spend Saturday night either at a hotel in the city or, more often than not, at their cabin located on Seneca's western shore.

Young Butler loved spending time there during the long summer break between school years. Their stone cabin stood near to the shoreline, a dozen miles south of Bellehurst Castle, a mansion built in the late 1800s by Captain and Mrs. Collins who still lived there.

Driving past Bellehurst on their way to the cabin always brought to mind local folklore. Many believed the four-story mansion was haunted. One man had died during construction and some thought his ghost still wandered the huge stone edifice. Another man went insane when confronted by the specter of his dead co-worker, or so folks said. Even as a young boy, Butler did not believe in ghosts. Later, he would have doubts.

Rural folk tales notwithstanding, his parents' monthly absences were an accepted part of life. He spent those days with a grandmotherly housekeeper, Mrs. Elliot, a childless widow redolent of freshly baked bread and lilac sachet. His parents would return home from their private excursions, faces flushed and bursting with happy energy. It was an unremarkable aspect of his life; a brief, predictable interlude that allowed him a bit more freedom of action than what he enjoyed when his parents were around.

On that particular Saturday morning in July, a week following his fourteenth birthday, his parents kissed him goodbye, climbed into their new 1906 Pierce-Racine touring car, clattered off down the street and never returned, vanishing from his life without warning.

The remaining summer was a kaleidoscope of solemn faces and quiet assurances from Mr. Albright, his father's attorney, an older gentleman who was also a family friend. Neighbors and acquaintances dropped by regularly, but as fall approached, the repeated phrase "One must never give up hope" sounded less and less hopeful.

Then, in late August, Mr. Albright announced that Butler would not begin ninth grade at the local high school. Instead, he would attend St. George's Academy, a full-time Jesuit boarding school for boys, grades nine through twelve. His parents were Protestant, members of St. Bartholomew's Episcopalian Church. Nevertheless, Mrs. Elliot—who had stayed on—told him St. George's was the best place for him, "under the circumstances."

Mr. Albright put it another way. "Leaving your friends is difficult, I know, but we have little choice. There are few boarding schools in the vicinity and St. George's has an excellent reputation. It's also the closest. As your guardian I intend to visit regularly. I don't want you to feel as though you've been forgotten." He then explained, "Your parents were without other living relatives. And while you have no financial worries, neither do you have aunts or uncles who might look after you."

"But what happened to Mother and Father?" he remembered asking. It had been his constant question, one nobody answered to his satisfaction.

"We don't know for sure, Robert. Their automobile was parked under the covered shelter beside the cabin and the sailboat was not at its mooring."

"Did it sink?"

Mr. Albright shrugged. "We think so. There were sudden thunderstorms that weekend. The lake can be treacherous during those times."

"But if you don't know for sure, then they might be alive, stranded somewhere."

"I suppose that's possible, but I doubt it. Your father is a resourceful man. If they were stranded, we would have heard from him by now."

"We could still search for them."

"Yes, we are doing that. There are a dozen boats out there right now, but it's a big lake."

Later, when he understood more, he realized what Mr. Albright meant. Glacier-formed Seneca Lake was indeed big: three miles wide, forty miles long, and more than six hundred feet at its deepest point. It was an enormous body of water nestled in the middle of vast woodlands, orchards, and vegetable farms.

In the days and weeks following there were brief mentions of his parents at church, but no funeral, no significant acknowledgement of their passing other than an announcement in the local newspaper. Most people accepted the disappearance as part of a natural order, an unfolding of 'God's mysterious plan for humanity.' It was an idea his mind would not absorb. Why would God do such a thing? He was not a bad kid and his parents were good people. In Butler's mind, God's plan—if indeed He had one—didn't make sense.

The next four years at St. George's Academy comprised another phase of his life. There he made new acquaintances and learned the intricate subtleties of schoolboy ritual, including one in particular whose recollection always produced a smile.

Every building at St. George's featured a Latin phrase, a slogan intended as a motto for that particular edifice. Chiseled into the great stone arch leading to the dining hall were the words: *Fidem Scit...* He Knows the Faith.

Segregated boys—like those at St. George's—tend to formalize their disdain for rules and practices over which they have no control. In this case the plain but nutritious dining hall fare had captured the imagination of a previous generation of students. Those lads—some long dead—often pronounced the Latin phrase other than what its originators had intended. Their mischievous irreverence gave rise to an old and honored breakfast utterance. Every school morning, as they marched two-abreast under the archway and into the dining facility, freshman boys would mumble: *"Feed 'em shit."*

By his second year he had outgrown initiation rituals and, minor transgressions notwithstanding, had become the focus of Father Leo's attention. The demanding Jesuit priest stressed three key principles: the need for candor when dealing with others; mankind's obligation to acquire knowledge; and, the importance of mental discipline. The good Father also had a passion for athletics.

St. George's, like most schools, required student participation in sporting events. Young Butler knew he possessed above-average physical abilities. Interestingly, he took no pleasure in the more social activities such as football, baseball, and basketball. Instead, he pursued the solitary pleasure of distance running, spending long hours on the track and, in all but the foulest weather, gliding his way down the narrow dirt roads that linked small communities. In the spring of his senior year Butler ran 1500 meters in four minutes and eight seconds—a school record. That same summer at the London Olympic Games, Mel Sheppard won a gold medal in the 1500-meter event, covering the distance in four minutes and three seconds.

"God has given you a gift," Father Leo told him. "And Harvard would like you to join their cross-country team."

"I have no interest in Harvard. I want to attend St. Bernard's."

Father Leo did not seem surprised at Butler's interest in the priesthood, but neither did he express much enthusiasm for the idea.

"I am pleased to hear that, Robert. You possess a good heart and a bright mind. But consider this: You have lived in the company of priests for almost four years, week in and week out, seldom leaving school grounds. This place has become your sanctuary from life's misfortunes. Other than Mr. Albright, you've had little contact with anyone beyond these walls. In short, you have no practical knowledge of adult life outside St. George's. Studying theology at St. Bernard's would be more of the same."

"That's okay. I like the privacy."

"Yes, I am aware of that, but please hear me out, Robert. Attend Harvard for one school year—two semesters. That's all I ask. If, after one year you still feel the same as you do now, then so be it."

It had taken more coaxing and some hard-nosed cajoling—activities that no doubt added to the soft-spoken priest's growing collection of gray hair—but Harvard's acceptance of Butler's application signaled the beginning of a new life.

When Mr. Albright arrived at his high-school graduation ceremony—alone—Butler realized his parents were not coming back. The secret hope, harbored since his first days at St. George's, gave way to uneasy acceptance. Four years was a long time for them to stay away. If they were still alive, he told himself, they would never have missed high school graduation.

But nagging doubt remained.

8

Margaret watched the two gray warships slip farther and farther behind, each trailing huge geysers of white water that rose and fell at measured intervals: seagoing bloodhounds intent on destroying their underwater quarry.

Off to her left the stricken troopship tilted deeper into the sea, its main deck nearly awash. Dozens of men wearing life vests crowded the rails, waiting their turn to leap overboard and swim away before the vessel sank.

"Heaven help those poor soldiers," someone behind her said.

"They'll be rescued. I'm certain of it," another suggested.

"I hope to God you're right."

"Pity about the horses," a male voice observed. "They look like fine animals."

"I'm sure they are," a deep voice answered. "The U.S. Army takes the best mounts for its cavalry troops."

"Damned shame..."

The voices gradually muttered to pensive silence. Margaret looked away from the doomed vessel, her eyes again finding the warships as they became specks on the horizon.

"Well, I guess that's that." The words came from a different speaker, nearer.

But it wasn't. They remained at General Quarters for another two hours, swaying periodically as the *Mongolia* continued its zigzag course. The sun climbed higher and the wind increased but the hats worn by Margaret and Beatrice remained in place, held firm by silk scarves looped over the crowns and tied under their chins. Margaret felt the tightness in her muscles loosen and she began to feel more at ease.

"My feet hurt," Beatrice whispered, lifting one foot, setting it down, and then raising the other.

"So do mine."

Margaret wore comfortable walking shoes but they did not seem to help; she was unaccustomed to standing in one spot for long periods. Shifting her weight now and then hadn't helped much; her calves and the soles of her feet ached. *Serves you right. Just be thankful you weren't dumped into the sea like those unfortunate soldiers.*

The loudspeaker crackled: "Secure from General Quarters. Secure from General Quarters. The smoking lamp is lit."

"Thank goodness. I was ready to *collapse* from exhaustion."

"Don't exaggerate, Beatrice. Remember, I've seen you dance for hours on end."

"That's not the same thing, and you know it."

Everyone was moving now, untying the straps of life jackets and dispersing from muster stations. Some gathered in small groups, lighting each other's cigarettes and chattering between puffs. The deck was suddenly crowded with soldiers of all ranks, some nudging their way through the milling throng in an effort to get somewhere else, others continuing to chat and smoke their cigarettes. Margaret hadn't realized there were so many on board.

"Look, there's Lieutenant Butler," Beatrice said. "I wonder who he has with him."

Butler moved toward them, his tall athletic frame sliding easily through the uniformed assembly. A younger man accompanied him—a soldier wearing a single chevron on each sleeve and not quite as tall—someone Margaret had never seen before.

Earlier that morning Major Gregory, a subdued Lieutenant Butler at his elbow, had met Margaret and Beatrice at the entrance to the dining room. Smiling amiably, the Major had asked if he and Butler could join them for breakfast. Remembering Butler and their troubling prior conversation, Margaret's first impulse was to find some excuse to decline. As her mind worked, the contrite expression on Butler's face made her hesitate. Beatrice filled the brief silence by announcing that she and her sister would be delighted to have breakfast with their newfound acquaintances.

During pre-breakfast coffee, Butler had shared his earlier mealtime experience in the enlisted men's galley, mentioning a Private First Class Someone in the process. What was the soldier's name? It came to her then: Jack Mayo. She wondered if the nice-looking young man was the same person.

"I see you managed to keep your feet dry," Butler said to Beatrice.

"That is *not* amusing," Beatrice said, stamping her foot lightly. "You and Major Gregory share a morbid sense of humor. We could have just as easily been sunk, just like that other troopship."

"My apologies, Miss Jerome. My intent was to lighten the atmosphere."

"You know what they say about good intentions."

The young man spoke to Beatrice. "Miss Jerome, I read somewhere that humor is a natural defense mechanism. It allows human beings to cope with extraordinary situations over which we have little or no control."

Beatrice stared at the young man, but said nothing.

Margaret was slow to recognize the glazed look in her sister's eyes. *Oh, my. Beatrice seems utterly captivated.*

"Ladies, please forgive my oversight," Butler said. "And permit me to introduce a new-found friend."

Lieutenant Butler's companion was indeed Jack Mayo, as Margaret had suspected. What she did not expect was Beatrice's sudden abandonment of her irritated mood. Bea and Jack Mayo couldn't stop looking at each other, their eyes darting away and then just as quickly returning, filled with something akin to rapt bewilderment. It occurred to Margaret that she was observing something extraordinary—the first moments when two people realize they are attracted to one another.

Butler probably noticed it as well. He moved apart from the young man, took Margaret's elbow lightly, and then eased her away, allowing the younger couple to be in closer proximity. It wasn't much. Still, Beatrice and Jack seemed to notice little but each other; an isolated island for two amidst the flow of passengers swirling around them.

Margaret looked at Butler as he continued to eye the couple, an expression of consternation knitting his forehead.

"Is something wrong?" she whispered.

"They appear smitten with each other."

"Yes, it seems so."

"I never anticipated something like this."

"Nor I, but why does that concern you?"

Butler turned away from the couple and looked into her eyes. "I think Jack is a nice enough fellow, but he's an enlisted man. He will be confined to the lower decks for most of the voyage." He paused for a moment. "I can't seem to do anything right. First, I've gotten off on the wrong foot with you, a situation I have yet to correct. Second, I have introduced your sister to a difficult situation. If they are as taken with each other as it seems, then she and Jack will have little or no opportunity to meet without incurring the wrath of a priggish Army officer, several of whom I have already had the displeasure of meeting."

"Wrath? I don't understand. What do you mean?"

"Miss Jerome, the Promenade Deck is restricted to officers and civilians—it's off limits to enlisted soldiers except during drills or official business, like now. Some of my fellow officers take the privileges of rank quite seriously. Jack would get into trouble, even face disciplinary action, should his idle presence on this deck became noticeable."

"Why, that's absurd!" Margaret felt color rising in her cheeks. "For goodness sake, we're Americans. I've never heard of such a thing."

"Miss Jerome, the Army is a unique society with its own rules and regulations. Every soldier is required to obey them, regardless of rank or personal preferences." His eyes reflected embarrassed misery. "I am truly sorry. I should have thought this through."

They heard footsteps and turned just as the couple approached.

"I need to get below, Lieutenant," Jack said.

"I understand."

Margaret said: "It was a pleasure meeting you, Private Mayo."

"The privilege was all mine, Miss Jerome."

They lingered over goodbyes for a moment and then Jack Mayo strode away, becoming lost in the dwindling crowd. He looked every bit the soldier: proud and erect, marching off to duty. She turned to Beatrice whose eyes had also followed Jack's departure.

"He seems like a nice young man," Margaret said.

Beatrice appeared oblivious to the comment. Then she turned toward her sister, her eyes shining. "What did you say?"

*

When Margaret first boarded the passenger-liner-turned-troopship, the prospect of a dangerous ten-day Atlantic crossing had created a sense of melancholy anticipation and more than a little dread. *Lusitania's* fate and the possibility of drowning in a cold, dark sea was never far from her thoughts. Honoring an obligation to her dead brother, a task that might cause her own death was one thing, but the thought of endangering Beatrice was unbearable. The recent troopship sinking worsened her feelings of guilt and sense of impending doom. Margaret remembered wishing for a powerful draught, a magical potion that would let her sleep through the entire voyage. Now, at last, this impromptu and rather hazardous Atlantic crossing was almost behind her.

"Hello, Margaret," Butler said.

They had spoken frequently after the submarine attack, mostly at meals but also other times, pausing for conversation when opportunity presented itself. Margaret had sensed his interest and, despite their disastrous first conversation, had responded with polite courtesy. It had taken her a while, but she now understood how he could despise those who had initiated the war, but care deeply for those affected by the consequences. It was, she had to admit, a compassionate attitude; one much closer to her own than she was ready to openly acknowledge. Now, following dinner this evening—their last night at sea—he stood waiting on deck outside the Officers' Dining Room. Beatrice exchanged greetings and then moved away, standing just out of earshot.

"We're scheduled to arrive at Le Havre tomorrow morning," he told Margaret. "I must take breakfast early and then disembark with the troops, so we probably won't see each other after this evening."

Margaret did not know how to respond, so she remained quiet but attentive.

"I wish you'd reconsider going to Paris. Now is not a safe time. Is it possible to conduct your business from somewhere west of the city… Versailles, perhaps—or even Plaisir?"

Margaret shook her head. "I wish that were so, but it isn't. We must discuss this matter in person, with an individual at the American Field Service office in Passy."

"I see." He continued to meet her gaze, then he said, "I'm sorry we didn't have more time together. I wanted to ease your concerns about me and my opinions."

She studied his forlorn, almost handsome face. He had tried so hard to smooth out their rough beginning—by no means a wasted effort—but she had forced herself to remain neutral, unwilling to allow herself the luxury of forgetting her obligation to Michael.

Margaret now believed she had a better understanding of what had compelled her to undertake this dangerous voyage. Surely the idea of a shared consciousness was not that far-fetched. If such a thing was possible, could it extend beyond this life? Why else would she have defied her father? Why else had she assumed the responsibility for claiming Michael's remains? In a manner she could not explain, this had become a commitment she could not ignore.

Margaret felt a sudden rush of impotence, a powerful longing to change the unchangeable. Regardless of how she might want to, focusing her attention on Lieutenant Butler was an option she could not explore, not now; perhaps not ever. This tantalizing encounter would end in the worst possible way—in limbo—a potentially interesting story without a middle or a conclusion... or even a beginning.

"You *have* eased my concerns, Lieutenant Butler...Robert. Sharing company with you made this journey more pleasant than it might have been. Under different circumstances..." Margaret left the sentence unfinished, not sure what should come next. Finally, she extended her hand. "Take care. Good luck to you."

The disappointment in his eyes was unmistakable. It was obvious he wanted something more promising than a winsome smile accompanied by a goodbye handshake. She was tempted to suggest an exchange of correspondence, but then held her tongue.

His features changed, assuming the firm expression of a man who knows he must accept an unpleasant reality. He took her hand and held it for a moment. "Yes, I understand. In any case, I wish you and your family well. And please be careful, Miss Jerome."

Then he turned and strode away.

She kept her eyes on him until he stepped through a hatchway and vanished from sight. Her shoulders slumped and Margaret turned her gaze outward, past Beatrice to the watery expanse stretching to the horizon. The gray swells mimicked the gloominess that never left her completely.

Yet, another part of her mind prodded and poked and refused to set aside a nagging sense of unfinished business.

After she had taken care of Michael's remains, when that sad obligation was satisfied, Margaret wondered if it might be possible to contact Lieutenant Butler. A brief letter expressing her appreciation for his company aboard ship would not be presumptuous. In hindsight, she regretted not giving him her Paris mailing address.

However, if another opportunity presented itself...

9

Looking down from the *Mongolia's* Promenade Deck, Le Havre's Pier Escale reminded Margaret of the scene at Hoboken eleven days earlier.

Except for minor differences in attire, the cheering throng looked strangely familiar. It seemed like the same troupe of actors and musicians had taken a faster ship across the Atlantic to reprise their earlier roles. Many also waved tiny American flags, but larger furls dominated the scene here. The French tricolor and the U.S. flag—dozens strung on poles or hung vertically from windows and balcony railings—bathed the wharf in a fluttering sea of red, white, and blue. In a musical twist 'Yankee Doodle' and 'Over There' took second billing to *Quand Madelon* and *La Marseillaise*.

Similarities aside, this was not Hoboken. The wide expanse of Pier Escale contained far too many silent women standing in huddled clutches. Their bodies swayed in unison keeping time with a dirge perhaps only they could hear. Wearing long black dresses, knitted shawls, and tight-fitting headscarves that framed pale-as-death faces, their gaunt expressions reflected an odd mixture of half-wild torment and faint hope. Their sad, watchful eyes seemed intent on the two lines of American soldiers striding down gangways and forming into companies four ranks deep.

As the troops stood at attention, rifles shouldered, an ever-rising wail overwhelmed the sound of cheers and band music. The lament swelled to a moan, a grieving crescendo unlike anything Margaret had ever experienced. Her ears throbbed from the sound and she felt a quick tremor of premonition; a sense that something amazing or wonderful or terrifying was about to happen.

Pandemonium struck without warning. The women mourners ducked beneath the roped cordon and rushed toward the soldiers, their arms outstretched. Approaching the front ranks, they fell to their knees on cobblestones and then grasped the legs of men who stood at stiff attention. The women's cries rose to an anguished howl.

"Remercier Dieu! Remercier Dieu vous êtes venu!"

The quavering tone of that sad litany conveyed depthless human misery and desperation borne of unimaginable loss and suffering. Margaret's hands tightened on the ship's rail, her wide-open eyes struggling to comprehend the sight of so many war-widows thanking God, not once, but repeatedly.

Most soldiers never moved. They stood rigid amidst the black surge, eyes staring straight ahead, lips drawn into tight thin lines, brows wrinkled in embarrassment and silent consternation, unsure how to respond to such overwhelming displays of emotion. A few men kneeled and stroked the shoulders of distraught women, attempting to comfort the inconsolable.

Gendarmes gently took control and eased the hysterical women away.

As order returned to the quay, Margaret knew she would never forget those pale, tear-streaked faces or the supine bodies racked by depthless grief. Still clutching the rail, she felt those images sear themselves into her memory, a companion piece hanging beside her own grieving work.

The American ranks shivered to attention, probably anticipating a command Margaret could not hear above the crowd noise. Then, as one, the soldiers pivoted left and marched in crisp rhythmic step, an armed procession gliding toward still larger crowds lining Boulevard Strasbourg.

For one breathless moment the panoramic scene took on a finely honed clarity: a grandly staged *concertato* with perfect tone and tempo. The black shimmer of grieving women, the helmeted ranks moving as one, the sunshine colors of fluttering flags, the pitiful wails, the measured tramp of boots on cobblestones, the uplifting music, the cheering crowd: all the grim and glorious trappings of war became a grand triumphal that flowed and coalesced into a pageantry of contradiction.

Blinking away a film of tears, she fought to take in fresh air as her heart swelled and throbbed inside her chest. If this was the essence of a great war—the cause of both wretched agony and joyous enthusiasm—if, as Lieutenant Butler believed, a feuding and self-serving monarchy had wielded the tainted baton that orchestrated such a monumental tragedy, then they and all their kind were beyond redemption.

*

Citing the urgent need for surgeons, a harried balding major at the replacement depot—a vast assemblage of squad-sized tents located two miles north of Le Havre—gave Butler a hand-written order directing him to Chaumont, headquarters of the American Expeditionary Forces.

The trip from Le Havre to Paris took six-hours. After locating another convoy, Butler endured twelve additional hours, one hundred and sixty miles of cramped travel, before he arrived at Damremont Barracks; an impressive group of two-story brick buildings surrounded by a high wrought iron fence.

The sluggish journey—over dusty roads jammed with a clanking array of camions, horse-drawn wagons, and motorized vehicles of every description—had taken all night. At dawn, an Adjutant Corps lieutenant-colonel at AEF Headquarters expressed surprise that Major Simmons, the balding officer at the replacement depot, had ordered Butler to Chaumont. The desperate need for surgeons existed not at headquarters, where battle action was non-existent, but rather at Base Hospital Number 15 near Meaux.

"This must be someone's idea of a joke," the lieutenant-colonel muttered. With a new set of orders Butler set off for Meaux, a small town nestled on the Marne River, more than a hundred miles in the opposite direction.

Now, after bouncing over many of the same cluttered roads, he stood in an office facing the hospital's commanding officer, a full colonel named Greevly. Butler, weary and unshaven, wore a travel-wrinkled uniform that one might charitably describe as unkempt.

Colonel Greevly read Butler's orders, looked up, leaned back in his chair and then fixed Butler with an inquisitive gaze. "I now know *who* you are, Lieutenant, but I am not quite sure *what* you are." The Colonel's voice carried an edge, a tone reminiscent of a displeased schoolmaster.

Butler thought he understood the Colonel's irritation. *I should have cleaned up before reporting in, but there was neither time nor opportunity.* Still at attention he said, "Sir, I apologize for my appearance. I've traveled a half-dozen roads during the last thirty hours. Authorities in Le Havre ordered me to Chaumont, apparently by mistake; and then, just as quickly, sent me here."

The Colonel rose from behind his desk. He was short, a little thick around the middle, and his trimmed gray hair was thinning. The inquisitive look dissolved into an anticipatory glare, warming to his subject. "Were you indeed?" He rocked on the balls of his feet, a middleweight boxer preparing for another round, and stared at Butler through wire-rimmed spectacles.

Butler felt perspiration gathering in his palms. The Colonel's demeanor reflected quiet malice, much as a child might anticipate squashing an insect. He sensed there was something more to the Colonel's displeasure than the slovenly appearance of a new arrival, but had no idea what it could be.

The Colonel said, "In case you didn't know, most career Army men are disdainful of the Medical Corps. 'Chancre mechanics' is one of their more colorful epithets. They share the opinion that we are pretentious civilians at heart, unworthy to wear the same uniform as 'real' soldiers. Your appearance re-enforces that belief and discredits those of us who take pride, not only in our work, but in military service as well." The Colonel arched an eyebrow and leaned forward. Clearly, he expected a response.

Butler remembered a *mea culpa* phrase from his training at Camp Gordon. "I have no excuse, sir."

He felt a sudden rush inside his head. A swelling tide of frustration and annoyance that threatened to burst forth—unfamiliar emotions produced by the bone-deep weariness of a long, difficult journey; exhaustion further exacerbated by knowing the Colonel was rightly upset. He took a deep, calming breath and remained silent while embarrassment gave way to tired acceptance.

Why did some things never seem to change? While justified, Colonel Greevly still exhibited the same distressing traits as had certain others he knew: chiefs of surgery at Mount Sinai Hospital for example, individuals who admonished interns who failed to show respect for the exalted status of their professional betters.

Apparently, the Colonel disliked unkempt uniforms, especially when worn by junior medical staff, and was not hesitant about voicing his displeasure. Butler had not expected the same punctilious attitude from Army doctors. He wasn't sure why, but he had assumed that professional soldiering during risky wartime service might engender a closer kinship among its members, particularly medical practitioners.

Did the unique nature of war and wartime surgery inhibit such camaraderie? Perhaps, but he also realized that reporting to his commanding officer looking like a penniless vagabond might be construed as 'conduct unbecoming an officer and a gentleman'.

The phrase triggered the memory of a classroom lesson in military justice learned during training. Baron Wilhelm von Steuben had first articulated the 'conduct unbecoming' phrase while training George Washington's ragtag army during the American Revolution; words subsequently codified in the Rules and Articles of War. Even with the passage of more than a century, the United States Army still used *Conduct Unbecoming* to describe all manner of unacceptable behavior.

Colonel Greevly glared at him a moment longer, then turned and faced a large map tacked to the wall behind his desk. "Look here," he said.

Butler followed the Colonel's gesture and studied the map of northeastern France. A red line snaked in a top-left to bottom-right diagonal, its wiggling northwest-to-southeast geometry distorted by a large bulge aimed at Paris. The Colonel's index finger touched the westernmost point in the bulge.

"The German trenches are twenty miles from where we now stand. That means the enemy is within fifty miles of Paris."

"Sir, I didn't realize they were that close."

"It seems there is much you don't know, Lieutenant."

"On that issue, sir, we are in complete agreement."

Colonel Greevly ignored Butler's comment. "In any case, their latest offensive has run out of steam here, on the north bank of the Marne River near Chateau Thierry." He tapped a spot on the map at the southernmost edge of the German salient. "The American battalion in that sector is dug in on this side of the river. They have need of another ambulance surgeon, so I'm sending you to Lucy-le-Bocage. It's a village close to our trench line. The dressing station is situated nearby." He turned, sat at his desk, took pen and paper, and began to write. A minute or so later, he handed Butler a written order. "When you arrive, report to Captain Peckham."

"Yes, sir."

"Sergeant Hollenbeck—the soldier outside my office—will show you where to collect a helmet, gas mask, and other field items." He ran his gaze over Butler's shabby uniform. "Unfortunately, you don't have time to change or press your uniform. Several trucks carrying replacements will be leaving within the hour. Your driver will know where to drop you." He paused for a moment, then said: "You say you've been on the road for thirty hours?"

"Yes, sir. More or less."

"Have you eaten lately?"

"Not since noon yesterday, sir."

"Get yourself something to eat. The officer's mess is open. They might ignore your disheveled appearance and recognize you as such. The Sergeant will point it out and then show you where to meet your transportation. Do you have any questions?"

"No, sir."

"Then you are dismissed, Lieutenant. Good luck."

Butler saluted. The crisp gesture was parade ground perfect. "Thank you, sir."

The Colonel returned Butler's salute. "Don't thank me, Lieutenant. You'll soon discover that I've done you no favor."

10

"Say, give us a fag, Jimmie lad. I'm fresh out."

A tall, rather thin corporal eyed the speaker, a slick-sleeve private with the knocked-around face of a bare knuckle brawler, and frowned. "Fresh out? There's a whole pouch of Bull Durham in yer shirt pocket. I saw it there with my own eyes."

"Bull Durham, sure." The private waved a hand dismissively. "But you've got tailor-mades, Jimmie boy. Four packs of Chesterfields, no less." He smiled. "I saw you put 'em in yer kit just before we shoved off."

"So what if you did. They're mine and I intend to smoke every last one. You want a fag, roll your own."

"Ah, Laddie. Your selfish ways are breakin' me heart."

Butler smiled at the exchange. He sat next to the tailgate inside a canvas-topped Dodge truck. Seven enlisted men occupied narrow plank benches facing each other, the wooden stocks of Springfield rifles resting on the floorboards between their legs, metal barrels crooked in forearms. An equal number of duffle bags along with Butler's luggage cluttered the narrow space separating the two rows of soldiers. An infantry captain had exercised the privilege of rank and sat up front, occupying the passenger seat beside the driver.

Butler turned and eyed the scenery as it receded beyond the tailgate. A green sweep of farmland rolled away, almost to the horizon. The knee-high vegetation looked like wheat but it could have been oats, rye, or something else. It was pleasing to look at—late afternoon sun on grassy fields rippled by a summer breeze—but he had no idea what sort of crop it might be.

An irregular thumping in the distance interrupted his sightseeing. Conversation inside the truck stopped.

"French seventy-fives," Corporal Jimmie muttered. "There's a battery near Mont-de-Bonneil."

Butler spoke to the soldier: "Is that where you boys are headed?"

"Nah. This gang is off to Coupru." He tilted his head toward the truck's cab. "At least, that's what the captain told us. Where're you headed, Doc?"

"Lucy-le-Bocage. I understand we have a dressing station there."

The Corporal nodded. "Yeah, I've been to Lucy Lay. It's a couple miles north of where we're going."

Butler could not restrain his curiosity. "How do you know that place? Were you wounded?"

The Corporal nodded.

"Seriously?"

He shook his head. "I was lucky." Corporal Jimmie indicated a spot just below his right rib cage. "Bullet passed clean through. Nicked my liver, but not much else. Spent an easy seven days in Meaux." He looked at the others, all of whom appeared awed by the Corporal's revelation. "Then they stuck me with these greenies." He pointed a finger at the knuckle-faced private who had asked for a cigarette. "Except for that character. He's an ignorant Mick, but he's no rookie."

"Were you wounded, too?" Butler asked the private.

The Corporal's short guffaw echoed from the canvas top. "Wounded? That's a laugher! Private Cohan is fresh from three days in the guardhouse."

"Now, Jimmie. Don't be talkin' outa school. It wuz all a big misunderstandin', and that's God's Holy Truth."

"You got drunk and punched a sergeant. *That's* the truth."

"A friendly scrape between old chums, nothin' more."

"You and your sergeant pal might have sold that Persian rug to the colonel. I figure that's why you two got off so light, but that old shirt don't wash clean. Not with me."

Butler clasped his hands together, eager to question Corporal Jimmie about his wound, but that was unlikely. The soldier was now engaged in a heated debate with Private Cohan over the difference between a 'friendly scrape' and a 'bar room brawl'. Butler leaned back and resumed his survey of the French countryside.

In *War Surgery*, Dr. Delorme had described the unique wound tracks left by different types of bullets as they passed through human flesh. According to Jimmie's description and quick recovery, it was probable the Corporal's wound had come from a German 'S' bullet—a pointed cylinder—rather than a projectile having a blunt nose. In all likelihood then, the man had fallen victim to someone firing a machine gun, not a Mauser rifle.

The truck's gears downshifted as it slowed and turned left. A minute later it stopped.

"Lucy-le-Bocage," the driver yelled. "This is your stop, Lieutenant."

After dropping the tailgate, Butler jumped onto a narrow dirt road and retrieved his luggage: a full musette bag fitted with a single carrying strap, and his brown leather suitcase. He lifted the hinged tailgate and clanged it shut. Then he stood there for a moment, looking into the truck's dim interior. Then he said: "Good luck, boys. I hope never to see your smiling faces ever again."

Laughter greeted his remark. "We don't want to see you either, Doc," Corporal Jimmie answered. "Not until the war is over."

"Fair enough."

The Corporal stomped his foot on the truck's wooden bed. "All clear. Let's go."

The Dodge turned onto the main road and headed off in a clash of gears, trailed by wispy clouds of gray-brown dust. A short distance away, it came to a 'T' and turned south.

Butler stood on the side of a narrow dirt road, placed both hands above his kidneys, and stretched. As he worked blood into stiff muscles, he took in his surroundings.

The road on which he stood led to a tiny, rubble-strewn village. Fifty yards away, almost hidden under a mature copse of chestnut trees, stood a small scattering of dirty-white Army tents.

For the first time since he disembarked the *Mongolia*, Butler realized he was actually standing on French soil. He had knowingly waded into the great tide of human events. The unstoppable flow had swept him up and deposited him on this ancient plot of land, a skeptical volunteer participating in a conflict he did not believe in. Familiar questions arose: *what lay beyond... where will I be when this is over...?*

He shivered as a momentary quiver zippered along his spine.

Walking toward the grouping of tents with luggage in hand, his back warming to the sunshine, Butler tried to forget that third unexpected question, one he had never asked himself: *will I survive?*

11

"After you get settled," Captain Peckham said. "I'd like you to become familiar with our sector of the American trench line. Tomorrow morning would be a good time."

"Yes, sir."

"You can also forget the 'sir' unless the brass is around. My first name is Woodrow but I prefer Woody."

"Okay, Woody. I'm Robert."

"Robert—not Bob or Bobby or Rob or Robbie. Am I right?"

"You are."

The tent—large enough for a cot, footlocker, small desk, and two chairs—smelled of mildew and dry grass. Peckham scratched his scalp then smoothed sandy hair with fingers. "Okay, Robert. Aren't you going to ask me why you need to visit the front line?"

"I assumed you would tell me if you thought it was important."

After his unpleasant experience with Colonel Greevly, Butler did not want to antagonize his new commanding officer. On the hour-plus truck ride from Meaux he had decided to listen and obey his superiors—no questions asked. At first glance, Captain Peckham appeared cordial but it was too early to make that judgment.

"I think becoming familiar with your new home is important. Don't you?"

"My new home? I thought this was my new home," Butler said.

Peckham shook his head. "No such luck, pal. Field medical

stations are located adjacent to the trenches, close to the point of enemy contact. Your particular station is a canvas-covered dugout about a half-mile east of here. The Second Battalion of the 23rd Infantry Regiment occupies our sector of the line. If you happen to be a Civil War buff, then you might be interested to learn that the 23rd was once the 14th Connecticut. The Nutmeggers fought in every major engagement of that war. At Gettysburg, they were positioned in the center of the Union line and helped repel Pickett's charge."

Butler nodded appreciation. "Very impressive, but do they still call themselves Nutmeggers?" He remembered—too late—his determination to keep his mouth shut.

"Not any more. Haven't you heard? The Civil War is over."

"I seem to remember something like that," Butler replied. "I think my father might have mentioned it."

"Your father?"

"Yes. His father—my grandfather—joined the 108th New Yorkers when he was seventeen. As a boy, I remember watching those old veterans march in a parade. My grandfather had passed by then so he wasn't among his old comrades."

"No kidding? That must have been interesting."

"It was, but it wasn't at all like I'd imagined."

*

In the summer of 1905, the year before his parent's unexplained disappearance, the three Butlers piled into their automobile for a trip to Rochester. The occasion was the 40th anniversary marking the end to what some folks called the Civil War and others called The War of the Rebellion.

There were brass bands and speeches, pretty girls in fluted skirts and puffy blouses, cotton candy and hand-pulled taffy—all the exciting sights, sounds, and activities a 13-year-old boy might anticipate. But what Butler had looked forward to most of all—more than the rides or the music or the rollicking clowns—was the Old Timers parade. In his mind's eye he pictured neat rows of blue-clad Union soldiers marching in perfect unison, the warm air vibrating with the synchronized beat of their measured steps.

However, the actual parade was not like that at all.

What had seared his memory were the long, somber ranks of gray-bearded men as they shuffled down Main Street toward fairgrounds nestled beside the Genesee River. Many limped; those missing a leg lumbered by on worn wooden crutches; still others had lost an arm or a hand or an eye; a few occupied rickety wheelchairs, pushed along by younger volunteers. Rather than the crisp attire he had imagined, many of those old men wore their original issue Federal uniforms and forage caps, now faded and shabby and dusty with age. When they lumbered past where he and his family stood, the mixed aromas of tobacco smoke, musty clothing, and old newspapers smelled like… history.

Given the lighthearted atmosphere of their surroundings, the unexpected solemnity of those worn-out marchers had sent a quiver up his spine. Stunned by the sight of all those decrepit and mutilated soldiers, young Butler had shifted his stance in an effort to avert his eyes. At that moment he felt a gentle hand on his shoulder.

"Don't turn away, Robert," his father had told him. "Look them in the eye." The soft voice continued. "Those are Rochester Boys— veterans of Antietam, Chancellorsville, and Gettysburg. They have seen the Elephant—experienced first-hand the fear and horror of close combat. Without them, there would be no United States of America. Without them, there might not even be a you or a me."

His father had paused for a moment, his eyes focused on the passing troops. Then, "My father—your grandfather—passed away before you were born. His name was Robert. We named you after him. It was your grandfather who told me about the Elephant, about the terrible events he'd witnessed as a boy. Had he lived, your granddad would be marching alongside those men today."

"He would?" young Butler had replied.

"Yes. I know they seem old to you, and they are, but remember this: Your grandpa fought alongside those men in order to save the Union. They suffered through an ordeal we cannot imagine. Someday you will better understand what I'm talking about. Meanwhile, you must show them the respect they earned and deserve. Look them in the eye, Robert; and clap your hands as they march by."

*

Butler had never forgotten that moment. Now, more than a decade later, he wondered how many of those old soldiers, the amputees and infirm, had since passed on. He also wondered if his presence here would make any difference at all.

Butler submerged the memory, then he said, "On the other hand, this current war isn't over yet, is it?"

"No, not quite. Anyway, your dugout is where the battalion's wounded gather. Your job is to apply emergency care and then put injured men onto stretchers for transport here. You are the first line of treatment."

"I understand."

On board the troopship, Colonel Dawes had provided detailed explanations of how the wounded were collected, treated, and passed on to aid stations and base hospitals.

"In the meantime," Peckham said, retrieving a darkly tinted bottle and two glasses from a bottom desk drawer, "I'll introduce you to the staff. Our happy little band numbers thirty-eight: two surgeons—you and yours truly—twelve orderlies, four ambulance drivers, and twenty stretcher bearers."

"*Twenty* stretcher bearers?"

"I know what you're thinking: that's a high number, but consider this. We routinely assign four men to a stretcher. This station has five stretchers in total. We use four men because bearers also become casualties. Shell fragments, mostly, but snipers, too. The armbands don't seem to make a difference to the Germans. In fact, men wearing red crosses are preferred targets. Anyway, we need a minimum of two men per stretcher to carry the wounded; assigning four bearers gives us some slack."

"That makes sense."

Without asking, Peckham poured an inch of whiskey into two glasses and then added a dribble of water from a metal canteen. A light, peaty aroma filled the small space. He slid one glass towards Butler.

"Do you drink scotch, Robert?"

"Yes, on occasion."

"Then you're in luck. We get our whiskey ration from the British officer's mess. I'm told those gentlemen are quite particular about their booze." He raised his glass. "Cheers."

Butler picked up his drink, repeated the toast and sipped whiskey. The scotch was redolent of old wooden casks and something else he couldn't quite define—a heavy complexity of smoky flavors unlike any he had ever tasted.

"I'm impressed," Peckham said.

Butler was not sure how to respond. "Oh?"

"You didn't ask for ice."

"I figured ice boxes might be scarce out here."

"Ice boxes? My friend, *running water* is scarce out here. There's a lone pump in the kitchen of that building across the way. It draws water from a cistern in the cellar. When the cistern runs dry, as it tends to do this time of year, we fill buckets from the communal well in the town square. It's great fun, more so when dodging sniper fire."

"Should I even ask about toilet facilities?"

"I think you already know the answer."

"Outhouses?" Butler was surprised to learn that this charming little village was not unlike much of rural America, places without the benefit of modern plumbing. Since Europeans were more advanced culturally, he had likewise assumed they were ahead of America in creature comforts as well. Yet, that did not appear to be the case, at least not here, a scant fifty miles from Paris, the most elegantly cultured city in the world.

"They're out back."

"I see."

Peckham smiled. "Unfortunately, sanitary facilities in the front lines aren't quite as luxurious. Open slit trenches are the norm. Sometimes covered by a tent fly."

"I'll try to restrain my enthusiasm." Butler changed the subject. "It seems quiet. I hear artillery every now and then, but it's far off. I expected more activity."

"Aid stations seem to operate at one of two extremes: we're either overworked or idle. Learn to appreciate the latter; it's a rare occurrence."

Another question formed in his mind. "I assume that, primitive living conditions excepted, we have modern medical tools and equipment."

"We have enough to do the job, which does not include major surgery. Our primary goal is to get the wounded stable enough to survive the five-mile ambulance ride to the field hospital at Nogent. After additional treatment, they go by rail to the base hospital at Meaux. The severe cases are sent to one of the seven major hospitals in Paris."

"And the others?"

"We treat their wounds and either return them to duty, or send them to Nogent. As you can see, we have little room for recuperative patients. The recoup tents can hold a dozen casualties at most. We limit their stay to twenty-four hours."

Butler recalled Colonel Dawes's advice regarding *triage*. "What about the mortally wounded?"

"If they are unconscious, leave them alone. The hopeless cases go on the ambulances last."

"And if they are in extreme pain?"

"Then you will administer three grains of morphine sulphate and, should the same misfortune ever befall you, pray to God someone returns the favor."

Butler took another sip of whiskey.

There it was again, that cavalier attitude toward human life. First Colonel Dawes and now Woody Peckham. Unable to let the comment pass, he said: "Shouldn't we at least make an effort to save them?"

Peckham smiled, a forlorn upturn of his lips. "That question tells me you have no idea what to expect out here."

"That's probably true."

Peckham took a long, last swallow of his whiskey. "Don't worry about it. When the time comes, you will understand and act accordingly."

"And if I can't... or won't?"

Peckham's expression hardened. "Then, Robert, you are not suited to battlefield surgery. You might be more comfortable serving at one of the hospitals. If not, then you should give this up, take the next boat home and return to whatever it was you were doing, because you'll be of little use over here."

He had now received the same advice from two different sources, yet Butler continued to struggle with the concept of mercy killing.

The idea offended his sense of responsibility. The worst moral offense a medical doctor could commit was to play God when it came to the life of another human being. Yet, that's what his superiors had told him to do, and the U.S. Army's Medical Corps expected him to act accordingly.

Butler nodded, more acknowledgement than acceptance, and then swallowed the last of Peckham's excellent scotch whiskey.

12

It proved impossible to secure rail passage to Paris until all the American troops and most of their equipment had cleared Le Havre. Margaret then booked a first class compartment for herself and Beatrice on the one o'clock train.

Late that afternoon they arrived at Gare de l'Est. An aging porter gathered their trunks, placed them onto a small cart, and then escorted them outside the station. He whistled for an elegant black fiacre and loaded their luggage.

As Margaret watched, the cobblestones beneath her feet suddenly undulated. Instinctively, she grasped the side of the carriage as a soft boom echoed in the distance.

The young horse emitted a throaty snort through his nostrils.

"*Calme mon bravei cheva,*" the driver's soothing words had a calming effect on the animal.

The porter scowled and mumbled what sounded to Margaret like an obscenity.

"Was that one of those bombs they warned us about?" Beatrice whispered, her eyes glistening.

Margaret swallowed once before replying. "Yes, I think so." She looked around, but saw no signs of panic or distress.

"Take no mind," the porter said. "The Boche have no souls."

"Does this happen often?" Margaret asked.

"A few times each day, sometimes not." He shrugged in that

uniquely Gallic way. "It is the war."

He then assisted both women as they stepped aboard the carriage. Margaret thanked the old gentleman for his courtesy and placed a one-franc coin into his gloved hand.

"Your French is very good," Beatrice murmured as the porter moved off. "I almost understood everything you said."

"Hotel Lutetia," Margaret told the driver.

"*Oui, mademoiselle.*"

The bay gelding responded to the light touch of reins and they were off, clopping toward St. Germain de Pres.

Margaret closed her eyes, took in measured drafts of air and tried to relax. The ground had physically *shaken* beneath her feet, an eerie sensation unlike any she had ever experienced. *What I need is a long, hot bath followed by a quiet dinner and a good sleep; preferably in a bed that does not sway in time with the ship's movements or quiver beneath me from an explosion.*

She opened her eyes and tried not to think about tomorrow and the task of claiming Michael's remains. No doubt Beatrice had similar thoughts. As they turned onto Boulevard Ney, she said: "Even with a good night's sleep, I'm not sure I want to look at Michael. Not when he's… you know, not alive."

Margaret was not sure how to respond, so she remained silent.

"Anyway," Beatrice continued, "do you think we *should*—just to make sure it's really him'?"

"I don't think that will be necessary. The Army seldom makes mistakes about such things. Besides, his casket is sealed by now."

"I pray God you're right. I want to remember Michael as he was. I couldn't bear to see him… maimed."

Maimed? A momentary shudder. That possibility had never occurred to Margaret.

They continued on their way without speaking further, a weary silence melding with the rhythmic clop of the gelding's hoofs and the thin clatter of metal-rimmed wheels rolling across ancient cobbles.

Margaret did not want to think about the details associated with relocating Michael's casket—not yet. There would be time for that tomorrow when they visited the American Field Service headquarters in Passy. Nor did she want to think about the scene on Pier Escale and those somber, haunting images. And she certainly did not want to think about the possibility of more bombs dropping out of the sky unannounced.

She gazed at the passing scenery and pushed dark thoughts from her mind. Taking in the city's unique architecture, she forced herself to recall her near-obsessive study of French history.

There was the work of Thomas Carlyle, of course. His acclaimed three-volume history was a classic. Likewise, Jules Michelet's *Histoire de France* was lesser known but quite interesting, providing a perspective different from what one might expect from a traditional historian.

Slowly, memories of happier times from their summer vacation five years earlier poked through the gloom clouding her mind.

Back then, her first impression of Paris was all she had imagined it to be—glittering and elegant and reeking of Gallic arrogance. The obvious charm of the city was unrivaled, but her fondest memories drifted to Amiens, a much smaller town sprouting from the River Somme's rich fluvial plain. The narrow streets lined with brick houses—a hue more burgundy than red—returned faint echoes from centuries past. On her solitary strolls Margaret ambled across hand-hewn granite cobbles worn and polished by countless hooves, wagon wheels, and tramping feet. Visiting the wooded expanse of Madeleine cemetery and standing beside Jules Verne's impressive tomb gave the author a tangible sense of existence Margaret had not found in dry biographies.

More than anything however, the magnificent 13th century cathedral had marked her soul with its indelible stamp of ages past. Staring up at the three-layered interior and soaring choir loft, her clothing dappled by sunlight bleeding through stained glass images, Margaret could almost hear the low mutter of ancient prayers whispered from shadowy cloisters. Thick stone walls echoed tales of Albigensian crusaders pillaging Languedoc, and soft, grateful murmurings for Louis IX's piety. She also heard, or imagined, muffled groans as flagellants whipped themselves with knotted leather thongs in a forlorn attempt to ward off the horrors of plague—a Black Death that would eventually claim more than a third of Europe's population.

Back home in St. Louis, during those reflective moments when she daydreamed about what it must be like to live in France, she invariably pictured Amiens, an unexpected haven in the sleepy little province of Picardy. Margaret felt her body relax as the recollections faded. With luck, she would visit there again, perhaps with someone she loved.

But not this trip.

Amiens was under siege by the German Army. She would come back another time; when the war was over and civility returned to Europe.

She stifled a yawn and her eyes took in the wide boulevards. They were less crowded today and the few *habitants* appeared more somber than they had in her recollections. Paris appeared nervous, unsure of herself, a city anticipating either disaster or reprieve in equal measure.

"It's a lot *quieter* than I remember," Beatrice said.

"Yes, I noticed that too."

"Didn't Major Gregory say the Germans were fifty miles away?"

"Yes, that's what I remember."

Beatrice pursed her lips. "The war is a lot closer than I thought."

They crossed Rue de Rivoli and entered the Tuileries. Margaret expected to see the gardens filled with young lovers peering into each other's eyes and married couples enjoying time with their families. But there were no blankets spread upon the lush grass, no picnic baskets brimming with food and bottles of wine. Instead, a handful of women occupied benches and watched children at play. A scattering of sad-eyed old men sat nearby, absently smoking cigarettes.

One man, younger than the others, captured her attention. Gaunt-complexioned and bearded, he wore a black, ill-fitting suit, white shirt, black tie, and a matching beret. Medals hung from colorful ribbons attached to his left lapel. He trudged along the walkway with the aid of wooden crutches, his empty left trouser leg folded up and pinned to a spot behind his thigh. He paused for a moment and their eyes met. His expression reflected an emotion Margaret had never seen before. It was not sadness, gaiety, or anger; neither was it anything in between. His undecipherable, haunting gaze followed her as they glided past.

Moments later the horse-drawn carriage crossed the River Seine at Pont Royale. From Rue du Bac it turned left onto Boulevard Raspail and came to a stop alongside an impressive stone building.

Margaret stifled another yawn and checked her watch. Eleven hours had passed since they had first arrived at Le Havre.

"At last," Beatrice sighed.

Margaret knew exactly how her sister felt.

13

The bronze sign mounted on the gate outside the three-story mansion at 21 Rue Raynouard still carried a glistening hint of morning dew.

American Field Service
Service Automobile Américain
Aux Armées Françaises

"My goodness," Beatrice exclaimed, as the taxi entered the grounds and parked near the entrance. "I didn't expect this."

"Nor did I," Margaret admitted as her eyes took in the magnificent chateau. The mid-morning sun accentuated the mansion's elegant stone architecture.

Margaret paid the driver; then she and Beatrice walked up wide stairs to a set of double doors. Once inside they strode across a marble floor and approached a uniformed young man sitting behind a reception desk in the middle of a spacious foyer. He looked up and rose to his feet as they approached.

"Good morning," Margaret said.

"Americans! What a pleasant surprise. Good morning to you as well, ladies. Please allow me to introduce myself. I am Carleton Keogh."

"My name is Margaret Jerome and this is my sister Beatrice."

"A pleasure to meet you both. How may I be of service?"

"I have a letter from Lieutenant Colonel Andrews regarding our brother. Would it be possible to speak with him?"

"I presume your brother is attached to the American Field Service?"

"*Was* attached. He died five weeks ago."

Keogh's voice changed to one of somber concern. "I am sorry. Please accept my deepest sympathy."

"Thank you."

A hint of recognition passed across his face. "You said your name is Jerome. Was your brother's name Michael?"

"Yes. Did you know him?"

His expression shifted to one of mild surprise. Margaret thought she understood Keogh's reaction. Her father had sent a cable informing authorities of the family's intention to return Michael's body to America. They were probably expecting Michael's parents, not his sisters.

"Yes, I did," Keogh replied. "We were acquainted and had several mutual friends. Once again, please accept my sympathy for your loss."

"Thank you, Mr. Keogh. Now, about Colonel Andrews..." Margaret left the sentence unfinished.

The young man's eyes dropped to an appointment register and his index finger moved down a series of written entries. "I expect the Colonel in about forty minutes. He has a number of meetings scheduled here in his office, but he might be able to see you before he leaves for his next appointment." He looked up. "Would you care to wait?" Before Margaret could respond, Keogh added: "Better yet, would you like to walk the grounds? The gardens are quite nice, particularly this time of year."

Margaret looked at her sister and received a slight shrug.

Beatrice had been quiet all morning, hardly speaking at breakfast or during the short taxi ride from the hotel. Margaret recognized and understood her silence. The reason they had come to France, the subject they had shied away from during their Atlantic crossing, now lay before them, stark and unavoidable.

"Yes, Mr. Keogh. That would be better than just sitting, I think."

"Let me show you the way." He led them through the long foyer to a set of French doors and onto a terrace with artfully crafted balustrades. "After your little tour of the gardens, please wait on the verandah near the fountain. It's there to our right, just below. I'll inform the Colonel of your arrival."

"Thank you."

The wide terrace overlooked a parklike setting. In the middle distance to their left, poking above the trees, stood the top third of the Eifel Tower. The spacious rear grounds—at least five acres Margaret thought—were indeed beautiful. The chateau, sited on a gentle rise above the river, showed evidence of professional landscaping: specimen trees and various flower gardens encapsulated within a manicured lawn that swept toward the quay and the gray waters of the Seine. Looking down the hill, Margaret counted seven ambulances parked along the cobbled Quai de Passy.

"I didn't expect to see so many soldiers," Beatrice remarked.

"Nor did I."

Several buildings located a short distance from the main house thrummed with activity. Men in Army uniforms worked at various tasks, some tending ambulances while others received instruction.

"Didn't Michael say this was a civilian affair?" Beatrice said.

"Yes, he did."

"Well, I don't see many civilians about."

Margaret agreed. Despite the pastoral ambiance, the estate looked more like a military training facility than the home of a civilian ambulance corps.

They descended wide stairs, strolled among the statuary and paused beside several gardens, enjoying early summer blooms but speaking little. After a while they returned to the verandah and approached a white marble bench situated beneath the green umbrella of a mature plane tree. Margaret smoothed her long dress and sat. Twenty feet away, the fountain gurgled and glittered in bright sunlight.

"Sit down and tell me about Jack Mayo," Margaret said, wanting to discuss a topic other than the reason for this visit. "You haven't spoken a word about him since we left Le Havre. Are you going to write to each other?"

Beatrice's face brightened and her eyes glowed. "Yes, we are."

"You seem taken with him."

Beatrice sat down beside her. "Oh, Margaret! I am, truly." Her smile faded. "But we had so little time together."

"But you saw him every day, Beatrice. Sometimes for hours on end."

"It didn't *seem* that long. There was so much to talk about. We enjoy the same books, prefer the same music. My Goodness, Margaret, he even likes Browning!"

"Which one: Elizabeth or Robert?"

"Both!"

"I see. But how did he manage to have so much time on his hands?"

"His sergeant took pity and rescheduled Jack's shipboard duties to late evening. That left Jack with a couple of free hours during the day."

"That was considerate. But I'm curious. Whenever Jack showed up, the both of you disappeared. Where did you two sneak off to?"

"Jack wasn't allowed to spend casual time on some of the upper decks, but we always found a reasonably quiet place."

"And?"

"We talked. Sometimes we just held hands and enjoyed each other's company."

Margaret touched her sister's forearm. "Bea, someone once wrote that sorrow is born in the hasty heart. Are you being hasty about this? Have you been swept up by the times... by a nice young man sailing off to war? If not, then how could something every girl dreams about happen so quickly? And why now?"

Beatrice studied her folded hands for a moment, then looked up. "I've thought about that, too. And you could be right. I think being among so many young soldiers facing danger affected me in some strange way; made me more susceptible to someone quiet and charming. Do you think I'm behaving like a foolish schoolgirl, going tipsy over a handsome young man in uniform?"

"No one but you can answer that."

Beatrice sighed. "Yes, I know. But the thought of being with Jack *feels* right to me, truly it does. I think about him constantly. Sometimes, I miss him so much it *hurts*."

Margaret squeezed her sister's forearm. "Then I'm sure things will work out for you both. The war can't last forever."

Lieutenant Butler's image popped unbidden into Margaret's consciousness. She looked away, her eyes moving down the green lawn, coming to rest on the flat sheen of the River Seine. She regretted not being more encouraging. He had tried so hard to overcome her initial displeasure. Early on Margaret had sensed his tendency toward introspection so it must have been difficult for him to make the effort, but he had tried, nevertheless. In hindsight she could have been more receptive to his discreet advances but it was too late for that now. Romantic opportunity had presented itself, and then fled when she failed to encourage his polite attention.

A movement caught her eye.

An older man in uniform emerged from the chateau and stepped onto the terrace. He paused for a moment his eyes searching for someone. When he saw Margaret and Beatrice, he descended the wide stairs and strode toward them.

They rose as he approached.

"Pardon me," he said to Margaret. "Are you Miss Jerome?"

"Yes, I am Margaret Jerome. This is my sister Beatrice."

"I thought as much. You and Michael share a strong resemblance." He bowed slightly. "I am Colonel Andrews. It is indeed a pleasure to meet Michael's sisters, but I deeply regret the circumstances."

"Thank you, Colonel. Did you know Michael well?"

"Yes, I did. He was one of the finest young men I had the privilege to command."

Margaret started to speak, but found herself without words. Her aching sense of loss returned, rushing in like a chilling tide that doused her warm remembrances of Lieutenant Butler.

The Colonel, probably sensing her discomfort, changed the subject. "Well, how do you like our home?"

Margaret found her voice. "It's lovely, but this isn't what we expected."

"Nor did we, actually," the Colonel said. "The Hottinguer family owns the property. They graciously donated this chateau, the grounds, and the surrounding buildings for the duration of current hostilities. We have room for offices, sleeping quarters, and messing facilities for about two hundred men."

Beatrice said, "That's another thing. We didn't expect to see so many soldiers. Michael led us to believe the American Field Service was a civilian organization."

"It was, but when America entered the war an agreement was

struck with the French government. The Field Service is now part of the American Expeditionary Forces. However, we continue to provide ambulance support to the French Army, as we have since the war began."

"I'm not sure I understand that," Beatrice persisted. "Are you telling us Michael was a civilian assigned to the American Army?"

The Colonel shook his head. "There are civilians on staff, and your brother was one of them, initially. Understandably, new arrivals from America knew little or nothing about the workings of the French army. To remedy that situation, college graduates like Michael attended the French officer training school at Meaux prior to their assignment to a military unit. When the AEF took over, the U.S. Army offered Michael—who was still a civilian—a commission. He became a lieutenant, head of an ambulance section detached to Field Service. The commission was temporary of course, one that would expire at wars end."

"This is all news to us," Margaret admitted. "We thought he was a civilian who drove an ambulance for the French."

"In the beginning he was exactly that. Later, he was part of an American ambulance unit attached to the French Army, but this time serving as a military officer commanding a medical support detachment. As I said, things changed when America joined the allies."

"But that was months ago," Margaret said. "I wonder why he never mentioned it in his letters."

"Maybe he did," the Colonel suggested. "German submarines have claimed a number of ships crossing the Atlantic. A great deal of cargo, including mail, was lost." He paused and rubbed his chin. "On the other hand, it would be unusual for a submarine to sink an empty ship returning to America. They tend to prey on fully-loaded supply transports on their way here."

"That explains the odd wording in the telegram we received," Beatrice suggested. "We assumed whoever sent the telegram thought Michael was in the Army. Now, it turns out to be true, after all."

Margaret touched a spot just below her breasts, hoping to quell the first tendrils of unease now gathering inside her abdomen. Not telling his family about joining the Army was so unlike Michael. Had he decided to spare mother and father who worried constantly about his safety? That presumption fit with the tone of the letters they'd received during the past few months: his words were more guarded and carefully chosen, a son reluctant to reveal all that was happening to him.

"In any case," Colonel Andrews continued, "Lieutenant Jerome tended to downplay his service to France. He was quite unpretentious, actually. Maybe he didn't think it was important."

Lieutenant Jerome? How odd that sounded.

Margaret—born only a few minutes ahead of her fraternal twin—had nevertheless thought of him as her 'little' brother, as though the age difference was much greater. Was that natural? She didn't know, but *Lieutenant* Jerome sounded so... *grown up.* "That could be so," she said.

The Colonel's observation made sense. Modesty had always been a part of Michael's character. Nevertheless...

Beatrice, unsatisfied, pressed on. "I just don't understand why we didn't know about the Army commission. Why would Michael not mention something so important?"

"I cannot answer that, Miss Jerome."

"This is all so strange," Beatrice muttered.

Yes, it was strange, but it was not a question they could resolve now. Margaret redirected the conversation. "In any event, Michael was driving an ambulance when... it happened. Is that part correct?"

The Colonel nodded. "Sadly, yes. He and those around him died from the blast effect produced by an explosive artillery shell."

Margaret felt her knees quiver. "What can you tell us about that?"

"All I know is what was written in the report submitted by the French officer commanding the infantry unit to which Michael was attached. Your brother's death occurred near a contested crossroads west of Lassigny. There were no survivors so the commanding officer's report is based on after-the-fact observations."

"Yes, we understand that. However, our family would be grateful for any additional information you could provide."

"I'm sorry, but everything I learned regarding your brother's death is contained in my letter."

Margaret pursed her lips, still unsatisfied. Surely, someone must have more information about Michael's activities over here. His first letters had been cheerful and newsy, full of interesting tidbits. Then something changed. Michael wrote little of his personal life, closing a door that had once been open. Did he confide more personal thoughts to a journal or diary? Margaret desperately hoped so. She did not want to travel all this way and then return home with unanswered questions.

She tried another approach. "Did he have close friends?"

"Yes, of course. Michael was well-liked."

"Any one or two in particular?"

The Colonel did not respond immediately. Then he said: "Yes, Lieutenant Gurney Shaw. I understand he and Michael attended the same college. Yale, I think. They arrived here together—traveled on the same ship I believe—and were close friends. Gurney knows as much about Michael as anyone."

"How difficult would it be for us to speak with Mr. Shaw?"

"Not difficult at all, unfortunately. Lieutenant Shaw is recuperating from wounds at the American Ambulance Hospital in Neuilly."

"You said 'recuperating'. Does that mean he will recover?"

"Yes, the doctors are quite optimistic."

"Is his condition serious?"

"Difficult to say for certain. Last week he suffered multiple fractures and lacerations to his left leg; deep and painful injuries typical of shrapnel from a trench mortar. If a sequestrum doesn't develop, then his wounds should heal."

"What on earth is a sequestrum?" Beatrice asked.

"Oh, sorry. It's a bone infection; one that often leads to sepsis— blood poisoning," the Colonel replied. "It's a fairly common occurrence, I'm afraid."

"Well, we must hope for the best." Margaret paused and thought for a moment. "As I recall, Neuilly is a suburb, not far from here."

"That's right. The hospital is on Boulevard d'Inkermann, about three miles away. I'd be happy to provide transportation."

"Yes, thank you. But first, I would like to begin arrangements for Michael's return."

The Colonel blinked several times, his confusion evident. "Arrangements for his return? I'm not sure I understand what you mean."

"We intend to take Michael's remains back to the United States, as stated in my father's cable to you."

"Cable? Miss Jerome, I received no such cable."

Margaret felt another pang deep inside her stomach—a hollow, wrenching sense of foreboding that approached nausea. She swallowed several times, determined to calm herself. Finally, she said, "You didn't?"

"A cable is not something I would forget, Miss Jerome." He was neither defensive nor confrontational, but like a gentleman expressing an unpleasant fact, rather gently.

"No, of course not," Margaret replied. A woozy rush joined the gut-twisting sensation and the world tilted before righting itself. Something was wrong.

"What did you do with him?" Beatrice whispered, her voice tinged with fear and uncertainty. "What happened to our brother's body?"

The Colonel's response seemed to echo from a great distance.

"We did what his last will and testament instructed us to do, Miss Jerome. Two days after his death, we interred your brother's remains with full military honors. His body rests in the cemetery at Suresnes, alongside those with whom he served."

The world quivered and slid out of focus and Margaret sensed the total absence of sound. She had become a voiceless mute encapsulated inside a translucent globe, safely removed from the clamor of life's random perplexities. It took a moment before she realized she had stopped breathing.

14

Beatrice sat heavily, slumping onto the marble bench.

Margaret took several deep breaths and tried to ignore the weakness in her knees. She remained standing, desperate to regain control of the riotous thoughts churning through her mind. She clamped her jaws shut, attempting to make sense of the Colonel's words.

"You *buried* him?" she finally said. "Am I to understand Michael is buried *here*—in a *cemetery?*"

"Yes, of course."

The Colonel's matter-of-fact response left her speechless once again. In the fleeting moment between heartbeats, the entire rationale for her voyage evaporated. How could this be? Margaret's deepest instincts told her that Michael belonged in the family plot back home—yet, according to Colonel Andrews, his will had specified the opposite.

Doubt began to fog her mind. Had she really sensed Michael's clearly-felt urging? Was her decision to use her father's steamship tickets a rainy-day illusion borne of grief and guilt arising from her inability to discern her twin brother's violent death?

"This just isn't fair," Beatrice wailed softly, dabbing the corner of one eye with her silk handkerchief. "We've come all this way for *nothing.*"

Margaret forced herself to concentrate, to quell her sense of confusion and replace it with understanding and clarity. Was

Beatrice's observation correct? Had their voyage been nothing more than a fool's errand?

"Is that true, Colonel?" she said, regaining something of her composure. "Can we do nothing about this?"

He raised both hands to his waist, palms upward. "Please try to understand, ladies. Your brother left a valid will. His instructions regarding last remains were specific and unambiguous. We had no choice in the matter. In truth, your father's cable would have made no difference. The legal will of the deceased would have been honored, regardless of his family's wishes."

Margaret nodded. The will was problematic. Had Michael written it under duress—during a particularly difficult time? Had he later experienced a change of heart? If so, then effort and determination could sometimes overcome the unexpected. All it took was a glimmer of opportunity, no matter how faint, and unflagging effort to see it through. If she genuinely believed Michael wanted burial alongside the graves of his grandparents, then returning home without her brother's remains was unthinkable. If a way existed to rectify the situation, then she intended to discover it.

Margaret said, "But the issue can be re-visited, can it not? I mean, diplomatically?"

The Colonel's expression cramped and his tone of voice took on an edge. "I suppose you could explore that avenue via the American Embassy. A French court would ultimately decide the matter; however, they could not easily ignore the wishes of the United States government regarding disposition of an American soldier's remains. On the other hand, neither can a court defy the law by negating a properly executed last will and testament of the deceased. Is it your plan to pursue this matter, Miss Jerome?"

Plan? What plan? How could I have planned for this?

"Colonel Andrews, I have no idea what I'm going to do next.

Michael's decision has come as a great shock to us. We never expected anything like this."

The Colonel's expression smoothed. "May I make a suggestion?"

"Of course."

"Take a day or so before you decide on a course of action. Visit the cemetery at Suresnes; it's just across the river. Speak with Gurney Shaw. Give yourself an opportunity to think this through—to reflect on Michael's final request. He surely understood how this decision would affect his family. Knowing your brother, I find it difficult to believe he acted as he did without considering the effect it might have on those back home. Disinterment of his remains is not an option you should pursue unless you are positive it's the right thing to do."

Margaret's gaze shifted. It followed the sloping lawn and then paused at the Seine, flat and pewter gray as it slid northwest toward Honfleur and the English Channel. The Colonel's suggestions made sense. After all, time was not a factor. They could remain in Paris for as long as it took to resolve this matter. Besides, she could do nothing until she explained the situation to her parents. Informing them was necessary, of course. However, Margaret understood that *what* she communicated was more important than *when.* Regardless of how her parents felt about the steamship tickets—were they still angry?—the *tone* of Margaret's letter, along with a personal viewpoint, would have an impact on how they might resolve this unexpected dilemma. A few days, even a week, would make little difference.

She met the Colonel's inquisitive gaze. "You offered transportation, did you not?"

"Absolutely. I will make a car and driver available to you for the remainder of the day."

"That is generous, perhaps more than we deserve."

"Not at all. I'm delighted to do so."

"Thank you, Colonel."

"You're welcome. If I may ask, where do you plan to go?"

Margaret considered the question for a moment. Then she knew exactly what she and Beatrice must do. "We will first go to Suresnes and see where Michael is buried. From there, we will visit the American hospital. That is, if Gurney Shaw is well enough to receive visitors."

"I believe he is. I will call Neuilly and let them know of your arrival later today."

"Thank you, Colonel."

"May we talk again before you make a final decision?"

"Yes, of course."

"Excellent. Give me a few minutes to arrange for a car and driver."

*

Their transportation turned out to be Colonel Andrews's personal automobile, a glistening black Mercedes touring car. The driver, a soldier introduced as Corporal Iverson, answered her unspoken question.

"The car doesn't really belong to the Colonel," he informed them. "The Frog government lets him use it."

"How thoughtful of them," Margaret said.

"That's nothing," Iverson added. His face turned toward the back seat, but his eyes remained on the road. "Mrs. Vanderbilt—that rich lady from New York—donated ten Ford ambulances."

They drove across a stone bridge west of the city proper, through a small cluster of buildings, and then up a steep hill. As they neared the cemetery, Margaret felt her hands begin to tremble.

"This is called Mount Valerien," Iverson again volunteered. "Someone told me Napoleon had big plans for this site."

Margaret clutched her hands together and somehow found her voice. "What sort of plans?" she asked, trying hard to overcome her growing apprehension.

"A home for old soldiers, I think, or a place for the families of dead heroes. Something like that. Anyway, Waterloo kinda upset those plans."

"I imagine so," Margaret offered.

Following another minute of silence, Corporal Iverson said: "The cemetery is coming up on our left."

Margaret's heart pounded, threatening to burst through her chest. Her feet became restless, first one foot moving forward or backward, then the other, wanting to take her somewhere else; but she forced her ankles close together, ashamed of her growing desire to flee, to have Corporal Iverson turn the car around and return to... *where?*

She turned and looked at her sister. Beatrice, her face unnaturally pale, stared straight ahead, unblinking.

As they approached the main entrance, Margaret noticed a scattering of fresh plantings; beech and oak, mostly. The young trees and scores of new white crosses gave the impression of fresh life sprouting from the earth. It was an odd image for a cemetery; but then she reconsidered. Resurrection of the soul was indeed a new beginning, was it not?

Corporal Iverson parked beside wide steps leading to an iron gate. He looked at Margaret. "Did the Colonel tell you where your brother's grave is located?"

"Yes, he did," she murmured.

Iverson stepped from the car and opened the rear door. "I'll wait here until you get back. Take all the time you want."

She and Beatrice made their way slowly up the wide gravel path then turned left. Margaret, a lump rising in her throat, counted rows and crosses as they moved hesitantly through the grounds. Fresh sod squished beneath their feet. 'We have burials every morning,' the Colonel had told her. 'Please watch your step. The sod might be soft in places.'

It was, indeed.

Margaret stopped. "Here he is."

She stared at the plain white wooden cross, indistinguishable from so many others, and felt her knees tremble as she read the inscription.

1894-1918
Michael Patrick Jerome 2d Lt AEF
Chevalier du Legion d'Honneur
Mort pour la France

"It's true," Beatrice muttered. "Michael is really gone. I didn't believe it until now. I always thought we'd see him again." Her voice trailed away. Her shoulders began to shake as she cried.

Margaret felt tears gathering in her eyes and overflowing down her cheeks. Beatrice had echoed her thoughts exactly. Despite the telegrams and letters, Margaret had not quite accepted her brother's death. It was all a frightful mistake. She and Beatrice would sail to France and find Michael alive and cheerful. The three would have a great laugh and ridicule the ineptitude of bumbling bureaucracies.

Later, in private, she would tell her brother all the things she should have told him but never did; of how ignorant it was of her to blame him for the numerous failings of society. He would listen and smile and tell her he understood, and then make a silly joke about 'backward' twins.

But here, in this beautiful and dignified place, staring at his name carved into a simple wooden cross, all her hopeful rationalizations crumbled. Her brother would never hear what she desperately needed to tell him. Nor could Michael help her understand how he had passed from this life without her sensing his death. Did she lack a vital perceptive element that made her oblivious to her twin brother's fate? Or was it the great geographical distance that had separated them?

As her body trembled and sobs escaped from her throat, a soft atmosphere of timeless continuity formed around her. She could feel Michael's unique presence, but this time he was in the company of many others, he and they sharing a long moment in eternity. Michael and all those ghostly ranks existed everywhere at once, cohered spirits gathered in a place just beyond her vision.

The closeness she had shared with Michael since their first moments of life persisted, but she also knew that he was now part of a larger existence. Unlike her disquieted feelings on that rainy day back home, Michael's spirit exuded a sense of peace.

Unsure of what she might be feeling, Margaret's blurred gaze wandered among perfect rows of crosses, brilliant white markers rising from an immaculate green carpet, her moist eyes searching.

If she focused hard enough and long enough…

She held her breath, waiting, but nothing happened. As her lungs again took in air, the unearthly feeling ebbed away.

Standing on that quiet hill overlooking the great southerly loop of the River Seine, Margaret's heart finally accepted what her brain knew to be true: One might share a life with another human being, but the living could never share a death.

Margaret wasn't certain how long they stood there, dabbing tears from their eyes. Eventually their sniffles grew quiet and her grief surrendered to weary depression. She and Beatrice looked at each other and then embraced—a long, affectionate hug, one they had shared so many times before with Michael—three souls bound together by their parent's flesh and blood and the unyielding bond of sibling love. As she hugged Beatrice, faint hope refused to yield. *Put your arms around us, Michael. Just once more...*

She waited for his familiar touch but felt nothing but the soft breeze. He was no longer a living element of her life and his absence intensified an aching void.

"Now we know for sure," Margaret whispered.

She felt Beatrice nod, a wordless end to lingering hope. "Let's say a prayer for Michael," Margaret suggested.

Afterwards, they turned and retraced their steps across the still-damp sod.

*

On their way to the American Hospital at Neuilly, Beatrice broke a long silence. "What does Knight of the Honor Legion mean?"

"I'm not sure," Margaret replied wearily. Every muscle in her body felt drained of energy, but Beatrice's question revived an earlier curiosity.

The inscription on Michael's cross puzzled her as well. It almost certainly meant something significant. Walking back to the Colonel's automobile after prayer, she had taken note of names and inscriptions carved into other crosses. All contained the phrase *Mort pour la France*—Died for France—but none she saw contained the words *Chevalier du Legion d'Honneur*. Obviously, the French government considered Michael a 'Knight of the Honor Legion'—whatever that meant. The words piqued Margaret's curiosity. She said, "We will ask the Colonel. I'm sure he knows what it means."

"It's a French medal," Corporal Iverson again volunteered from the front seat. "A real doozy. I think it's the highest award Frogs give to a foreigner."

"Really?" Beatrice said. "What on earth did Michael do to deserve such a medal?"

The Corporal shrugged. "Can't say, Miss Jerome. You'll have to

117

ask the Colonel about that."

Beatrice muttered, "I don't understand *any* of this. First he joins the Army, then he gets a medal, and then he decides to be buried here… in a foreign country. What else don't we know? What else did he keep from us?"

Margaret didn't reply. Instead, she felt a slow flush of troubling anticipation. *What else did he keep from us?* The haunting question wouldn't stand still. It danced through her mind, a slippery presence she could not quite grasp.

"We're here," Corporal Iverson announced.

The car stopped at the curb near the hospital's main entrance.

According to Colonel Andrews, the man they were about to visit—Gurney Shaw—knew more about Michael than anyone. Was that possible? Could a stranger be more cognizant of Michael's frame of mind than his fraternal twin? She didn't think so. Not sensing his death had been a shock, but Margaret still believed she and her brother had shared something akin to a spiritual third consciousness. It was a conviction reinforced by the memory of a teen-aged ice-skating party.

On that bright and brisk winter morning, she and Michael had met a group of friends at one of the ice-covered ponds in Forest Park. The boys went off to play crack the whip but Margaret stayed ashore, choosing instead to join other girls who stood around a log fire, chatting. She was in the middle of sharing a silly tidbit of high-school gossip, her back toward the undulating line of boys skating across the pond, when an icy shudder far different than one might expect from chilly weather made her stop in mid-sentence. In that frozen moment, long seconds before she heard Michael cry out in pain, she knew something dreadful had happened to her brother. Turning, she saw Michael on the far side of the pond, sitting on the ice, his companions standing over him. Michael had taken a bad spill—had broken his wrist—and she had somehow known of his plight the moment it had happened.

Margaret's experience at the cemetery had been different. She had never felt dread, nor had she sensed the otherworldly hint of a premonition. What she had experienced on Mount Valerian was the familiar tonal resonance of her brother's spirit; a presence communicating a message she had yet to decipher.

Stepping onto the sidewalk, Margaret felt a deepening chill icing its way through her body: a sense of change not unlike the first early-morning frost of an approaching winter.

15

"The Colonel called earlier," Gurney Shaw said to Margaret. "He told me you might be dropping by."

Gurney, a pleasant-faced, slender man about twenty-five years old, wheelchair bound and wearing an elegant blue silk dressing gown over matching pajamas, smiled at them. His left leg, immobilized by a plaster cast, rested on a horizontal extension attached to the wheelchair's seat. If one ignored morning apparel and the unmistakable aroma of disinfectant, one might easily picture Gurney Shaw as a pale-complexioned office administrator of some sort; certainly not a man who drove an ambulance in and out of harm's way. On closer inspection however, the wizened nature of his gaze would invariably lead one to question and then abandon the Mr. Milquetoast presumption.

"I would have recognized you in any case," he continued. "You and Michael look remarkably alike. But then, why shouldn't you?" He shifted his attention to Beatrice. "No question about it. You three definitely share a strong family resemblance."

Margaret said, "You are not the first person to make that comment, Mr. Shaw."

"It's not *Mister* Shaw; not anymore. I am now *Lieutenant* Shaw, a temporary minion of the United States Army. But let's not dwell on stuffy formality. With your permission, let's make it Gurney, Margaret, and Beatrice."

"Michael was a lieutenant, as well," Beatrice said. "We didn't know about his military rank until today. It seems that particular letter may have been lost."

Gurney shook his head. "To my knowledge Michael sent no letter regarding our change in status from civilian to military, so I doubt it was lost. I believe your brother decided not to tell his family about the Army commission."

"Why would he do that?" Beatrice asked; her voice more plaintive than demanding.

Gurney's eyes flicked away, his reluctance evident. Finally he said, "Would you mind wheeling me outside? It's a nice day and I enjoy the sunshine."

They were standing in the main wing of a brightly lit ground floor hallway at the rear of the hospital. Outside, patients and nurses nearly filled the courtyard's trimmed lawns—neat greens divided into three large sections by gray concrete paths.

"Of course we wouldn't mind," Margaret said. She was still thinking about Gurney's answer to Beatrice's question. This was so strange. Michael was not secretive and had never concealed anything important. Had he changed that much—or were there other reasons?

She steered Gurney's wheelchair through wide-open doors and outside where other wounded soldiers enjoyed warm but not yet oppressively hot weather. Dozens of men, many in wheelchairs but a few moving about with or without crutches, spilled onto the expansive, neatly trimmed lawns. White-clad nurses and orderlies moved easily among their charges.

The murmur of a half-dozen dialects and language filled the air. "I didn't realize this was an allied hospital," she said.

"Few people do," he replied. "Not only do they care for French and English soldiers, but we also have men from French colonies: Senegal, Algeria, Morocco, and even a few from Annam."

"Annam?" Beatrice said. "Where on earth is that?"

Gurney smiled. "Indochina."

"So it really is a *world* war, isn't it?" Beatrice murmured.

Margaret found a relatively secluded spot beside a white-painted wooden bench. She parked the wheelchair and sat facing Gurney, Beatrice at her side.

"You said Michael never informed us about joining the Army," Margaret began. "Why would he keep something like that from us?"

Gurney studied them, his brown eyes moving from her to Beatrice and then back to Margaret, perhaps weighing the implications of sharing what he knew. He expelled air from his nose, apparently arriving at a decision.

"To begin with, what we saw is difficult to explain to someone who wasn't there. The war wasn't at all like the *Iliad* or Caesar's commentaries. Books and college lectures failed to prepare us for the mind-shattering din of an actual battlefield, for the inability to hear a man's shouted voice, even though his face is inches away from yours. You can see his lips move, but the ceaseless clamor overwhelms everything. I believe the horrors we witnessed gave Michael an urgency of purpose he had never felt before. I also believe he discovered a sense of individuality. That, I think, made him determined to follow his own path, no matter where it might lead."

Follow his own path? Margaret opened her mouth, wanting clarification, but then hesitated as Gurney continued.

"There was one particular conversation that stands out. It occurred during one of the few quiet times we shared at the front. We had parked our ambulances side by side and sat on the running boards facing each other. 'Gurney,' he said to me, 'I've spent my whole life trying to satisfy the expectations of others. It took a terrible war to make me realize that life is much too short to chase someone else's dream. Even under ideal circumstances, that other person will always be disappointed.'

"I asked him what he planned to do, you know, after the war. 'I'm not sure,' he told me. 'I've half a notion to remain in France. I could grow a beard, frequent left-bank coffee houses, and have passionate discussions about obscure topics. I might even become a disgruntled writer-in-exile like one of those fictional characters we read about in college.' Then he smiled. 'Assuming, of course, that I'm still alive and able to grow a beard.'

"The words might not be exact, but that's close to how he felt. I believe Michael experienced a newfound sense of freedom, a discovered opportunity to live and do work that was meaningful, like driving an ambulance, but also important to himself as well. For the first time in his life perhaps, Michael was thinking and acting on his own behalf, without regard to family obligations."

Margaret said, "I'm not sure I understand what that means."

"Really? What did Michael do before he joined the Field Service?"

That was an easy question for Margaret to answer. "He was learning the family business, gaining an understanding of each function by working in various departments. When the time came, he would succeed our father as president of the company."

"And before that he was at Yale, where we first met and became close friends."

"Yes, Michael took a degree in commerce."

"That's what I mean," Gurney explained. "He was doing precisely what was expected of him: the dutiful son following in his father's footsteps."

"But he graduated *cum laude*—with honors."

"Of course he did. That was Michael—heart before head—doing what others expected of him rather than what *he* wanted to do."

Gurney's remark resurrected a memory that struck Margaret like a soft blow to the abdomen. She turned and spoke to Beatrice. "Did I ever tell you what Michael told me on the day he left for France?" she asked.

Beatrice shook her head.

"Michael said that he and I were a backward pair; a mismatched set of twins."

"I don't understand," Beatrice said.

"He called me the Doer while he was the Dreamer. He said he envisioned, but I accomplished. He said Father should be grooming me for the business, not him."

"What a strange thing to say," Beatrice told her.

Margaret nodded. It had indeed been an astonishing revelation, an admitted contradiction of sibling roles she too had felt but could not articulate. Margaret had wanted to talk more about the 'mismatched pair', to explore the different nature of their abilities, but Michael had never clarified his thoughts, even in his private letters to her.

As the sole male offspring, everyone naturally assumed he would carry on with the business Father had started. She could not remember a single discussion offering Michael a future other than that. Had he resented it? Did he want to do something different with his life? If so, what might it have been? Margaret realized she didn't know, and the reason she did not know was because she had never asked. Like everyone else in the family, she had made certain assumptions regarding Michael's career. Did her preconceived notions prevent her from sensing what Michael truly felt?

Those thoughts reminded her of the change in tone that began a month or so before his death. Rather than cheerful and filled with interesting observations, his letters had taken on an uncharacteristic mix of regretful melancholy. At the time, she felt that Michael was on the verge of revealing something important, a special insight, but could not find the right words. It further saddened Margaret to realize she might never learn what had troubled him so.

She shifted in her seat, trying to find a more comfortable position.

"Why did he get that medal?" Beatrice asked Gurney, changing the subject. "The one inscribed on his cross."

"You wondered about the medal, did you? I thought you might."

"Yes, we did," Margaret replied. "What does Knight of the Honor Legion mean?"

Gurney studied his hands for a moment, and then looked at her. "The medal is called the Legion of Honor. France inducted Michael into the Legion with the rank of *Chevalier*—Knight. Higher ranks are given to Frenchmen, or to the president of another nation."

"For Heaven's sake. What on Earth did he do to earn such an award?" Margaret asked.

"Michael would say he was doing what was important to him: removing wounded men from the battlefield, loading them onto stretchers or into ambulances, and evacuating them to an aid station or field hospital."

"What would *you* say," Margaret persisted.

"I would say your brother risked his life on many occasions to save the lives of French soldiers and was recognized for his efforts."

Beatrice spoke up. "Is that how he died?"

Gurney nodded. "Having been one of them, Michael realized how important it was to get wounded men to an aid station quickly. He never wavered in that commitment."

"One of them?" Margaret sensed something deeper behind the phrase. "What do you mean?"

Gurney shook his head and frowned. "I forgot. Michael probably never said anything about that either."

"Are you telling us Michael was *wounded*—injured in *battle!?*" Margaret began to feel a sense of unreality. Were they discussing Michael or someone else?

"Yes, on two different occasions. He spent nearly five weeks right here, alongside other soldiers."

"On *two* different occasions? In *this* hospital?" Margaret suddenly lost her voice. An invisible bellows had sucked all the air from her lungs. She gasped softly and took several deep breaths. Then, in a calmer tone, "Why weren't we notified?"

"Michael wanted it kept confidential. In certain matters of a personal nature, the French Army can be quite accommodating."

Margaret looked at her sister. Beatrice's open-mouthed expression reflected bafflement, a mood similar to her own feelings. "This doesn't make any sense, does it?"

Beatrice clamped her lips shut and then shook her head.

She turned to Gurney and paused, studying his face. He looked much paler than when they first arrived. Crow's feet squeezed the corners of his eyes and his mouth formed a tight line. She touched his arm. "Are you in pain?"

Gurney's lips turned upward, more grimace than smile. "Is it that obvious? Sorry. There's quite a bit more you need to hear, but that will have to wait. My keeper has arrived."

"There's more?" Margaret turned as a middle-aged nurse approached carrying a small porcelain tray containing a syringe and hypodermic needle.

"You always schedule your arrival just in the nick of time," Gurney said to the nurse.

"That's why I'm so invaluable, Lieutenant." To Margaret she said, "This injection will make him drowsy for several hours. I think you should say your farewells until the next time."

Gurney shrugged and spoke to Margaret. "Nurse Tuttle is right.

Morphia knocks me silly. Can you come back tomorrow? I'd like you to meet someone."

"Another of Michael's friends?" Margaret asked.

"Yes, I suppose you could say that. A person who knew him even better than I."

"Really? In that case, I'm sure we can."

"Then here we go," Nurse Tuttle said, placing the tray on the bench next to Beatrice.

The nurse worked with professional efficiency. She opened Gurney's robe, undid the buttons of his pajama top, and then slid one side down, exposing a portion of Gurney's upper left arm. She then scrubbed a spot on his thin white shoulder with an alcohol swab and administered the narcotic. The effect was almost immediate. He smiled and his eyes took on a faraway look.

The nurse slipped the used syringe and porcelain tray into a leather pocket in the seat's back. Then she rearranged Gurney's pajama top and robe, grasped the handles of his wheelchair, and smiled at Margaret and Beatrice. "I must return him to his ward."

"We understand."

"It was a pleasure meeting you ladies," Gurney slurred. He waved lazily as Nurse Tuttle wheeled him away.

Margaret raised her hand and returned the wave.

"I don't know what to say," Beatrice remarked. "I'm more than a little stunned by all this."

"So am I," Margaret admitted.

She turned and her eyes roamed across the lawn to where dozens of soldiers still enjoyed bright sunshine. *There's quite a bit more*, Gurney had said. What did that mean? And who was this other person Gurney wanted them to meet—an unnamed someone who knew Michael better than did his best friend?

Margaret felt an unsatisfied urge, a maddening itch in a place just beyond her reach. Her heart yearned to find answers to unexpected questions, to grasp an understanding of realities that challenged strongly-held assumptions regarding her special relationship with Michael. What had once seemed so clear was now a muddle.

The more she pondered what Gurney had revealed—and the odd nature of what she had sensed from somewhere beyond—the more unsettled she became.

Obeying an impulse Margaret rose and stepped onto the lawn, leaving Beatrice who remained seated. Walking slowly, she made her way among the wounded men, acknowledging their long glances with a nod or a smile. She hadn't realized there were so many amputees. Most were missing a single extremity; others had lost matched or mixed pairs of arms and legs, feet and hands. A few suffered horrifying disfigurement.

As soldiers acknowledged her presence with a word or a smile, Margaret also noticed a peculiar similarity, a subtleness of expression she had first observed on the face of the one-legged *poilu* at the Tuileries Gardens when she and Beatrice had first arrived in Paris. Gurney Shaw exhibited that same odd characteristic as well. She hadn't really thought about it until now, but there was no mistaking it.

Regardless of coloring or nationality, the face of each wounded man bore the wise, ageless expression of one who had suffered and endured a unique ordeal. Their searing brush with mortality had left a tempered core, an inner self absent the romantic delusions of the uninitiated. Her brother had likewise suffered, probably as much as the men among whom she now walked. Michael's war injuries had thrust him into this unique fraternity, a comradeship where bleeding on a battlefield was the sole rite of initiation.

Had Michael perceived a truth beyond the pain of his wounds? Had he accepted the inevitability of death? Had he glimpsed its approach and then modified his will so that his body could remain among those with whom he had shared so much? Did he truly desire rest in foreign soil—to spend eternity on that high, hallowed place so far from home?

A lump rose in her throat, quick and hot and surging: an emotional shiver bringing with it profound understanding. Here among the scores of wounded, what she had experienced on that dreary afternoon finally became clear.

For the first time since learning of Michael's death, Margaret knew with certainty what she must do... what Michael wanted her to do. It was not what she had thought—not at all—nor was it something her family might easily accept. Nevertheless, the clarity of that insight came as a tonic.

She felt her back stiffen, her mind filling with the determination necessary to face a heartbreaking prospect.

16

Margaret had not slept well, tossing for hours, unable to quell the persistent flow of questions arising from the previous day's conversations with Colonel Andrews and Gurney Shaw. There was a great deal more ambiguity in Michael's life than she had once believed possible.

A part of her sensed their unique connection, a mystical bond unlike any other. However, sibling envy sometimes tested that assumption. As a man, Michael had benefited from certain advantages not usually accorded females, some of which she had accepted, albeit reluctantly. Margaret had raged at laws and social rules that limited her choices. When police officials jailed suffragists Alice Paul and Lucy Burns for the 'crime' of wanting to vote, Margaret's frustration boiled over. Poor Michael had suffered the worst of her outrage.

Another part knew her brother was not to blame for bigotry or the tacitly sanctioned segregation practices and condescending manner of others. Nor had he exhibited the social arrogance she found so appalling in too many men their age. Still, his sympathetic demeanor made him a handy foil. At those times he had quietly absorbed her vexation, often agreeing with what she said but unable to change the prevailing attitudes of the day.

Yet, while she could often share a portion of his moods, Michael had something more: an extraordinary sense of perceiving more of

Margaret's feelings—abilities beyond her own.

Nevertheless, they were different people. While Michael had been affable and not prone to confrontation, Margaret rarely backed away from a potential argument. And when it came to personal matters, Margaret believed she was much better at concealing what she truly felt.

That is, until yesterday.

She and Beatrice sat opposite each other in the Lutetia's dining room. Margaret broke a small piece from a croissant and topped it with a chunky smear of orange marmalade.

She placed the butter knife on a small plate and looked at her sister. "What are you thinking, Bea?"

"I'm still confused, and a little upset, too." She took a sip of tea before continuing. "I don't understand why we didn't know any of this. My goodness Margaret, our brother became a soldier, twice wounded in battle! And the *medal*...!" She paused for breath, her expression a mixture of youthful consternation and puzzlement. "We all have our little secrets, yes; but the Michael I remember wouldn't keep such things to himself."

"And Gurney Shaw said there was a lot more," Margaret reminded her.

"Yes, he did. I have no idea what he meant and that *frightens* me."

Margaret felt anxious as well, but she would never admit to such fears. Someone had to remain calm, to keep control of their emotions. She was the eldest, by a few minutes in Michael's case, but it was still her responsibility.

"What else do you suppose there might be?" Beatrice asked. Her red-rimmed eyes reflected the haunted look of one anticipating the worst of all possible outcomes, an innocent defendant unjustly convicted of a crime, fearfully awaiting the judge's sentence.

Chewing her croissant, it occurred to Margaret that neither she nor her sister had slept well. In an odd way however, Margaret felt she was beginning to understand Michael's behavior. The notion had developed overnight while she tossed in bed, repeatedly fluffing her pillow, waiting for an uneasy sleep that finally arrived near dawn. As the words formed, Margaret began to explain her thoughts.

"Listen to us, behaving as though Michael committed a great outrage. Stop and think for a moment. What did he really keep from us? That he was a soldier? His work as an ambulance driver didn't change—he still served with French troops. Maybe he considered the Army commission a formality. What else: that he was unselfish and brave? That he risked his life to save others? Is that so surprising? Our brother was never one to toot his own horn. Did you really expect him to tell us such things? To puff himself up in letters? Of course not. The Michael we knew and loved would never do that."

Beatrice leaned back in her chair, the haunted look slowly giving way to one of thoughtful acceptance. "Yes, I suppose that *could* explain some of it, but what about his will and the burial? How do you explain that?"

"I'm not sure I can," she admitted, "not completely."

It was a truth she had no choice but to accept. Prior to learning of his will, Margaret had been positive regarding what she had assumed Michael wanted; that is, to have his body returned home for burial. Her subsequent experiences at the cemetery and hospital clearly contradicted what she had once believed.

"Anyway," she continued, "whatever else we learn today will be in keeping with Michael's character. I have no doubt about that. We may be surprised, but if we are, then we should ask ourselves why."

"What do you mean?"

"Bea, do you think Michael really wanted to attend Yale? To study commerce? Was he happy working for Father?"

"I don't know. I never thought about it."

"Exactly. Neither did I. Did Michael ever tell us, either way? Did we ever bother to ask?"

"Well, no. I just assumed…"

"Mother and Father probably did the same thing: assumed what we thought Michael wanted. Suppose our assumptions were wrong."

Beatrice took another sip of tea. Finally, she said: "Maybe we didn't understand Michael as well as we thought."

Margaret dabbed marmalade on another bite of croissant. "I believe we knew Michael's heart, his essential goodness, but you have a point. It seems none of us knew everything that went on inside his head." Another possibility occurred to her. "Do you think Michael was unhappy all this time and I—we—never knew it?"

"Please don't say that."

"But suppose he was. What does that tell you about us?"

"We are *not* a bad family. I refuse to believe that."

Deep inside Margaret agreed, even though the dark memory of sibling envy continued to haunt her. Had her mind somehow compensated for such unsisterly thoughts, creating the illusion that she and Michael were closer than they really were? If so, it was a possibility she was reluctant to share with her sister. Instead, she talked around the subject. "No, I suppose that's true. But maybe you and I pay too much attention to what *we* want and not enough to what others might need."

"Does that mean we're self-centered?"

"Would that surprise you?"

"No, I suppose not."

"We also take too much for granted. Sometimes I think we behave like honeybees—focusing on what's under our nose—oblivious to everything else."

Beatrice half-smiled but offered no comment.

Margaret swallowed tea—the same Lady Grey brand Beatrice had chosen—a dark brew hinting of citrus. Her mind sifted through the events of the last six weeks, searching for a way out of the emotional dilemma she now faced.

Years ago, Margaret had come upon *The Tale of the Monkey's Paw*, a reprint of an earlier short story written by someone whose name she no longer remembered. However, she had never forgotten the moral of that rather frightening story: *Be careful what you wish for.*

They finished breakfast in silence. Margaret touched a napkin to her lips and checked the time. "We still have two hours before visitors are allowed in the hospital. What would you like to do until then?"

"I don't know. I feel like taking a nap. I didn't sleep well. Are my eyes as red and puffy as yours?"

"Yes, they are."

Except for several pleasant interludes aboard the *Mongolia*, she and Beatrice had been in a state of mourning since hearing news of Michael's death. Margaret wanted to improve their mood before meeting with Gurney. But witless gaiety was clearly not appropriate when visiting wounded soldiers in hospital. Nor could she totally ignore the grief that squeezed her heart without letup. To avoid chronic depression—if that was possible—Margaret knew she had to re-establish a semblance of balance between those two emotional extremes.

An idea popped into her head. "I don't want to take a nap. We can nap all we like on the voyage home. Bea, we're in Paris! I know it's not the best time, but we've been cooped up for nearly two weeks. Why don't we do something between now and when we have to meet Gurney?"

"But I don't *feel* like doing anything."

"Neither do I, but that's the point! We should."

Beatrice did not look convinced. "What do you have in mind?"

"I don't know. How about re-visiting Sacre-Coeur? It was under construction the last time we were here and the basilica wasn't open to visitors. But now it is. We could go inside and say another prayer for Michael. While we're there, we could also look around. If I remember, the view is spectacular. It might raise our spirits."

Beatrice shrugged, apparently indifferent to the prospect. "I don't feel much like sightseeing."

"Neither do I, but we should try to think about something other than how bad we feel, at least for a little while."

Beatrice lifted one shoulder half-heartedly. "Well, if you insist…"

"I don't insist. But let's do it anyway."

Outside, the liveried doorman whistled for a cabriolet.

"*Montmartre*," Margaret told the driver. "*La basilique du sacré coeur.*"

They rode without speaking, the silence broken by the sound of iron-rimmed wheels and shod hoofs clattering over granite cobblestones. The early morning air was already warm but the cabriolet's fringed black leather roof shielded them from the sun.

Twenty minutes later the two sisters stepped from the cab, turned, and looked across the city.

Margaret's breath caught in her throat.

High atop Montmartre hill, standing in the shadow of Sacre-Coeur's brilliant alabaster domes, all Paris stretched down and away, magical and magnificent, a dazzling city trembling with memories of a turbulent history. Margaret imagined Genevieve defying Attila's hordes; the coming of Charlemagne, Joan of Arc, and Charles VII— gray and golden years of iron and empire; a churning parade of individuals and events that ultimately led to the Bastille,

Robespierre's Terror, and a bloody end to French monarchy. Her gaze took in the elegance of Eiffel's tower—a lacy spire piercing the horizon—and finally came to rest at the Invalides where Napoleon's body lay in a crypt beneath the yellow dome.

From up here it was all so beautiful—and so illusory. In the streets below, shuttered and silent like a house abandoned by its owner, Paris lay stripped of gaiety. The City of Light no longer glittered. Lovely and intemperate Paris had become a shadowy refuge for the wounded—a gathering place haunted by widows and orphans and sad old men silently puffing on brown cigarettes.

Contrary to what she had hoped, neither the basilica nor the breathtaking view lifted her spirits. Instead, the visit left Margaret with an even deeper feeling of melancholy.

Beatrice had been right. This was not a good time for sightseeing.

17

"Have you heard the news?" Gurney Shaw's deep-set eyes were alive with excitement as both fists pounded the arms of his wheelchair.

Nurse Tuttle pushed Gurney's wheelchair down the center of a wide hallway where an overflow of wounded men lay head to foot in cots jammed alongside either wall.

"Have you heard the wonderful news?"

"Settle down, Lieutenant. You'll tip over."

Nurse Tuttle approached and stopped. "He's all yours," she said to Margaret, rolling her eyes. Then she turned and strode back down the crowded hallway from which she'd come.

Margaret said: "Gurney, I have no idea what you mean."

"Haven't you read *Le Petit Parisien*?" The lighthearted expression became one of disappointment, as though a great and glorious revelation had unexpectedly burst forth and nobody noticed or cared.

"We generally don't read Paris newspapers. They tend to be political and therefore boring. Now, tell us what's gotten you so excited."

Gurney drew a deep breath. "We've pushed the Germans back across the Marne."

"That's nice," Beatrice said. "But I'm not sure what that means."

Gurney blinked several times, his jaw agape.

Margaret explained. "I'm afraid we're uninformed when it comes to military matters. I assume you mean the Marne River."

Gurney closed his mouth, his knitted forehead reflected distress at their admitted ignorance.

"Does that mean the artillery bombs will stop falling on Paris?" Margaret added.

His expression softened. "Yes, perhaps it does."

"Then that *is* wonderful news," Beatrice said. "Two days ago at the train station, the ground actually *shook*, but the sound came from far away. We've heard several more, but none that shook the ground like that first one."

Gurney adjusted his position on the wheelchair. "The Germans call it the Paris Gun," he told them. "It can lob a two-hundred-pound shell more than fifty miles. It's not accurate, but people in the northeast section of the city seem to get the brunt of them."

Margaret said, "If what you just told us about the Marne is true, then could the worst of the bombing be over?"

"Yes, but it's more than that," Gurney said, his voice rising. "If we push east and north from Soissons and Chateau Thierry, the German Army will have to abandon Rheims. And if we continue pushing, this offensive could end the war."

"End the war? Are you serious?"

Margaret could not quite get her mind around the idea. Ever since Michael had announced his intention to join the American Field Service and drive ambulances in France, genuine concern for his safety had dampened her initial enthusiasm. At first, she was pleased about his impending departure. Margaret was full of ideas about how to improve the family business. With Michael in France, her father might pay more attention to her suggestions.

Then, haunted by a growing sense of shame, Margaret had agonized over her jealousies, a sense of guilt that had plagued her for the past two years. Now, could the war that had claimed her brother's life be nearing an end?

"Yes, I believe so," Gurney replied. Then the excitement drained from his face.

"Is something wrong?" Margaret asked.

"Offensive operations mean more troops out in the open. Casualties will rise—significantly."

Beatrice shot a frightened look at Margaret. "Oh, my."

Margaret was still mulling Gurney's comment about the war. It was too late for Michael—a bitter truth beyond denial—but not for others. The faces of all those young soldiers aboard the *Mongolia* came to mind; among them were Robert Butler and Jack Mayo. Were they in danger? She had no way of knowing except through Beatrice, assuming Jack wrote to her as promised. Besides, what would Jack know about Robert?

"Have I said something wrong?" Gurney asked.

Beatrice said, "We have friends in the Medical Corps, two nice gentlemen we met on the voyage. Naturally, we have concerns about their safety."

Margaret said nothing.

Did she really think of Robert Butler as a casual friend or might there be something else? His face had winnowed its way into her mind on several occasions since that last evening at sea—those gray eyes lightly flecked with green, calm and clear and absent of guile—images that surprised her by the intensity of their unexpected appearance. She had not encouraged him while aboard ship. Now that he might be in danger... She looked at her folded hands. The knuckles were white and bloodless. With effort, she forced herself to relax.

"I have a pal or two down in Chaumont," Gurney said. "That's where AEF Headquarters is located. If you give me their names, I'll ask my friends to have a look at the assignment list. If either of those two gentlemen are posted to a base hospital, then it should be fairly easy to find out which one."

"That would be wonderful." Beatrice took pen and a small tablet from her purse. She turned to a fresh page, neatly printed two names, tore it loose and handed it to Gurney. "We have rooms at the Hotel Lutetia. You can call us there if you find out anything."

Gurney folded the note and, with obvious effort, slipped it into the side pocket of his dressing gown. "I'll telephone my friends later this morning."

"Thank you so much," Beatrice said.

Margaret remained silent. Why had she not objected when Beatrice added Lieutenant Butler's name to her list? Was it merely curiosity or did she experience something else? Were there other emotions at play; feelings she had unconsciously suppressed or ignored? She had considered writing to Lieutenant Butler once they tended to Michael's remains, but had not figured a way to obtain his location. With Gurney's help that might no longer be an impediment.

Gurney was smiling at her. "I'll call you the moment I find out anything."

"Thank you," she managed to say in a clear voice.

Nobody spoke for a moment. Just then another thought occurred. Margaret had wondered about her father's missing cable. Would Gurney's friends at Chaumont know what might have happened to it?

She said, "My father sent a cable to Colonel Andrews regarding disposition of Michael's remains. Apparently, it's been lost or mislaid. Do you suppose your friends could look into that as well?"

Gurney's smile faded and a shadow slid across his pale face. "Your father's cable wasn't lost. A friend of ours, a classmate posted to the Signal Corps at Chaumont, received it late one evening shortly after Michael's death. He took a risk and told me what it contained."

"Oh? I'm not sure I understand."

He took a deep breath, let it out slowly, then set his jaw. "Michael and I belonged to the same fraternity at Yale. So did our mutual friend. The three of us initially drove ambulances. When America joined the war, the Army offered options to those of us with college degrees. Our friend, an engineer, chose to serve in the Signal Corps.

"Michael and I continued to work together, doing our jobs on and off the battlefield. The longer we worked, the more we realized we might not survive. Michael understood this. Even so, I was surprised when he asked me to read the amended Last Will and Testament. 'Do you really expect to die?' I asked him. 'What about your plans for growing a beard? What happened to prowling left bank coffee houses? And what about living in a writer's garret above a sleazy bistro?' He just smiled. 'How did you know about the sleazy bistro?' he said. 'I never mentioned that part.'"

Gurney looked away for a moment and smiled, his eyes growing moist with the recollection. He blinked several times, and then looked at Margaret.

"I didn't want to, not immediately, but Michael was insistent. 'This is important,' he told me. 'And you are my best friend. I want you to sign and bear witness.' I simply could not refuse him.

"When I learned of your father's cable and what it contained, I took it upon myself to see that Michael's burial request was carried out without complication. I made sure the message was intentionally misplaced so that Michael could be laid to rest as he wished."

Margaret took a deep breath before speaking. "I didn't realize it was that easy to divert a cable." Her voice was much sharper than she'd intended.

"It is not as difficult as you might believe. We exchange thousands of messages. Now and then, one or two are often lost or misfiled."

"I see. What about my father's cable? Where is it now?"

"In a file drawer, somewhere at 21 Rue Raynouard."

"I presume Colonel Andrews knows nothing of this?"

"That is correct."

"And if I pursue the matter?"

"Then my friend at AEF Headquarters would be in a great deal of trouble."

"As would you."

Gurney nodded. "As would I."

"You wouldn't deny involvement?"

"Of course not. My obligation to honor Michael's last request was clear. I have no regrets."

"And Mr. Keogh, the young man at the reception center. I presume he's involved in some way. Is he the one who 'misfiled' the cable?"

Gurney shook his head. "I am not going to share any more particulars, Margaret. I alone bear full responsibility for this."

Margaret wasn't sure how to respond to this unexpected bit of news. Regardless of the cable, her brother's will probably bore far more weight than did her family's desires. Besides, Colonel Andrews had told them Michael's burial had occurred two days following his death. Her father's cable would have arrived too late to have any effect on Michael's final instructions. In fact, the cable would have complicated rather than changed the situation. She also believed Gurney's intervention had not been malicious. Rather, it was an act of respect—a final obligation rendered by one close friend to another. Those thoughts tended to soften her initial outrage at Gurney's presumptive act.

She looked at Beatrice. "What do you think?"

"If we pressed the lost cable issue, would it make any

difference?"

"I don't know."

"Then let's say Michael's amendment took precedence over father's cable. That would be the truth, wouldn't it?"

"Yes, I suppose so."

Margaret looked at Gurney. A thin sheen of sweat made his skin appear oily. "It's not my place to approve or disapprove what you did, but I understand and appreciate your motive. As far as we're concerned, the issue of the lost cable is closed."

Gurney shook his head. "I sincerely appreciate your consideration, but you should tell your family everything. There have been enough secrets, don't you think?"

He was right, of course. Margaret did not want to add another layer of ambiguity to Michael's life. "Yes, I suppose so." She spoke to Beatrice. "When the time comes, we will tell Mother and Father about this, just the way Gurney told it."

Beatrice nodded agreement.

Margaret said: "Well, that clears up one issue."

Yet, the biggest issue of all remained.

Had influenza not altered his plans, her father would have sailed to France, met Colonel Andrews, and then promptly ignored Michael's last wish. In the end, he would have done what he had set out to do: retrieve his son's body. Mike Jerome was an imposing individual, a man whose physical presence commanded attention. Without question, his desire would have prevailed. Nothing would have kept him from claiming Michael's remains.

Interestingly, that had been Margaret's initial reaction as well. She had come to France to bring her brother's body home, to return it to where his family thought it belonged. Like her father, she too would have ignored her brother's final request.

Yet, it was clear Michael had felt otherwise. Overcoming that obstacle would not have been easy.

The physical presence of his will, a legal document that contained explicit burial instructions, was problematic. That, in and of itself, would be difficult to overturn. But what about those other, rationally unexplainable experiences? Margaret found herself struggling with an unexpected dilemma. Whose wish should she honor: Michael's or her family's? Could she really ignore her brother's last desire on Earth?

In death, Michael had wanted to remain in the company of his fellow soldiers. Her brother's final resting place was far from home, yes; but did Michael's family have the right to deny him one last measure of love and respect? She did not think so.

Somehow, Margaret would have to do what she had once believed was unthinkable: convince her parents to leave their son's remains where they were—in the foreign soil of a land far from home.

The weight of responsibility caused her shoulders to sag. She sat for a moment, unmoving, then finally addressed the purpose of their visit. "Gurney, yesterday you told us we should meet someone who also knew Michael."

"I haven't forgotten about that, Margaret. Let's go outside. She's waiting for us in the courtyard."

Beatrice's head jerked, awkwardly. "*She?* Did you say 'she'?" Her eyes grew wide.

Gurney nodded. "Give me a little push and let's go outside."

After what Margaret had learned about Michael, the existence of a 'she' was not surprising. Her brother had withheld information regarding his wounds and decorations; nevertheless, some of his letters had provided subtle clues about his personal life. At the time, Margaret suspected that something important had occurred. When he did not elaborate, she had written and asked for more details.

However, Michael chose not to embellish those points, nor had he ever provided additional specifics.

As she slowly wheeled Gurney outside, Margaret felt her shoulders tense as the prospect of another unknown made her wary of what she might next discover.

18

"There she is," Gurney told them, "on the bench to our left."

A slim, attractive young woman dressed in a white nurse's cap and uniform stood as they approached. When Gurney carefully maneuvered his cast and attempted to rise from his wheelchair, the woman smiled and shook her head.

"*Monsieur fou*," she said quietly, placing a restraining hand on his shoulder. She gently eased him back into a sitting position and then gave him an affectionate hug followed by a kiss on each cheek.

"I am not a crazy man," he said, blushing slightly. "Merely one who is temporarily chair bound." He turned. "Margaret and Beatrice," he said, indicating each sister with a courtly sweep of his arm. "This is Anna-Elise du Chatelet, the person I told you about yesterday." He then spoke to the young lady. "Anna, these are Michael's sisters."

Anna-Elise took the initiative. She stepped toward Margaret. "I would have recognized you without introduction," she said. "And I am truly delighted to meet you both," she added, smiling at Beatrice. Her English was near-perfect, with but the slightest hint of Gallic accent.

Margaret returned the greeting but Gurney's attempt to rise in Anna's presence remained stuck in her mind. Yesterday afternoon when she and Beatrice first met him, he had politely acknowledged them but remained in his wheelchair. Margaret had not given it much thought at the time. After all, with his leg fully encased in a cast, she did not expect the courtesy. But clearly, Anna-Elise had earned something more; had attained a status not achieved by the Jerome sisters. His obvious respect for the young nurse worsened the tension knotting the muscles between her shoulders.

"Now that you've been properly introduced," he said, "I shall return to my ward and allow you ladies some privacy."

Margaret opened her mouth to object, but Gurney swiveled his chair, turning the wheels in opposite directions. Then, both arms working in quick rhythm, he rolled his way toward the open door. "Have a nice chat," he said, glancing over his shoulder.

"Such a nice gentleman," Anna said, as Gurney departed. Then she gestured toward the bench. "Shall we make ourselves comfortable?"

Margaret sat beside Beatrice, facing Anna-Elise who had taken up a white wooden chair. "Is Gurney's wound as serious as it seems to be?"

"Yes, quite so. Artillery bomb fragments cut and broke the tibia in several places. Gas gangrene infected the foot and calf, but surgeons cut the diseased tissue away. Sadly, even if the injury heals without further complication, Gurney will always need use of a cane."

"Further complication? What do you mean?"

"Bone infection and sepsis are always a danger, but the surgeons are hopeful for a full recovery."

"I see." Margaret's gaze softened as she took in the sight of wounded men.

They looked more like individuals now, no longer an anonymous gathering of the infirm. The tension in her shoulders eased as a profound sense of compassion returned, an emotion first aroused by the sight of all those black-clad women at Pier Escale, a feeling reawakened by the stunning reality of so many battered and limbless young men. Although she could never share their special kinship, never experience what they had known, Margaret now had a deeper appreciation for their sacrifices.

She sighed, then turned and looked at Anna: "It must take a great deal of courage to be a soldier, to accept the possibility of painful wounds, to awaken each day with the knowledge that there might never be another."

Anna's blue eyes—the lightest, clearest azure Margaret had ever seen—remained sad. "Yes, that is so. But death, I think, is not their greatest worry. Neither is the possibility of painful wounds."

"I don't understand. How is that possible?"

"I shall try to explain," Anna said. "You see, every soldier knows that none can escape death, that Charon ferries a boat upon which all will someday make passage, each in our own time. Nor do they long despair the loss of limb or eyesight. One can endure even those terrible afflictions. What soldiers fear most, what they dread above all, is facial disfigurement—to become a nightmare to their children; to see wives turn away in revulsion. Inside, they are the same men, but outside..." She paused and shook her head, an infinitely melancholy gesture. "To be pitied by those they love—to suffer silent exile—that, not death, is what a soldier fears most."

From the corner of her eye, Margaret saw Beatrice's eyes widen. Suffering and dying came naturally to mind when one thought of war, but facial disfigurement raised psychological issues neither sister had discussed. "Is that a common injury?" she asked, recalling the two or three cases she had noted on her first visit.

"More so than one might think."

"Was Michael... disfigured?" Beatrice's voice quavered.

Anna shook her head. "His uniform was a little burned—singed?—from the hot flash, but there were no other marks."

Margaret felt the beginnings of another shudder. "If Michael's uniform was burned, then how could he remain unblemished?"

"The doctor said Michael died from the crushing weight of air pressure. In such cases death is instant and without pain. *Concussion*: that was the word he used."

Margaret had avoided thinking about specifics. But now she had no choice. According to Anna, Michael had died instantly, had not shivered in agony while awaiting the inevitable. Margaret silently thanked God for His mercy.

Is that why she had not felt his passing? Had his death been so sudden that he was gone before realizing it? Perhaps. Then again—she studied the young nurse sitting across the table.

Who is this woman? What might have occurred between her and Michael? Were they more than patient and care giver? Might they have been romantically involved? If so, what secrets had Michael shared with her that he had withheld from his fraternal twin?

"Did you treat Michael when he was wounded… I mean *before*?"

"Yes. At first he was one of many in my care." Anna looked directly into Margaret's eyes, her expression open and without guile. "Later, we became much more to each other."

Anna-Elise wore her hair in a single braid partially tucked behind her cap. The combination of unblemished fair skin, dark hair, and incredibly light blue eyes radiated youthful health and vigor.

But there was more than glowing superficial beauty. Anna exuded strength and quiet charm. Her observation regarding the dreadful after-effects of facial disfigurement had also revealed a mind capable of compassionate reasoning. It was easy to see how Michael had become attracted to this bright young woman. Or had their relationship developed into something more than physical attraction?

"Michael didn't tell us much about his life over here," Margaret began. "We knew nothing of his Army service, his wounds, and certainly not about the Legion of Honor. And, as you probably know from Gurney, we had no inkling of your relationship."

Anna nodded. "Michael and I talked about that many times. I said to him: 'Why must you keep such things private? You have done nothing to embarrass yourself or your family. *Au contraire.* You have proved yourself the equal to any soldier many times over. Revealing personal things would not be shameful.' He would smile and say: 'Yes, you are probably right.' But he could not bring himself to do it."

"We don't understand that part," Margaret admitted. "Michael was never a secretive person. Do you know why he kept such things from us?"

"Not for certain, but I have a suspicion. As you know, Michael was proud of his family. He told me of your father's journey from Ireland—sailing alone to America as a boy of fifteen—not merely a survivor, but one who became a successful businessman as well, much admired by his workers and rivals alike—a truly honest man who never forgot from where he came."

"Yes," Beatrice acknowledged. "Father told us about his voyage to America many times."

"Michael spoke of your mother's family as well; those ancestors who fought in your war between states. And he told me of his sisters—two bright, beautiful young ladies who educated themselves and devoted much of their time to worthy causes. He also spoke of you Margaret, his twin; a strong woman who refused to accept a lesser place in a masculine society."

"He told you about that?" Margaret asked. "About the arguments I had with our father?"

"Yes. He was especially fond of the story about a big march and the lady on a white horse."

Margaret had never forgotten the breakfast conversation and was about to reply, but her sister interrupted.

"I *remember* the lady-on-a-horse story," Beatrice exclaimed, a wide smile spreading across her lips. "I thought Father would have a *stroke!*"

19

The Woman's Suffrage Procession, Margaret remembered, was the topic of Nellie Bly's article in the March 8 issue of the *Woman's Journal*.

In the spring of 1913, Inez Milholland, her white cape draped across the haunches of an equally white horse, spearheaded a suffrage parade in Washington, D.C., clopping down the middle of Pennsylvania Avenue, leading a throng of eight thousand women. Groups of male bystanders—sometimes aided but never hampered by policemen who lined the route—jeered and harassed the marchers.

The front-page report contained numerous photographs, including one of Inez Milholland astride a huge white horse. Margaret, unable to contain her delight, smiled as she read Nellie Bly's account of the event over breakfast.

"Why do you insist on reading such rubbish?" her father asked.

Margaret looked up from her reading.

"Rubbish?" Is that what you think about the right of women to vote?"

"Yes, I do," he said, setting his own newspaper aside. "And I'll tell you why. Most women, given the opportunity, would vote for a Handsome Harry over a better-qualified candidate. They'll choose to believe the lies of an attractive slick-talker rather than the simple truths of a plain looking man. And they'll do it every time."

"Maybe so, but aren't all politicians slick-talkers?" Margaret retorted. "Even the not-so-handsome ones?"

"I'll give you that, Maggie, but politics is serious business. We can't have every dreamy-eyed scullery maid and washerwoman stuffing the ballot box."

"Inez Milholland isn't a scullery maid *or* a washerwoman. She's a college graduate... and a lawyer."

"Then she ought to have sense enough to not scamper around Washington wearing a silly cape. And atop a horse, to boot! Why, I've never heard of such a thing!"

Michael sat between them, his head moving back and forth between father and daughter as the heated discussion raged.

Finally, Margaret turned to her brother.

"What do you think, Michael?" she asked, hoping to enlist him as an ally.

"I agree with Father," he answered, surprising her. Then he continued. "It just wouldn't do to have a bunch of handsome *amateurs* mouthing familiar lies. Being a successful politician requires the skills of a *professional* liar."

Her Father had smiled at the first part of Michael's comment. He was not smiling after the second.

20

"So did I," Margaret said.

Anna began to speak again, but Margaret had a sense of what might come next. Before Michael left for France, the growing tension between father and son had been obvious.

"Michael told me he came to France contrary to his father's wishes. There were many *désaccords*—disagreements that bothered him greatly. Yet, Michael could not abide what his father wanted and chose to go his own way. I think he was displeased because your father could not, or would not, understand why Michael needed to come here." She shrugged. "But I cannot say for sure."

"I remember a few of those discussions," Margaret admitted. "In Ireland my father's people lived under British rule. He despised the notion of royalty and their presumption of power over common people. Father believed Europe was tainted by its history of feudalism, religious persecution, and hereditary monarchies. This latest war was solely the product of royal minds addled by centuries of interbreeding. 'It's *their* war, not ours,' my father once said. But Michael saw it differently. He wanted to help the French people—to aid those who suffered."

"And so he did," Anna said. "The service Michael gave to France had great worth. He also found much satisfaction in the difficult work needed to save our wounded *poilu*. Yes, there was the disagreement—such are common between fathers and sons, mothers and daughters—but what troubled Michael was much different. I sensed a deep troubling in his soul."

A deep troubling in his soul... what did that mean? "I don't understand," Margaret managed to say.

"Nor do I. The last few months of his life were indeed strange. He seemed to turn away; a little from me but much more from everyone else, especially from Gurney, his best friend. He spoke not as much and brooded more. The lives he had saved, the wounds and medals he received... all seemed to mean nothing. I tried many times to change his mood, but I failed at every turn."

"Medals?" Margaret asked. "You said medals—the plural. We know of the Legion of Honor. Were there others?"

"Oh, yes. France also awarded Michael the Croix de Guerre and the Insigne du Blesse Civil—the latter on two occasions, one for each wound. There is also an American medal. They are with his personal things which I have for safekeeping."

"Personal things? What sort of personal things?"

"His uniform, medals of course, family letters, photographs, and a journal which he kept."

"A journal?" Margaret sat erect as an excited flush swept through her body. "May we read it?"

"Of course. But I brought nothing of his with me today. I must go to my post soon."

Margaret was not sure how to ask her next question, so she approached it directly, as she did most things in life. "Anna, you used the word 'safekeeping'. Does that mean we can have Michael's belongings... take them with us back to America?"

"Yes. I have things for you and your family, and some other things I shall keep for myself, all of which we can talk about later."

Margaret couldn't help but wonder what those 'other things' might be. She had forgotten to ask Colonel Andrews for a copy of

Michael's will. Margaret resolved to remedy that oversight the next time she saw the Colonel.

"When would it be convenient for us to see them?"

"Tomorrow is my off day. Could we meet at my home, say eleven o'clock? We could talk, have tea and take lunch together."

"Yes, that would be nice."

Anna took a pencil and a small white card from her purse. "This is where I live," she said, writing on the card. Then she handed it to Margaret.

Except for the question regarding facial disfigurement, Beatrice had said little. Now she stared at her hands and shook her head, a gesture ripe with poignant melancholy. "Something must have happened to Michael that we don't know about... something he couldn't or wouldn't share." She raised her head and looked at Anna. "Do you have any idea what that might have been?"

Anna shrugged. "Michael saw much of the war. Perhaps too much."

They sat in silence while Margaret struggled with her thoughts.

At times during the past forty-eight hours Margaret had had the eerie impression they were discussing a stranger. Michael was her twin brother, yes; but he was also a friend and trusted confidant—his thoughts an open book. Had his prior behavior been a charade? Had Michael, like his twin sister, always kept certain things inside? Was he likewise unable to share his deepest and most profound feelings?

Cognizant of her own flaws, Margaret was reluctant to accept the possibility that Michael could have experienced similar traits. Rather, she tended to believe Gurney. The war had changed Michael in some fundamental way. As a result, Anna—this quiet young woman, this stranger, really—had come to understand more about her brother than anyone in his own family. She remembered a line from a poem about 'seeing ourselves as others see us' and wondered: would such power be a gift or a curse?

On impulse, Margaret reached across the table and grasped Anna's hand in both of hers. "Tell us about you and Michael."

Anna's eyes grew moist, but she smiled, as one remembering a pleasant, once-in-a-lifetime interlude. "There is much to tell," she said. "But there is little time today. Tomorrow I will share with you all I have."

*

No longer beneficiary of the Colonel's automobile and driver, Margaret and Beatrice found other means of transportation. Soon after their meeting with Anna, the one-horse carriage returned them to Hotel Lutetia. During the ride from the hospital, both had agreed it was time to notify their parents about the unexpected situation they now faced.

Striding into the elegant lobby, they found an unoccupied desk with two chairs. Margaret took a seat behind the desk; Beatrice sat on the side chair.

Using complimentary hotel stationery, Margaret found a pen resting in a groove near an inkwell. She thought for a moment, carefully loaded the pen with ink, and then began to write. Several minutes later, she studied the brief letter:

Hotel Lutetia
45 Boulevard Raspail
St. Germain des Pres – Paris
July 24, 1918

Mr. & Mrs. Michael E. Jerome
21450 Ladue Road
St. Louis, Missouri, USA

Dear Mother & Father:

Beatrice and I hope you have recovered from your illness and are feeling well. As you probably know by now, we arrived in France safely but our voyage was not without incident—more on that later. Following a somewhat delayed train ride from Le Havre, we have taken rooms at this hotel.

As planned, we met with Colonel Andrews who gave us disturbing news. In accordance with Michael's Last Will & Testament, military authorities interred his remains at Suresnes, a military cemetery near Paris.

We learned other things as well: He suffered wounds on two occasions while rescuing French soldiers from the front. For his service, the French Government awarded Michael two medals: the Legion of Honor and Croix de Guerre. All this came as a great surprise to us.

Given the presence of his Will, I believe disinterment of Michael's remains from where they now rest would ignore his final wish, an act we should not commit hastily. I realize this is not what we originally intended, but what, if anything should we do?

Beatrice and I are well and will remain in Paris until we hear from you.

Love from both of us,

Margaret & Beatrice

She handed Beatrice what she had written. "How does this look to you? Have I covered everything?"

Beatrice read the note and handed it back. "Yes, it looks fine."

Margaret rose and approached the concierge, a short, graying man with neatly trimmed mustaches. He smiled and raised an inquisitive eyebrow. "How may I be of service?" he asked.

"I wish to send a cable to America," she told him.

"*Oui, Mademoiselle.* That I can arrange without difficulty."

"It is rather long for a cable."

"Do you have it prepared?"

"Yes."

"May I see it to count the words?"

She handed the concierge the single sheet of stationery.

He took the note, removed pince-nez from his waistcoat, fastened them to the bridge of his nose, and began to read, his eyes seeming to pause at each word. A moment later, the concierge removed the reading glasses and raised his eyes to Margaret. Then he bowed—a brief, elegant gesture.

"*Mademoiselle* Jerome, you and your family have my greatest admiration and respect. Please have no worries about this message. I will personally see to it immediately."

"*Merci beaucoup*," Margaret said. She opened her purse, intending to offer a gratuity.

The concierge shook his head and took one step backwards. "*Je suis honoré être de service.*" I am honored to be of service. Then he turned and strode toward the front desk.

As she made her way to the elevator where Beatrice stood, Margaret wondered how her parents would react to the cable. Were they still angry with her? Father could be headstrong at times, maddeningly so. But he had also surprised her on a number of occasions. Mother's reaction was equally difficult for Margaret to ascertain. In short, how they might actually respond was unpredictable.

Filled with fresh uncertainties, Margaret followed Beatrice into the elevator where the uniformed operator stood waiting.

21

Every soldier in the American Expeditionary Forces carried, among other things, a small canvas pouch, either attached to a webbed belt or fixed to an easily accessible place on his uniform. Inside the pouch were two roller bandages holding absorbent material. Lightly stitched into the fabric of each dressing was a safety pin. Waxed paper sealed and protected the entire kit. A small ampoule of iodine enclosed in a cardboard tube completed the package. If wounded, this kit provided the soldier's first opportunity for treatment.

In theory, that is.

One by one, Butler removed items from the field-dressing pouch of Private Dottle. First came six pieces of hard candy, then four tailor-made cigarettes, and finally the stale, crumbly remains of several biscuits. The wax paper—intended to protect sterile dressings from contamination—now kept the Private's cigarettes safe and dry.

"What happened to your roller bandages and iodine?" Butler demanded.

"I lost 'em... sir."

"Really? How tragic." He retrieved a replacement set from a nearby rack holding medical supplies. "These, and nothing else, belong in your field dressing kit."

Private Dottle did as instructed, grudgingly, and found other places to store the candy and cigarettes. The soldier's attitude was one degree short of insolence. Colonel Greevly, who had recently taken issue with Butler's slovenly appearance, had been right: unless they were in dire need of treatment, regular soldiers thought little of the Medical Corps. No matter. Butler could not allow these men to discard medical kits.

"I'm going to put a tick mark by your name, Dottle." He retrieved a clip board hanging from a nail on the wooden tent post and made a note on the sick list. "The next time I find this pouch empty of bandages, you or the man you're carrying had better be wearing them. Otherwise, you can explain yourself to the company commander. I'm sure the captain, more likely the first sergeant, can find ways to impress upon you the importance of a sterile first aid kit."

"Yes, sir." Dottle mumbled.

They stood inside the dressing station, a sandbag-enclosed dugout partially carved into the side of a low hill. A gray canvas tarp suspended from wooden poles served as a roof. The tamped dirt floor was large enough to contain a folding examination table, a small rack holding medical supplies, and a narrow portable cot. Beneath the cot was just enough room for Butler's suitcase and personal belongings.

Private Dottle was not the first man he had ragged about an empty dressing kit, nor would he be the last. Still, Butler hoped his random inspections would become common knowledge among the soldiers. Sniper fire and the whine of ricochet occurred regularly and he did not want men to run short of bandages should one of those rounds find its intended target.

The main Allied trench line lay on the opposite side of the hill, about forty yards away. Less than a half-mile beyond that ran another long series of trenches occupied by Germans. Sniping at each other was a daily occurrence.

"Now, what is your complaint," Butler asked.

"It's my leg, Doc." Private Dottle unwound his left puttee and pulled up one leg of his trousers. "Trench rabbit got me last night while I was asleep."

Butler concealed his discomfort. During the first terrible years of the war, vast numbers of dead soldiers had lain abandoned on the battlefield. The rat population, feeding on thousands of unattended corpses, increased tenfold. Now, even after implementing much improved field sanitation procedures, rats were as common as houseflies. As a surgeon Butler had cut into living flesh, unbothered by the sight of exposed organs and free flowing blood. But for reasons unknown to him, the thought of rats feeding on human beings caused his stomach to churn.

The bite on Private Dottle's calf, an oblong-shaped series of tiny punctures, looked fresh. Butler cleaned the wound with cotton soaked in hydrogen peroxide, swabbed the wound liberally with iodine, and applied a bandage. Finally, he removed a syringe and hypodermic needle from a black leather kit and pulled in half a milliliter of anti-tetanic serum from a small, rubber-stoppered bottle.

"Roll up your sleeve," Butler told him.

Private Dottle eyed the needle and frowned.

"This might hurt," Butler said, swabbing the soldier's arm before injecting the serum, "but lockjaw would hurt a lot worse."

The soldier rolled down his sleeve, a sour expression on his face.

"I want to see you again tomorrow morning," he told the Private.

"Yes, sir." Dottle bent down, rewound his puttee, and left.

Butler followed him outside into cloud-dappled sunlight. The farmland, its vegetation pounded flat by countless vehicles and boots, sloped gently westward toward Lucy-le-Bocage, a gray cluster of buildings about a mile away. He sighed and ran fingers through his hair.

Treating rat bites was not exactly the work Butler had expected.

He was an experienced surgeon; he should be doing more than administering treatments more suited to the duties of a medical orderly. Nevertheless, he was determined to put a pleasant face on it. After all, the rat bite was certainly important to Private Dottle, and that was all that really mattered.

He lowered his gaze. A short distance away two groups of four stretcher-bearers sat cross-legged on olive-drab blankets spread upon the ground, a telltale sign that a bridge game was now in progress. Small canvas rectangles supported by upright poles protected the card players from the sun's rays. For some odd reason, the Army called these makeshift awnings 'flys'. His eyes ranged across the two groups while his mind associated each man with a name. 'It is important to call individuals by their name,' Peckham had advised. 'It's polite and shows respect.'

Other than random sniping, Butler had heard no sustained bursts of gunfire. Artillery rumbled constantly from the north and east, the sound remote and impersonal: a minor skirmish in an unimportant country far away. However, there were growing signs that the status quo was about to change.

For the past two days he had observed soldiers arriving just after sundown. These men were not merely a smattering of replacements, but two companies of fresh troops from another regiment. They shuffled past his dressing station in single file and disappeared into the trench complex to the south; a solemn parade accompanied by the muted clump and clatter of boots and equipment. Soft gray moonlight bounced from their rimmed helmets and whispered voices heightened the sense of anticipation. He wondered how many more might be on the way.

Butler turned toward the sound of approaching footfalls.

Two soldiers assisted a third man. The middle soldier, his gray, dirty face twisted in a grimace, hopped along using one leg, his arms slung across the shoulders of his comrades.

"Here we go, Wink," one of the soldiers said to the wounded man. "Doc'll fix you up good as new."

"Lay him down inside," Butler directed.

They eased the wounded man onto the examination table. "What happened?" Butler asked.

The same soldier spoke again. "Old Wink here ran into some trouble a cupla days ago. The Heinies spotted his patrol and popped them with trench mortars. Wink got lost and was left behind. We gave him up for dead, but old Wink finally made his way back to our lines this morning."

"I got tired waiting for you sorry asses to come get me," the wounded man said. He looked at Butler. "I got a hunk of Kaiser iron in my leg."

"Let's have a look." Butler took sheers and cut through filthy trouser material. He peeled away the cloth and exposed a horrifying sight. A squirming layer of gray maggots totally concealed the soldier's wound.

"Sweet Jesus," one of the other soldiers hissed.

Butler washed his hands and slipped on a pair of rubber gloves. Using squares of purified tow soaked in hydrogen peroxide, he gently swept the maggots onto the dirt floor. Private Winkleman's two friends, muttering in disgust, quickly squashed them under their boots. When he pried open the injury, Butler saw a wound surprisingly clean and absent of fleshy debris. The vastus medialis, deeply lacerated and oozing blood, glowed pink and revealed no sign of infection. The undamaged muscle fibers looked firm and nicely grained. Buried within lay a blue-black edge of metal.

"I'm sending him up to the aid station," Butler told the Private's two comrades. "You can return to your unit."

"Will he be okay, Doc?"

"He'll be back before you know it."

One of the soldiers laughed. "Thought you had yourself a long vacation, did ya, Wink? Hah!"

Both soldiers left the tent, still chuckling.

Butler flushed the wound with more hydrogen peroxide and cleaned the surrounding tissue thoroughly. A surgeon at the Evacuation Hospital would remove the metal fragment and further treat the injury.

"This will sting a bit," Butler said.

He swabbed the area with iodine. The soldier's posture stiffened but he did not utter a sound.

Butler applied a field dressing and secured the bandage with a safety pin.

"That will do until you get to the Evacuation Hospital. Now, tell me your full name, company, and service number?"

As the soldier spoke, Butler wrote the following on a manila tag:

Winkleman 270554, Herbert J.
PVT, Co. K, 23rd Infantry
July 17, 1918, 8:20 A.M.
G.S.W. Left Medialis, Éclat, Iodine Dressing
Lt. Butler, M.O.

Without thinking about it, he had used the Medical Corps terms for gunshot wound and explosive shell fragment. The manila tag contained one hole through which looped a long doubled string. He tied the tag to a button on the soldier's tunic. "How do you feel?" Butler asked.

"Pretty good, I reckon."

"I saw no permanent damage. You should be fine once surgeons remove the shrapnel."

Butler turned and stepped outside just as Olsen, a tall Swede from Duluth, approached with three other stretcher-bearers. "Private Winkleman is ready to go," he told them.

"We'll carry him nice and gentle, Lieutenant," Olsen said.

The four *brancardiers* easily transferred the wounded man onto the canvas stretcher. Then, one bearer on each corner, they left the dressing station and began the one-mile trek back to Lucy-le-Bocage. As they walked down the slope toward the rear, the bearers in front raised the stretcher slightly, keeping it level. The second group of bridge players—now joined by Winkleman's two companions who stood watching—looked up, waved to their comrades as they walked past, and then continued with their card game.

Back inside the dugout, Butler cleaned the examination table and thought about Private Winkleman, his first actual combat casualty. What had Colonel Dawes said aboard the *Mongolia*? Butler smiled as he recalled the Colonel's words: 'In battlefield surgery, one hopes to start out slow and then taper off.' Well, he had certainly fulfilled the first part.

The sudden drone of a large motor interrupted his thoughts. A piercing whistle followed by two near simultaneous explosions— thunderous and soul shaking—blotted everything from his mind. A force unseen flung him into the examination table which overturned, scattering instruments and disinfecting materials across the dirt floor. Disoriented, his ears ringing, Butler's mind grasped a single phrase: *German aeroplanes!* From a great distance came shouts and painful cries. He grasped one of the tent poles, pulled himself upright, and felt his knees wobble. Shaking hands touched various parts of his body. He found himself bruised but unhurt. Then he stumbled outside, paused near the dressing station's entrance, and took in the scene.

A lone biplane, now hardly more than a double-hyphen in the

blue sky, turned back toward the German lines. Butler shifted his gaze. Two craters about six feet in diameter—wispy steam rising from their centers—marched down the slope, the first not more than two dozen yards away. All evidence of the bridge game had vanished. Instead, players and spectators sat on the ground or staggered unsteadily on wobbly legs. Playing cards littered the ground. The tent flys and neatly spread blankets now resembled discarded rags. Farther down, Olsen and his stretcher-bearers lay awkwardly positioned beside their patient, five crumpled bodies frightfully close to the second bomb crater. A few soldiers arriving from the nearest trench moved cautiously towards the two groups. Butler went back inside the dressing station, retrieved his musette bag, left the dugout, and jogged towards the stricken men.

It had happened so *quickly*...

Calm had become chaos in the flutter of a hummingbird's wing. As he approached the first group, a bitter thought occurred: He had started out slow enough, but the tapering off part was nowhere in evidence.

*

Sitting on an ammunition box across from his commanding officer, Butler silently tallied the casualties.

Olsen, the big Swede from Duluth, was dead as were his three companions, all four stretcher-bearers killed by bomb fragments and concussion. Butler could do nothing for them. The bridge players and Private Winkleman's two friends had fared much better, suffering bruises and contusions. The vastly unlucky Winkleman however, lying prone on the stretcher, survived but took another, far more serious wound.

"They will probably take his arm at Meaux," Peckham said, long hours later. "The brachialis was shattered beyond repair. Any more delay will cause gas gangrene."

"I thought as much," Butler replied.

"You did all you could. It was just bad luck."

"Yes, I suppose so."

Was it really that simple? Was luck all that mattered in life? If so, then it was grossly unfair. What sort of logic allowed an arbitrarily selected individual to avoid misfortune and survive disaster? What about those less fortunate? Were they simply out of *luck*?

Butler imagined a bizarre scene: Human souls stood single file in a celestial waiting room. When their turn came for the opportunity to live a mortal life, each soul reached into a magic hat and took a colored token. Depending on the color drawn, that soon-to-be-born human being would have more or less luck than did one of his or her contemporaries.

Is that how God allocated good fortune—by mere chance? If so, how many colors did He use, and which were His favorites?

"Anyway, you're short one stretcher team," Peckham continued. "I'll get you another from Meaux."

"Okay, thanks. By the numbers of fresh troops I saw, it looks like activity might be picking up."

"I suspect that might be the case."

The long summer day had finally surrendered, giving way to darkness. Butler felt an enormous weight pressing on his back and a cramp had settled in his shoulders. He rose, stretched and rubbed his face with both hands. "I guess I'll get back to the dressing station."

"Why not sleep here tonight?" Peckham suggested. "There's room."

Butler felt a stab of resentment. Was Woody Peckham feeling sorry for him? If so, then Peckham could take his sympathy and shove it. Butler retrieved his medical rucksack and looped the strap over his helmet, then diagonally across his chest. "I appreciate the offer," he said, keeping his voice casual. "But my place is up there."

168

Packham nodded but said nothing.

Outside, a gibbous moon hung in the eastern sky. Butler paused to study Earth's pale companion. Tonight it looked drab and yellow with age—centuries older than the one he remembered back home. How could that be? Did it appear so ancient because Europeans had been staring at it far longer than their upstart cousins who exhibited so little understanding of history? Or had the sudden reality of war tarnished his perspective? He continued walking along the dirt road that passed through Lucy-le-Bocage. A few minutes later Butler heard the familiar rhythmic clang of steel on steel.

The hamlet, abandoned by most of its residents, boasted a solitary blacksmith shop. Someone, probably the owner, was working late. The ringing clamor reminded Butler of Eamon's Forge, a shop located at the sleepy crossroads near Dresden, a village on the western shore of Seneca Lake.

Eamon's open-air forge stood adjacent to a cavernous stone barn. Inside, wood plank shelves attached to high walls contained all sorts of interesting items: horseshoes, individual boxes filled with spikes, hasps, hinges, and a variety of miscellaneous items the purpose of which remained mysterious to young Butler. From the beamed ceiling hung wagon wheel rims and ornate black ironworks, each piece suspended on hooks or gently swaying on whisper thin wires.

Outside, underneath a roofed enclosure open on four sides, Eamon Sligo, like generations of blacksmiths before him, spent his working hours pounding glowing steel into new shapes, either functional or beautiful and sometimes both. As the soft-spoken muscular Irishman once explained to a curious city boy, Eamon Sligo was both a farrier and a blacksmith. 'Farriers make horseshoes, trim hooves, and shoe horses for a living,' he once told Butler in a rolling brogue. 'Blacksmiths make horseshoes too, but they also fashion many other things as well.'

When working at his forge Eamon Sligo's tireless motion exactly matched that of the Frenchman Butler now approached. As he paused to watch, Butler felt a strange collusion of events. So many things reminded him of home; and so many other things did not.

The clanging stopped.

Lucy-le-Bocage's blacksmith was much older than he had appeared from a distance. The old man looked up at Butler—wizened brown eyes above drooping gray mustaches—nodded a brief acknowledgement and then turned away from the anvil. Standing close to the fire he continued his work, left hand clasping long iron tongs while the other pumped a bellows.

Butler watched as a flattened metal stub turned red... orange... yellow.

The old man released the bellows and reached for his hammer.

As the clanging resumed, Butler found it impossible to ignore what had bothered him since the aeroplane attack. Had the German flyer toggled his switch a heartbeat earlier, then bombs would have struck the dressing station and he would not be standing in the moonlight watching an old smithy pound metal. Instead, his dead body would be inside a canvas sack, alongside those whose luck had also run out. The pilot's hesitation—a mere split second—had spared his life, had taken instead the lives of four stretcher-bearers and claimed Private Winkleman's left arm. Just a matter of luck Peckham had told him—nothing more, nothing less. Had Butler plucked one of God's favorite colors from the magic hat? He didn't think so. The truly fortunate do not lose what he had lost.

The rhythmic clanging stopped. The blacksmith plunged hot steel into a wooden bucket three-quarters filled with water. Hot metal cooled with a sizzling, steamy hiss. The old man set hammer and tongs aside, slowly removed his leather apron and hung it on an iron peg driven into a thick wooden post.

"*Le temps pour aller,*" the blacksmith muttered.

Yes, it was time for Butler to go, too.

They nodded silent goodbyes and Butler continued toward the dressing station, walking alongside his moon-shadow up the long slope. He arrived just as the first artillery shells struck the forward trenches.

"Take cover!" someone hollered from the distance. The high-pitched voice trembled with panic.

Butler tensed, his body frozen for just a moment. Then primal instinct took hold and he quickly found his foxhole, tumbled inside, and lay on the bottom, inhaling the earth's dank aroma. He clutched his helmet with both hands and drew his knees close to his chest, suddenly aware of his own rapid heartbeat as it pounded his eardrums.

A moment later the earth shuddered beneath him, groaning itself awake, enraged by the countless prods from unseen tormentors.

22

He cowered at the bottom of a hole in the ground, powerless and terrified.

Artillery shells rained from a dark sky, sleek conical shapes descending in long arcs, a chorus of baleful whispers growing louder and louder until they slammed into the earth, seeking to rip his soul from its frail human cocoon. Hot fumes assaulted his nostrils—vile, sulfurous vapors reminiscent of hellfire and retribution. The ground beneath him trembled and then disappeared. For one horrible, gasping moment Butler imagined himself falling into the bowels of Hell, a condemned sinner forever damned. A heartbeat later his body slammed back to earth, knocking him breathless. He lost control of his bladder and warm wetness soaked his crotch. Revulsion swept through him, a fleeting humiliation lost amidst waves of gut-clenching fear.

Incandescent yellow globes penetrated his squeezed-shut eyelids and an insane cacophony assaulted his eardrums. Thunderous cracks from exploding shells vibrated through his mind, slivering rational thought into a billion witless shards. A giant hand pressed against his back—hot, quick and insistent—thrusting him deeper into the dirt and then instantly relented.

Stop it! Stop it now! His mind roared in protest, a voice outraged and wildly desperate. Yet, nothing but a whimpering dissent echoed inside his head.

He tried to concentrate on something else—to focus his thoughts on a pleasant memory from quieter times, but the incessant bombardment was a raging presence impossible to ignore. It persisted without pause, an iron-splintering demon ignorant of reason or remorse, angrily hurling great clots of earth into the sky. Heavy smatterings of dirt and debris fell upon his back and pinged against his helmet.

Ages passed; a grinding, deadly epoch no living creature could possibly survive. Butler suddenly realized he was going to die; this he knew with absolute certainty. Soon, one of those lethal missiles would plunge mindlessly from the hollow blackness and plop beside him, its arrival preceded by a shivering hiss. In a single moment everything he was and all he hoped to be would disappear in a silent, volcanic flash. Mysteries would remain unsolved, questions unanswered, the faint glimmer of romantic potential snuffed out. He imagined an ethereal voice whispering in his ear: *Thank you for visiting Earth. Please deposit your colored token into the magic hat near the exit. Better luck next time.*

How odd it seemed: Minutes—or was it hours—ago he had wet his pants and groveled at the prospect of certain death. Now he made light of it. Curled like a fetus at the bottom of a roofless womb, eyes squeezed shut, fingers locked over his helmet, Butler found himself both terrified and amused by life's unending supply of cruel absurdities.

A mad cackle emerged from between clenched teeth.

He had come all this way; through a life filled with tragedy, uncertainty, and possibility; a life aching with potential.

And all of it had been meaningless.

23

On the first day of the September following his graduation from St. George's Academy, reluctant but determined to honor his commitment to Father Leo, Butler took the now-electrified Cambridge Horse Railroad from Boston's South Station to Harvard Square. Wearing a new suit and carrying an equally new leather suitcase filled with mostly new clothes, he trudged into a world clanging with eye-popping discoveries.

Chief among those were scotch whiskey and the unexpectedly pleasant company of genteel young ladies from nearby Wellesley College. While his introduction to the former presented no obstacle to the priesthood, his attraction to the latter—and vice versa—now made that career option unlikely.

St. George's measured time in predictable segments, but time at Harvard was much less so.

Following two years of required undergraduate study, Butler entered the four-year medical school. His decision to forego the priesthood vindicated Father Leo's belief that Butler's path through life would indeed venture beyond the confines of St. Bernard's Divinity College. In Butler's mind the switch from potential priest to aspiring medical doctor was a minor fall from piety, one that surely allowed him plenary indulgence.

On his twenty-first birthday, Butler kept a previously arranged appointment with Mr. Albright, meeting the ageing attorney in New

York City.

"I believe it's time you learned the source of your income," his soon-to-be ex-guardian told him. From the Waldorf Astoria he and Mr. Albright stepped into bright sunshine, walked five blocks up Park Avenue, turned left at East 54th Street and made their way to the offices of Swain & McGonigle, located on the sixth floor at 535 Madison Avenue.

"Who are these people?" Butler asked as the elevator operator took them to one of the upper floors.

"Swain & McGonigle look after your late father's business affairs."

"I thought my father was an engineer."

"He was also an inventor. Swain & McGonigle are Patent Law attorneys. In accordance with your father's will, you are now the legal owner of his patents, all of which continue to produce substantial income."

Following introductions, Mr. Swain—a neatly attired, bespectacled man with thinning red hair—led them to an oak-paneled office. Once seated the attorney explained each paragraph of his father's will.

"Your late father's inventions will eventually become obsolete," he told Butler. "However, assuming you are not a witless spendthrift, you will have become financially independent, even moderately wealthy, before that happens. You are a fortunate young man," Mr. Swain concluded.

"Is that so," young Butler replied.

"I understand how you feel," Mr. Albright told him. "You'd trade it all for something you can't have: your mother and father, alive and well. But that's not a possibility. Accept your good fortune and do your best to cope with what life has presented."

"As always, Mr. Albright, your advice is appreciated."

"On a related subject: What would you like me to do about your house?" he asked.

Butler had visited the residence he no longer shared with his parents once since leaving for St. George's. What he remembered most about the visit was unease. The house didn't feel the same without his parents. That warm sense of home, of belonging to a special place, was gone. The big Victorian was void of life, absent of joy and passion; an empty haunt occupied by silent ghosts. He had no desire to see it again.

"What do you suggest?"

"The current renters have expressed interest in the property."

"Are they good people?"

"Yes, I've known John and Alma Hollenbeck for most of their lives. They've offered a fair price."

"Then you should sell it to them."

Mr. Albright nodded. "What about the cabin on the lake?"

The summerhouse was really a spacious two-bedroom stone residence, complete with running water via a well, indoor plumbing and a modern septic system; a place rich with memories, much like his now forsaken home on Orchard Avenue. But, like his about-to-be-sold home, the intimate sense of belonging no longer existed. His first impulse was to dispose of it as well, to sever all ties with the past, to leave his ghosts behind.

But then he hesitated. "What shape is it in these days?"

"A caretaker drops by regularly. It's been well maintained and rents out during the summer months."

Butler had last visited the cabin on Seneca Lake the weekend prior to his parent's disappearance. He wondered if he would ever see it or sail the big lake ever again.

If—as the Iroquois legend told—the distant sound of intermittent thunder was the Great Spirit continuing to mold the earth, then the deep lake had certainly shaped Butler's life in ways he would never have foreseen. Were better times to come? He desperately hoped so.

Butler knew he had lost something essential, a vital element key to the well-being of a human soul. What he missed was that warm, wonderful sense of family, the pleasant comfort of his own special niche in the world. Having been part of something larger than himself had once provided the spiritual foundation upon which he had built his early life. But then, without warning or preamble, it was gone. When his parents vanished so did his feeling of belonging.

The physical companionship he now enjoyed with others did nothing to mitigate his sense of loss. Over the years he had become a spiritual nomad, a solitary wanderer searching for another place to call home.

"Let's maintain the status quo for a while longer," he told Mr. Albright.

He could not let the past go; not completely, not just yet.

24

The German bombardment lightened perceptibly and then slowly died away, the fading grumble of a satiated monster returning to its lair. Butler thought about Peckham and the aid station near Lucy-le-Bocage. Canvas tents offered no protection against artillery blasts. Had they made it to their shelters in time? And what of the old blacksmith and the hot metal he had worked so diligently to shape?

"Stretcher bearer!"

The panicky, high-pitched voice sounded far away. Butler raised his head and peered above the rim of the foxhole. Pale light glowed in the eastern sky. Had he lain there all night? Had he fallen asleep? He looked over his shoulder. The dressing station was gone, replaced by two huge craters. No sign of the examination table, cot, or medical equipment was visible. Nor were there any signs of his remaining staff.

"Stretcher bearer!"

The cry was insistent, a call Butler was unable to ignore. His musette bag, filled with medical supplies, was still looped across his chest. He stood—slowly and reluctantly—and shifted the bag to one side. Then he slipped from the hole, crawled on his belly toward the main trench line and then rolled feet first into the narrow excavation.

According to the map he'd observed at battalion headquarters, this end of the trench cut eastward toward the Bois de la Roche and the hamlet of Vaux. Butler moved forward, but then paused at the

178

sound of gunfire. Directly ahead, a half-mile away, came the familiar snap of individual Springfield rifles and German Mausers mixed in with rapid, coughing bursts from French-made Chauchats—an automatic rifle used by the Allies. Given his direction of travel, the exchange of gunfire was happening near the Roche Woods.

A hundred feet farther along, he stopped again. An artillery shell had struck this portion of the line. The narrow trench now featured a wider, circular depression. On the far side Butler found a Springfield rifle, bayonet affixed, the weapon snapped in half at the wooden grip just behind the bolt, two pieces held together by a leather sling. Whoever owned that rifle was absent from the scene. So was everyone else. The trenches were empty.

Where is everybody?

He knew the answer: They were off in the distance, firing those shots. *Had men survived that terrible artillery barrage, then left the relative safety of these trenches and attacked over open ground?* He shuddered. How could mortal human beings summon such raw courage? It did not seem possible.

As he continued along the trench, he came face-to-face with two soldiers carrying a third man between them. They saw each other at almost the same time.

"Thank God!" the wounded soldier cried. "I thought you'd never come."

He quickly ran his eyes over the soldier who spoke. "Where are you wounded?"

"Both legs. Pretty bad, I think."

"Set him down, boys. Let's take a look," Butler said to the wounded man's companions.

He scissored away mud-encrusted trousers and examined the soldier's wounds in the growing light. The soldier grimaced and twitched with each touch but remained silent. Artillery shell fragments had peppered both legs and fractured the right patella. Blood seeped from the wounds. He cleaned and immobilized the right leg with a small, temporary splint. Then he swabbed each laceration with iodine and applied bandages.

"How painful is the knee?" Butler asked.

"It's pretty bad, Doc."

Butler removed a half-grain morphine tablet from a tin. "Open up. Put this under your tongue."

He inked a large 'M' on the soldier's forehead and then completed a manila tag, which he tied to the man's uniform.

"If you don't see any of my stretcher bearers," he said to the unwounded men, "then you two must carry him to Lucy-le-Bocage. Do you know how to get there?"

Both nodded.

"Okay, off you go."

They lifted the wounded man, one Private Haskins, and prepared to carry him in the same manner as before.

"Just a minute," Butler said. "Where is everybody?"

Private Haskins gave him a bleary smile. The morphine had already taken effect. "Why, haven't you heard? 'B' company of the Twenty-Third is attacking through the Roach Woods."

Roach Woods?

As he had on other occasions, Butler marveled at the American soldier's propensity to mispronounce—sometimes intentionally—French names.

"It's not Roach," the taller of the two unwounded men said. "It's pronounced Row-*shay*." The soldier looked at Butler, his expression reflecting sympathetic understanding. "Don't mind old Haskins, Doc. He's one of them hillbilly clod kickers who don't know no better."

Butler nodded. Neither pronunciation was correct, but he said nothing. To the Doughboys who fought there, it would always be the

Roach Woods.

Private Haskins spoke, his voice slurred. "No matter whatcha call it, there's a lot of dead and wounded men up ahead, Doc. I believe you'll need more than a few roller bandages. The Krauts were throwing potato mashers."

"How many wounded?"

The men exchanged troubled glances. Finally, the taller of the unwounded men said, "Hard to say. Most were dead or close to it when we passed through."

Butler's dressing station no longer existed and he needed to establish another one, probably nearer to the new front line, somewhere ahead to the east or southeast. Assuming, of course, the new line held.

He said: "When you get to Lucy-le-Bocage, tell Captain Peckham where I'm headed. Also tell him I need medical supplies and stretcher bearers—as many as he can spare. If Captain Peckham isn't available, find an officer and tell him."

The tall soldier acknowledged with a quick nod and then all three moved slowly towards the rear.

Butler picked up his musette bag and looped it over his head and across his chest.

Like most front-line trenches, this one sloped upwards, being wider at the top than the bottom. It also featured a two-foot high shelf carved into the forward side. The eighteen-inch wide step was both a firing position and facilitated climbing out of the deep trench into the open.

Hesitating for just a moment, Butler stepped onto the ledge, pushed himself up and out, and then strode purposefully toward the Bois de la Roche.

25

Margaret looked up from the document, unable to conceal her surprise. "Is this all there is—three pages? I expected much more."

When Colonel Andrews had first told her about Michael's Last Will and Testament, she naturally assumed her brother had drafted and then legally executed an entirely new document, thereby superseding the original will filed by the family attorney. Obviously, that was not the case.

"It's a codicil," Colonel Andrews explained. "I apologize if I didn't make that clear when we first spoke. What you have is a Certified True Copy of the original codicil Michael filed with the Adjutant General's office."

Margaret and Beatrice sat in one of the drawing rooms presently serving as the Colonel's office, a bright and airy space located on the second floor of the Hottinguer mansion fronting Rue Raynouard. It was their second visit to the American Ambulance Field Service headquarters in as many days.

"We were probably in shock," Margaret said. "Learning of Michael's burial caught us unprepared. I'm not sure I remember everything you told us."

"That's certainly understandable," the Colonel offered. "In any case, a codicil augments or amends rather than replaces a previously executed will. In short, that means all the existing provisions of the original document remain unchanged, except for the three items noted."

"Yes, of course," Margaret replied.

The first item addressed his burial. It was a straightforward narrative, written in clear, concise language that left no doubt regarding Michael's intent. The second allocated his military life insurance benefit plus ten thousand dollars from his trust account to an entity called the War Survivors Fund. The last page, recently dated, provided a modest but comfortable monthly stipend for Anna.

"Each of us has a will," Beatrice volunteered. "Father saw to it that the bulk of our individual trusts remained within the family in the event of death. The trust has a special name, but I've forgotten what it is."

Colonel Andrews smiled but did not respond.

"What is the War Survivors Fund?" Margaret asked. "I've never heard of it."

"It's a privately managed benevolent organization that provides financial assistance to the widows and children of French soldiers killed in action."

"That sounds odd. Why exclude American soldiers?"

"Because American soldiers have a $4,500 death benefit, a sum provided by the United States government. France cannot afford such generosity. Millions of French soldiers have died... the best and ablest of an entire generation."

"And the $4,500 amount is the life insurance mentioned in Michael's will?"

"Yes, plus the ten-thousand from his trust."

"I understand."

Indeed she did. The image of black-garbed widows huddled together on Le Havre's Pier Escale was still fresh in her memory, as were those joyless women in the Tuileries who looked after their fatherless children. Michael's bequest would help provide for those unfortunate survivors.

"Miss Jerome," the Colonel said to Margaret. "Regarding another subject, the topic we discussed during your first visit. Have you decided on a course of action regarding your brother's remains? When last we spoke, you were unsure."

She met the Colonel's inquisitive gaze. "Yesterday afternoon I sent a cable to my parents informing them of the situation. I also indicated we should fully consider Michael's wish before we decide anything. What happens next is up to them, I suppose."

"Do you have an inclination about how they might respond?"

"I believe my father's first impulse might be to proceed with his original plan. When Beatrice and I left America, our family was of one mind regarding Michael's remains. We were positive he'd want to rest in the family plot, beside the graves of our grandparents. Now, considering his new will—and other things—I want to believe our family would respect Michael's last request. However, I'm not sure my parents would understand his reasoning."

"And the War Survivors Fund?" he asked, reverting to the original subject.

"I don't see how we could reasonably object. The money belonged to Michael. The organization he chose as beneficiary is certainly worthwhile. As to the monthly bequest to Anna…" Margaret shrugged. "She obviously provided a great deal of support and comfort during his time in hospital. If our brother wanted to recognize her efforts in some material way, then I see no reason, legal or otherwise, for dispute. I have no doubt my parents will agree."

Margaret re-folded and inserted the three pages back into the envelope Colonel Andrews had given her upon their arrival. "May I keep this?"

"Of course. I made a Certified True Copy for you. I believe the Army Judge Advocate's Office sent executed originals to your attorney in St. Louis."

"I see." Margaret looked at her sister. "Is there anything else we need to discuss with Colonel Andrews?"

"No, I think we've covered everything."

Earlier, Colonel Andrews had confirmed their rights regarding Michael's property—the items Anna held in 'safekeeping'. While Margaret anticipated and hoped that no significant conflicts would arise, she also wanted to be sure of her claim should Anna prove uncooperative.

Finally, as she had promised Gurney, Margaret had not raised the issue of her father's cable, a private communication purposefully intercepted and misplaced by him and his friends. Beatrice had likewise remained silent in that regard. Given Michael's will—codicil—there was little point in divulging Gurney's well-intentioned conspiracy.

Margaret stood and extended her hand. "Thank you, Colonel Andrews. You've been helpful and generous with your advice and counsel."

"It was my pleasure," he replied.

Outside, Margaret checked her watch. It was time to meet Anna Elise for tea and lunch. As a carriage pulled to the curb, concern that Anna might dispute the family's right to claim Michael's possessions tarnished, perhaps unfairly, Margaret's positive first impression of the young French nurse. Fair or not, her brother's personal effects belonged to his family and Margaret resolved to stand firm on that issue, regardless of what Anna might believe.

26

Police Superintendent Fernand Raux frowned at the prospect of again having to visit the unsolved murder of Lieutenant Guy Jean Aubray. He lit another Gauloises and blew smoke toward the ceiling. His neatly cluttered office, located in a non-descript building on Avenue Mozart, overlooked a small park.

What had again brought the matter to his attention was the recent arrest of the late Lieutenant's widow, Lizette Aubray. According to witnesses, Madame Aubray had knifed one Pacu Mirković, a man reputed to be her Serbian pimp. The stab wound was superficial, requiring disinfectant and a few stitches. Mirković did not press charges and her release from custody was imminent.

Earlier in the day, Raux had spoken to Madam Aubray. It was obvious the woman now existed at a much lower social level. The once-fine clothing, now faded and worn, hung from her frame in untidy folds. In the period following her husband's unsolved murder, the woman's status had sunk from marital disrepute to common whoredom—a loathsome existence where pimps and prostitutes lived lives of mutual abuse, often maiming, and sometimes murdering each other.

As he remembered from previous reviews, they had discovered Lieutenant Aubray's carefully positioned body on the Quai de Passy. That was about five months ago. Since then the case had grown cold. Nevertheless, Raux had questioned Madame Aubray again, hoping to unearth new information.

Dirty, unkempt, and reeking of the gutter, she was not recognizable from the mildly attractive woman he remembered. 'It's too late,' she had told him, her croaky voice ravaged by alcohol. 'You will never catch him now.'

He wondered about that comment. Did her remark suggest the murderer was dead, or did she mean that too much time had passed since her husband's death? He tapped ash from his cigarette into the elephant-foot ashtray, recalling more of their last conversation.

"Explain yourself," he had insisted.

"He's gone," she rasped. "Pffft! Just like all the others."

Raux had pressed her hard, even a bit cruelly, but further questioning produced incoherent mumbles and spittle-flecked profanities. Clearly, the woman was marginally deranged, her mind and memory corroded by absinth and opium and God knew what else. It was a human tragedy befitting Victor Hugo—perhaps Dumas.

He sighed.

A few more months, he told himself. I will hold the case open for a little while longer. If nothing develops, then I shall give it up.

Not entirely satisfied, he returned the file to the Open and Unsolved drawer of his desk, and then directed his attention to the next case.

27

The war's cutting edge had moved on, leaving behind a shattered landscape pocked with artillery shell craters, churned earth, abandoned trenches, and broken coils of barbed wire. In the early-morning quiet Butler picked his way across open ground. He was utterly alone.

Fifteen minutes after leaving Private Haskins and his two companions, Butler stumbled upon scores of soldiers—both German and American—their bodies cluttering a five-acre sized field adjoining the Bois de la Roche—Private Haskins's *Roach Woods*.

'You'll see for yourself,' the bleary-eyed soldier had told him.

It was a horror beyond words.

Aboard the *Mongolia* Colonel Dawes had explained, in great detail, the mutilating effect of explosive artillery on human bodies. Butler had prepared himself for what he thought was the worst possible battlefield conditions; still, the ghastly reality left him stunned with disbelief.

The word 'slaughterhouse' was wholly inaccurate. In those places, mankind had organized the process of death; efficiently butchering cattle and sheep before hanging their carcasses in neat, uniform rows. But the scene near the Bois de la Roche defied imagination.

Far from orderly, the dead lay in random scatterings—some whole, others a cruel disassembly of limbs and mutilated torsos—

bodies desecrated without pattern or purpose. In rare cases what remained was not recognizable as human; a bloody tangle of woolen brown clothing or leather accoutrement offered scant evidence of human origin. And everywhere, permeating the air like a malodorous fog, hung the stench of human feces and the burnt metallic reek of spilled blood. Unlike heroic tales from antiquity, this battlefield held no glory, no dignity; only a gruesome banquet for legions of rats and flies and crows.

During the early stage of the war, the unexpectedly large numbers of dead had overwhelmed both sides. Abandoned like tattered laundry, the dead had remained on the battlefield for months, their bodies reduced to skeletons by vermin and rot. Would these dead soldiers also suffer a similar indignity? Butler swallowed and moved on, careful of where he stepped.

Most soldiers had died instantly, the result of concussion, a trickle of blood from a nostril or ear providing a telltale clue, but others had suffered grievous wounds. There were clear signs that a few had lived for a time before death claimed them as well. Evidence of their last agonizing moments—fingers clawing the earth, boot heels digging fruitless grooves—told a solitary tale of each man's death.

One soldier lay facing the sky, his lower body folded backwards in half just above the pelvis, legs splayed in a wide 'V', booted toes pointing in opposite directions, head and shoulders wedged in between. It was an impossible position, even for a double-jointed contortionist. Blood had pooled just below the soldier's belt and several rats tugged and gnawed on exposed viscera. Butler shuddered at the sight and fought to quell a rising sense of revulsion. His worst nightmare, rats feeding on human remains, had become a terrible reality.

He forced himself to approach the body. All but the largest rat waddled away. The huge gray rodent—the size of a house cat—turned and stared at him with tiny red eyes. The creature bared yellow teeth, its pointed snout and whiskers twitching in a crimson snarl. Then it opened its mouth and uttered a menacing shriek. Butler stopped abruptly, shocked and horrified by the rat's unexpected aggression.

At that moment the soldier's eyes slid open and he fixed Butler with a long, pleading stare. The dry, cracked lips formed a voiceless appeal. *Help me...*

A mixture of shock and black fear surged through Butler, clutching at his heart like the icy hand of a long-dead ogre raised from a grave. He staggered backwards and nearly tripped over another corpse, then turned and stumbled away, desperate to escape the unspeakable horror.

Moments later a semblance of self-control forced itself into his consciousness. A deepening sense of shame and self-loathing slowed and then halted his retreat. What in God's name was he doing? A wounded soldier needed help. The man in question had no chance of survival, but that irrefutable fact meant nothing. Stunned by the enormity of his cowardly act, he turned and retraced his steps.

On the way back to the mangled soldier, Butler stooped beside a dead captain and took the officer's sidearm—a Model 1911 Colt .45 caliber semiautomatic pistol. He pulled the slide halfway back and saw the brassy glint of a chambered round.

The large gray rat, still feeding, turned at Butler's approach and immediately repeated its aggressive behavior, this time leaving its meal and creeping menacingly toward where he stood. Butler felt an icy calm settle through his bones. He pulled back the hammer, thumbed the safety off, sighted down the barrel and squeezed the trigger, exactly as the range sergeants at Camp Gordon had instructed.

The impact of the heavy slug caused the scavenger to explode in a crimson mist of blood and fur and tissue.

He set the pistol down and approached the mutilated soldier, determined to apologize, to beg forgiveness, or to do the unthinkable: ease the man's pain with a lethal dose of narcotic. But it was too late. The soldier—freshly spattered with rat's blood, slimy gobbets, and furry clumps—was beyond anyone's help.

Butler forced himself to accept his disgraceful act. He had clearly failed, both as a surgeon and as a soldier; even as a man. Had the sight of rats feeding on a living human being spooked him that much? He wasn't sure. However, the scene before him reflected the stark difference between these fallen soldier's display of courage and Butler's cowardly behavior as a surgeon.

He turned away and resumed his search for signs of life, hoping for an opportunity to redeem his spineless act. He blinked away angry tears, overwhelmed by a profound sense of shame.

*

The field and adjoining woods ended at a one-lane dirt road cut parallel to a shallow depression on the opposite side. He crossed both and approached a woodlot sheared by artillery fire. Not one tree stood erect. A few stumps remained, jutting from the earth like shattered bones.

His eyes swept the unfamiliar landscape.

Beyond lay a wheat field, wide swaths of golden tassels mashed flat by tramping boots. A quarter mile away a house and several outbuildings loomed above the ruined field like gray limestone sentinels. Somewhere beyond the farm a muted chorus of gunfire popped and stuttered—hollow, distant mutterings rising and falling with the intermittent breeze.

As he approached the farmhouse, an American soldier emerged from a doorway, his rifle resting in the crook of one arm. "I thought that might be you, Doc."

Butler studied the soldier's face but could not recall seeing him before. The man either recognized Butler or noticed the red Geneva Cross armband on his left sleeve. As he drew closer, the soldier saluted, a casual touch to the narrow rim circling his British-style helmet.

Butler returned the salute. "I'm Butler. Who are you?"

"Coburn, sir. Harold J."

"Are there wounded men here?"

"Yes, sir. They're inside the house."

"Show me."

Private Coburn slung the weapon over his shoulder, adjusted the leather strap, and then led the way into a kitchen void of furniture. Butler counted eleven men in various positions. Two, either unconscious or asleep, lay on the bare wooden floor. A half-dozen men slouched against one wall and three more sat on the ledge fronting a craggy stone fireplace. Most had arm, shoulder, or leg injuries. Every man wore a bloody, hastily applied roller bandage over his wounds. None had manila tags indicating medical attention.

Butler turned to Private Coburn. "Are you the lone guard?"

"Yes, sir. I was told to wait here until help came."

"I see." Butler frowned, then addressed the soldier. "Listen, Coburn. I need you to find an officer. Tell him where we are and that we have eleven wounded that require evacuation. Each ambulance can carry four stretchers in a two above two rack, so we require three ambulances. Do you understand?"

"Yes, sir. But you'll be here by yourself. Suppose the Heinies counterattack?"

"Let me worry about that. We need those ambulances, and quickly. On your way—now!"

"Yes, sir."

Private Coburn scurried out and Butler turned his attention to the wounded.

He examined each conscious man, mentally categorizing wounds. As he worked, Butler realized he was performing *triage*, if not formally then certainly *de facto*, precisely as Colonel Dawes had described during that second day aboard ship. After his appalling performance in the field near the Roche Woods, Butler was surprised to discover the categorization process had come to him automatically.

Satisfied the walking wounded did not require immediate medical attention, Butler focused on the two men who appeared to have more serious injuries.

The first unconscious man had suffered a head wound. Butler removed the bloody field dressing and saw the dull edge of a metal fragment protruding from the frontal bone, above and an inch or so left of the metopic suture. Apparently, the éclat had pierced the soldier's helmet and then lodged in his skull. Without an x-ray, Butler could not determine the fragment's length or the extent of brain damage, if any. He checked the man's pulse: slow but steady. There was nothing he could do here; the patient required the facilities of a proper hospital. Butler swabbed iodine on the wound and applied a fresh bandage.

The second man's tunic lay open and his fully unbuttoned shirt lay outside his trousers. A field dressing protected the soldier's abdominal wound, but it looked dry, absent of seepage. Fearing the worst, Butler removed the bandage. A round puncture wound, slightly right of the navel, had clotted. Butler carefully turned the man and noted a similar-sized exit hole opposite the first. He then studied the tunic and shirt. Using his finger to smooth the cloth, Butler saw that both entry holes closed completely. A pointed bullet had passed through cleanly, neither tumbling nor bringing with it any significant fragment of the uniform's contaminating material. That was good.

The soldier's pulse was slow but firm, not at all thready—another good sign.

The wounded man opened his eyes and blinked several times. "I'm gut shot, Doc. Don't waste your time on me. Tend to the others."

"What's your name?" Butler asked.

"Herb Vogel."

"I won't kid you, Vogel. You *are* gut shot, but the bullet went through cleanly."

"So what? Gut shot is gut shot. I'm goin' West and that's that."

"Don't quit on me just yet."

"I'm not givin' up, Doc. I just understand how it is, that's all."

Butler remained squatted on his haunches and stared into the soldier's eyes. "Listen to me, Vogel. The small gut is not in a fixed position like your heart or lungs. They move around, like greased rubber coils. Sometimes a pointed bullet pushes them aside on its way through the body. Can you see how that might happen?"

Vogel squinted and frowned. "You mean like pokin' your finger through a tin can full of night crawlers?"

"Yes, something like that. You might have a few intestinal nicks or punctures, but they often close spontaneously—that is, of their own accord. Your pulse is good, which means the bullet didn't sever any major blood vessels."

Vogel's eyes narrowed. "Are you tellin' me the truth?"

"I am not in the habit of lying."

"Then you're sayin' I'll be okay."

"No, not quite. If what I believe did indeed happen, then, with a simple procedure, you have a good chance of pulling through once you get to a hospital."

Butler's primary concern was the extent of damage caused by the bullet's passage through the soldier's viscera. Lesions of the hollow intestinal organs were far more serious due to potentially massive leakages of purulent fluids. Mixed with blood from the wound, they tended to pool within abdominal cavities—in Vogel's case, the right iliac fossa. As they accumulated, swelling and muscular tension would force septic fluids into the peritoneum. Once absorbed, life-threatening infection was certain. Relieving the pressure would lower the risk of peritonitis and increase Vogel's chances of survival.

"What kind of procedure?" the soldier asked.

"Blood and poisonous fluids are building up inside your abdomen. I need to drain the wound. The longer we wait, the bigger risk you have for infection." Butler smiled, trying to put the soldier at ease. "Compared to being shot, this will be a piece of cake."

He turned to the group of wounded men. Several were looking at him with apparent interest. "One of you fetch a glass container of some kind."

Butler said to Vogel: "Believe me; you won't feel much at all."

He loosened the soldier's belt, unbuttoned the fly and tucked the fully opened trouser front out of the way, exposing the lower abdomen completely. From his medical kit Butler took a razor and shaved a six-inch square just above the pubic arch. Then he swabbed the entire area with a one percent solution of Procaine. "This will numb the spot where I need to place the drain," he said to Vogel. "It might still hurt a bit, but not too much."

One of the wounded soldiers, his arm in a makeshift sling, approached holding what looked like a clean, 16-ounce Mason jar. "Will this do?"

"It's perfect. Thanks." Butler set the jar beside Vogel.

He took a sealed waxed paper pouch containing a length of quarter-inch rubber tubing and a bottle of iodine from his kit. Butler then swabbed the shaved area with disinfectant. There were no rubber gloves in his kit so he rinsed his hands and dipped the scalpel in an alcohol solution. It wasn't perfect but it would have to do.

"Here we go," Butler said. "Just relax. This won't take long."

He made a half-inch incision in the abdominal wall just above the pubic arch, near the center of the shaved area, into which he inserted one end of the black rubber tubing. The other end lay halfway inside the glass jar. A mixture of blood and yellow-green fluid slid from the tube into the jar. After a few minutes, it slowed to a drip. About four ounces lay in the bottom.

Butler gently probed the lower abdomen with his fingers. The muscles yielded easily under slight pressure, another good sign. There was nothing else he could do at the moment. If no complications developed over the next day or so, then the soldier would probably recover fully.

He dressed the wound, leaving the rubber tube in place. Then he said: "You must lie still until the ambulances arrive. Take no food or drink at all. Do you understand?"

"But suppose I get thirsty."

"You can rinse your mouth with water, but do not swallow. Your life depends on it." He took a manila tag from his medical kit. "Now, tell me your full name, service number and unit."

He completed the tag with the following entry:

G.S.W. Abdomen. Perforating.
Murphy's Incision. Iodine Dressing. Lt. Butler, M.O.

He attached the tag to Vogel's uniform. Then he stood, stretched and surveyed the room. Picking up his kit, Butler approached a soldier with a leg wound. "You're next," he said.

*

As he already knew from initial examination, the less seriously injured soldiers were not in mortal danger; most of their wounds were painful but superficial, the result of explosive artillery fragments. The first of three ambulances arrived just as Butler completed his treatment of the last wounded men.

After supervising the loading, Butler spoke to the driver of the remaining ambulance, a dark-haired corporal. "Where are you taking them?"

"Evac Six," the driver replied.

Butler translated the response: Evacuation Hospital Number 6. "I don't know where that is."

"Chateau-Thierry, about two miles down this road." The driver pointed in a southeasterly direction.

"Where am I now?"

The driver studied him for a moment. "Vaux is on the other side of that rise. Say, Lieutenant, are you lost?"

"That would appear to be the case."

"Where did you come from?"

"A field dressing station about a mile this side of Lucy-le-Bocage."

"And you hoofed it from there?"

Butler nodded.

The driver turned and pointed in the opposite direction. "Lucy is about four miles that way."

Butler wasn't sure where he should go. Captain Peckham—assuming he was still operating an aid station—had probably followed the advance as it moved eastward. He had no inkling where Peckham's current location might be, but he was certain that someone at Chateau-Thierry could direct him to the 23rd Infantry's new command post. From there, it should be an easy matter to rejoin his detachment.

"Do you mind if I hitch a ride with you back to Evac Six?" he asked.

"Climb in, Lieutenant. I'll have you there in a jiffy."

Riding in the passenger seat, Butler could not help but reflect on the events of the past eight hours. As Colonel Dawes had predicted, Butler had used *triage* to segregate individual cases. However, could he administer a lethal dose of morphine to a hopelessly wounded man with equal ease? The lingering experience near the Bois de la Roche now challenged his once automatic response. The concept was not quite as repulsive as he once thought.

Recalling the informative lectures aboard the *Mongolia* also reminded him of Margaret Jerome. He pictured her face and wondered again why he found her memory so compelling. Was it merely the color of her eyes and the unmistakable reflection of an inner strength? Was it the inquisitive intelligence of a lady who would challenge the ignorant assumptions of fools? Perhaps it was all those things. Yet, her manner also suggested hints of a passageway she never left unguarded. Where might the key to that mysterious place be? If he was lucky enough to find it, would she allow him access to her innermost feelings? And what might he discover there?

He also wondered where she might be at this early hour. Parisians were not, as a rule, early risers. A sit-down breakfast would be difficult to find before eight or nine o'clock. Had she and Beatrice completed arrangements regarding their brother? Were they on their way home? Butler felt an ache; an inconsolable sense of loss.

The wishful pang was a rare sensation for him.

With Father Leo's help, Butler had learned to fine-tune his mind and then follow where logic and fact led. Those early lessons, applied soon after the disappearance of his parents, had shaped his outlook on life. Butler's subsequent personal and professional conduct was not unlike what his Jesuit mentor might have predicted:

a demeanor more intellectual than emotional.

However, Butler's attraction to Miss Jerome was not what he'd come to expect of himself. Nor was his shocking behavior towards that unfortunate soldier in the Roche Woods. Those two events undermined his once unshakable sense of who he was: a man governed by his head rather than his heart.

He studied his clasped hands.

Perhaps he wasn't as imperturbable as he once thought.

Chateau-Thierry, a large village or a small town, lay in a shallow depression surrounded by gentle hills turned golden-green with ripening grain. Most of the buildings lay to the north of the Marne River. The ruins of a large gray chateau overlooked the town, its square tower reminiscent of a medieval castle. The driver approached an imposing stone church and eased into a circular drive, parking close behind the two preceding ambulances. Grim-faced orderlies unloaded wounded men and carried them inside.

"Welcome to Evac Six," the driver said.

"What is this place?"

"It used to be a Catholic seminary. Saint Somethin' or Other."

"I see. Well, thanks for the lift."

"My pleasure, Lieutenant." The driver left to assist his companions.

After the ambulances were unloaded Butler walked up concrete steps and into the building. In the main hallway a doctor examined medical tags, the same ones Butler had previously tied to each wounded man. One by one, the doctor—a man he recognized from the *Mongolia*—directed patients to a specific ward. A few minutes later, Major Gregory looked up. A smile crossed his face as he approached, right hand extended.

"Doctor Butler. I wondered if you were one and the same with 'Lt. Butler, M.O.' written on those treatment tags."

He took Major Gregory's offered hand. "It's good of you to remember me, sir. There were a lot of surgeons aboard that particular troopship."

"Yes, but only one Lieutenant Butler from Mount Sinai Hospital who became infatuated with an attractive young lady." He examined Butler's face and disheveled uniform. "Where on earth have you been?"

Now conscious of his appearance, he brushed dust and small particles of debris from his tunic. He could do nothing about the dried blood.

"My apologies, Major. It seems I blundered my way from Lucy-le-Bocage to a farmhouse near Vaux. That's where I treated those wounded men. One of your ambulance drivers gave me a ride."

"Following the American advance, were you? Alone? That's quite interesting, but I can't say I'm surprised."

"It's much less adventurous than what you might think. Last night, while I lay quaking in a foxhole, an artillery bombardment destroyed my dressing station. Later, a soldier told me of wounded men near the Bois de la Roche. Apparently I got lost along the way." He chose not to elaborate.

"Not by much. Vaux is adjacent to Roche Wood."

"Pure luck, sir."

"I see." The Major rubbed his chin. "So, they have you manning a dressing station, is that correct?"

"Yes, sir."

"That's not much of a challenge for someone with your experience, is it?"

"Perhaps not, but it has its moments."

Major Gregory's eyes reflected skepticism. "Look, Butler. I'm overwhelmed by casualties and have desperate need for qualified surgeons. Who is your commanding officer?"

"Captain Peckham, sir. We're attached to the Twenty-Third Infantry's Second Battalion."

"I have no idea where they are but I know someone who does." He turned and summoned a nearby orderly. "Take Lieutenant Butler to the officer's mess. After he's eaten breakfast, hand him over to Captain Evans." Then to Butler: "George Evans is the hospital adjutant. He'll arrange transport to wherever you need to go." He extended his hand. "Good luck, Doctor. I hope to see you again, soon."

He took the Major's hand. "Thank you for feeding me, sir. And for the ride back to my unit."

"Not at all. Now, if you'll excuse me, you brought a lot of work to which I must attend." Without another word, he turned and strode away.

Butler said to the orderly, "I haven't eaten in a while, but I need to wash up."

"Come this way, Lieutenant."

As he followed the orderly down a wide corridor, Butler wondered if Major Gregory had sufficient authority to have him transferred. It was an intriguing possibility, one he found both exciting and problematic. Duty in an evacuation hospital would provide unique opportunities to further develop surgical skills and expand his medical knowledge; goals he had pursued with single-minded diligence. Evacuation hospitals were also miles behind the front line, away from battlefield squalor and the constant threat from artillery bombardment.

Butler wasn't sure which potential outcome pleased him most.

Did he favor duty in an evacuation hospital because it offered professional opportunities, or was it merely a way for him to escape the horrors of a battlefield?

28

"Automobiles?" Captain George Evans said. "Sorry, there are none available just now. They're being used as ambulances, ferrying wounded to the train station." The hospital's adjutant, stocky and middle aged with thinning brown hair, sat behind an ancient wooden desk, smoking a cigarette fixed to an ivory holder. He eyed Butler's filthy uniform. "Looks to me like you had a rough go of it."

"Not as bad as some, Captain."

The carnage near the Roche Woods was still fresh in Butler's mind. He suspected the memory would never disappear, not completely.

The Captain blew smoke towards the ceiling. "Oh, I can imagine. Last night's thrust was a surprise to everyone. I believe they briefed Major Gregory, but few others were. Apparently this is the beginning of our long-anticipated drive to eliminate the German salient."

"All the more reason for me to find Captain Peckham, sir. Do you know where his aid station might be?"

"I believe your unit has moved to the outskirts of Mont-Saint-Pere."

"How far away is that?"

"About five miles east of here, give or take. They should have bivouacked close to the main road."

"In that case, sir, if you point me in the right direction, then I'll be on my way." Butler was not looking forward to an early-morning hike along a dusty road, but there was little choice.

Captain Evans tapped his cigarette with an index finger, knocking ash into an already filled metal container. "As I said, there are no automobiles available. However, I do have a motorcycle with a sidecar. They're uncomfortable—hard on the ass—and insanely dangerous, but it's marginally better than walking."

Butler had never ridden a motorcycle sidecar but the prospect was preferable to traveling on foot. Last night's bombardment had robbed him of sleep. The hot breakfast of coffee, oatmeal, and crisp bacon—a welcome and satisfying meal—did little to assuage his weariness.

He stifled a yawn. "The motorcycle sounds fine to me, Captain. Thank you."

"Fortuno!" Evans called.

The adjutant's ground-floor office occupied one room of a residence adjacent to the hospital. A stocky, dark-complexioned soldier appeared in the doorway.

"Yes, sir?"

"The Lieutenant needs a ride to Mont-Saint-Pere. Take him there and come straight back. No detours." Evans looked at Butler: "After suffering under German occupation, the French are deliriously happy to have the Krauts out of their homes. Being generous country people they show their gratitude by offering food, wine and other spirits at every opportunity, but especially when American soldiers dawdle near a village square."

Butler smiled. "One must never be rude to one's hosts."

"Exactly." Evans spoke to Fortuno. "No lingering, understand?"

"Yes, sir."

Evans rose, and extended his hand. "Good luck, Lieutenant."

"Thank you, sir."

A sleek, wire-wheeled Indian motorcycle stood just outside.

Butler climbed into the mud-spattered sidecar and settled in, his posterior hardly more than a foot above the cobblestone street.

"Hang on, Lieutenant."

They left Chateau-Thierry and rumbled eastward, following the north bank of the Marne River to the village of Gland. Evenly spaced Lombardy poplars lined both sides of the road, graceful columns rising like leafy green sentinels toward a clear blue sky.

Fortuno exchanged honks and waves with several ambulances headed in the opposite direction. As they drew closer to the front, the Indian sped by dead horses, their swollen bodies covered by a shimmering carpet of black flies. The huge draft animals lay scattered on both sides of the road, their legs stiff and unnaturally extended. Artillery blasts had eviscerated a few and their exposed entrails lay in greasy blue chains. As they passed by, the stench of putrefaction hung in fumy pockets, sickeningly heavy odors separated by spheres of untainted air.

Among the horses lay a few dead soldiers. Medical personnel assigned to the graves detail attended the corpses, sliding each into a white canvas sack. Butler hoped others were doing the same for the dead near the Roche Woods.

Beyond Gland the river road swung north over rising ground. They passed more fly-infested animals and foul air, skirting around wrecked vehicles and myriad equipment discarded haphazardly like broken toys. Craters left by explosive artillery bracketed the dirt road.

Fortuno zipped through Mont-Saint-Pere, slowed, and then stopped alongside a stone building. Three ambulances and several tents stood nearby.

"Here ya' are, Lieutenant."

Butler climbed stiffly from the sidecar. "Thanks for the ride."

"Sure beats walking, doesn't it?"

"Yes, barely."

Fortuno chuckled, tossed Butler a relaxed salute, turned the three-wheeled motorcycle around and roared back toward Chateau-Thierry, pulling a swirling cone of dust as he accelerated.

Captain Peckham looked up as Butler entered the building. A startled expression crossed his face. "My God, Robert! I thought you were dead."

"Close, but no cigar."

"So I see. Happily, I might add." He rose and they shook hands. "Take a chair and tell me what happened to you after the shelling stopped."

Butler removed his tin helmet, unslung the musette bag and plopped into a wooden chair. Then he related the details of his post-bombardment excursion to the farmhouse near Vaux, the subsequent visit to Chateau-Thierry and his meeting with Major Gregory.

"I first met the Major on board the *Mongolia* and we spent some time together. I like him. He seems like a nice gentleman. I never expected to see him again."

"The Regular Army Medical Corps is a small community," Peckham volunteered. "Most of us are acquainted with or know one another by reputation. I've heard the Major's name mentioned, but never had the pleasure."

Butler decided that candor required him to reveal the entire conversation. "Major Gregory was interested to learn what I was doing: that is, working in a field dressing station. He told me he needed surgeons and asked for your name."

"I'm not surprised. We generally use interns or first year residents to man dressing stations. It's a seasoning process, a hint of things to come before introducing them to combat surgery. You happen to be an exception. Sorry, Robert, but we were short-handed. It couldn't be helped."

Butler ran fingers through his hair. "I understand. Anyway, now that I've returned to the fold, where do you want me?"

Peckham leaned back in his chair. "You look tired. I suggest you catch a few hours' sleep. Word is we're going to continue our attack sometime tonight. Things are quiet at the moment but that will change. Better get some rest while you can."

"That sounds like an excellent idea. But first, tell me the latest. What's going on in our sector?"

Peckham rose and refilled his cup from a metal pot resting on a small gas burner nearby. "Would you like some coffee?"

"No, thanks."

"The Germans occupy Jaulgonne," Peckham began. "It's the next village up the road, about two miles from here. French and American units are dug in west and south of the town. Our casualties have been fairly high and we expect more of the same later on. As bad as we think it might be, I hear it's much worse up around Belleau Wood. It's rumored the Marines may have lost an entire regiment."

Butler nodded but said nothing. If he remembered correctly, approximately two thousand men comprised a regiment. If what Woody said was true, that was a staggering loss indeed.

"Anyway," Peckham continued, "after you've rested a bit, I'll show you where to set up a dressing station."

"Okay," Butler said.

He was going back to the line, a reality he expected but did not relish. Would there be another artillery bombardment? Probably, but there was nothing he could do. Would his bladder fail once again? Butler hoped not, but he didn't really know.

"Where can I get a change of clothes and another personal kit? Everything I own went up in smoke last night." Other than the dried mud and bloodstains, Butler did not feel it necessary to reveal additional details regarding his need for a change of clothing.

Peckham studied him for a moment. "We look about the same size. I could loan you a razor and a spare uniform until yours are replaced."

"I appreciate that. Where can I get a new suitcase and new uniforms?"

"You can buy a new suitcase in Paris, if we ever get leave. In the meantime you'll have to make do with a duffle bag. I'll take care of the requisition. Uniforms and equipment 'Lost in Battle' is a common occurrence. The regimental quartermaster is a friend of mine so it shouldn't take long to get you fixed up with new gear."

Butler stood and retrieved his tin helmet and musette bag. "Sounds like you have it all figured out, Woody."

Peckham expelled air through his nose. "I wish that was true," he said.

*

Butler strolled along the sidewalk of a deserted street lined with fully-leafed mature hardwoods: elm and maple and a scattering of oak. Substantial two-story houses stood on oversized lots, their gray clapboards aged and weathered by too many untended years. They appeared empty and void of life. Parlor windows, once wreathed in folds of milky lace, now stared vacantly as he drifted by. The bulky silence felt ponderous and absolute, an atmosphere totally void of rustle, whisper or buzz.

He turned toward a familiar house, made his way through a picket gate and then ambled up a sidewalk bordered on either side by disused flower beds. Climbing wooden stairs onto the porch, he opened an unlocked front door and stepped into the foyer. Further inside he passed through spacious, high ceiling rooms absent of furniture and decoration. Everything looked both familiar and strange; images warped by an imperfect pane of glass.

The slowly unfolding scene, sepia-toned and dusty with time's passage, left him forlorn and puzzled. *This is a wonderful old house in a pleasant neighborhood. Why is it vacant and abandoned? What happened to the people who once lived here?* He stood for a moment, waiting in the breathless silence, hoping for a response.

He felt a firm hand on his shoulder and the dream dissipated into beige fog, leaving the question unanswered.

"Up and at 'em, Robert." The voice belonged to Woody Peckham.

Butler sat up, swung his bare feet to the wooden-plank floor and rubbed sleep from his eyes, still troubled by the lingering memory of his former home on Orchard Street.

"Feeling better?" Peckham asked.

In spite of the dream, Butler felt surprisingly rested. "Yes, much." He checked his pocket watch: four o'clock. "Six hours is more than a nap," he said. "Why did you let me sleep for so long?"

"Get it while you can. That's my motto." Peckham left the small bedroom and clomped downstairs.

Earlier that morning, before availing himself of Woody Peckham's cot, Butler had shaved and taken a makeshift bath, his first in several days, and then stepped into fresh underwear. Now, as he climbed into more of Peckham's clean clothes—which fit quite well—Butler mulled the recurring dreams.

They had started soon after his arrival at St. George's Academy and each followed a similar pattern: He was alone in a vaguely familiar place, wondering where everyone had gone. The locale varied—sometimes the house on Orchard Street, other times the cabin on Seneca Lake—but the theme never did. At college Butler realized those particular dreams were a manifestation of the unresolved mystery surrounding the disappearance of his mother and father. In the decade-plus since his parents vanished, the dreams had become less frequent and eventually stopped. Why had one suddenly reappeared after two years?

He fastened the Sam Browne belt around his waist, and then looped the thin strap through the right shoulder epaulette of his borrowed tunic. The image of Margaret Jerome glided across his mind's eye: auburn hair and clear blue eyes that understood all the ambiguities cluttering his life.

Did her polite rejection reinvigorate his desperate sense of abandonment back when his parents disappeared all those years ago? Perhaps, but why should it? He and Margaret were strangers to each other, hardly more than casual acquaintances. The answer came almost immediately: Like his parents, Margaret Jerome was an unresolved matter. And, not unlike those older feelings of irretrievable loss, thoughts of Margaret left him melancholy and pensive; a man haunted by a gloomy pessimism borne of tantalizing but unfulfilled possibility.

His Jesuit schooling notwithstanding, Butler was not immune to deeply felt emotions. Beginning in his third year at Cambridge, he'd had a long affair with Adele Byington, a pampered divorcee twelve years his senior. Their relationship had grown, peaked and gradually declined over a two-year period, finally ending in a quiet, amicable parting. With Adele, Butler had experienced his first taste of passion—or was it lust? In the last weeks of their relationship, both came to realize that romantic love was not what had attracted one to the other. Not surprising, when the passion cooled, likewise did the affair.

Yet, what he now felt towards Margaret was much different. The physical attraction was certainly part of it, but those feelings had a great deal more depth, more... *texture*. Had he fallen in love? Butler was reluctant to answer that question. He also realized it was a situation he must resolve one way or another lest she become one more ghost wandering through his dreams. The challenge filled him with determination. Unfortunately, *how* he intended to confront the issue was not clear.

Peckham looked up from a stack of paperwork as Butler entered the small office.

"Thanks for the use of your bed—and everything else," Butler said, spreading his arms. "Your uniform fits me perfectly."

"My pleasure, Robert. But I must say: it looks better on you than it does on me." Peckham set aside his paperwork and stood. "Let's visit the regimental mess tent and have an early supper. Afterwards, I'll take you to your new dressing station. I fear it's going to be another busy night."

Butler fingered his musette bag. "I'm short of bandages and tetanus serum. In fact, I'm out of everything."

"Easy enough to fix. We'll replenish your supplies and then eat. Follow me."

It was past five o'clock, the summer sun still high, but the spacious regimental mess tent was not crowded. Inside, the air hung thick with the odors of cooked food, trapped heat, and human sweat. Perspiring attendants garbed in long white aprons served pan-fried sausages, baked beans, fresh-baked bread and strong coffee. Butler's stomach emitted a hollow growl. He hadn't eaten since his bacon and oatmeal breakfast.

Several more officers drifted in as he and Peckham ate. Most looked haggard and pre-occupied, the strain of combat evident on their faces. They gobbled their food quickly, reluctant to pause and savor what might be a last meal on Earth. Then, pushing empty plates aside, they leaned toward each other, foreheads nearly touching, and spoke quietly among themselves. Butler couldn't hear specific conversations but the tense urgency in their voices was unmistakable. Each man looked determined, but certainly not eager.

Butler stared at his plate while he chewed.

What was it like to be an infantry officer: to huddle at the bottom of a filthy, vermin-infested trench under constant threat from enemy snipers and artillery bombardment; to watch the sweep second hand climb inexorably towards the numeral twelve—zero hour; to stand, one foot on the firing step; to blow your shrill-sounding whistle and then lead men into a fiery cataclysm reeking with horrors no human being should be forced to endure? From what internal reservoir did they draw such awesome courage? Was it merely the result of intense military training or were such men born to fight, the modern offspring of age-old warrior clans?

As he ate without tasting his food, Butler studied the small group of determined soldiers and wondered how many of them would pass through his dressing station tonight, either wounded or dead.

"The faces change," Peckham said quietly. "But the slaughter never ends."

Butler refocused his gaze. Had Woody read his thoughts?

After supper an ambulance took them farther up the river road to within a half-mile of the front.

"Wait for me," Peckham ordered the driver.

They walked across a trampled wheat field, down a shallow ravine and up an easy rise. Before they reached the top, Peckham dropped to his knees. Without thinking, Butler followed suit. His, or rather Woody's, clean uniform hadn't remained so for long. They crawled fifty yards, slipped over the crest, and then tumbled into a crater three feet deep and ten feet across.

"Keep below the rim," Peckham advised. "During daylight there might be German snipers hidden in that little wood just beyond our line." He pointed toward a group of trees about five hundred yards to the northeast.

"Where is the dressing station?" Butler asked.

"You're in it."

"This… *hole?*" Surely, Woody was pulling his leg.

"Given the cramped confines of our trench line, this crater is the best option. Don't be overly concerned. This spot is temporary. Once the advance begins, either tonight or just before dawn, you'll want to move forward and gather up the wounded. Later on, sometime before dark, I'll send a stretcher team to keep you company." Peckham smiled, a wry, apologetic upturning of his lips. "One team is the best I can do, Robert. I've had to send most of my bearers up to Soissons. They're having a bad time of it up there—much worse than here, I'm told. Sorry."

Meeting Peckham's steady gaze, Butler felt a growing sense of camaraderie, a soldierly kinship far more complex than his feeling of professional respect toward his commanding officer. "If that's the best you can do chum, then no apology is necessary."

Woody continued. "Pay a visit to the battalion's CO, Colonel Trask. Let him know where you are. He might suggest a less primitive location for you to wait, but I doubt it."

Butler nodded.

"Okay, then. Well, good luck. See you in the funny papers." Without another word, Peckham slid out of the hole and crawled back the way they had come.

Butler unslung his musette bag, now fully replenished, leaned against the slanted wall of the crater and tried to relax. The sun still hung well above the horizon and he began to perspire lightly. At this time of year in Picardy, nightfall wouldn't occur until after ten o'clock. Butler gazed at the deep blue sky and inhaled deeply. The warm air held lingering traces of death, burnt gunpowder and freshly turned earth.

You'll want to move forward and gather up the wounded.

He thought about the phrase and its unspoken implication. Sometime between ten P.M. and dawn, Woody expected him to leave the relative safety of this crater and follow the troops as they advanced, trailing just behind the attacking force, exposing himself to enemy fire and treating wounded men along the way. Could he actually do such a thing? He pictured the faces of those infantry officers gathered in the regimental mess: hard-eyed, determined soldiers whose courage was beyond question.

It was a difficult fact to admit, but he was not cut from the same sturdy cloth as those men. They were like heavy-duty canvas duck, impervious to all weathers. Compared to them he was muslin gauze, fluttering at the slightest breeze.

Remembering the terrors from last night's bombardment and his cowardly reaction at the sight of a mutilated but still living soldier near the Bois de la Roche, Butler found it difficult to believe he would ever satisfy Woody Peckham's high expectations.

29

The two-horse carriage stopped beside a block of adjoining residences facing each other across a cobbled, tree-lined street: a sun-dappled thoroughfare within easy walking distance to the Paris Opera House. The three-story homes, each constructed of gray limestone with chimneys rising above slated mansard roofs, appeared well maintained. Although similar, individual façades reflected one or more unique architectural touches. A few shops were visible, several below street level, their entrances located at the foot of iron-banistered stairways. Colorful awnings sheltered two sidewalk cafes at either end of the block, on opposite sides of the street.

"What a delightful little neighborhood," Beatrice remarked.

It certainly was. The quaint setting reminded Margaret of a finely rendered picture postcard from a less-troubled era.

Margaret was eager to read Michael's journal, but then an uncharitable thought popped into her mind: Had her brother's monthly stipend provided Anna with the means to live in such pleasant accommodations? A silent admonition followed almost immediately. What Michael did with his income was no business of hers.

Margaret suppressed a frown, displeased with her negative assumption regarding Michael's nurse and friend, a woman about whom she knew nothing.

After paying the driver Margaret and Beatrice mounted the wide stone steps of Number 19 Rue Joubert and stood before a set of tall, finely-crafted double doors. Each side appeared to come from a single slab of dark wood, perhaps mahogany. The center panel of each door displayed an intricately-carved series of leaves, flowers, and vines. A black wreath hung on the leftmost side.

Margaret raised and then dropped a polished brass knocker, twice. A moment later Anna answered, opening the right hand door. Her bright smile and the absence of a nurse's uniform made her appear much younger.

"Ah, you are exactly on time. How nice to see you again."

She ushered them into a large foyer. Then, after closing the huge door, she led them a few steps down the hall, turned left through an archway and glided into a comfortable parlor at the front of the house.

"This is a lovely room," Margaret said, genuinely impressed. She quickly took in the elegant furnishings and other appointments. Contrary to her intentions, she again wondered about how such nice appointments came to be here.

"*Merci*. If you like, I will show you more after we have had our tea. Sit, please."

Margaret and Beatrice sat beside each other on one of two facing sofas near a stone fireplace. Anna took a seat opposite, close to a delicate china service resting on a table between them. Margaret controlled her impatience. She wanted to discuss the purpose of their visit—the disposition of Michael's personal effects—but she also knew that Europeans had their own customs when it came to matters of hospitality. She took a deep breath and forced herself to relax.

"Have you always lived in Paris?" Margaret asked.

"Yes. My grandfather purchased this house many years ago. My mother was born in the master bedroom upstairs, as was I."

"How interesting. Do you live here with your parents?"

Anna shook her head. "They have a country home near Blois, to the southwest. It is their home for most of the year, except when they visit friends here in the city. They are a little more distant from the war, which is good."

"I see." Obviously, her family was far from destitute. Anna's response satisfied Margaret's unflattering curiosity regarding the house and its furnishings. It also explained Anna's educated diction, genteel mannerisms and expensive but understated clothing: garments much like what Margaret wore when she expected daytime visitors.

She studied the room as Anna poured tea. Fresh flowers carefully arranged in vases filled the parlor with summertime aromas. Fine paintings hung from two walls and wonderful antiques—porcelain figurines and what looked like delicately jeweled Fabergé eggs—filled a small array of shelves.

Yet, there was something about the décor that eschewed stuffiness and formality. Margaret felt comfortable sitting here and she realized why: the room glowed with vitality and reflected the tastes and unique personal touches of a refined young lady. She and this French woman—separated by geography and culture—seemed to share similar tastes. Margaret's initial discomfort with Anna as an unknown person in her brother's life eased somewhat, but did not disappear entirely.

As they sipped tea, Anna expressed curiosity about their voyage across the Atlantic and listened wide-eyed as Margaret told her about the troopship sinking, the plight of soldiers in the water, depth bombing the German submarine, and the sad fate of so many fine horses. Neither Beatrice nor Margaret spoke of their conversations with Jack Mayo and Robert Butler, respectively.

Finally, Anna broached the purpose of their visit. "As I told you at the hospital," she began. "I have things for your family which belonged to Michael, but there are certain other things of his which I shall keep for myself."

"Yes, I remember," Margaret said, not wanting to start an argument, but determined to make her position clear. "And I understand your feelings, Anna. But we are Michael's family. We are legally entitled to his possessions. Please consider that."

"Be assured that I have. You are indeed Michael's family. This I understand and respect. But sadly, like so many women in France these days, I too have become a widow—Michael's widow. With my loss come certain obligations... and privileges."

"His *widow!*" Beatrice exclaimed with a start. A dribble of tea slid down the side of her cup and into the saucer. "You and Michael were *married?*"

Margaret said nothing. Her shoulders drooped as bewilderment gave way to resignation. For reasons she could not comprehend, Michael had deliberately excluded his family from one of the most notable events of his life; deprived them of sharing his happiest occasion. Of all she had learned about her brother, this latest revelation was the most heartbreaking and troubling.

Twins were supposed to be closer, sharing a spiritual bond much as they had physically shared the warm intimacy of their mother's womb. Yet, she had discovered this immense chasm—a great unknown that separated one conscious mind from another—a human limitation that twins could presumably overcome.

She had not perceived her brother's deepest feelings and the realization left her with the same frightening sensation she had first experienced in the waters off Mackinac Island, and then again upon hearing news of Michael's death. There was no bottom to her life, no solid ground upon which to stand. Margaret leaned her back against the sofa, seeking comfort from its solidity.

Anna said: "Yes. We married three weeks before his death. Our ceremony took place at the Basilique Sainte Clotilde. It was a small affair. My family and a few of Michael's friends attended."

"Gurney never mentioned that," Margaret observed quietly.

"Perhaps Gurney did not feel he should speak. As I told you before, Michael had changed, became less cordial. He and Gurney grew a little apart. Besides, it was my duty alone to inform you of this special love between your brother and myself."

"A *little* apart...?" Margaret exclaimed. "Gurney didn't tell us about that, either," she added, uneasily.

Anna lifted one shoulder slightly, then let it settle back.

Margaret said nothing for a moment, while she tried to gather her thoughts. "Did you know of Michael's will?" she asked. "About his wish to be buried in France?"

"No. I would not allow him to talk about such things."

"Were you surprised by what it contained?"

"Not at all. Michael had a special affection for the wounded men he removed from the battlefield. He also felt for the widows and orphans of all those who did not survive; his gift to them was in tune with those feelings. That Michael desired burial among his fellow soldiers also came as no surprise. What did surprise me was the bequest. I had no knowledge of that until so informed by his colonel."

Margaret remained quiet so Anna continued.

"Gurney told me of your father's cable and what he did to conceal its existence. Knowing that, I expected the arrival of your father and mother. That is why I did not write or send Michael's things to his family. What your brother and I did together, and how we felt about each other, was something to be told directly, one person to another. In these matters, speaking face to face is much better than words on paper. I asked Gurney to remain silent until I could meet with your parents in private."

"I think I understand," Margaret said. To her surprise, she did.

"That is good. However, instead of Michael's parents, his sisters arrive. This I did not expect, but in other ways your presence makes what I have to say easier." Anna shrugged. "On matters concerning children, fathers and mothers hear what they want to hear. In my heart, I knew this news would be most disturbing, and I begged Michael not to keep plans of our marriage from his family. It was not proper behavior for a son to deny his mother's dream. I asked him to wait until all could join us here. Then we would be together, one family celebrating a joyous event.

"But Michael did not want to delay our marriage. He said German submarines would hinder ocean travel and it could take months for everyone to gather in Paris. I loved him, so I did what he asked. He promised to write of our marriage but the war took him before he could find the words. Perhaps we should have done other than what we did, but it is too late for that now. Like yours, my family is also quite sad. They loved Michael like a son, as though he was their own flesh and blood. But my parents did not understand his thoughts." She paused and offered a wistful smile. "Sometimes, neither did I."

Margaret sighed, an utterance mirroring her feelings of bewildered melancholy.

"Anna," she began, "I can understand how Michael could fall in love with you and propose marriage. We hardly know each other but I honestly believe your chosen work is evidence of a good and caring heart. You are also intelligent, refined, and beautiful. Everything one could hope for in a sister–in–law. I also believe your grief is as deep and sincere as ours."

"Thank you for that. I feared you would not understand how much I loved your brother, and how much he loved me." Anna's eyes became moist with tears but did not overflow.

"Believe me, I do understand. But what am I missing? Why would Michael keep so much, even his marriage, from his family? Why did he grow distant from his best friend? What I *don't* understand is what happened to him."

Anna turned away and blinked several times. Then she looked at Margaret. "I do not know more than what I told you yesterday. But, as you will read in his journal, something caused Michael deep regret. It seemed he wanted to make amends."

"Make amends?" Margaret asked. "What does that mean? Make amends for what?"

"This I cannot explain. He makes mention of it in his journal, but gives no reason."

Reminded of Michael's journal heightened Margaret's curiosity. Might his written words hold clues to the mystery of his silence? "The journal. May we see it?"

"*Certainement*," Anna said. "Please follow me. I have laid out Michael's things in the next room."

They rose, crossed the foyer, and then entered the dining room located opposite the parlor.

A magnificent rosewood étagère dominated the wall to her left. The matching dining table and chairs could seat eight guests in comfort. Someone, presumably Anna, had carefully folded back the delicate white-lace tablecloth. The exposed half held an assortment of objects, most of which Margaret recognized.

"This is Michael's uniform," Anna explained, touching a neatly folded brown woolen tunic. Five ribbons, each about an inch wide and a quarter-inch high, were pinned above the left breast pocket, arranged two over three. "And these are his decorations." She opened five black leather cases of varying wallet-sized dimensions, one at a time. The three larger cases held bright medals. The remaining two contained identically colored ribbons.

"Oh, my goodness," Beatrice murmured.

Margaret noticed that the color of the ribbon in each leather case matched those on Michael's uniform. She said, "Could you explain what they mean, please?"

"Yes, of course. Anna touched the first case. This is the Silver Star award, given to Michael by the American Army," she began. The bright metallic star hung from a ribbon with red, white, and blue vertical stripes. "I am told it is a high decoration, one given for bravery."

Anna's fingers moved to a five-armed silver Maltese cross attached to a scarlet ribbon. "This is the *Legion d'Honneur*, a noble order of great prestige, one created by Napoleon Bonaparte in 1802. Michael's rank was *Chevalier*, a Knight."

"We saw that carved into his cross at Suresnes," Margaret said.

"Yes, it is customary," Anna replied.

She touched the third medal, a bronze Latin cross superimposed on two crossed swords attached to a green ribbon with thin vertical red stripes. Pinned near the ribbon's center was a tiny silver star. "The *Croix de Guerre* was awarded by General LeGotte, who commanded the infantry division in which Michael served. Thus, the star."

Her hand moved to the smaller boxes, each with identical ribbons having blue and gold vertical stripes of equal width. "These are the *Insigne du Blesse Civil*, given in recognition for the wounds he received."

Margaret studied the decorations closely. The medals and ribbons were obviously of high quality. She wondered if Anna planned to keep them for herself. *I certainly would,* Margaret admitted.

Anna left the award cases open.

Her hand moved a stack of letters bound with a wide blue ribbon. "These are what Michael received from you and his parents. And in here," she continued, pointing to a photo album, "are pictures, including those taken at our wedding. "Finally," Anna said, "this is Michael's journal." She held a thick, weather beaten diary that looked about eight inches square.

Margaret recognized the faded cover, once a rich brown leather and the gold-embossed initials: MPJ. She had given it to Michael prior to his departure for France. 'Keep a journal,' she had suggested. 'You never know. You might become famous one day and your biographer could make good use of it.'

Michael had chuckled at her suggestion. 'My own version of *Caesar's Commentaries*' he had remarked, referring to the wartime journals of Julius Caesar. 'I could call it *Michael's Mutterings*.'

They had shared a laugh over his play on words. Sadly, her brother would garner no recognition worthy of a biography; nothing of Michael would survive except a few personal items, a photo or two, and the memories of those who would never forget him.

"That was my going away gift," she informed Anna.

"Yes, he told me that."

"May I see it?"

Anna handed her the diary without speaking.

Margaret ran her fingers over the soft cover. The leather showed signs of wear: usage scuffs and faded spots touched by moisture. But it was clean and showed evidence of recent care.

"Did you rub the leather with Neat's foot oil?" Margaret asked, looking at Anna.

"Yes, it was needed."

Margaret's fingers trembled as she gently opened the journal. Several pages were puckered, a characteristic of paper accidentally dampened then dried; some pages showed faint smears of fingerprints and brown mud. On others, the ink had run in a few places, evidence that Michael had written those entries while sitting or standing in dampness. Michael's silent presence emanated from every word.

Beatrice moved closer and Margaret slowly turned the pages, reading words written in her brother's familiar hand.

30

Margaret scanned the first few pages: entries detailing Michael's arrival in France and his posting to the American Ambulance Field Service. His first paragraphs reflected enthusiasm and hopeful expectations of new adventures.

Not wanting to appear rude by reading every single word, she turned pages quickly, hoping to find clues to her brother's changed behavior. Now and then, she paused to read, noting how the lighthearted tone of his early entries had gradually turned somber.

November 2, 1916 – Thursday
Verdun is saved. I thank God for that.

The five-month battle took a grisly toll and we did not have ambulances for all the wounded. Many gas-blinded men, their eyes thickly bandaged, walked to safety led by a medical orderly, each wounded man's right hand on the shoulder of the one in front, staggering to the rear like drunkards in a strange neighborhood. Pain and unbearable suffering have reduced young soldiers to shuffling old men, aged long before their time.

Several pages later...

January 15, 1917 – Monday

Burying the dead is always a sad affair, but even more so when it rains.

Many of the deceased are not afforded the final luxury of an unpainted wooden coffin. In those instances a canvas sack encases each body which we place on a low platform made of planks, and then drape with a French flag.

Two small boys, one bearing a cross and the other a container of holy water, stand wet and shivering while a priest utters the final benediction in Latin. Then comes our turn.

First, we remove and fold the flag. If we are lucky, the dead are in coffins, which we lower with ropes. Those in sacks are usually stiff with rigor and the lowering is easier than it is for men whose death occurred days ago. The latter almost always slip through the ropes and splash limply into a hole containing several inches of muddy water. When that happens, someone must climb into the grave and reposition the body so that it rests properly, if not with dignity.

Often there are two services: one in English or Latin for Christians and another in Arabic for Mohammedans—soldiers from colonies in French Morocco and Algeria—whose graves are nearby, each facing Mecca. Still, once wrapped in canvas shrouds or encased in coffins, I cannot tell one dead soldier from the other without their nametags. Presumably, God can tell the difference and will pass judgement as He sees fit.

She skipped a few more pages...

April 20, 1917 – Friday

A cold mix of rain and snow hampered our drive east from Auberive to Mont Sans Nom, but the weight of massed French artillery made the Infantry's work easier. Around ten a.m.

Wednesday, my presence near one of those batteries and the arrival of a German artillery shell coincided, causing my luck to run out.

One moment I was tending to the wounded, the next I was among them, flat on my back, ears ringing, staring into the silent gray sky. There was no immediate feeling of injury, only a sense of dazed confusion and disbelief. When I tried to rise, pain struck—-agonizing waves that left no room for other thoughts.

For the first time since my arrival, I rode in the back, not the front, of an ambulance, my pain dulled by morphine. Not being able to see where we were going or what dangers lay on the road ahead was less nerve-wracking than I imagined, no doubt a result of the drug. Now, safe at the American Ambulance in Neuilly-sur-Seine, I am grateful to God for a dry bed, hot soup, and regular doses of morphine.

I am also thankful for the company of a new-found friend—Guy Aubray—an artillery officer. He was standing close by me, concerned about injuries to the men in his battery, when the same German shell wounded him as well. Here at the hospital our cots are side by side and conversation with him helps pass the time. He is a delightful young soldier, not quite my age, ebullient and quick to laugh at the foibles of others, including himself. His perfectly trimmed mustaches—of which he is quite proud—are full and waxed with upward pointed tips; so immaculate they might have come from a costume shop.

Aubray had applied for the Cavalry School at Saumur but no appointment resulted. He lamented: "I saw myself as a cuirassier, resplendent in plumed casque, mounted on a fine stallion. Alas, it was not to be." Then he frowned. "A tragic waste of fine mustaches."

And then there is Anna, one of my nurses. I hesitate to say more. Like many soldiers, I too have grown superstitious. I shall write about her sparingly, if at all.

Margaret turned the page and continued reading.

April 28, 1917 - Saturday
My wound is nearly healed. Sometime next week, the hospital will evacuate myself and Aubray to our respective units. I will miss his company.
Earlier today his wife Lizette brought us a treat—bread and cheese and a wonderfully dry Lillet from Podensac; food and bottle discretely tucked away in an oversized cloth handbag. As we sipped our contraband, Miss Hilda Beck—a volunteer Red Cross nurse from Chicago—happened by. The bottle was out of sight, but the lemony-hued liquid in our glass tumblers was evidence of our infraction. "Well," she said, her brow knitted in consternation. "It seems our water supply has become contaminated. I must remember to speak to the administrator about this." Then she moved on.
Such compassion and understanding greatly eases the slow, painful process of recuperation.
Lizette left us soon after. She appears older than her husband, more... experienced. She seems devoted, but Mme. Aubray does not visit as often as my friend would like. "It is the war," he confided to me, his demeanor unnaturally somber. "The war has changed everything."

Margaret, conscious of Anna's silent patience, skipped many pages, moving well past the halfway point in her brother's journal.

January 13, 1918 – Sunday
A new year finds me once more wounded and recuperating at Neuilly-sur-Seine. Yet, I consider myself lucky. There are a half-

dozen ambulance hospitals located throughout the city. Medical authorities could have sent me elsewhere. I look forward to seeing Anna again, but regret the circumstances. It could be fate or merely my imagination, but I believe something extraordinary might come of this.

She turned the page.

January 14, Monday

I had a surprise visitor today. My friend Guy Aubray strode into our ward, resplendent in an immaculate uniform adorned with his Croix-de-Guerre and red-enameled wound star. His mustaches, as usual, were perfectly trimmed and freshly waxed.

After handshakes and warm greetings, I asked for the latest war news. He shook his head. "Such a waste. That old fool Anthoine continues to dally, fearful and reluctant to act. Petain should have sacked him long ago and given Fourth Army to a real general." He raged on for a few more minutes before pausing. "Forgive me," he said with his familiar good humor.

Then, reaching into his kit, Aubray produced a silver flask. He wiggled the container slightly. "Napoleon brandy," he announced, "some of the ninety-nine vintage from Saint Jacques." He poured a generous amount into each of two water tumblers ("A sacrilege, but I had no room in my haversack for snifters.") passed one to me and kept the other for himself. He swirled the amber liquid and then took an appreciative sniff. "To our fallen bothers," he said, leaning forward and touching my glass with his. We drank a solemn toast to those who were no longer among us.

We sipped his excellent cognac and spent a pleasant hour together, exchanging stories of our remarkably similar lives before the war. His family owns four hectares in the Loire Valley near

Vouvray where they have cultivated Chenin grapes for nearly a hundred years. "A tradition which, God willing, I hope to continue." He shrugged when he learned that I did not plan to follow in my father's commercial footsteps. "Each of us much follow our own path."

Our long, pleasant conversation was marred only when I asked about Lizette. "She is well," he muttered. Aubray said nothing more and I sensed they might be drifting apart. I feel so sad for my friend. He deserves better.

Margaret skipped many pages, not wanting to keep Anna waiting.

March 19, 1918 – Tuesday
This is a momentous day, the happiest of my life. Tonight we had dinner at Le Moine Affame. At a quiet corner table I asked Anna to marry me. She consented, clear evidence that her normally good judgment has failed. The joy I feel is beyond description, a warm tenderness marred by a thin wisp of anxiety. This terrible conflict has left me with few illusions. Death might easily claim me as it has so many others. Should Anna become pregnant, I dread leaving her with a fatherless child. I have seen far too many widows and orphans. The possibility that my wife and child might number among that sad gathering fills me with despair.

I am delirious with joy, but I do not deserve such good fortune.

Close to the end, Margaret read...

June 5, 1918 – Wednesday
The stubborn defense of Chateau-Thierry by American troops has stopped the German drive to Paris. Before C-T, some of my French associates had politely questioned the mettle of American soldiers. Not so Aubray. My dear departed friend had never questioned

America's mettle.

He has been gone two months and how he died continues to haunt my conscience. I can say no more about this, but I shall carry the burden of his death for as long as I live...

Margaret frowned at the puzzling last paragraph. She read on.

June 8, 1918 – Saturday
After visiting Sacre Coeur, Anna and I walked a little way down Montmartre hill and turned into the Rue des Abbesses. The narrow street was crowded with two-wheeled carts and chattering housewives, each bargaining to fill their shopping baskets for the fewest francs. Wonderful aromas filled the morning air—-fresh bread, earthy smells from just-picked vegetables and ripe fruit—-all accompanied by the silken babble of earnest voices. There, in front of two old men playing violins, stood a young girl hardly more than twelve or thirteen years old, solemnly dressed in black with a white handkerchief loosely knotted about her throat. She held a small pewter bowl containing a few coins and sang about Le Petit Enfant, of the little blue-eyed Alsatian boy, shot dead by evil Prussians, Monstres Odieux, because he shouted 'Vive la France!' and threatened them with his wooden gun. "Is that a true story?" I asked Anna. She shrugged. "If not, it will be soon. The people will make it so." Then Anna added to the girl's meager coin collection with a few from her purse.

Among artichokes and haricots and sweet red berries, the voices of children breathe new life into old hatreds.

Then she read Michael's final entry.

June 23, 1918 – Sunday
I have much to be thankful for—Anna is first among them—yet

the happiness she brings to me cannot fully overcome the despair that continues to follow me, inseparable as a shadow. The cruel choice I faced has left me with a wretched secret I can never reveal. Without dear Anna, who knows to what depths I might have sunk?

I have sought forgiveness through prayer and deed, yet the stain on my soul remains. Only God can wash it clean.

Margaret closed the book and held it to her breast with both hands, blinking away tears that threatened to overflow onto her cheeks. The tone of his later entries were ripe with melancholy and regret. What was Michael trying to tell them? What did he do that had haunted him so. What act required divine forgiveness?

Had the horrors inflicted by one human being upon another caused him to make a terrible choice... one that had forced him into brooding reticence?

Margaret looked at Anna. "Do you know what Michael was keeping to himself?"

Anna lifted one shoulder, a half-hearted shrug. "Who can say? Many terrible things happen on a battlefield—shameful acts one can never forget."

"Yes, I suppose that's true."

The war had profoundly changed her brother and his death left many unanswered questions. However, one thing was certain: Anna had been Michael's earthly redeemer; rescuing him from desperate remorse.

"May I keep this?" she asked, holding up the diary.

"No... I cannot part with that."

Nor can I, she wanted to say. Instead, "My parents would like to read what Michael wrote. Is that possible?"

"Yes. I made books."

Margaret's brow knitted slightly. "Books?"

"I have them here." Anna took four thin volumes from one of the étagère's polished shelves. "These, and everything on this table, are yours to keep. All will easily fit into Michael's suitcase, which you may have also."

"All?" Beatrice asked. "You mean *everything*, including the uniform and medals?"

"Yes. When I explained, the French and American authorities were most understanding. They provided medals for each of Michael's families—those in America and those in France." She handed Margaret the four volumes. "And these I give to you: one book for each member of Michael's family."

She placed two copies beside the medal cases and handed the others to Margaret and Beatrice.

Margaret, curious about the 'book', returned Michael's diary, reluctantly, and took a thin volume exquisitely bound in rich brown leather. Embossed into the front cover were two flags, American and French, mounted on crossed staffs. Margaret turned to the title page and read:

The Wartime Journal
of
Michael Patrick Jerome
2d Lt A.E.F.
1894-1918

The facing page contained a head-and-shoulders photograph of Michael in his American Army uniform. He looked happy and hopeful, a young man anticipating a future he would never live to experience. As she turned to the next page, Margaret could not help but notice the quality of the paper—it had a thick, almost linen-like texture.

A brief introduction followed. It described particulars of Michael's brief life: his birthplace, education, and volunteer work with the American Ambulance Field Service, along with his subsequent commission as a Second Lieutenant in the American Expeditionary Forces. A final paragraph noted his decorations and the circumstances of his death.

It was obviously the product of someone who loved Michael, someone who wanted to preserve forever the memory of who he was and what he did. With effort, Margaret forced down the lump forming in her throat.

After a moment, she asked: "Did you write the biography, Anna?"

"Yes, but Michael's words are exactly as he wrote them."

"What a marvelous thing to do," Margaret added, slowly turning pages. "I don't know what to say. How could you have accomplished this in so short a time?"

"My father has an old friend who prints books. He did me a great favor."

"I don't know how to thank you. What you have given us is so much more than we expected."

"I am happy that you think so."

"Oh, I do. Anna, you have done our family a great honor."

As she studied the sad face of her brother's widow, Margaret's initial concern about who this woman might be began to dissipate. Clearly, Anna had loved Michael deeply. She had cared for him, soothed his wounds and, when he died, took the time and effort to preserve his memory. The more she thought about it, the more Margaret began to accept that Anna was indeed a part of their family. How could anyone think otherwise?

31

"Stretcher bearers coming in. Hold your fire."

The sun had slipped behind the western hills and purple twilight crept across the sky. He had been gathering wool and the voice, vaguely familiar, jolted him alert..

Hold your fire? Butler, sitting alone and unarmed at the bottom of a shell hole, found the suggestion mildly amusing. "Come ahead," he replied.

Scuffling sounds approached his position; a moment later three soldiers scrambled into the crater, one of whom he recognized.

"Hiya, Lieutenant," Jack Mayo said, adjusting his tin helmet. "Long time no see."

To Butler's great surprise and pleasure, the day was turning into a minor reunion of USS *Mongolia* passengers. Earlier this morning came the unexpected encounter with Major Gregory at Chateau-Thierry. Now, at days end, Jack Mayo had tumbled in unexpectedly. "What are you doing here?' he asked.

Using his thumb, Mayo tilted his helmet towards the back of his head. "Beats me, Lieutenant. I must have taken a wrong turn somewhere down the road. How far is Kansas City?"

Mayo's fellow travelers chuckled and Butler smiled, enormously pleased to see the young soldier.

"Well, when you figure out how to get there, let me know." He motioned toward Mayo's companions. "Who are your friends?"

Mayo introduced the new men: Rotelli, a dark-complexioned Italian from Manhattan's East Side; and Hanssen, a blond Scandinavian from St. Paul. As he shook hands, Butler remembered Olsen, the jovial Swede from Duluth. A bomb dropped from a German aeroplane had killed him and his three companions as they lugged a wounded man to the rear. Who was it they were carrying? Oh, yes: Private Winkleman, Butler's first combat patient, a young soldier whose bad luck would eventually cost him an arm. The sudden violent deaths of his four stretcher-bearers had occurred less than forty-eight hours ago. It seemed much longer.

"Before I forget," Mayo said, reaching into his rucksack. "Captain Peckham sent you a present." He gave Butler a small square parcel wrapped in waxed paper. "He said this might be your last chance to eat for a while."

Butler unfolded the waxed paper, exposing a thick sandwich.

Butler hid his confusion with a tiny smile. Instinctively, he knew the gesture was more than a courtesy, more than concern for Butler's eating habits. The snack was a nice thought, one Butler appreciated, but what else might Woody have in mind? It took a moment before he understood.

At Camp Gordon, Butler learned that his paramount obligation as an officer, second only to duty, was to look after the soldiers under his command. *Take care of your men and they will take care of you.* It was a proposition that made good sense, a lesson he had not forgotten. By sending a sandwich, Woody Peckham was taking care of his newest surgeon. The sandwich also reminded Butler that Woody expected him to take care of the three soldiers gathered at the bottom of this shell hole. Through no fault of his own, Butler had lost four of his earlier charges, thanks to a German pilot. He vowed to do better this time.

He looked up. "Have you men had your supper?"

All three nodded.

"We just came from the mess tent," Mayo told him.

"Slum stew," Rotelli said, frowning.

"The sandwich is all yours," Mayo added.

Butler took a bite and began to chew. He recognized the sharp taste of mustard but the meat had an unusual, rather gamy flavor. "What am I eating?" he asked after swallowing the first mouthful.

"Monkey meat," Rotelli said. "Same stuff was in the slum stew."

Butler nodded and continued eating.

To feed vast numbers of her soldiers, France imported tons of canned beef from Argentina. Quartermasters routinely issued that ration first to French and then to Allied units. Because of the brand name—Madagascar—French soldiers mistakenly believed it came from the island of that name. Further, the vile taste convinced them the tins really contained monkey meat, not real beef. Butler had heard the story from other Doughboys on several occasions, but—as far as he knew—this was his first actual encounter with the product. The heavy slathering of mustard on his sandwich camouflaged but failed to overpower the nasty flavor.

"Tastes kinda like hog swill, doesn't it, Lieutenant?" Rotelli observed.

Butler took a swig from his canteen before answering. "I'm not sure, Rotelli. What does hog swill taste like?"

Everyone laughed, including the Italian, who gave Butler an appreciative nod.

Butler finished the sandwich and took another long drink of water. Then he covered his mouth and belched softly. The ghastly essence returned—a powerful aftertaste markedly stronger than the original flavor. Somehow, the process of ingestion the meat had unleashed strange new powers.

He mumbled a 'pardon me' and then eyed the three soldiers. "Are we expecting more men?"

A stretcher team usually consisted of four bearers, a man at each corner, one hand grasping the wooden pole extending from a canvas sleeve, leaving the other free to maintain balance. Mayo and his two pals had brought three stretchers with them. Three active stretchers required twelve bearers. Ideally, he needed nine additional men. In a pinch he could make do with three more: two men on each stretcher. That is, if he didn't lose anyone to hostile fire.

Mayo shook his head. "I don't think so. If we're it, then we can handle but one stretcher. If it comes to that, we'll take turns carrying the light end."

The light end, Butler knew, was the 'foot' of the stretcher.

Woody could spare but a single team, less one man. By sending three stretchers he was telling his surgeon to find other means. Butler chewed on his lower lip. Could the fighting at Soissons be that much worse than what had occurred at the Bois de la Roche? Apparently so. In any case, one stretcher team simply would not suffice. It was clear he would require infantrymen to augment his meager staff. That is, if any were available.

"It's sorta crowded in here," Rotelli observed.

The crater's bottom was four feet across, sloping upwards to a ten-foot diameter. The men sat equidistant from each other, helmets a foot or so below the rim with their boots almost touching. Any movement to ease from one position to another resulted in contact. The stretchers lay outside.

Rotelli continued. "There's another crater about a dozen steps away. I saw it when we was coming in." He said to Hanssen: "Hey Swede, want some more leg room?"

Hanssen shrugged and looked at Butler. "Is that okay, Lieutenant?"

Rotelli's suggestion made sense from several perspectives. First, they were indeed stepping on each other's boots and probably would be until they moved out. Second, should a soldier need medical attention between now and when the attack commenced, there was little room to attend his wounds. Third, and Butler was reluctant to admit this, he wanted to chat with Jack Mayo—privately—about the Jerome sisters, one in particular. Finally, the distance between them would not be a problem; he could easily maintain voice contact.

Butler rose and peered over the rim. A smaller crater lay ahead and to his left. "It's thirty feet away, Rotelli."

"Close enough, Lieutenant. Don't ya think?"

Butler resumed his sitting position. "Probably." He looked at Rotelli and Hanssen. "Are you sure about this?"

Both men nodded.

"Okay. Take off."

The two men prepared to leave.

"Go together," he told them. "And move fast."

Rotelli and Hanssen scrambled from the crater. A few seconds later Butler heard Hanssen's quivering voice.

"Oh, God!"

Rotelli's voice was much firmer. "Shit!"

A soft thump followed the mild expletive. Butler raised his head and looked toward the second crater. "What's wrong?"

Rotelli said: "There was a boot in our hole... with a leg attached. I got rid of it."

Mayo rose up. "Hey, Rotelli. Ours or theirs?"

"Theirs."

Mayo sat back. "Then I'm not going to worry about it," he muttered.

Butler remained silent, unwilling to voice agreement. He had arrived at the front a week ago. To his bewilderment and dismay, Butler realized he already exhibited casual acceptance of death and dismemberment, his mind easily adopting an attitude common among veteran soldiers.

The brutally disfigured bodies littering the field near the Roche Woods had shocked him. But repeated instances of such carnage had also inured him to the sight. It was a protective mechanism, or so he believed—a necessary mental adjustment unique to men in combat.

Was it likewise common among those who provided medical treatment under such conditions? If so, those psychological transformations had taken residence inside his head rather quietly, without his conscious knowledge of their stealthy approach. Is this what Colonel Dawes meant when he described war's 'cruel reality' during those shipboard educational sessions? Or did he mean something else: something Butler did—or, more accurately, did *not* do—for that horribly mangled soldier from whom he'd fled in terror?

He swallowed as the familiar sick churning in his stomach returned.

His conduct was an act he could not suppress from memory. Uncomfortable with the recurring image, he changed the subject.

"So, Jack, I see you ended up with an American unit after all."

"Yeah," Mayo replied. "It seems I worried about nothing. All of us, except for that Harlem regiment, ended up in the AEF."

"Harlem regiment? You mean Negros?"

Mayo nodded. "They ended up with French troops."

Butler frowned. Had Pershing partially given in to Foch's demand to blend American soldiers into units commanded by French officers? Or were there other reasons?

"Anyway," Mayo continued. "Here I am."

"Yes, I see that." Butler decided to breach the subject of the Jerome sisters without preamble. "Have you heard from Beatrice yet?"

"No. I wrote to her two days ago. That's when I received my unit assignment and mailing address."

"I was thinking of dropping Margaret a note. Do you know where they are staying?"

"Yeah, I sure do. Got something to write with?"

Butler retrieved notebook and the stub of a pencil from his tunic pocket.

"You can write to her in care of the Hotel Lutetia in Paris."

Mayo recited the address from memory and Butler wrote everything on a clean page.

"They should be there for at least another week, maybe longer," Mayo added. "What they're trying to do, I mean regarding their brother, might take more time than they realize. The French look at these things differently."

"You may be right about that." Butler studied the address. "Hotel Lutetia. That's interesting."

Mayo returned a blank stare. "How so?"

Butler was sorry he had spoken. Now he would have to explain without sounding like a know-it-all. He tucked the notebook and pencil away. "Back when Paris was a mud and thatch military settlement at the far reaches of the Roman Empire, it was known as Lutetia."

"Really? That *is* interesting. I'm impressed."

"Don't be. Committing historical minutia to memory is a hallmark of pretentious Ivy League schools, including mine. Reciting such arcane tidbits at social gatherings, preferably in Latin or Greek, is often mistaken for actual intelligence."

Mayo chuckled. "Maybe so." After a moment he said: "I wonder if Beatrice knows about the Roman name."

"I have no idea."

"Maybe I'll use that in my next letter. Those two ladies are difficult to impress."

Indeed they were, especially the elder. Butler, however, did not share that opinion with his young friend.

"I probably shouldn't be saying this," Mayo began. He paused and eyed Butler, clearly waiting for a response.

"Saying what?"

"Well, Beatrice told me a little about her family. It might explain some of Margaret's behavior."

"Is that so?"

Mayo nodded. "You see, everyone considered Michael special. To hear Beatrice tell it, he was everything sons and brothers are supposed to be, and then some."

"Guys like that make it tough on the rest of us."

"Yeah, I know. Anyway, I got the impression that when Michael went off to France it was like everybody placed a bookmark in their lives, hoping to pick up where they left off at some future time. But it didn't work out that way, not for Margaret."

"I sensed that as well. But it isn't unusual for twins to feel empathy for one another. There are documented cases of uncanny psychological connections. For example, one twin knowing the other was in distress, even though miles apart from each other."

Mayo nodded. "I read about that somewhere." His next words came slowly, obviously reluctant to divulge what he knew. "Beatrice also told me about your first meeting aboard ship. I gather it wasn't the best way to start things off."

"Jack, my boy, that's an understatement. Both sisters wore a black rosette on their clothing, but I didn't connect it to a family member. During dinner, I unwittingly shared my opinion regarding the stupidity of this war. Had I known about their brother, I would have kept my fat mouth shut. Unfortunately, that particular horse had already fled the barn. That's why I asked you for her address. I've been trying to smooth things out between us, but it's been tough sledding."

"I wouldn't give up," Mayo suggested. "Her sister was upset with you, yes, but Beatrice thought Margaret understood and that your comments weren't personal."

"Really?" The news surprised him and he could think of no response. If that was true, then another *mea culpa* might not be appropriate. As he thought more about it, Butler decided to forgo another apology. The next time he had a few private moments, he would write a nice, chatty letter.

For the first time since his arrival on French soil, Butler felt optimistic. Would they exchange letters? The possibility made him smile. "Well," he said finally. "In that case, I *will* drop her a line or two and see what happens."

Mayo nodded. "It couldn't hurt. And it might do you some good."

"Maybe so."

It was time to change the subject.

"Earlier this afternoon," Butler began. "I took a little tour of this place."

It had taken great effort to leave the safety of the crater, but he felt compelled to orient himself relative to the front line. It was also his duty to inform the battalion's commanding officer of his whereabouts, as Woody had suggested.

Afterwards, he'd spent a few hours walking the front-line trenches, talking to a few of the men, asking if they required anything in the way of medical attention. He had also considered moving in closer. The battalion command post was the one building best suited for an aid station, but it was already at capacity. The other alternative was to find a spot in an equally crowded trench. It took a moment, but he finally realized that Woody Peckham had selected the best available location.

"Oh? Find out anything interesting?"

"I spoke with Colonel Trask, the battalion commander. He told me that two of his infantry companies, together with a battalion of Algerian *spahis*, were going to attack Jaulgonne at oh-four-hundred, immediately following a half-hour artillery barrage."

Mayo checked his watch. "That's about seven hours from now."

"More or less. I was thinking we should give the assault troops a two or three minute head start, then tag along behind to gather up the wounded."

"If it's anything like last night, we'll have a hard time keeping up. One stretcher won't be enough."

"That's what I plan on telling the Colonel. I suspect the CO will not be pleased. He will be even less enthusiastic when I ask him to spare nine of his soldiers to help man stretchers."

"I don't envy you, Lieutenant. When are you planning on doing this?"

"Now, I think. Let Rotelli and Hanssen know what's planned for tomorrow morning. Meanwhile, everyone should try to get some rest."

"I'll tell them," Mayo said. "Good luck."

"See you in a bit," Butler said.

32

He slid from the crater and crawled toward the battalion command post, an abandoned stone house about a hundred yards to the east. Dusk shrouded the landscape with deepening purple gloom and the first eager fireflies signaled the coming of full darkness.

Displeased with his slow pace, Butler cursed himself and swallowed his fear; then he rose and began a slow trot, his body bent at the waist. There was little cover and he felt completely vulnerable.

A few minutes later he nodded to the guard and stepped inside the command post. Heavy cotton duck covered the windows and several small kerosene lanterns provided illumination. Butler scanned the room and saw the battalion commander hunched over a table, studying a map. The Colonel was talking with two other officers, captains, neither of whom he recognized. Butler approached and stood nearby. He didn't have long to wait.

After the two officers left, the Colonel turned and raised an eyebrow at Butler's presence. Then a tiny half smile curved one side of his lips. "We don't see many doctors this close to a front line trench," he began. "And this is your second trip in just a few hours. Why does that make me suspicious, Lieutenant?"

"Probably, sir, because of what I'm about to request."

The Colonel's almost-smile remained unchanged. "Is that so?"

"Yes, sir. I've come begging."

The smile faded. "Every soldier comes begging now and then,

Lieutenant, including battalion commanders. What is it you need?"

"Sir, I have three stretchers but only three bearers. If I'm to fully man all three stretchers, then I'll need nine additional men to help carry wounded from the field."

"Nine men? That's nearly a whole squad. I'm afraid that's not possible. I took quite a few casualties last night. I'm not at full strength as it is and we're expecting the Germans to put up another tough fight."

"Then could you spare three men? That would put one pair on each stretcher. Two men will tire much faster than four, so they couldn't go as long without rest, but I could make that work."

The battalion commander didn't respond.

Butler stepped closer to the CO. "Colonel, if you expect a tough fight, then you're going to have casualties. I'll need all three stretchers to keep up. Even three might not be enough. But the faster we get wounded men treated and off to a field hospital, the better chance they have to survive and recover."

"And if you lose a man?"

"Then I'm down to two stretchers... or less."

The pale yellow glow from nearby kerosene lanterns had transformed the Colonel's normal complexion into a dark golden mask. The lines and shadows around his eyes and mouth emphasized the challenge and strain of having to make life-and-death decisions. And now Butler was asking the CO to make another difficult choice: reduce the assault force by a squad, or leave his wounded men in the field, unattended, for much longer than he desired. Butler was grateful the issue was not his to resolve.

The Colonel didn't answer immediately. A moment later he turned and spoke to a major who stood close, listening.

"What do you think, Harry? Do you suppose we could spare four or five men; troops who are a little under the weather? Perhaps a file clerk or two?"

The Major stepped closer. "That might be possible, Colonel. We have a few mild cases of dysentery that could slow us down. We'd be better off if they tagged along behind."

"I see what you mean." The Colonel turned and spoke to Butler. "I presume you have ample quantities of paragoric in your rucksack?"

"Yes, sir."

A teaspoon of camphorated tincture of opium in a glass of water was the standard treatment for diarrhea.

"Okay, then." He turned to the Major. "Do what you can to get the doctor the men he needs."

"Yes, sir."

Butler couldn't leave without expressing his thanks. "Colonel, I understand how difficult this is and I sincerely appreciate your consideration."

The Colonel nodded. Then his lips turned down, the look of a man pondering an important but unresolved detail. Without another word, he turned and leaned over his map.

"Follow me, Lieutenant," the Major said.

33

The gently undulating field rolled away and then vanished abruptly into pre-dawn fog, appearing to end at a sheer cliff bordering an invisible sea. The illusion brought to mind medieval images of a flat earth terminating at the far edge of the world; a place beyond which, many then believed, lay vast emptiness.

But this particular field did not end. It continued on and on, a lacerated countryside grudgingly revealed as they stepped carefully through the mist. Butler led the way. His stretcher teams followed a few steps behind, ghostly figures wandering through a phantom world populated by watchful gray shadows.

American artillery shells preceded them: soft whisperings passing high overhead in long woeful arcs, then crashing somewhere in the distance ahead, consigning their terrors to an unseen enemy.

Where was the German counter barrage?

Butler checked his pocket watch without breaking stride. Less than twenty minutes had elapsed since a dozen shrill whistles had signaled their attack. A few minutes later, his mouth brackish and tasting of old pennies, Butler had arisen from the crater and followed the advancing troops, a few steps ahead of his stretcher teams.

The shuffle and muted clanks of many soldiers, a great armed horde plodding steadily forward, reached his ears. Unable to see them, Butler followed their sounds, a blind man wandering a strange land, fearful of losing his way. He wished for a compass; a moment later he wondered why. Presumably, someone up front knew where they were supposed to go. Butler certainly did not. The biblical phrase 'blind leading the blind' popped into his head.

He knew the Germans often pre-registered their artillery, firing rounds ahead of time to determine impact points. That meant the enemy didn't need visual observation to fire their cannons accurately. Given a specific azimuth, wind conditions, and caliber of weapon, they knew exactly where each explosive shell would land.

What are they waiting for?

A small rise loomed from the mist; its smooth edge obstructed by a bulky shape. As Butler drew closer the indistinct mass became a soldier crouched behind low cover. The man held a Springfield rifle in both hands, bayonet affixed.

Butler stopped beside the man and dropped to one knee. "Are you wounded?"

The soldier turned and stared, eyes wild with panic, his mouth a thin bloodless incision drawn across his face. Then he turned away and continued to look in the direction of the advancing troops.

"I asked you a question," Butler said, his voice louder.

The soldier ignored him.

"He's scared shitless," Rotelli said.

"I know this guy," one of the recently conscripted bearers said. "His name is Kleppermann. He's from B Company."

"All right, Private Kleppermann," Butler said, his voice sharper. "Get on your feet and come with us."

The soldier looked at Butler, his eyes reflecting a mixture of fear and hatred. Dirt-encrusted knuckles whitened as he gripped the weapon tighter. He shook his head and looked away.

"Lieutenant," Mayo said. "Can I have a word?"

"In a minute," Butler replied. Private Kleppermann had disobeyed a direct order. He could not let that stand.

"Now... *please!* If you don't mind, sir."

The urgency in Mayo's voice caused Butler to shift his attention. Jack Mayo was making a desperate 'come here' motion with his hand. He looked at Kleppermann once more, then rose and joined Mayo who had moved a few yards away.

"What's so important?"

Jack Mayo's voice was a raspy whisper. "Lieutenant, none of us are carrying weapons. Kleppermann has a loaded rifle with a fixed bayonet, and he's scared half out of his mind. If you push him too far he's liable to use it—on you, and then on the rest of us."

The possibility that Private Kleppermann would react violently to his order had not occurred to Butler. There were stories of course: tales of officers and NCOs shot by terrified or disgruntled enlisted men, but the verbal reports were second or third hand. Could such a thing actually happen to him? He looked over his shoulder. Kleppermann had not moved.

Butler's outrage began as a small ember, a single coal in the pit of his stomach that slowly expanded into a white-hot lump. A malingering soldier had flagrantly disobeyed his direct order, but Jack Mayo wanted him to back off from further confrontation.

Why?

A sudden realization struck him: Jack Mayo thought his lieutenant wasn't up to the job—that he wasn't a *real* Army officer, merely a sawbones with a commission. Putting it bluntly, Mayo probably believed that Lieutenant Butler was a fraud—a make-believe Army officer with scant legitimacy and even less credibility.

He looked at the stretcher-bearers and studied each man's face. None would look him in the eye, preferring to inspect their boots or shift uncomfortably from one foot to the other, their silence confirming what he suspected.

Butler turned and quickly retraced his steps. Kleppermann, still crouched, never bothered to look up. Almost before he realized what he was doing, Butler swung the side of his boot squarely onto the soldier's buttocks. The swift, unexpected blow launched the Private upward with such force that the edge of his tin helmet thunked onto his nose.

Yelping, Kleppermann reached to straighten his helmet and relieve the pain. At that moment Butler leaned over and snatched the rifle from the Private's other hand.

"You miserable son-of-a-bitch!" Butler roared. The profanity burst from his lungs suddenly and without premeditation. "If you want to hide your cowardly ass back here, then do it without a rifle. None but *soldiers* are permitted to carry arms into battle."

Private Kleppermann stared at him wide-eyed, helmet askew, his expression a mixture of surprise, awe, and shame. A thin trickle of blood ran from one nostril, stopping at the curve of his upper lip. Butler, holding the Springfield with one hand, turned his back on the Private and stalked away, once again following the diminishing sounds of advancing troops.

"Awww, Lieutenant," Kleppermann whined.

Butler concealed his rage and growing anxiety. He rarely used epithets and was not in the habit of physically attacking other human beings. Such conduct was degrading and unbecoming. Compounding those social offenses was the fact that he, a commissioned officer, had struck an enlisted man. Far worse, he had done so in the presence of other enlisted soldiers. What on earth had gotten into him? Had he punished Private Kleppermann in a perverse effort to redeem his own cowardly act in the Roach Woods? If so, then he had exacted unfair retribution, punishment that others should have inflicted on Butler.

Shame and self-rebuke further dampened his initial anger. He had lost his temper, showed weakness in front of men for whom he was responsible. Without breaking stride, he turned, not sure what to do next.

To his amazement they were following him: Mayo, Rotelli, Hanssen, and the six new bearers gathered up during his visit to battalion headquarters, every man maintaining his rapid pace. Leading the group was Private Kleppermann, a short step behind Butler's left shoulder. The swelling at the bridge of his nose magnified the soldier's worried expression.

"I wasn't shirking my duty, Lieutenant," Kleppermann pleaded, walking quickly to keep pace. "My ankle got twisted around and I wuz just restin' a bit. I dint want my leg to seize up or anything like that. I'm not a coward. Honest."

Butler, struggling to understand what was happening, ignored the Private.

"I carry my load. Ask anyone who knows me, Lieutenant. But it wuz this damn fog. Can't see a blamed thing. I got a mite spooked."

That was probably closer to the truth. Butler remembered a similar feeling, a sense of not knowing what unseen horrors might lay before him. Like most individuals he could usually cope with a known situation, even though it might be dreadful. The unknown however, was something else. Hidden perils lurking in dark corners resurrected ancient demons from ages past and gave new life to mankind's oldest fears, childhood terrors instilled by bogeymen— those imagined and those incarnate.

Up ahead, the rattle of advancing troops slowed and muttered to a stop. The battalion had probably reached its first checkpoint. Officers and NCOs were no doubt straightening their lines prior to resuming the assault. The encounter with Kleppermann had taken minutes, so his medical team was not that far behind the forward wave. To Butler's surprise, keeping close to the advancing troops was now immensely important to him.

An approaching shadow loomed from the mist, a lumbering hulk, massive and ghostly. It soon took the shape of a bear wearing a helmet and three stripes. The rifle in the sergeant's hand looked like a child's toy.

Kleppermann muttered, "Oh, *shit!*"

"Where the hell have you been, Rookie? Off hiding somewhere?" The sergeant's voice sounded like wet gravel rolling around in a hollow metal drum.

"No! You got it all wrong, Sarge." Alarm caused Kleppermann's voice to increase an octave higher than before.

"Bullshit!" The gravel in the metal drum became more agitated.

"I twisted my ankle. The Lieutenant and these other fellas came along and helped me out." Kleppermann turned and looked at Butler, his eyes pleading. "Ain't that right, Doc?"

"Probably a minor sprain," Butler said, addressing the sergeant. "Not at all serious."

Was his response a bald-faced lie or was he merely giving Kleppermann, and possibly himself, the benefit of doubt? He hoped it was the former. Butler was amazed at how easily he had accepted the soldier's unlikely claim.

"Is that so?" The sergeant did not sound convinced.

"See? Just like I told ya, Sarge."

"And I suppose you got the bloody nose when you slipped and fell. Turnin' yer ankle, of course."

Kleppermann quickly wiped away the blood trickle with his sleeve and checked the smear. Then he smiled. "Right. Now you got it. Clumsy Kleppermann. Twisted my ankle and fell smack on my face."

The sergeant's eyes narrowed. "And the Doc here, he's holdin' onto yer rifle so's to ease the strain on your messed up ankle."

Kleppermann's smile vanished.

Butler said: "The sergeant is right." He tossed the rifle, a two-handed gesture, exactly like he'd seen inspecting NCOs do at Camp Gordon. "It's time you carried it yourself, Private."

Kleppermann caught the weapon smartly, checked the action, and held it diagonally across his chest.

The sergeant shifted his gaze from Kleppermann to Butler and then back to the Private. He made an over the shoulder gesture with his thumb, a jerking motion toward the advancing front. "Get back up where ya belong."

"Yes, Sergeant."

Kleppermann double-timed forward, jogging easily, his rifle at port arms. He soon disappeared into the fog.

The sergeant turned back to Butler. "A miraculous recovery, don't cha think?"

"So it would appear."

"With all due respect, Doc, that was the biggest bullshit story I have ever heard in all my years in the Army."

"Really? I am truly surprised. I thought you would have heard much taller tales by now."

The sergeant's lips turned up and he uttered a growling rumble Butler assumed was a chuckle. Then the huge soldier turned and strode back the way he came.

Butler adjusted the straps on his rucksack and followed.

Admitting to Klepperman's falsehood didn't quite absolve him— striking an enlisted man was inexcusable—but he felt better knowing the soldier would not face charges of cowardice. After all, Butler's own behavior under fire was not much better. There was but one difference between him and Private Kleppermann. Butler was luckier: nobody saw him wet his pants.

Nor had anyone seen him abandon a mortally wounded soldier.

34

The sun eventually burned away the mist revealing a small settlement. The clutter of stone farmhouses and outbuildings brought to mind the weathered and crumbling remnants of an ancient civilization—the broken stones and walled ruins of a warring society long vanished and forsaken by history.

For reasons unknown to Butler, German artillery had never materialized to a volume sufficient to stop their advance. Kept busy treating a steady flow of wounded men, he did not realize this until much later in the day. The bloody tide of casualties peaked, waned and finally stopped just before nine o'clock that evening. By then Jaulgonne was in allied hands and his exhausted stretcher bearers finally had time to rest. They lay nearby, eyes closed, sweat-and-dirt-streaked faces drawn and lax and vulnerable.

Nightfall was still more than an hour away. He was tired and his appearance unkempt but there was something he still needed to do. Butler washed and tried to make himself a little more presentable before calling on Woody Peckham.

"I wanted to tell you about this before you got word through the grapevine," Butler said, concluding his verbal report on the kicking incident. "Sorry I was too late."

The two men sat inside a tent, facing each other across a battered field desk.

"I understand," Peckham replied. "In the Army nothing travels faster than a juicy story about an officer."

"Anyway, my apologies for not getting to you sooner. It couldn't be helped."

"We were all busy."

"What happens to me now?"

"What do you mean?"

"What charges will I face?"

"You expected charges?"

"Woody, I struck an enlisted man. My conduct is grounds for reprimand, perhaps a court-martial."

"You got a recalcitrant soldier to do his duty. That's what officers are supposed to do. Admittedly, your method was somewhat unorthodox—it's usually sergeants who do the actual ass-kicking—however, the result was the same."

"But there were witnesses."

"None of whom have come forward to register a formal complaint."

Butler knew that Jack Mayo, Rotelli, and Hanssen would not be among the complainants. However, the soldiers recruited from battalion headquarters would doubtless jump at the chance to point their fingers at an abusive officer. Either way, he deserved whatever punishment higher authority imposed.

"Maybe not yet," Butler conceded, "but it won't be long before one of my 'volunteer' stretcher-bearers informs the battalion CO, as well he should. When that happens, you might find yourself in hot water—harboring an unfit officer as it were. I wanted to prepare you for that."

Peckham shook his head and smiled, his face reflecting the infinite patience of a dedicated schoolteacher attempting to explain a simple concept to a slow-witted but otherwise likeable student. "Oh, Robert my young friend, they have already done that. They told

Colonel Trask the whole story. And in great detail, I might add. One witness corroborating, and sometimes elaborating, the account of another."

The tired smile on Woody's face did not match the seriousness of his words. Obviously, Butler was missing something important. "I don't get it."

"Those soldiers told on you, all right. However, not in the manner you think. They *respected* what you did. Sure, you were rough on the guy in question. But when this unnamed soldier decided to do his duty, you gave him back his rifle. You topped that off by not reporting him to his sergeant. Keeping your mouth shut impressed them a hell of a lot more than the kick in the pants."

Butler frowned. Something didn't make sense. "If that's true, then why mention the incident in the first place? Why not keep the whole affair under their hats?"

"Perhaps to cover their butts. If the soldier in question decided later to file a complaint and called them as witnesses, they didn't want to be accused of withholding evidence of your alleged misconduct. I suppose they kept the soldier's name out of it to preserve confidentiality, but if this character decides to make an issue of it, then they expose him. I have a hunch the soldier understands this and has decided to let bygones be bygones. In plain English, the issue is closed."

"Is that what the Colonel said?"

"More or less. I was also told that, after your 'volunteers' left the headquarters tent, the Colonel had a pleasant little chuckle. He thinks you might make a pretty good officer some day—for a sawbones, that is."

"All because I kicked an enlisted man?"

"No, for motivating a laggard; for giving a frightened soldier the benefit of doubt; for offering him a chance to reclaim his self-respect."

"You make it sound almost humane."

"There's damn little evidence of humanity over here, Robert. We take what we can when it's available."

Peckham turned in his chair, raised the lid of a wooden footlocker and extracted a dark green bottle along with two glasses. "You look like you could use a drink. As a matter of fact, so could I. It's been a long day."

He dribbled whiskey into each of two small tumblers, added a spot of water from his canteen, and then slid one across the desk. The familiar aroma of smoked peat filled the tent.

Butler, relieved but still troubled by the unexpected development, took the offered glass. "I was going to ask you about this scotch the first day we met at Lucy-le-Bocage. When was that? A week ago?"

"More or less."

"It seems longer."

"Time flies like an arrow," Peckham said.

"I'm impressed. That sounds like Nietzsche."

"Does it, really?"

"You don't know?"

Peckham shrugged. "I have no idea."

Butler shook his head and smiled. "What about the scotch?"

Peckham held the bottle so Butler could read the label. "It's Glenturret. This particular brand, I was told, comes from the oldest distillery in Scotland and is the preferred beverage of Her Majesty's Royal Scots Greys."

"You remember that and not who uttered the famous quote?"

"Unlike you, Robert, my brain does not have the capacity to store and recall worthless minutia. It has room for essentials and little else." He smiled and sipped his drink.

Butler swallowed whiskey, guiltily savoring the harsh complexity of flavors and the warmth growing in his belly.

After brooding over the potential consequences of his outrageous act for most of the day, Butler had reached the conclusion that an official reprimand, court-martial, and dismissal from the Army was an inescapable probability. He was prepared to accept that outcome. After all, he clearly deserved punishment—if not for booting Private Kleppermann in the ass, then certainly for what he'd failed to do on that dreadful morning near the Bois de la Roche.

But now, the unsmiling face of military justice would turn elsewhere. Relief and guilt struggled to gain supremacy, finally settling for an unsatisfying draw.

Peckham set his empty glass on his desk. "It seems that our next major objective is Roncheres."

Butler finished his drink and stared at the empty glass. "Is that so?"

Peckham nodded. "I don't believe Pershing is going to stop this drive until he pushes the Germans across the Aisne River."

"I thought the French were running this war."

"They are, but old Blackjack can be quite insistent. The old warhorse has clamped the bit between his teeth and he's off at full gallop."

"Is he now? How long do you suppose this will take?"

"A few months, more or less."

"Really? Then what?"

"Well," Peckham said, drawing out the word, "I think the Germans will quit. Then we can all go home and live out the rest of our lives in contemplative gratitude."

"Not all of us," Butler said, remembering the carnage he had witnessed.

"No, in war it's never all of us, unfortunately. But most of us will survive and that has to be good enough."

Butler eyed the bottle of Glenturret and thought about asking for another drink. Deciding against it, he set his glass on Woody's desk and stood. "I'd better get back," he said. "Thanks for the booze."

"Try not to think about it too much, Robert."

"Think about what, Woody? My bad conduct, or the scores of dead and wounded men I saw today?"

"Both. Fretting over either is pointless. What's done is done. We're here, we have a job to do, and that's that."

"I never realized you were a fatalist."

Peckham shrugged. He looked paler and thinner than he had when they first met. For a fleeting moment his soft brown eyes reflected melancholy bewilderment, the expression of a man who had unwittingly traded a clean, comfortable life for one filled with squalor and deprivation. Butler had never seen so much emptiness on Woody's face, but he immediately understood what he saw, recognizing a reflection of his own sad image trapped forever in a fun-house mirror. In that bizarre carnival universe, he and Woody were exiles; two outcasts who futily practiced medicine in a hopelessly infected world: a lunatic planet banished to a quarantined sector of the Milky Way.

Then Woody smiled crookedly and his eyes took on a gently determined glare.

"I am not a fatalist, Robert. But I know one thing for certain: It will be up to those who survive this obscenity to make sure nothing like it ever happens again. Modern weapons—aeroplanes, explosive artillery shells, and machine guns—will make any future war a political option too horrible to contemplate."

"Do you actually believe that?"

"I have no choice. And neither do you, chum."

It was a prospect Butler had never considered. Had he lost the surgeon's cool objectivity; personalized war's cold indifference to human suffering? Maybe he could no longer see beyond his own savage guilt—no further than gassed lungs vainly struggling for air, hay wagons mounded with amputated limbs; countless lives cut short in their prime. Was it possible that something good might emerge from this ghastly calamity? If so, then a future absent of organized conflict might indeed be worth the appalling misery of today. A lasting peace might justify the irreplaceable loss of all those bright hopes and secret dreams.

He clung to that idea, wanting passionately to believe, much as a desperate man caught in a river's swollen torrent clings to a floating log. Woody was right. Not believing in a better future, giving up and letting go, was unthinkable.

Butler looked at his friend. "For once in your life, Woody, you might be right about something."

"Of course I'm right," Woody said. "After all, *I* am a seasoned Captain; an officer and a gentleman by presidential decree; a medical doctor of renown. You, on the other hand, are a half-made Lieutenant with horse shit on his boots."

35

July's heat staggered into August, continuing to enfold Paris in a sweltering blanket. Daytime street traffic, which had increased as the allied offensive gathered momentum, dwindled to previous levels.

"I'm surprised we haven't heard from Mother and Father by now," Beatrice said, between bites of a breakfast croissant. "When did you send the cable?"

"A week ago yesterday."

"That's what I thought."

Margaret sipped tea. Time had passed so quickly.

At Anna's suggestion, Margaret and Beatrice had volunteered to work at the American Ambulance hospital in Neuilly-sur-Seine. They spent a few hours each day rolling bandages and reading books, newspapers, and magazine articles to recuperating soldiers. Margaret sometimes assisted nurses in rehabilitation efforts, providing an arm or shoulder to soldiers as they tested legs that were not quite ready to bear full weight. Slowly walking the halls lined head-to-toe with occupied beds gave Margaret a sense of closeness to her brother and a clearer understanding of what he must have suffered. Had Anna provided similar comfort to Michael? She believed so. Volunteer work also helped pass the time while she and Beatrice nervously awaited a response from their parents.

They visited daily with Gurney Shaw who remained in hospital under continuing treatment. Unfortunately, as everyone feared but prayed would not happen, Gurney developed a sequestrum. The infection turned septic, necessitating amputation of his left leg just below the knee. It was a crushing blow but Gurney seemed oddly at ease with his condition. "Everything always works out in the end," he whispered, soon after awaking from the ether, a reaction Margaret found baffling.

Privately, they fretted over his medical situation, a condition that stubbornly refused to show significant improvement.

On those evenings when all three women were unoccupied, they had extended discussions over quiet dinners. Anna proved to be an excellent cook, preparing special dishes from various provinces. Although meat was scarce, often nonexistent, there was no practical limit to what Anna could accomplish with vegetables and a variety of seafood.

Her specialties included *bouillinade*, baked fish and potatoes in a white wine sauce, a recipe from Languedoc; *cotriade*, a savory Brittany stew concocted of eel and sardines among other things; *moules au Roquefort*, mussels in a tangy Roquefort sauce, a dish known throughout France. Then, of course, there was always freshly baked bread—round, crusty loaves called *boules.*

Margaret was pleasantly surprised at how quickly she and Beatrice became adept at cleaning fish, chopping vegetables, and mastering the art of *mirepoix sauté*. She was equally pleased to discover something else: She no longer thought of Anna as a stranger, the foreign woman who had married her brother. Rather, Anna had slowly become a friend, warmly connected through their mutual love for Michael.

Gurney had also grown closer as a male friend. However, he did not share in the private coziness the women enjoyed, nor did he seem to expect it, given his inability to leave the hospital. He brooded much more than was apparent before the amputation, which surprised no one. It was, Margaret thought, a normal reaction to the loss of his lower leg.

"Do you suppose they are still angry with us?" Beatrice asked.

"Us? You mean me, don't you? I'm the one who stole their steamship tickets."

"Yes, you did, didn't you?"

Margaret shrugged. "Anyway, I hope not."

"What do you suppose they are thinking—or doing?"

"I'm not sure, but one thing is certain: Our parents are up to something."

"Maybe today we'll find out what they have in mind. Aren't cables delivered earlier than the daily mail?"

"Yes, I believe so." She checked her watch. "It's time we left."

As they prepared to leave, the Lutetia's concierge approached and stopped beside Margaret. He carried a silver plate upon which lay a blue envelope.

"Miss Jerome, a cable has arrived from America. It is addressed to you."

"Thank you, *monsieur*. It's one we have been expecting."

"I thought as much," he replied.

Margaret reached for her purse but the concierge smiled and shook his head. He set the plate on the table beside her, bowed, and then backed away.

"Such a nice man," Beatrice remarked.

"He is indeed."

Margaret took the envelope, broke the seal with a finger and extracted a single sheet.

"What does it say?" Beatrice asked. "Read it, aloud."

Margaret scanned the cable. "It says: *Mother and I arriving in Paris on or about August 19 via Liverpool. Please arrange lodging at the Lutetia. We are well. See you soon. Love, Father.*"

She handed the cable to Beatrice. "Here, read it yourself."

Beatrice glanced at the text and then rummaged through her purse. She finally produced a small calendar. "The nineteenth is on a Monday. How long do you suppose they will want to stay?"

"I'm not certain, probably two weeks more or less."

Beatrice replaced the calendar. "That means we'll be here for another month, at least."

"Are you surprised they decided to come over here?"

"Not at all. What choice did they have?"

"None, really. This is not a situation Father could easily accept. And coming here without Mother was not possible."

"Hardly. She would have insisted on keeping to their original arrangement."

"You mean, before they got sick and I ran off with their steamship tickets."

Beatrice smiled. "That *was* rather impudent. But you were always the bold one," she added. "I still remember that big argument you had with Father—the one about those women who marched in Washington." She paused and her expression changed to one of thoughtfulness. "It seems to me you were never satisfied with the way things were. You always wanted more."

Margaret shook her head. "No, I never wanted more—just *as much*. I never liked the idea of being treated like chattel when it came to voting—or anything else for that matter. What about you? Don't you want the same privileges as those pompous dimwits in Washington who presume to know more about things than everyone else?"

"Yes, I suppose so."

Margaret sensed hesitation. "But?"

"Well, since you asked, what I *really* want is to settle down with the right man and raise our children. Having the opportunity to vote would be nice, but it's not exactly the most important thing in my life. Is that so *bad*?"

"No, I suppose not." She thought about Beatrice's comment for a moment. Then she said, "And you think Jack Mayo is the right man for you?"

Her sister beamed. "Yes! I'm *sure* of it now. I've thought and thought about it until there's absolutely no doubt in my mind. Jack and I are absolutely *perfect* for each other."

"Well, I hope you're right."

"I *know* I'm right," Beatrice said.

Margaret checked her watch. "It's time we left for the hospital."

Beatrice said: "When are we going to tell them about Michael and Anna?"

"Right away, I think. After they've had a chance to rest. Then we'll all get together in one of our suites. We need to be alone for that."

"I'm afraid they're going to be upset and disappointed. What do you suppose they'll do afterwards?"

"I wish I knew. I just hope Father doesn't rush off and stir up a hornet's nest before thinking this through."

"He's been known to do that."

"I remember. Poor Michael. It seems Father had always been either enormously pleased or terribly upset with him. There was seldom a middle ground."

"Will he try to get Michael's will overturned?"

"Probably so."

"What's the matter? You have a funny look in your eyes."

Margaret wasn't sure how to address what troubled her, so she began on a cautious note. "I'm not sure, Bea. Ever since we visited Michael's grave I've had a strange feeling about, you know, digging him up. It doesn't seem right. The more I think about it, the more I believe we should leave him be."

Beatrice frowned. "So far from home?"

"It's what he wanted. We should respect that."

"Maybe so, but what about Father? He's pretty set in his ways. Getting him to change his mind won't be easy."

"No, it won't. Our father is a hard case, but what about you? What do you think about this?"

"I just don't know what to do, Margaret. I'd like to have him close so we could visit his grave and place flowers near his headstone on his—your—birthday. But then I never really thought about *digging him up*. That seems wrong, like desecration or something." She sighed. "It's a worrisome situation."

"Yes, it is." Margaret placed her napkin on the table. "In any case, we should make their hotel arrangements before we leave. Are you ready?"

"No," Beatrice smiled. "But let's pretend I am."

"Don't be a goose. You enjoy working at the hospital as much as I do."

"Not quite as much," Beatrice corrected. "But enough."

Margaret smiled. "That will do nicely, for now."

36

They returned from the hospital later that afternoon and, as was their routine, stopped at the front desk. It was another muggy day and Margaret was looking forward to a bath and a change of clothes.

The clerk smiled as they approached. "Good afternoon, ladies. I have mail for you today. One moment please."

The clerk turned away and examined a small wire basket filled with a dozen or more letters. "Ah, yes. Here they are." He handed Margaret two envelopes.

"Who are they from?" Beatrice asked, her face flushed from the heat.

"This one is for you. It's another letter from Jack Mayo."

Beatrice, her eyes suddenly bright, snatched the letter. "And the *other* one?"

Margaret felt a warm glow, a sensation unlike the malaise associated with summer heat. "It's from Lieutenant Butler."

"I knew it! I just *knew* he would write to you."

Almost without realizing it, Margaret's lips had creased into a pleasant smile. She immediately felt foolish and uncomfortable.

"Don't try to hide it," Beatrice said as they entered the elevator. "You're *pleased* he wrote, aren't you."

She was indeed. Why not admit it? "Yes, I am. But I wonder how he knew we were here."

"Perhaps Jack told him."

"That must mean they are together, or close by each other."

"Yes, that must be it."

Inside their suite, Margaret went to her bedroom, sat on a chair, slit the envelope with a thin metal blade, then opened and quickly read the brief letter.

Roncheres, Picardie
July 29, 1918

Dear Miss Jerome:

I hope this letter finds you and Beatrice well and that arrangements regarding your brother Michael are proceeding satisfactorily.

As you might expect, the work here both challenges and despairs anyone who finds himself close to men wounded in battle. The fighting goes on—we advance steadily each day—but the casualties rise in proportion to our progress. If we cross the Aisne River, they say the Kaiser might quit the war. One can hope.

Do you recall Major Gregory? Well, it seems fate has thrown us together once again, along with Jack Mayo. Major Gregory now commands Evacuation Hospital #6, presently located at Chateau-Thierry but will soon move forward again. Jack is a member of my field team, serving as a medical orderly/stretcher bearer. I believe he has written several letters to Beatrice.

I am not sure when or whether I may get leave, but I hope we can meet again, either in Paris or St. Louis after the war. If this is a possibility, please let me know. In the meantime, kindly give my regards to Beatrice. I wish you and your family well.

Sincerely,
Robert Butler

Margaret raised her eyes and looked through lace curtains to the bright sky beyond the window. It was a nice first letter—a little sad, as one might expect under such terrible circumstances, but also cautiously hopeful. There was no question in her mind about answering his letter, but what should she say?

Staring out the window, Margaret allowed her mind to drift. Without effort, a memory flickered and came alive.

*

It became clear to Margaret that, even while hating those responsible for starting the war, Lieutenant Butler harbored no animosity for those now entangled in its tragic consequence. After dinner one evening Beatrice excused herself leaving Margaret and Robert Butler alone. "Would you like to take a stroll around the deck?" he suggested.

She had agreed and after several unhurried turns, much of it in not-unpleasant silence, Margaret heard music coming from the dining room.

"Come with me," Butler said. "I do believe some unscheduled entertainment might be in the offing."

As they drew nearer the dining room, Margaret heard voices engaged in song.

"Shall we find out what's going on?" he asked.

The dining room, cleared of meal service, now had the appearance of an informal lounge. The vocals came from a quartet of soldiers accompanied by three others: one playing a ukulele and two mouthing harmonicas. The musical group stood and performed in one corner, facing two dozen or so spectators scattered about the room, a few stood but most relaxed on chairs. As Butler led them to a pair of unoccupied chairs, everyone joined in singing the final lines of a familiar chorus:

So prepare, say a prayer,
Send the word, send the word to beware;
We will be over, we're coming over
And we won't be back 'till it's over, over there.

"I know that song," Margaret said, joining in the vigorous applause. "Nora Bayes made a recording."

"It's become very popular these days," Butler replied.

"More! More!" The shouts came from somewhere to Margaret's left. Soon, the small room reverberated with the chant: "More! More!"

A member of the quartet raised both hands and gestured 'settle down'. The room became hushed. After a brief huddle with his fellows, several heads bobbed in the affirmative. The ensemble then resumed their original positions and began another familiar tune, the quartet singing in near perfect harmony. In fact, the septet sounded much better than one might expect from a presumably impromptu gathering.

Once again, the opening lyrics slid effortlessly into a sadly sweet chorus in which everyone joined:

Pack up your troubles in your old kit bag,
And smile, smile, smile!
While you've a Lucifer to light your fag,
Smile, Boys, that's the style.
What's the use in worrying?
It never was worthwhile.
So, pack up your troubles in your old kit bag,
And smile, smile, smile!

The incongruity of the moment was difficult for Margaret to

ignore. On the one hand they were sailing into dangerous waters toward a horrendous conflict in which millions had already died. Yet this same group now gathered in jovial companionship, singing and smiling, happy young men without a care in the world. During a pause in the music, curiosity overcame her neutral attitude regarding Lieutenant Butler's attentions.

She turned toward him. "I like the music—it's nice and unexpected—but there is one thing I don't understand."

"What is that, Miss Jerome?"

"Well, why on earth would someone bring their ukulele when going off to war?"

A look of informed understanding filled his eyes. "For the same reason my roommate brought along his tennis racquet."

"Tennis racquet? Are you joking?"

"No, I'm not. This is a unique experience—a historical first. American soldiers are sailing off *en masse* to fight in a European war; a conflict most of us don't really understand. We want to believe it's not as awful as newspapers make out; that it will be over quickly. But there's also the possibility that everything we've read about is true. So we hedge our bet by carrying with us favorite mementos from happier times, little things that offer comfort; that remind us of home and the lives we left behind."

His words struck a responsive chord, a previously hidden truth she found impossible to ignore. There had been no reason to do so, but packed inside Margaret's luggage was her most cherished possession: a gold locket shaped like a unicorn, a sixteenth birthday gift from her father. 'Never stop believing in magic,' he had told her. 'Magic and hard work is how we Irish survived.' After a moment he'd added: 'But it was mostly hard work.' What had compelled her to carry the charm on her sad journey to France was something she could not explain. In that moment of quiet reflection, Margaret wondered what memento of happier times Lieutenant Butler carried with him.

"What special item did you pack?" she asked, now a bit more curious about this man with such confounding opinions.

A mixture of sadness and regret crossed his face, the glassy-eyed look of one recalling a valued possession irretrievably lost. He blinked, then studied his hands for a moment before folding his arms across his chest; then he met her gaze. "I brought nothing like that along," he told her. "Nothing like that at all."

*

Margaret emerged from her reverie, confused and unsure of what was happening to her. Why would she experience such warm feelings toward someone she hardly knew? And why, if she was indeed attracted to him, had she suppressed her emotions? Shunned him, in fact.

Part of it came from preoccupation with her own personal predicament; but Margaret also realized there was something more. Fear, perhaps? After so many years searching for the right man to share her life, was she now frightened by the unexpected prospect?

Margaret shook her head, hoping to clear it of uncomfortable thoughts. If there was ever to be a romance in her future, then she must not keep certain feelings tucked away inside the dark sack of secrecy. She had to share what haunted her thoughts when sleep failed to provide the comfort of temporary oblivion. The difficult act of sharing might lighten the burden she carried, but with whom might she confide? Not Lieutenant Butler—they hardly knew each other. In a moment the answer came to her.

Satisfied and somewhat relieved, Margaret decided to answer Robert's letter today. She would bring him up to date regarding her brother's situation, including the fact that she must remain in Paris for an extended period. She would also consent to a visit, should the occasion present itself.

Feeling better than she had in weeks, Margaret stood and began preparing for her bath, vowing she would not consciously hinder whatever might develop between her and the pleasantly persistent Lieutenant Butler.

37

"Don't leave me for the rats to gnaw on," the raspy voice pleaded.

The words halted Butler in mid-stride. Stark memories of a field near the Bois de la Roche sprang to mind. He located the soldier who spoke, walked a few steps, and then kneeled beside the wounded man. It took him a moment to recognize the pale face—now smeared with grime and twisted by pain.

Butler said nothing for a moment, astonished by the coincidence. There on the ground was the man he had kicked—when was that— two weeks ago? A month? He wasn't sure. Time had become fluid, slipping past him like an unseen current. Butler was positive however, of the soldier's name. It was one he was unlikely to forget.

"Leave you for the rats, Kleppermann? What makes you think I would do that?"

The soldier's eyes narrowed for a moment, then his expression cleared. "It's *you*," he said. "The one who booted me in the pants."

Butler nodded. "I am truly sorry about that, Kleppermann."

"Ahh, it wuz nothin', Lieutenant. Besides, that's all in the past. This is the here and now, and I've run out of chances. There's not a thing you can do to save me this time."

Kleppermann was right. Fragments from an artillery blast had torn open his abdomen. Mud-smeared viscera lay in greasy coils beside his right thigh. The other leg was acutely twisted and bent upwards at the hip socket to such a degree that the toe of Kleppermann's booted foot now pointed to his left ear. Shock and concussion should have killed the man long before now. That he was still alive and conscious was a remarkable testament to the human body's primal instinct for survival.

"I won't lie to you, Kleppermann. You're in a bad way."

"That's what I figured."

"What I mean is, there's not much anyone can do."

"You can give me something—put me to sleep. I mean for good. You can do that, can't you?"

Butler said nothing but his mind provided an answer. Yes, he could certainly do *that*. It was an option he should have exercised on another maimed soldier. Instead, he'd run away like a frightened schoolboy fleeing the class bully. Kleppermann's twisted body was weirdly reminiscent of that nameless unfortunate Butler had abandoned.

What had Colonel Dawes advised those long weeks ago? His interesting and informative lectures were like a distant event, an incident from a far more innocent time. The Colonel's words reformed in his mind: *Focus your efforts on soldiers who have the best chance of survival. Don't waste precious time on those whom fate has already condemned.*

Well, he certainly hadn't wasted time on that mortally wounded man near the Bois de la Roche. Was this another opportunity to do what he dreaded? Was God giving him an unwanted second chance? Perhaps. But enormous doubts remained, unresolved issues that seldom had satisfactory resolutions.

"I'm not sure I can do what you're asking, Kleppermann."

"Why not? I'm in terrible pain, Doc. And it's getting dark." He grimaced, took several quick breaths through clenched teeth, and then continued. "The trench rabbits will be chawin' on me long before I kick the bucket. Are you going to stay by my side for the next half-hour or so and keep them away?"

"No, I can't do that. There are other wounded I must attend to."

Kleppermann shuddered and then gasped as a spasm ripped through his body. After a long moment, he took another deep breath.

"Sure, an' I understand. That's yer duty. Ya gotta save thems that got a chance to pull through. Look, Doc, I wuz born to die here, I know that now. You saved me from bein' shot a coward an' I'm grateful. But ya can't save me from this. And we both know it."

It was true. This soldier had no chance to survive his wounds. All that remained for him now was a slow, agonizing death.

As he struggled with himself, Butler reflected on a troubling coincidence. By what perverse destiny had he become instrumental in the life—and now death, it seemed—of this unfortunate soul? Was it truly another chance or merely one more bewildering test of his morality? Butler was weary of such trials and desperately wanted God to get on with whatever fate He had in mind.

"What about it, Doc? Are ya gonna do right by me?"

That was the question at hand, wasn't it? Could he leave another man to suffer an agonizing end? Could he actually walk away without doing *something*?

No, not this time.

"Are you sure about this, Kleppermann? Once it's done, there's no going back."

The wounded man grimaced, moaned softly and then relaxed as another spasm racked his shattered body. "I've made my peace with God and I hold no earthly grudges. It's my time. Let's get on with it."

"Okay, then."

Moving deliberately, Butler took a small black leather case from his rucksack. He opened it flat and removed a tubular glass syringe.

Then he selected a needle, snapped it into place on the syringe's metal base and pulled in two hundred milligrams of morphine sulphate in solution, drawing from a small glass bottle capped with a rubber stopper.

As the liquid flowed, Butler felt growing discomfort in his stomach, a slimy black serpent unwinding in oily coils. He was about to administer a lethal dose of narcotic to a living human being. In so doing, he would violate the surgeon's most sacred oath. Might he also be committing murder?

Struggling to rationalize his decision, one stubborn question remained unanswered: Could a presumably merciful act be immoral as well?

He swallowed several times but his tongue and throat remained dry. Finally, he looked down and met Kleppermann's pain-racked eyes. "Are you ready?"

Kleppermann gasped. "Do it quick... now!"

Butler emptied the syringe, driving the needle through trouser material and deep into the large abductor muscle of the undamaged right thigh.

"God bless you, Doc," the dying man muttered.

Pain bled away from the soldier's face and his breathing became slow and measured. Soon Kleppermann's eyes took on a dreamy, faraway look. A moment later he smiled and his shattered body relaxed. "It's you," he whispered. Then breathing stopped, his pale, dirty face turned gray, and his eyes glazed over.

Butler stared at the dead man and wondered about the smile. Was it merely the effect of the narcotic or had the soldier, in those final moments of life, conjured a pleasant vision from his past: a relative or loved one. Or maybe he'd perceived a joyous vision beyond the limits of human perception.

Butler also wondered what great purpose Kleppermann's death

had served. Was the world better off without him? Did his passing satisfy a perverse requirement of a great cosmic tally sheet? With Kleppermann's passing, would the war end a week, a day, or even a minute sooner?

He raised his eyes and gazed across the darkening field, at the silent lumps that had once been thriving human beings. There was no dignity here—certainly no glory. Nor was there confirmation of faith: no flash of heavenly brilliance or blaring trumpets welcoming the vanquished into Heaven.

Butler was no stranger to death—patients had died under his care at Mount Sinai Hospital—but the death of multitudes in a great war, the mass slaughter of so many in such a short period of time, should have elicited some sort of divine outrage.

According to Father Leo, deliberately taking the life of another human being was the worst of sins. Such an act was doubly heinous for a surgeon. But where was God's indignation? Where was His 'terrible swift sword'? Butler waited, half-anticipating some manner of punishment but hoping for acknowledgment of extenuating circumstances, hoping for reprieve.

But nothing happened. No soul-searing thunderbolt came from the sky; no voice of doom proclaimed his eternal banishment to Perdition; nor did he hear soothing words of understanding. All Butler felt was a profound sense of loneliness, a hopeless futility more dreadful than all the imagined fears of Hell.

He shook his head, pushing away such thoughts. Then he quickly removed the used needle from the glass tube and placed both in the appropriate groves. He closed the case, slipped it into his rucksack and stood, turning toward the sound of footsteps. Jack Mayo approached with a stretcher team.

"Carry him back to the aid station," Butler said, motioning toward the dead soldier at his feet.

Mayo eyed the corpse. "But he's already gone, Lieutenant."

"I know. Just get his body off the field, *now!*"

Mayo looked like he was about to protest, but then paused. He studied the dead man, leaning hands on knees to get a better look. "I'll be damned," he muttered. Then he turned to his stretcher team. "You heard the Lieutenant. Load him up."

It took the stretcher team a few minutes to straighten Kleppermann's disjointed leg and pile slippery insides atop his ruined abdomen, but the bearers finally got the dead man's body onto the stretcher and began the slow trudge back to the aid station.

Butler slung his rucksack and resumed his search for wounded men. As darkness gathered around him, he detected the familiar scuttle of prowling rodents.

*

A dreary pessimism settled in his bones. The too-often repeated sights and sounds of war had become commonplace and familiar, no more extraordinary than snowfall in wintertime. He remembered reading somewhere that familiarity bred contempt. That might be so, but war also produced a numbing sense of timelessness, a feeling that the present would never end. Butler felt that he knew more now than he ever wanted to know about the fratricidal tragedy called war.

One of the more esoteric bits of acquired wisdom was his ability to distinguish quickly between the different sounds produced by Browning and Maxim machine guns; between Springfield and Mauser rifles; and between the growl of a Spad's Hispano-Suiza engine and the flat clatter of the Mercedes-powered German Fokkers. However, that quantum of potentially lifesaving knowledge gave him little comfort. They were, after all, killing machines, and he had seen too much of the dead and dying, too many ghastly sights made ordinary by mind-numbing repetition.

Nevertheless, what Butler now observed sent a hollow ache

through his belly.

Instead of being hidden away in ambulances, today's consignment of dead soldiers left the battlefield on the wooden bed of a dilapidated hay wagon; a creaking spoke-wheeled antique pulled by a bay mare. The newly slain lay intermingled; one atop the other, lifeless forms stacked in a lumpy pyramid five bodies high, sharing in death a physical intimacy most would have shunned in life. The mare appeared wearily accustomed to her gruesome task. Head down and loosely reined, she plodded behind a baggy-trousered old man, patiently following her master.

There was something obscene about the casual acceptance of so much horror, a sense of wrongness that filled Butler with subdued outrage. He stepped into the middle of the road and raised his hand.

"*Arrêtez,*" Butler said.

The wagon creaked to a stop. The Frenchman's lined face took on a quizzical expression.

Struggling to control his emotions, Butler spoke the words that expressed his utter despair over how the slain were treated. "Have you no respect for the dead?"

The old man shrugged, palms upward, and his flowing white mustaches twitched. "*Ne pas comprendre.*"

Butler took a deep breath. Then he mentally formed the words and repeated the question in French: "*Vous ne pas avoir le respect pour les morts?*"

The wizened eyes brightened with understanding. "*Ah, les morts,*" he replied, glancing over his shoulder for a moment. "*Monsieur,*" he said in a voice filled with patient acceptance, "*Les morts comprennent ce qu'il faut faire. Ils sont avec Dieu.*"

Butler stared at the Frenchman for a long moment, his sullen anger ebbing like a receding wave, exposing again the pessimism he could not seem to shake. Was the old man right? Could it really be that simple? Butler realized he didn't know, and the admission added a measure of ignorance to his sorry frame of mind. Unable to voice an appropriate response, Butler stepped to the side of the dirt road and motioned for the wagon to continue.

The old man turned and muttered soothingly to his horse, then tugged gently on the reins. The wagon jerked forward with a dry, rusty squeak.

A minute later Butler followed the funerary procession as it continued along the dusty lane.

38

Woody Peckham poured two fingers of amber whiskey into a small glass and then added a little water. "It was the right thing to do," he said. "What other choice did you have?"

Butler took the offered drink but did not offer a reply.

"You had none," Peckham continued. "Leaving Kleppermann for the rats or watching him die in agony weren't really choices. I think you understand that."

"Yes, I do; unfortunately. That's why I did what I did."

The whiskey slid down Butler's throat and sent a warm glow through his stomach. He savored the peaty aftertaste. "It seems the one pleasure I get these days," he said, studying the glass, "are these infrequent occasions when we sit together and drink a little of your excellent whiskey. It has come to be the singular event I look forward to without a sense of dread. What does that tell you?"

Peckham's face would benefit from the use of a razor and his filthy uniform needed mending. He looked more like a tired street urchin than an Army medical officer. Butler realized his own appearance was equally appalling, the result of too many hours working out of doors and too little rest.

Peckham said: "It tells me I am in the company of a decent man trying to cope with an obscene situation."

A decent man? Would Woody still hold that opinion if he knew about the dying soldier Butler had abandoned to a large, aggressive rat? Surely not. That disgraceful act was something he would never divulge to anyone. It was a private shame he would carry to his grave. *Every human being has at least one unshareable secret,* he told himself. *This will be mine.*

Butler studied his friend and was mildly surprised at what he saw. "You have similar doubts about our work over here, don't you?"

"Of course. Every wartime surgeon does. Our understanding of how to repair a mutilated human body is pathetically weak. Still, it's better than what it was a decade ago, and it will be even better a decade from now."

"I'm not sure I believe that."

"Oh? When was the last time you bled a patient to free the body of evil impurities?"

Butler took another sip of whiskey. "You may have a point."

"I fear you have lived too long in squalor, my friend. You've lost your *gaieté de coeur.* Maybe you've even forgotten how it feels to be a surgeon."

That was certainly possible. The daily dose of carnage had sapped much of Butler's youthful enthusiasm. As a doctor, he understood its effect on him. He also knew that the simple joy of being alive—what Woody had termed 'gaiety of heart'—was an enduring human trait, a natural optimism difficult to suppress. Left an orphan at fourteen, Butler had prevailed over difficult personal circumstances and, with help from Father Leo and others, had rejuvenated himself. Butler had no doubt he would do so again. That is, once his life and medical practice returned to something resembling normalcy.

Yet, intermingled with hopeful confidence was the presence of a void, a familiar sense of loss much like the emptiness he had experienced when his parents vanished. As he'd sensed all those years ago as a boy, Butler the grown man realized he had lost something irreplaceable.

However, the hollow feeling was not quite the same as what he had felt back then. In this instance war's inherent vulgarity had taken from him something different, something intimate and precious; an essential part of himself one might never miss until it was gone. What the battlefield had stolen was his unique innocence, a natural optimism and purity of spirit that passing time could never restore. And it had done likewise to Jack Mayo, Woody Peckham, and countless others he had never met. This terrible war had cut away something essential, leaving an invisible wound on the soul of everyone it touched.

He swirled the liquor in his glass.

"On my way here I stopped an old man leading a wagon stacked high with corpses, one body haphazardly piled upon another like so many bundles of dirty laundry. For reasons I cannot understand, his casual disregard for decorum offended me. I stopped him and asked, somewhat righteously I might add, why he exhibited such disrespect for the dead. Do you know what he told me, Woody?"

"I can't imagine."

"He told me the dead were with God and they understood what must be done."

"That sounds like a reasonable answer."

"I agree. The dead understand everything that ever was and nothing of what might be. How could I have missed something so simple and so profound?"

"Robert, you are taking this war much too personally."

"Am I?"

"I think so. None of this is your doing. That particular responsibility rests on the shoulders of others. You've become obsessed about what happened between you and the late Private Kleppermann. First you kicked him in the ass. Then you found it necessary to kill him with a vial full of morphine, something he *asked* you to do. I think you've blown this whole matter out of proportion. You are not the first surgeon to administer a lethal dose of narcotic to a mortally wounded soldier. And, sadly, you won't be the last. I think you expect too much of yourself."

"Is that so bad?"

"If it clouds your judgment then yes, it is. You are a military surgeon but you're also a man. In that regard, you are no better or no worse than any other soldier. Stop trying to be perfect."

"I never thought I was perfect."

"Maybe that's why you work at it so much. You don't seem to realize that war invokes its own set of laws—inflexible rules from which no one is exempt."

Butler had never thought about war in quite that way. Had he missed another obvious truth? Was he striving for an ideal that simply did not exist—a fool seeking an unattainable goal?

"In any case," Peckham continued, "our particular situation is about to change, and for the better it seems."

Butler felt a tremor of anticipation. "Really? In what way?"

"Your troopship pal, Major Gregory, has convinced those on high that our surgical skills would be better utilized at an evacuation hospital."

"*Our* surgical skills? Yours and mine?"

Peckham, seemingly unable to keep a smile from spreading across his grime-streaked face, nodded. "Not a field hospital, mind you, but an evacuation hospital. One of those places where they perform actual surgeries under sterile conditions."

"That's hard to believe."

"But true, nevertheless. Apparently there are far more casualties than the present number of surgeons can handle."

Butler let the news percolate for a moment. He had spent two months in the field, living and working in primitive conditions. He felt relieved and happy to be leaving. But he couldn't help thinking about those who remained behind: soldiers and stretcher-bearers, Jack Mayo in particular, who would have little or no opportunity to escape the battlefield's unspeakable profanity.

"Where will we be going? Back to Chateau-Thierry?"

"Yes, I believe so. There were discussions about re-establishing ourselves in Rheims, but the Germans are still too close."

"Can I take a medical orderly with me?"

A slight frown crossed Peckham's face. "I'm not sure. Who did you have in mind?"

"Jack Mayo."

"Another of your sailing buddies?"

"You could say that."

"I just did."

"Look, Woody. We can always use another medical orderly. Why not Jack? He's a good man and a known quantity."

"I see your point," Peckham admitted.

"Okay, then."

Peckham rubbed the stubble on his chin. "I don't know if Major Gregory would go along with that, given the shortage of stretcher bearers."

"But you'll make inquiries, won't you?"

"Yes, I will do that, but it's not a thing certain."

"Just make the effort. That's all I ask."

Peckham nodded and finished his drink.

Butler did likewise. "When is this transfer supposed to occur?"

"Our orders should be here in a few days, not more than a week at most."

"Meanwhile…"

"That's right. Back to the daily grind."

Butler stood, retrieved his rucksack and then donned his helmet, sliding the thin leather strap under his chin. "Once again, thanks for the booze."

"Under the circumstances, it's the least I could do."

39

The sun warmed his bare skin, soothing away aches and bruises like a patented herbal balm. Butler, wearing short white drawers and nothing else, sat in the grass beside the Ardre River, a small tributary of the Vesle, and languished in late afternoon sunshine.

He had bathed in the river, standing naked near a flat rock, crotch-deep in luke-warm water, scrubbing himself pink using a bar of brown soap and a softly bristled wooden-handled brush. Then he had shaved by touch and feel. After a long swim he left the river and let the August sun dry his body. Now, feeling incredibly clean and relaxed, he watched his stretcher-bearers as they romped or dozed nearby. All except Jack Mayo, who sat propped against a chestnut tree, writing a letter—to Beatrice, probably.

Margaret's letter had arrived sooner than he had hoped or expected. Surprisingly, it contained none of the reserved tone he remembered from their voyage. The half-dozen pages, written in neat, flowing script, related the circumstances surrounding Michael's burial at Suresnes and the anticipated arrival of her parents from America. Her surprise at what she and Beatrice had discovered was evident. Yet, Butler had also detected hints of pride mixed with melancholy disappointment at how little she actually knew about her brother's life in France.

Her words reflected something else as well: an undertone of personal interest, even affection. He wanted to believe such was possible. The letter ended on a far more positive note than he had a right to expect and tended to bolster what he hoped was true.

I would be delighted to meet with you, Robert, in Paris if possible, or whenever the next opportunity presents itself. In the meantime, please be careful. I look forward to hearing from you again.

Butler lay on his back in the short grass beside the softly gurgling stream, folded his hands on his chest and tried to temper the unaccustomed sense of well-being. He closed his eyes, contemplating the potential outcome of a future meeting, and eased into a soft, drowsy languor.

*

Butler stood on a familiar, pebble-strewn beach, smiling as a sailboat glided by. His mother and father stood on the deck just aft of the mast boom, facing the shore, one arm around each other's waist, the other gently waving to him. His parents appeared exactly as they had when their Pierce-Racine touring car had taken them away for the last time. Bright smiles creased their faces and he could see that they were enormously happy.

"Goodbye, Robert!" Their melodious voices carried across the water; a soothing harmony more reassuring than a Bach cantata sung by a heavenly choir. "Goodbye, son! We will always love you!"

He wanted them to stop, to tack the boat toward shore, but he knew that was not possible. As he returned their wave, the sailboat shimmered and lost solidarity. Then it became translucent and slowly disappeared like the fading of early morning mist. Butler again experienced a familiar emptiness, but this time it was different. The recurring sense of irretrievable loss no longer stung as it once had. He realized this was an important moment in his life, a major transition, one he must share with...

He awoke with a start.

*

"What?"

"Sorry, Lieutenant," Jack Mayo said. "I didn't realize you were asleep."

Butler rose on one elbow and looked up. "I must have dozed off. Did you say something?"

"Yeah. It's time we got back."

Butler retrieved his gold pocket watch from a neat stack of clothing nearby. There was just enough time to collect his team and get a bite of supper before returning to the trench line.

"Right. Gather them up, Jack."

Mayo, already dressed, turned and walked away.

As he slipped into his uniform, brushed reasonably clean but not pressed, Butler wondered about the dream. Despite his Catholic-flavored secondary education, Butler was not overly religious, nor did he believe in mysticism or supernatural omens. Yet, the images and unspoken message had given voice to feelings he had been unable to understand until now.

When Butler lost his parents, he had also lost his place in the world; much like a shipwrecked sailor cast alone upon the open sea. St. George's Academy and Harvard were fertile islands, as was Mount Sinai Hospital. He had touched upon those shores like a transient mariner, an amiable stranger pausing for a brief sojourn, learning and growing with the help of friends and mentors like Father Leo, and then moving on.

That first night aboard the *Mongolia*, he had told Margaret that joining the Army was the right thing to do given the circumstances. That was certainly the case, but there was more to it than altruism. Like those other places in his life, the Army was merely another island; a temporary respite from a journey of unknown duration. Butler knew he was striving for that elusive feeling of completeness—a solitary soul yearning to become part of a greater whole. Rather than islands, he sought a continent, a *home*; a great emotional landmass where he could set deep roots and pass his remaining years in the close company of someone he loved.

Butler adjusted his Sam Browne belt, shouldered his musette bag and then slipped on his helmet. Then he patted his pockets. Satisfied that everything was where it should be, he strode toward Mayo and the small gathering of stretcher-bearers.

Yes, his parents were gone and he could never experience those lost years—potential times together that had never occurred. But the dream of their passing hinted at the possibility of sharing a future with Margaret. With her by his side he would no longer be alone and adrift. With Margaret he could be part of something larger than himself. With her he could again share a unique wholeness of mind and spirit.

Perhaps he had grasped one of God's lucky tokens after all.

40

Returning from the hospital in midafternoon, Margaret and Beatrice stopped at the front desk.

"Do we have mail?" Margaret asked the clerk.

"Sorry, *Mesdames*, nothing today," he told them.

She was half expecting a letter from Robert but then realized it was too soon. Posts sent from the front usually took longer than normal to reach their destination. As did letters from the United States.

Walking toward the elevator, Margaret turned to Beatrice. "I was hoping to hear from Mother or Father. Their cable didn't provide any clue regarding Michael."

Margaret had booked a second suite for her parents—a set of rooms located on the same floor, two doors away. Not sure how long everyone would remain in Paris, she had arranged for an indefinite stay.

"Well," Beatrice said, "they're supposed to be here on Monday. I'm sure we'll find out then. Meanwhile, let's try to enjoy the weekend." Then she smiled. "It seems odd, but I'm actually looking forward to tomorrow evening. Aren't you?"

"Yes, I am."

The theatrical troupe from London's Empire Theatre had crossed the English Channel and was now at the Paris Opera House, ready to begin a three-night run of their hit operetta *The Lilac Domino*.

Through the gracious efforts of the concierge, she had secured two excellent seats for Saturday evening's sold-out performance.

"Hello, Margaret."

She turned toward the soft baritone of a familiar voice and then blinked several times. He was not an illusion. Her heart thumped with such intensity she was sure everyone could hear. Somehow, she managed to respond in a calm voice. "Lieutenant Butler. Robert. What on earth..." Her voice trailed off and she could think of nothing else to say.

Cap in hand, his gaze shifted slightly. "Hello, Beatrice." Then his eyes met hers again. "Both of you look marvelous."

She didn't *feel* marvelous. They had worked six hours at the hospital dressed in baggy white smocks over their clothing, rolling bandages and washing down operating rooms after surgeries. Like Beatrice, physical labor and summer humidity had transformed her dress into a frumpy sack. She was in desperate need of a bath and fresh body powder.

"Robert, how nice to see you again." Beatrice glanced beyond his shoulder. "Is Jack here?"

"No, I'm sorry. I couldn't arrange to get his time off for the same three days. But Jack will be in Paris next weekend and he sends you his best wishes."

Beatrice's smile faded. "Oh, I see."

"I'm surprised to see you, Robert," Margaret said, finally getting control of her emotions.

"And I am just as surprised to be here. A few men from my unit recently transferred to the evacuation hospital at Chateau-Thierry. Major Gregory took one look at us and decided we needed a day or so off. The remainder of our crew will get their turn next weekend."

"If your appearance is any indication, then I can understand why. You look tired. And you've lost weight, haven't you?"

His uniform hung in loose folds and his face appeared thinner than she remembered, the cheekbones more pronounced. Gray shadows under his eyes gave his complexion an ashen cast.

"Maybe a little," he replied.

"A little?" Beatrice exclaimed. "Poor Robert! Why, you're hardly more than skin and bones. Are you and Jack getting enough to eat?"

"Yes, most of the time. But that is a condition I intend to improve upon, and soon, which brings me to why I was standing here, waiting for your arrival. If you two ladies have no other plans right now, would you consider joining me in the lounge? I believe they are about to serve afternoon tea along with an assortment of those absurdly tiny sandwiches."

"Are you a guest here?" Margaret asked.

"Yes, for the entire weekend. I'm not due back until noon on Monday."

"I believe I'll skip tea," Beatrice said. "I need a bath and a change of clothes."

"So do I," Margaret added, reluctantly.

It was true. She certainly could do with a wash. Spending any time at all with Robert in her disheveled state was an appalling prospect. But she was also hesitant to leave, to let him out of her sight, fearing he might vanish like an apparition.

"You look fine to me," he told her.

She felt the beginnings of a warm flush.

"If you stay and have tea with Robert," Beatrice suggested, a glint in her eye, "then I can have the bath all to myself for a while. You can use it afterwards."

Margaret turned toward her sister. "But you're such a messy bather. That's why I always go first."

"I'll bribe the floor maid. After I'm finished, she'll make the bathroom sparkle. There, now you have no excuse."

Robert raised an inquisitive eyebrow. "Tea and the promise of a clean bathroom all to yourself? How could you possibly refuse?"

Margaret stared into his gray eyes and struggled with her quandary. She did not want to spend their first time alone together looking and feeling so unkempt. But neither was she willing to leave the company of this man, a stranger really, towards whom she felt the beginnings of... something.

As she stood there, wholly confounded, Beatrice decided for her.

"Well, that settles it," Beatrice said. "Enjoy your tea." She smiled and strode toward the elevators.

*

The *maitre d'* led them to a table, already set for two, located close to a wall adorned with a tapestry depicting rural life: men, women, and farm animals toiling in pastel harmony, tending fields and reaping the rewards of their silent labors.

"That looks like an antique," Robert said, after they took seats.

"It is. Seventeenth century."

"Are you an expert on French tapestries?"

Margaret smiled. "No. I asked the concierge and he told me it was a Gobelins *verdure*."

His eyes shifted toward the tapestry and then back to hers. "My French is far from perfect, but did you just say 'green goblins'?"

"Yes, but that's not exactly what I meant."

"Well, that certainly clarifies things."

She smiled. "Gobelins is the guild or trade name associated with a group of dyers who got together in the sixteen hundreds. The style is *verdure*—greenery—in this case meaning 'outdoors'."

He studied the tapestry for a moment, then turned and said: "Now I understand. It makes perfect sense."

A waiter rolled a teacart to their table.

"Do you have a tea preference?" Robert asked.

"Yes. Lady Grey, please."

The waiter spooned tea leaves from one of four porcelain containers into a china pot and slowly added boiling water from a samovar. He set the pot and a small strainer in the center of the table. Another waiter followed, his cart brimming with an assortment of small sandwiches artfully arranged on a silver tray.

Margaret selected one *foie gras* and one cucumber sandwich, each dainty triangle barely three inches at its longest angle.

"I shall now proceed to humiliate myself," Robert said.

He selected one of each variety, a total of six bite-sized sandwiches.

The waiter smiled, and then moved to the next table.

"You must be starving. Why don't you order a meal?"

"At four in the afternoon? This is France, not America. Eating a full meal this early would probably cause an international scandal."

"Are you suggesting the waiter wouldn't serve you at this hour?"

"Oh, he'd bring me food. But can you imagine what he'd think while doing so?"

"No, I can't."

Robert leaned toward her, his voice dripping with feigned Gallic contempt. "I will speak to the chef, *monsieur*, but all Europe shall hear of this outrage!"

Laughter burst from her lips without warning. Margaret quickly covered her mouth with a hand and scanned the lounge to see if anyone was staring. Fortunately, most people were polite enough to ignore her outburst. Unable to restrain herself, she continued to chuckle softly. Tearful amusement gathered in the corner of her eyes. Robert had captured perfectly the arrogant pretentiousness so common among France's upper classes.

"I believe that's the first time I've heard you laugh," he said. "It was delightful. You should do it more often."

As she dabbed her eyes with a small, lace-edged handkerchief, a pleasant, relaxed feeling settled over her. She had forgotten how good laughter felt. It had been a long time since it burst forth spontaneously. Margaret had always been quick with a laugh or a silly giggle but the warm gaiety that once lightened her heart had fled, chased away by her brother's decision to run off to war. His death had banished merriment from her life. Yet, here it was again, humor returned from exile, glowing with renewed vigor.

He was watching her, his eyes pleasantly intent.

She said: "Yes, I probably should. But it's difficult. Grief can be so overwhelming."

"I know, but consider this: That which does not kill us makes us stronger."

"What an interesting perspective. Yours?"

"No. I heard it from a Catholic priest who, if you can believe this, got it from his reading of Friedrich Nietzsche. Father Leo drummed those and similar homilies into my thick head. Remembering what he taught helped me get through a difficult time."

The melancholy expression she remembered from the voyage returned and then instantly left his face. Instinct told her something painful had happened to Robert—a life-changing event from his past, and it was clear the old wound still ached.

"An Irish Catholic priest who reads German philosophy? Isn't that sort of like the Pope extolling the works of Martin Luther?"

"Maybe a little. But Father Leo is a remarkable man, a wonderful soul who changed my life." His expression reflected warmth and concern. "Margaret, I realize you haven't had much to laugh about, but that old priest taught me to embrace humor whenever possible. He believed it had a cathartic effect. I think he was right. Used in the proper way at the right time, it can help us cope with difficult situations."

"Even during wartime?"

"Especially during wartime. Sometimes, humor is mankind's lone defense against lunacy."

"More Nietzsche?"

"No, Butler."

She studied his face and then looked away, feigning interest in the tapestry.

There was a subtle complexity to this man, a characteristic she had either missed or ignored. He was intelligent but not boringly so, and his quick sense of humor was neither churlish nor offensive. Most important of all, she felt relaxed and comfortable in his presence—a cozy familiarity usually reserved for someone she had known all her life. And there was something else; something she could not easily define.

Feeling his eyes on her, Margaret felt buoyed by his unspoken attention.

Lilting soprano laughter from a nearby table diverted her thoughts. She turned toward the sound.

Like a queen bestowing knighthood, a young woman wearing a buttercup yellow dress lightly tapped the shoulder of her gentleman companion, not with a sword but a folded silk fan, her round face clearly amused by whatever he had said.

Margaret looked at Robert and then studied the table setting. "I believe our tea is ready," she said. "May I pour you a cup?"

"Please."

"Milk and sugar?"

"No milk. A little sugar."

"How much is a little?"

"A half-teaspoon or so."

As she prepared their tea, pouring hot liquid through a strainer into delicate china cups, her curiosity became aroused. "I know so little about you, Robert. Tell me something of yourself."

"There is little to tell, really. Up until now I led a rather quiet life."

She was not ready to believe that. Not yet, anyway. "Then tell me what little of it there is."

As he spoke, Margaret noticed his reluctance to discuss parents or anything related to early childhood. The exception was when he briefly mentioned his years at St. George's Academy and Father Leo's positive reinforcement during a difficult time. When pressed about what happened earlier, he would pause, chew thoughtfully on a sandwich, and then nudge the conversation along a different course. Thus, his years at college, medical school, and Mount Sinai Hospital were rich with acquaintances, events, and humorous anecdotes. In short, Robert's life seemed to begin at age eighteen. Was he a foundling, a newborn left on the steps of a church? It was an aspect of his life Margaret wanted to explore, but she kept her curiosity in check. By exercising patience, she believed Robert would eventually share with her what he now held firmly within himself.

He slid cup and saucer towards her.

"More tea?" she asked.

"Yes, please. It's more flavorful than I expected."

"It's my favorite. Would you like another sandwich… or several?" She turned and searched for the waiter.

"No, thank you. I've made quite a spectacle of myself as it is."

"Don't exaggerate, Robert. You were very discreet."

"Is that so? How does one devour six sandwiches discreetly?"

"They were *little* sandwiches, but you managed quite well."

He smiled and stirred his tea.

Margaret expected him to be as curious about her background as she was about his, but he remained content with silence, apparently comfortable with the lull in conversation. Finally she said, "Aren't you the least bit curious about me?"

He held her eyes with a calm, steady gaze. Then he said, "Of course. But I already have a good sense of who you are. What I don't know is how you became such a thoughtful and caring young woman. Nor do I know what you want to do for the rest of your life."

The room suddenly felt warm. It was not what she had expected from him, not yet. Margaret had always hoped to meet a man who would look into her eyes and instinctively know who she was without her having to explain. Until now she thought it was the winsome hope of a silly schoolgirl.

"Feel free to skip any embarrassing details," he added.

Margaret's first impulse was to tell him there were many embarrassing details, but she managed to control that urge. She said, "Are details unimportant to you?"

"Oh, no, to the contrary. *Deus in singulis*—God is in the details."

"Another phrase from Father Leo?"

He nodded. "According to him, human beings are made in His image, so the details that comprise our lives are important. Or so he believed. What I meant was something a little different."

She waited while he appeared to be gathering his thoughts.

"What I'm trying to say is this: We are who we are. The details of how we got that way are important, but they should not determine what we might make of ourselves. The past is history but the future is an unwritten book. Why clutter those blank pages bemoaning events we can never change? Does that make any sense?"

Margaret let the words settle for a moment, then she said: "Yes, it does. In other words we should not allow an unpleasant past to prevent a happier future. Is that what you mean?"

His smile brightened the entire lounge. "Exactly. As individuals we tend to fret most about acts and events we can never undo. What is done cannot be undone, and wailing over life's inequities accomplishes nothing. Our minds understand this but we still allow the past to haunt the present and govern our future. I believe each of us would be happier if we focused more on what we are becoming and less on who we've been. Unfortunately, knowing isn't the same as doing."

He paused, an expression of mild embarrassment on his face. Then he said, "I was blathering. Sorry."

"No, not at all. You have an interesting philosophy. I'd like to give it some more thought."

"And I'd like you to forget the ramblings of a weary mind."

Now, more than ever, Margaret believed that some event in Robert's childhood continued to trouble him, an experience that refused his efforts to bury its memory. Instinct told her she must somehow discover and understand what it was, but she was unsure how to proceed without offending him or, worse, drawing tighter the heavy curtain he'd drawn between his past and the present. She paused for a moment, thinking. If Robert decided to share his deepest secrets, would he expect her to do likewise?

She said: "If you're weary, you should take a nap before dinner."

"Have I bored you numb already?"

"Of course not. But whenever I've had a busy day, a short nap always perks me up."

"Have you had a busy day?"

"Yes, Beatrice and I keep ourselves occupied. We do volunteer work."

"Is that so?"

"It is. We help out at the American Ambulance in Neuilly."

"You do volunteer work at Number One? Really?"

She nodded. "I'm curious. Why does everyone call it that?"

"Number One? Oh, I think I know what you mean. Well, the Army has identified, by number, each of its main hospitals. They do things like that. Everything must have a name, number and nomenclature—all nice and tidy. There are about seven here in Paris. Anyway, the one in Neuilly-sur-Seine was supposed to be a secondary school called Lycée Pasteur. When war came in 1914, we completed construction and used it as a hospital. Being first, the Army designated Neuilly as Base Hospital Number One. Number Two is the Blake Hospital on Rue Piccine. And so on."

"I see. Well, another mystery solved!"

"Glad to help out."

"And you deftly avoided my question about a nap."

"I am not going to waste my time off by taking a nap. I'll have a good sleep in a real bed tonight. But, since you also mentioned dinner, do you have plans for this evening?"

Afternoon tea was over and the lounge was beginning to empty. A few patrons still lingered, including the young queen in the yellow dress and her attentive knight, but it was clearly time to leave.

"I have no special dinner plans, and I would love to continue our conversation, but..."

"Why is there always a 'but'?"

"...I wouldn't want Beatrice to dine alone."

"Then why not have her join us? I'm sure she'd like to hear what Jack has been up to."

"Yes, she probably would. I never thought of that. Incidentally, what *has* Jack been up to?"

"No good, but I won't go into that now."

She poked his forearm affectionately. "I don't believe that. You are not a convincing liar."

"I will take that as a compliment. Anyway, after the three of us have a nice leisurely dinner followed by coffee or sherry in the lounge, Beatrice can make a graceful exit and we can spend another hour or so together."

"I don't know, Robert. Are you sure you can stave off hunger until eight o'clock?"

"I believe so. If not, I'll sneak off to a local bistro for a light snack. The streets are bustling with uncultured American Doughboys who shamelessly consume food at any hour of the day."

The memory of his humorous impersonation of French *l'aristocratie société* produced another smile. "All right. Eight o'clock, then."

As she prepared to leave, Margaret reflected on the time between now and eight o'clock this evening. Why did three and a half hours seem like such a long time?

41

If patrons occupying Lutetia's opulent dining room were an indicator of the times, then Paris had discarded her mourning clothes in favor of brighter attire—or so it appeared to Margaret.

Under glittering chandeliers suspended from high ceilings, tuxedoed gentlemen breezily conversed with jeweled and elegantly coiffed ladies. Each in turn responded with a smile or a frown or mild dismay; whatever seemed appropriate at that particular moment. Counts and countesses, if one could assume such from their colorful regalia, looked less akin to displaced aristocracy and more like extras from a Gilbert and Sullivan comic opera. Those self-esteemed personages sat at the best tables, regally sipping pink aperitifs while studiously ignoring those of less-noble birth.

A string quartet played Brahms, an odd choice given the circumstances. The selection corroborated the transcendence of art and music over tribal differences. Listening to the delightful sonata, Margaret wondered if correspondingly privileged diners in Berlin were nibbling *foie gras* and sipping French champagne. The irony of Parisians enjoying the works of a German composer while Berliners stuffed their faces with French cuisine fascinated her. If each could see the other at this moment, would they acknowledge the tragic absurdity of this great disaster they had visited upon themselves?

Probably not. Ignoring or superficially altering an unpleasant reality was much easier. Proof of such was evident. A year ago

England's King George V had issued a royal proclamation changing his family name from 'Saxe-Coburg of Gotha' to 'Windsor'. Likewise, his cousin Prince Louis Battenberg became Louis Mountbatten. It was all so silly, as though the act of adopting an English-sounding name could somehow erase generations of German ancestry.

Yet, their calculated pretensions could not alter the fact that Europe's three primary combatants—King George V of England, Germany's Kaiser Wilhelm II, and the now-deposed Tsar Nickolas II of Russia—were blood relatives; descendants of England's Queen Victoria.

Perhaps the long history of royal marriages between related family members had somehow affected the bloodline of certain offspring. That could explain the Kaiser's withered left arm. If so, then Robert's belief about feuding cousins being responsible for this war—an opinion he had shared during their first dinner aboard the *Mongolia*—was closer to truth than she was willing to admit.

The soft music floated above the hollow click of silver on china and the murmur of numerous conversations among the finely dressed civilians. As one might expect during wartime, those wearing military uniforms—British khaki, AEF brown, and French horizon blue—were equally represented.

"What uniform is that?" Beatrice asked quietly.

Robert looked up from the remnants of his dinner, a hearty serving of chicken in white wine, all of which he had consumed with marvelously restrained gusto.

"The soldier who just came in," Beatrice added.

Margaret turned her head slightly. A handsome couple stood at the dining room entrance. Both were resplendent but the man's attire commanded attention. Tall and mustachioed, he wore scarlet trousers tucked into gleaming knee-high black riding boots and a dazzling light blue tunic trimmed in silver braid. The medal-laden tunic—draped across his left shoulder like a cape—brought to mind the style reminiscent of a Napoleonic *cuirassier*.

"French cavalry officer," Robert said.

"I think he looks spiffy."

"The gentleman certainly stands out in a crowd," Robert agreed. "And, mounted on an equally impressive horse, he is also an easy target for enemy machine gunners."

Beatrice's eyes grew wide. "Oh! I never thought about that."

"Apparently, neither did the French cavalry corps."

"Is that why British and American uniforms appear drab by comparison?" Margaret asked.

"Yes. Brown and khaki are supposed to blend in with the countryside."

"Then why doesn't everyone change into something less conspicuous?" Beatrice asked.

Robert shrugged. "In some of the older European regiments, common sense has not yet prevailed over pride and vanity."

Beatrice shook her head. "War is so stupid."

"And a frightful waste of young lives," Robert added.

So far, except for brief exchanges like this, their little group had remained silent, preferring to bask in the dining room's pleasant atmosphere.

Margaret found herself meeting and holding Robert's eyes for long moments and then quickly looking away. The self-conscious behavior delighted Beatrice who sat and watched, the trace of a satisfied smile on her lips.

She regretted inviting Beatrice to dinner. There were so many questions she wanted to ask Robert—and things she wanted to confide—personal thoughts Margaret did not wish to share with her sister.

Tomorrow would present a better opportunity for an extended visit, or so she hoped. Margaret looked forward to seeing *The Lilac Domino*, but she also wanted to share more of Robert's company, a fact she could no longer ignore. It was an unexpected and pleasant discovery, one she embraced with lighthearted caution.

An idea began to form. Might Anna accompany Beatrice to the operetta? Or, better yet, she and Robert could see it together. Did he enjoy the theatre? She did not know. Remembering that he had practiced medicine in New York City, home to dozens of playhouses and theatres, Margaret looked at Robert.

"Do you like stage plays?" she asked.

He nodded. "Yes, I do."

"Do you have favorites?"

"I really like those wonderful musicals by George M. Cohan."

"I enjoy musicals as well. What about comedies and drama?"

"Yes, those, too."

"Do you have a favorite?"

He thought for a moment. "Not really, but I enjoyed seeing *H.M.S. Pinafore* at the 48th Street Theater a couple of years ago."

"The comic opera?"

He smiled. "Yes. And then there was Clara Blandick in *Madame Butterfly*. I didn't like it as much. She was fine but the story was a bit too tragic for me. I lean more toward the lighter works."

She looked at Beatrice who returned a curious look. *The Lilac Domino* was clearly a 'lighter work'. Attending the play with Robert rather than Beatrice was an intriguing possibility, an option Margaret vowed to explore at her first opportunity.

*

A few nearby diners pushed away from their tables and stood, chatting on their way out.

"Would you ladies care to join me in the lounge for coffee or, as the French say, a *digestif?*"

Beatrice rose from her seat, as did Robert. Margaret followed.

"This was a lovely dinner, but it's been a busy day," Beatrice said.

"You needn't rush off," Butler replied.

"Good night, Robert. Dinner was lovely." Beatrice smiled at Margaret. "See you in the morning." Then she turned and left them standing alone.

"That was considerate," Robert said. "But I can't say I'm disappointed."

He took her arm and they ambled out of the dining room. A few minutes later they found a comfortable settee in a corner of the lounge.

"Do you have plans for tomorrow?" Margaret asked, settling in.

"No, but I was hoping we could spend more time together."

"How would you feel about a museum visit?" Margaret asked. "The French are using the Grand Palais as a hospital, but just across the street is the Petit Palais which is still open."

"Really, despite the bombings?"

"Yes. I've learned they are featuring an exhibition by Georges Seurat."

Butler wrinkled his brow. "Seurat. Isn't he the one who paints using tiny colored dots?"

"It's called pointillism."

"Yes, I remember the term: much classier than *tiny little dots*."

"Classy is not what those first art critics thought. Pointillism was meant as a derisive term."

"I can understand why—all those little dots…"

"You're not supposed to stand that close."

"Ahh, now I get it: the farther away one is, the better it looks."

Margaret shook her head but could not prevent a smile from

creasing her lips.

"Just kidding," he said. "Is it a large exhibit?"

She opened her purse, retrieved, and then unfolded a colored advertisement. "If one can believe the brochure, *A Sunday on La Grande Jatte* and two of his Eiffel Tower renderings are on display, plus some others." She met his gray eyes. "I take it you might be interested?"

"It sounds like a pleasant way to pass a few hours."

A waiter approached and Margaret ordered sherry.

"Port," Butler said. "Is any of the'99 or 1900 available?"

The waiter nodded appreciatively. "I have a very nice '99 from Douro."

"Excellent."

Margaret could not contain her curiosity. "Where did you learn about Port wine?"

"From a trusted mentor."

"Might that be your Father Leo from St. George's Academy?"

He nodded.

Studying his relaxed features, Margaret sensed it might be time to probe a bit further into this man's background. His apparent reluctance to discuss the early years of his life during afternoon tea still intrigued her. If he continued to avoid questions regarding his past, might that end what she hoped was the beginning of... *something?*

She took a deep breath. "What was it like, growing up."

At that moment, the waiter arrived and set their drinks beside them. Butler signed the bill and then raised his glass. "What shall we drink to?" he asked, looking into her eyes.

The phrase 'a timely interruption' came to mind; words uttered by Major Gregory aboard the *Mongolia* during their first dinner together. Margaret had asked Robert to further explain his attitude regarding the war, but the soup course arrived before he could answer.

"Saved by the sherry," she said, picking up her glass and taking a sip.

He appeared confused by her remark. "What sort of toast is that?"

The sherry was quite good and the deep, fruity aftertaste lingered on her tongue. "Answer my question first."

"All right, I suppose it's time." He sipped port and then exhaled. "I had a great childhood," he began. "But it ended prematurely."

"Really? What happened?"

"Twelve years ago, on July twenty-first, my parents threw a grand party to celebrate my fourteenth birthday. It was a Saturday. All my friends from school and the neighborhood gang showed up bearing presents in gaily wrapped packages. My mother baked an enormous cake made with Hershey's cocoa, and my dad bought cases of Hires and gallons of ice cream from Kolb's dairy. We stuffed ourselves with cake and drank root beer floats until they came out of our ears. Then we played Pin the Tail on the Donkey and London Bridge and Nuts in May. It was warm, but not too hot—a perfect summer day.

"My parents used to spend private time together every now and then. Sometimes they would travel to New York City for the weekend, but most other times they would stay in the cottage we owned on Seneca Lake. On those occasions our housekeeper, Mrs. Elliot, looked after me. On the Saturday following my birthday party, the twenty-eighth, my parents took their monthly sojourn and went sailing. I did what I usually did on a summer day between school years: played marbles, fished in the nearby creek with my pals... normal kid stuff. As for my parents, I never saw them again."

Margaret gasped at the revelation "What happened?"

He shrugged. "Their sailboat probably sank during a

thunderstorm but no one really knows for sure. Seneca Lake is huge. If you stand on the northern shore and look south, the lake runs all the way to the horizon. They simply disappeared."

"How awful that must have been for you."

"Yes, but in a strangely unusual way. As the summer wore on, it was difficult for my fourteen-year-old mind to reconcile those weekends. One Saturday was the happiest, most fun-filled time I can remember; the next was a sea of sympathetic frowns, hushed conversations, and muttered speculation. Those two events kept getting mixed up inside my head."

He paused and took a measured sip of port.

"By September everything had changed. Instead of parents, I now had a guardian—Mr. Albright—my father's friend and attorney."

"Weren't their relatives?"

"No. Like me, my parents were only children. I had distant cousins somewhere out west, but no one knew who they were, and I needed a place to live other than in our big, empty house. Mr. Albright was kind and helpful, but I had few options. So I left my home and my school and my friends—familiar things I had known my entire life—and entered St. George's Academy. I lived there full time as a resident-student until I graduated high school."

"And Father Leo helped you get through that terrible period of your life, didn't he?"

"That he did. Father Leo understood and sympathized with my plight, but he was not a coddler. It was exactly what I needed."

"Now I understand why you hold him in such high regard."

He smiled. "And I'm not even Catholic."

Once again she experienced that now-familiar stirring, only this time she felt it growing, nourished by the affectionate vulnerability reflected in his eyes. What she now felt had a name; one she had tried to ignore but with limited success. The presumably rational arguments about why this could not be happening succumbed to the fierce assurance beating inside her chest.

He drained his glass and his eyes searched for the waiter. Clearly, Robert wanted another glass of port.

Margaret finished her sherry. She sensed that Robert was about to ask her to share some of her life, but Margaret was not yet ready to do so. She needed time to think about what he'd told her—and to understand better what she was feeling, now more strongly than ever.

She stood and Robert rose to his feet as well. "Hold on, Margaret. You can't leave now. I've told you a little of my story, so you should tell me a little of yours. Fair is fair."

She touched his forearm with her fingertips. "Time enough for that tomorrow."

He nodded, clearly disappointed, but perhaps also realizing their evening together was now at an end.

"Tomorrow, then," he said.

42

The Seurat exhibition, located in one of the smaller sky-lit galleries, was awe-inspiring but not as extensive as Butler thought it would be. In less than three hours he and Margaret had viewed all the Seurat paintings plus collections of fine porcelains and 18th century furniture once owned by French royals, some of whom had ended up on the wrong end of the guillotine.

"It's nearly noon," he suggested as they made their way out. "We could have an early lunch and perhaps visit the Louvre."

"We should not short-shrift the Louvre," she replied.

"I agree, but a little is better than none. And, we could always go back again tomorrow."

"Let's have lunch and talk about it."

They stepped outside, passed under the domed arch, and descended wide stairs. He looked across the street and took in the many-columned magnificence of the Grand Palais. His eyes swept across the statuary and the matching bronze quadriga atop each of the two wings and finally came to rest on a busy swirl of drivers and medical attendants unloading a staggered line of ambulances parked at the curb. The great hall, stripped of art and the promising glimmer of human potential, now housed the surviving wreckage of a great war.

He heard a sharp intake of breath as Margaret nearly missed a step. Butler's firm hold on her elbow was all that prevented a nasty fall.

Had the sight of all those ambulances reminded Margaret of her dead brother?

Butler hailed a passing fiacre. "Do you have any particular restaurant in mind?" he asked, wanting to divert her attention.

"Yes, I do," she answered. "Let's go to *Le Moine Affame* in Montparnasse."

"The Hungry Monk?" Butler said, helping her into the horse-drawn carriage. "Sounds interesting. Is it a favorite of yours?"

"No," she replied, her voice oddly subdued and a bit haunting. "I've never been there."

They crossed the Seine at Pont de la Concord and then took Boulevard Raspail as it cut through the heart of Montparnasse. As they clopped along the wide avenue, Margaret stared straight ahead. She seemed oblivious to her surroundings.

"I understand the catacombs are nearby," he said, hoping to dissipate her obvious gloom. "That could be worth a visit." Butler immediately clamped his mouth shut, horrified by the remark. The catacombs were an ancient ossuary containing the bones of millions of human beings. If Margaret had indeed been thinking about her brother, then his suggestion to visit a human boneyard was witlessly macabre.

Oddly, the faint trace of a smile crossed her lips and just as quickly faded. Puzzled, he turned away from her profile and, not for the first time, wondered what she might be thinking.

He remembered similar behavior aboard the *Mongolia*. At times she had seemed to retreat behind a wall of privacy; a sanctuary into which no one dared enter. He also acknowledged the same characteristic within himself. It occurred to him that perhaps everyone had a private refuge; a cloistered vault of secrets, riddles, and enigmas.

The carriage turned onto bustling Rue Daguerre and stopped beside a café nudged between a flower shop and a bakery. Several outside tables sat in the shade of a green awning. Butler helped Margaret to the sidewalk and paid the driver.

"Inside or out?" he asked.

"Let's have a look inside," she replied. It was the first words she had spoken since boarding the carriage.

White linen covered the tables, sparsely filled at such an early lunch hour, and each contained a slender vase holding a colorful trio of flowers. A waiter ushered them to a table near the window, one already set for luncheon, and they sat on black-lacquered wooden chairs covered with burgundy-hued cushions.

As they settled in, Butler studied the decor, as did Margaret who seemed intensely focused. Overall, the dining room was cozy and well-appointed. Several excellent sketches and oil paintings, grouped or hung singly, adorned the walls. Nevertheless, war shortages had eroded some of its original grandeur. Portions of the tablecloths were threadbare and the worn oak floor could have benefitted from refinishing. The overall ambiance, although quite pleasant, reminded him of a dignified, middle-aged woman dressed in her finest old clothes.

"I like this place," he volunteered. "It has a comfortable, lived-in feel."

Margaret smiled, but said nothing.

"If you've never been here," he asked a bit hesitantly, "what made you select this particular restaurant?"

She clasped her hands together and rested them on the edge of the table before answering. "This was my brother's favorite place," she told him. "He mentioned it several times in his journal. In fact, this is where he proposed marriage to his wife." Her eyes left his and roamed across the room. "I believe he was very happy here," she added.

"I see," Butler said, leaning back on his chair. "Did the ambulances remind you of him?"

"Not the ambulances, themselves. However, one of the drivers removed his helmet and wiped his brow with a handkerchief. He had dark auburn hair, exactly the color of my own. For a moment I thought…" She shook her head. "But of course it wasn't Michael. It couldn't be, but seeing that tired soldier who resembled my brother gave me quite a start. If it weren't for you, I would have taken a tumble."

"And then my question about lunch reminded you of Michael's favorite restaurant."

"Yes, it's funny how that happened. I planned to visit here with Beatrice anyway, but then came this impulse…" Her blue eyes glazed for a moment, but she quickly blinked them clear. "Anyway, here we are."

"Well, thank you for the privilege, Margaret. Sharing this special place with you means a great deal to me."

Butler thought about apologizing for the catacombs suggestion but her mood seemed lighter now so he decided to remain quiet. Only if she mentioned it would he offer an apology.

The waiter approached and they ordered white wine.

Margaret had written about her brother in letters; however, Butler knew little about him. "You wrote that Michael was in the Army. When did he enlist?"

"He didn't actually join the Army, not in the usual sense. In 1916, long before America entered the war, he and several of his friends from college signed on to the American Ambulance Field Service as volunteer drivers attached to French Army units."

"I know about the Field Service," Butler told her. "Several doctors and nurses took leave from their positions at Mt. Sinai and volunteered. I was tempted but the head of surgery advised me to complete my residency first."

"So how did you end up in the Army?"

He shrugged. "It just happened, I suppose. When we declared war on Germany, I wanted to serve and the Army seemed like a good idea at the time. Did something like that happen to Michael?"

"Not exactly. When President Wilson finally declared war, the Field Service became part of the American Expeditionary Forces. Michael and several of those early volunteers were offered temporary commissions." She paused. "I'm still not sure how all that happened, but his ambulance unit, although part of the AEF, still served with the French."

"I see. What did he do before joining up?"

"He worked at our brewery, preparing himself to take over when my father retired."

"Your father owns a brewery?"

"That he does."

"And Michael just up and left?"

"He did indeed. Lately though, I've come to realize that Michael was never interested in the business. He was playing a role: the dutiful son subordinating his own needs to those of his father. Volunteering to drive ambulances in a far-off country gave him a legitimate opportunity to explore other alternatives."

"I suspect your father was none too happy about that."

"He wasn't, not at all. But Michael knew how to frame an argument. Our parents taught us that, as privileged children, it was our Christian duty to help the needy and less fortunate. In fact, they set the example. Both actively supported charitable and other benevolent societies."

"And did you follow along?"

"Yes, grudgingly. At the time, our parish operated a soup kitchen in the Soulard neighborhood. Every Wednesday Beatrice and I served food or cleaned up afterwards. We hated the idea of working as scullery maids. What must our friends think? Our father found our embarrassment amusing. He called us the Surly Sisters of Soulard. But, as we began to see those unfortunates as individual human beings in need, our attitude changed."

"Was your brother involved, as well?"

"Michael coached Saturday morning sports programs at the orphanage. Still, I could sense he was looking to do something else with his life. The American Ambulance Field Service was a well-publicized endeavor, a noble cause everyone admired. When a couple of Michael's college friends invited him to join them, off he went."

"That happens sometimes. Each of us needs to find our own place."

"Yes, we do. And sometimes the result is not what we might have expected."

Butler recalled his own feelings of loss and unutterable despair when his parents vanished all those years ago. Michael's death must have struck the Jerome family like a bolt of lightning. What was Margaret feeling? Was losing a fraternal twin the same or worse than losing parents? Is this what had first attracted him to her? Did he somehow sense the presence of another wounded spirit? Or was it something else?

"And sometimes," Butler added, "things just happen."

The waiter arrived with their drinks. Butler lifted his glass and was pondering a suitable toast. Before he could speak the waiter returned, this time carrying a silver tray holding two small plates. "*Amuse-gueule,*" he said, placing small appetizers before each of them. "*Avec les compliments.*"

The dainty china plate contained a round slice of cucumber upon which lay a pink fold of smoked salmon topped by a fluted blossom of cream cheese from which emerged a miniature green sprig of what Butler presumed was some sort of edible weed. He wasn't sure what to make of it, so he stole a surreptitious peek at Margaret.

Her face radiated pure delight.

"Oh," she said, her eyes glistening. "What a wonderful surprise!"

*

Their lunch selections, limited by rationing, were nevertheless delicious and satisfying. Afterwards she had taken his arm—a good omen—and they strolled up Rue Daguerre. The effect of food shortages was evident here as well, especially in the covered market where vegetables were available but meat, butter, and baked goods other than plain bread were practically non-existent. The atmosphere of emptiness and privation was palpable.

"How sad," Margaret said. "Five years ago this street was thriving with all manner of goods. Now..." She shrugged, perhaps unable to express the gloom that seemed to permeate certain parts of the city.

"Then you are not a first-time visitor."

"No, I'm not. Our entire family sailed here on the *Lusitania*."

"Really? When was that?"

"In June of 1912. Three years later, German U-boats torpedoed it." She paused. "That summer was the last time we vacationed together as a family."

They continued walking arm-in-arm toward Rue Gassendi and then turned left at the big intersection. Up ahead was Montparnasse Cemetery, burial place of Guy de Maupassant. Butler, remembering his earlier gaffe about the catacombs, steered Margaret toward the curb where several carriages sat parked.

"Have you made up your mind about the Louvre?" he asked.

"Yes," she replied. "Let's save that for another time. Meanwhile, perhaps we should visit the cemetery or perhaps take an uplifting stroll through the catacombs?"

Despite the hint of a mischievous smile on her lips, Butler felt his cheeks grow warm.

"I am truly sorry about the catacombs remark," he confessed. "I was just trying to get your mind off the ambulances. You were so quiet and when we passed the sign, I said the first thing that popped into my mind."

"I understood what you were trying to do, but you mustn't tiptoe around the tragedy of my brother's death, no more than you would that of your parents. I know he's gone but I treasure the happy memories we shared. Besides," the smile had crept into her eyes, "that same idea occurred to me, as well. The thought of my dead brother and the prospect of touring the catacombs is a juxtaposition he would have found both macabre and wildly humorous."

"Humorous," Butler said. "Interesting choice of words."

"What do you mean?"

"The humerus, spelled differently, is the long bone that runs from the shoulder to the elbow. I imagine there might be several million of those lying around the catacombs."

*

Their time together was nearly over.

She and Robert had spent most of the weekend in each other's company, fleeting moments that began on Friday afternoon when they nibbled tiny sandwiches, sipped tea, and admired a lovely tapestry. Now, sitting beside him at a sidewalk café near the Tuileries, she reminisced and quietly marveled at how quickly the time had sped by.

On Saturday they took breakfast together, enjoyed a long morning walk, and then visited the Seurat exhibition. After lunch she and Robert walked slowly through the nave of Notre Dame Cathedral and stood transfixed by the magnificence of the South Rose window. Afterwards they strolled along the Quai aux Fleurs, talking about everything except the war, which seemed very far away. That evening, thanks to Beatrice, the two chuckled through *The Lilac Domino*, a delightful musical play Robert had clearly enjoyed.

'I have an unexplainable tolerance for loveable scoundrels,' he'd remarked during an intermission.

They left the opera house after the final curtain, walked arm-in-arm a short way up Rue de Mogador and then turned left at Rue Joubert. Before reaching Anna's house where Beatrice awaited, they slowed and then stopped beneath the leafy branches of a Linden tree. She felt a winsome pang, a sense that neither wanted their time alone together to end. They stood there without speaking, gazing into each other's eyes. Then, drawn together by invisible magnets, their lips drew closer. Even before they kissed, Margaret felt the warm tingle of an electric charge, a rushing sensation that left her dazed and breathless. Fortunately, shadows helped conceal the flush she felt rising in her cheeks. Another lingering kiss followed, and then others, his lips caressing the pulsing vein in her throat.

Somehow they had managed to disengage from each other, neither speaking, fearing words might burst the shimmering magical sphere that enveloped them.

Sitting in the parlor at Number 19 with Anna and Beatrice, the four had sipped sherry and talked for hours. Then came discovery that Robert and Michael had trod much of the same sad ground.

'Almost every town and village has been damaged or destroyed,' Butler had said. 'Many places are hardly more than a jumbled pile of broken stones.'

All agreed the war had exacted a terrible price, both in property—which hard work could rebuild or replace—but also in human lives, which could not, regardless of human effort.

'Nevertheless,' he continued, looking at Margaret. 'I would like to visit Picardy after the war. Perhaps we could see it together.'

'I would like that,' she replied, remembering her brief but memorable visit to Amiens.

On Sunday morning, the four met for a late breakfast followed by a visit to Michael's grave at Suresnes. Afterwards, Beatrice and Anna left them, promising to meet again that evening for Robert's farewell dinner. It was then, under his gentle questioning, that Margaret revealed everything she had learned about her brother since coming to France.

'I understand your disappointment,' he told her as they walked down the wide path toward the waiting carriage. 'I don't believe I could have kept such important things from my parents.'

Now, in mid-afternoon on Sunday, they sat at a sidewalk café near the Tuileries, lazily sipping white burgundy. As he looked across the boulevard toward the Jardin de Tuileries, she marveled at how much they had shared during so little time together. Studying his profile, Margaret had the sense that there might be more.

Then, like receiving a cue, he looked at her and said, "It was the mail. It was all that mail piling up on the small desk in the foyer." He sighed and appeared more relaxed; a great weight lifted from his shoulders.

"I'm not sure I understand, Robert."

"After they disappeared, and for the rest of the summer until the day I left for St. George's Academy, my parents continued to get mail. The usual sort of things: letters, circulars, church notices. Mail kept arriving, day in and day out—all addressed to Mister or Missus Butler, sometimes both. It got to a point where I didn't really believe what Mr. Albright and Mrs. Elliot kept telling me. How could my parents be dead? Who was going to read all that mail Mr. Albright came by to collect every Friday? Disregarding what they told me, I kept waiting for my mother and father to come home and read the letters Mr. Albright held in safekeeping." He smiled, but sadness filled his eyes. "Of course, they never did."

"I am so sorry."

"So am I. They were good people. I never stopped missing them."

Looking into his eyes Margaret finally acknowledged the warm stirrings she had begun to feel since that first kiss—long and lingering and aching with promise. That innocent intimacy in the shadow of a Linden tree had blossomed into something bright and deliciously secret. What she now felt had a name; one she had tried to ignore without success. The presumably rational arguments about why she couldn't possibly feel the way she did could not prevail against the fierce assurance beating inside her chest. Overwhelmed, she turned away, seeking to lessen the dizzying swirl of emotions threatening to overcome her good sense.

She felt his hand on hers and turned to face him again.

"My leave is up and I have to catch the train tomorrow morning, but this mustn't end. I think we both know that. It seems I have fallen in love with you, Margaret. In fact, I probably did so the first time we met. It's taken a while—a lot longer than I'd hoped—but now I believe you might feel the same way towards me. Am I mistaken?"

It took a moment to find her voice, but her response rang true. "No, Robert," she finally managed to say. "You are not mistaken."

A look of relief washed over his face, followed immediately by a loopy smile. "Please don't hesitate like that. You nearly gave me heart failure."

His features blurred slightly; no doubt caused by a tiny welling of tears in her eyes.

43

Butler stood on the station platform among dozens of soldiers—British, French, and American—a chattering, milling throng waiting for the early-morning train that would take them eastward toward the front.

Margaret had asked to accompany him to Gare de l'Est, but he had convinced her otherwise, preferring to say goodbye in a more private surrounding. Now, as he envied other soldiers embracing young ladies and sharing a few parting words, Butler wished he hadn't been so self-conscious. His strong aversion to public displays of affection had deprived him of her companionship and denied them rare moments, now lost forever. Belatedly, he realized that every minute with her was a treasured gift. He vowed never again to allow emotional insecurity to overshadow his feelings for her.

The train arrived and the huge locomotive hissed to a stop amidst billowing exhaust steam and the warm sooty aroma of burning coal. A quickly passing hailstorm of tiny cinders peppered the metal roof overhanging the platform. With one scheduled stop at Meaux, the train would travel the fifty-five miles from Paris to Chateau-Thierry in a little over two hours. Even with minor delays, he would arrive comfortably ahead of the noon deadline. While he looked forward to his new surgical duties, leaving Margaret had created much more than a restlessness of spirit—it had exposed an aching void in his life no other person could adequately fill. If he believed her, and he did without reservation, Margaret was no doubt experiencing the same sense of emptiness and loss. The realization that he had caused her similar distress made him feel worse.

He stepped aboard, found a seat near a partially opened window, stowed his luggage—a newly purchased brown leather suitcase to replace the one lost during that first artillery bombardment—and settled in. Fifteen minutes later the whistle sounded and the train jerked forward. Of all his journeys, great and small, none were gloomier than the one he was about to begin.

Two hours later the train arrived at Chateau-Thierry. There Butler discovered that the American advance had continued during his brief absence, taking the evacuation hospital with it.

A sergeant he didn't recognize now occupied what had been the adjutant's office.

"Evac Six moved out, Lootenant—the whole hospital, everything and everyone. They sent all the wounded to Meaux and then packed up and left, bag and baggage. Right now they're at Fere-en-Tardenois, a Frog village about twenty miles up the road."

"Twenty miles? How far have we advanced?"

The sergeant, a square-faced man about thirty years old, clamped a thin black cigar between yellow-stained teeth. "We occupy the towns of Bazoches and Fismes, just this side of the Vesle River."

"We've advanced that far?"

"Yep. We've kicked the Heinies back to where they wuz before their big drive to Paris. Word is, we're gonna rest a while before we push on."

"Rest? For how long?"

The sergeant shrugged. "Who knows?"

"When did the hospital move to… where did you say? Fere-en-Tardenois?"

"Yeah, that's the place. Saturday afternoon."

He had been with Margaret then, strolling along the Quai aux Fleurs, basking in the warm joy of her company. Now she was in a hotel less than sixty miles away, but could easily have been on another continent. With effort, he refocused his thoughts.

"I need to get up there, and quickly. Can you help me out?"

The sergeant puffed on his black cigar. "There's a convoy headed that way, Doc. Replacements mostly. It leaves in twenty minutes." He stood. "C'mon. I'll show you where they're loadin' up."

*

Butler pushed his plate aside and took a final sip of coffee.

"Now that you're finished with lunch, Robert, let's start with a quick tour of the place." Woody Peckham set knife and fork atop his empty plate and then spread his hands wide; a measured gesture encompassing the high-ceilinged interior of what might have been a storehouse. "This is our dining facility."

Butler smiled. "I already figured that out."

"Just checking. Paris nightlife has been known to addle the minds of the young and innocent."

"Is that so?"

"Oh, yes. Surely you know what I mean: free-flowing Champagne, the Follies, half-naked women dancing on tables…"

"I visited an art museum and Notre Dame Cathedral."

"Of course you did."

"In the company of a lovely young lady I intend to marry."

Peckham returned a knowing smile. "That is exactly what I meant. You have re-enacted the age-old story of the young soldier rushing off to fight a war in a strange foreign land; the tale of an innocent soul bewitched by a sloe-eyed, scantily-clad siren."

When Butler didn't respond, Peckham's eyes narrowed. "Oh, my God. You aren't joking, are you?"

Butler shook his head.

"Well then, who is she: a poor but beautiful Romanian exile of noble descent? Or have you fallen for an obscenely rich but not-so-beautiful Russian baroness eager to escape the clutches of vengeful Bolsheviks. Paris is lousy with displaced European nobility these days."

"Yes, so I've noticed."

Butler recalled his dinner with Margaret and Beatrice in Lutetia's opulent dining room. Primly segregated in tightly clustered groups, the grandly frocked nobility was out of place amidst those wearing more traditional attire. Yet, their masks of cultivated disdain could not conceal what Butler saw in their eyes: indignant befuddlement. Somehow, the war had created an outrageous situation; one that forced those of noble birth to share a dining room with *hoi polloi*—common people who had brazenly altered the centuries-old social status. What's more, they had done so without asking permission of their betters.

"Well, tell me about this woman who has obviously addled your senses."

"The lady in question is one I met on board the *Mongolia*."

"*Another* shipmate? What sort of floating glee club is the U.S. Navy operating these days?" Peckham raised his hand, cutting off Butler's response. "Never mind. I prefer to remain ignorant. Nevertheless, I can assure you that when your friend Jack Mayo and I find ourselves in Paris this weekend, we will *not* be visiting art museums, Notre Dame, or any other location even slightly tainted by European culture. I have a hunch young Mayo will have less refined diversions in mind."

Butler smiled. Woody Peckham didn't know it yet, but Jack had other ideas; plans involving a young lady, one who had also traveled aboard the 'glee club'. He was about to mention Beatrice, but then decided to remain silent. It would be more interesting if Woody discovered still another shipboard connection on his own. Thinking about it, Butler regretted he would not be there to see his friend's expression when Jack told him the news.

"You could be right, Woody. By the way, where is Jack billeted?"

Peckham's brows knitted slightly. "He decided not to stay."

"Not stay? What do you mean?"

"While you were meandering through the streets of Paris with your lady friend, Jack decided he preferred doing his old job out in the field."

"I don't understand."

"He didn't want to dig graves."

"What? Why was he digging graves?"

"Jack is an enlisted man, Robert. Back here, when enlisted orderlies are not busy helping surgeons, they do other tasks, like digging graves. Unfortunately, there are a lot to dig these days."

"Damn! That's my fault. I just don't think of Jack as an enlisted man. Nor did I ever imagine his duties might include grave digging."

"Neither did I. Anyway, Jack wanted to spend his time doing something more positive. He asked me if he could return to field duty. I spoke with Major Gregory, explained to him that Jack didn't mind arduous work, just *that* kind of work. Jack is a good man. I think the Major understood and let him go."

Butler pinched the bridge of his nose with a thumb and forefinger. He had tried to spare Jack from duty on the battlefield. Instead, he'd succeeded in putting the young man in a worse situation. Sometimes, the best laid plans—he looked up. "What about his weekend pass?"

"It's still on."

"Thank God." At least Jack would have the opportunity to spend time with Beatrice. He hadn't fouled that up. "I feel awful about this,

Woody."

"Don't blame yourself. I should have thought it through, but didn't. We were tired. Neither of us was thinking straight."

Their lack of foresight was distressingly obvious.

Peckham stood up. "Let's take that tour."

They stepped outside and approached the main building, a three-story affair constructed of gray limestone. A weathered bronze Latin cross stood atop a high steeple.

"What's the name of this place?"

"St. Crispin's Abbey. It used to be a Catholic monastery. The abbot and his monks had the good sense to abandon the place before the Germans arrived. The Heinies used it as a field headquarters. Now it's a hospital. After this is all over, I hope it becomes a quiet, peaceful monastery again."

"The sooner, the better."

"My thoughts exactly, Robert."

They went inside and climbed two flights of stairs to the top floor where a single door opened into a long, wide gallery. A thin wooden partition about eight feet high divided the room into two equal spaces. Natural light from a dozen windows, six on each wall, brightened the atmosphere. Each space contained about thirty iron cots in two rows separated by a center aisle—each neatly made up and covered with a brown Army blanket. There was enough room between cots to allow access to the patient by doctors, nurses, and orderlies. No more than a half-dozen patients occupied beds.

Woody turned to Butler. "To the left is Ward A. Ward B is to your right. These are our recovery wards. We have beds for sixty-four patients."

Butler noted the empty cots. "Why aren't there more patients?"

"We just got set up. Besides, this is an evacuation hospital, remember? After surgery and a day or so to recover, we send them off to base hospitals."

"Yes, of course."

Butler's train to Paris the previous Friday had contained three passenger cars rigged to carry stretchers. Satisfied with the abundance of nurses and orderlies, he had nonetheless made his presence known and then let his mind become fully occupied with how he might meet Margaret at the Lutetia.

Woody led the way down the same set of stairs. The second floor housed Operating Rooms 1 and 2, each separated by an aisle and fully enclosed by the same type of thin wooden partition material that delineated Wards A and B on the floor above.

Painted dazzling white, each OR contained three porcelain surgical tables covered by thin oilcloth mats, scrub sinks, an oil cook stove upon which sat a rectangular copper basin—doubtless used for sterilizing instruments—and an adjoining lavatory. The remaining second-floor space contained X-ray equipment, a patient preparation area, and a post-surgical recovery ward lined with a dozen or so cots.

The ground floor was now absent altar, pews, and other vestments. Nothing of a religious nature remained except stained glass windows depicting biblical scenes. Likewise partitioned, it served as an administrative and reception area for incoming patients. It also housed two smaller wards, D and E, used respectively for burn cases and soldiers temporarily blinded by chloroethyl sulfide, a yellow compound commonly referred to as mustard gas.

They stepped outside and Peckham led him down a gravel walkway toward a much smaller stone building.

As they crunched down the path, Butler said: "It's impressive, but I expected the operating rooms to be a lot busier."

"That's how it seems to go around here," Peckham replied. "It's either uncontrolled mayhem or, like now, peacefully quiet. I prefer the now."

"So, what do I do until mayhem arrives?"

"Get yourself settled in." He pointed a little distance ahead. "I'll show you where we put your stuff." Peckham smiled. "You're going to love this. Each member of the surgical staff now occupies a monk's cloister: a tiny room with just enough space for a single cot, footlocker, and a wooden chair. Appropriate, don't you think?"

"Compared to the field, it sounds luxurious."

"Yeah, I suppose you're right. Anyway, you've got a little time to spare. Major Gregory won't let you operate on your own until he's satisfied with your proficiency—specifically, combat injury surgical treatment and sanitation methods."

"Let me guess: wound debridement and the Carrel-Dakin procedure."

Peckham nodded. "I'm glad to see you haven't wasted all your time wallowing in French culture."

"There was a Colonel Dawes aboard ship. He devoted several lectures to new techniques, including debridement and Dakin tubes."

"Interesting. Do you have any practical experience along those lines?"

"There weren't many combat casualties aboard the *Mongolia*."

"That's what I thought. But have no fear, my friend. Major Gregory will soon attend to the practical aspects of your education."

Inside the smaller building, Peckham opened the door to a ground floor room. Early afternoon light poured through a tiny square window. Butler's new luggage rested on the floor beside a narrow cot.

"This is yours," Peckham said.

Butler unslung his musette bag and set it on the narrow bed. "I brought you something."

Tucked among personal items were two cylindrical objects wrapped in heavy brown paper. He removed both and handed one to

Peckham. "In payment for past considerations."

"Is that what I think it is?"

"If you think it's a bottle of Glenturret whiskey, then yes, it is. One for you and one for me."

"How did you manage to find it?"

"The Black Market has all sorts of interesting things for sale."

"Some of them illegal, no doubt."

"I didn't ask."

Peckham unwound the paper covering the cylinder and stared at the darkly tinted bottle. Then he looked at Butler and extended his hand.

"Forget all the bad things I said about you, Robert."

"It will be difficult, Woody, but I'll try." He removed the brown wrapping from his bottle and twisted the cap until the cork popped. "Do you suppose the good monks might have left behind a glass or two before they left?

"Let us pray they did," Woody replied.

44

Soon after finishing his welcome back drink with Woody Peckham, Butler left his new quarters and took loan of an idle ambulance. Following directions provided by a helpful driver, Butler drove to Chery-Chartreuve, a tiny village eight miles closer to the front. He was about to park near a ten-foot pole atop which fluttered a white flag embossed with a large red Geneva Cross, but then had second thoughts.

In addition to their use of poison gas, the Kaiser's army routinely bombed Allied aid stations. The German penchant for dropping explosive shells on wounded men was one reason so many Frenchmen considered Hun soldiers uncivilized brutes.

Butler parked some distance away and made a note to speak to whoever was now in charge about the risks associated with flying such a conspicuous banner from a flagpole.

He found Jack Mayo slouched on a faded sofa chair set beside a brown canvas tent—tunic open, eyes closed—apparently dozing. Butler stopped a few feet away, not wanting to awaken him. The chair had seen better days. Tufts of horsehair padding leaked from worn spots in the wide armrests.

Mayo opened his eyes, looked up and squinted.

"Is that all you've got to do?" Butler asked, moving closer.

Mayo smiled, rose to his feet, and began buttoning his tunic. The pleasant demeanor did not fool Butler. His young friend appeared quieter, more subdued than normal. Butler thought he understood why.

"Hello, Lieutenant."

"Relax, Jack. I have come not to scold but to apologize."

"Apologize? What for?" He continued with his buttoning.

"For placing you in a tough situation. I forgot how things are for enlisted men posted to rear areas. Digging graves and burying the dead wasn't what I had in mind when I requested your transfer."

"I know. It didn't occur to me, either."

"I wanted you to understand that."

"And I do, really. Forget it." He finished buttoning and met Butler's gaze. "So, did you manage to square things with Margaret?"

"Yes, I believe so."

"Good. How is Beatrice? Did she get my letters?"

Butler studied the young orderly. Mayo looked tired and drawn but his red-rimmed eyes reflected no animosity or hard feelings. Still, there was something else: an undertone of discomfort or apprehension. Butler decided not to press his concern.

"Beatrice is fine. She got all your letters and is eagerly awaiting your arrival."

"No kidding? Did she really say that?"

"She didn't have to. When I showed up without you, she looked ready to cry."

The exhaustion of an overworked and dispirited soldier drained from his face. He said: "Did she really?"

Butler nodded.

"I feel bad she was upset."

"Well, you can remedy that in a few more days."

A quick smile. "Say Lieutenant, did you ever notice the way Beatrice emphasizes certain words in a sentence?"

Butler had, and he nodded again. It was a vocal characteristic he found mildly annoying, an opinion he kept to himself.

"I love that about her," Mayo continued. The smile grew and his eyes glistened. Then he looked away, embarrassed. The smile faded.

"You were right, Jack. Margaret and Beatrice will be in Paris a lot longer than originally planned. They're even considering staying until this thing is over."

Mayo kept his gaze averted. Finally, he said: "Maybe we could all go back home on the same ship. Like when we came over here. Wouldn't that be something?"

"Yes, it would."

At that moment Butler felt closer to Jack Mayo than he had at any time during their brief association; a warm, familiar sense of brotherhood. Somehow they had become connected, not by blood but by something quite different. Instinctively he knew what Jack was feeling, understood the thoughts now flooding the younger man's mind.

Butler too had a powerful urge to abandon this terrible war, to forsake the daily revulsions, to purge those ghastly sights and sounds from his memory, to return to his own country and settle in a peaceful, sunny borough where he could begin a new life with Margaret. But he could not leave the here and now—not yet. To abandon soldiers who needed his surgical expertise was something he could never do, not again, regardless of the consequences. Like Jack, he had shared far too many horrors and walked too many hazardous miles with such men. He could not turn away from them, no matter how desperately he wanted to.

"I know how you feel, Jack."

Mayo turned to face him. "Do you?"

"Yes, I think so. God willing, I'm going to marry Margaret. I'd do it tomorrow if I could… and she would probably consent. But I would have to leave here first and that's not possible. I simply couldn't do it. I must stay until this thing is finished. Or until it finishes me. And so do you."

Mayo's eyes glazed and he stared through Butler.

Jack Mayo appeared to focus on a compelling vision that lay elsewhere—a revelation whose inevitability was beyond doubt. The young soldier had the look of a man who had stumbled upon an irrefutable truth, an overwhelming certitude beyond anyone's ability to refute.

Jack's eyes refocused and a strange look of acceptance settled in his eyes. He said, "Well then. It looks like we're stuck here for a while, Lieutenant."

"I am, for sure. And so are you—at least until Friday, anyway."

Mayo's entire demeanor relaxed at the prospect of seeing Beatrice again, and Butler saw a little of the young man's familiar good nature return. A half-hearted smile further lightened his expression, but the strange look in his eyes remained.

45

"Is that clock accurate?" Beatrice asked. "What time do you have?"

Margaret flicked her gaze toward the eight-day longcase timepiece standing in one corner of the hotel lobby, its lustrous walnut bulk flanked by potted palms. It was approaching four o'clock.

"Yes, it is. And it's ten minutes later than the last time you asked. Try to calm yourself."

"I *have* tried, but it's no use."

Margaret shared her sister's nervous anticipation. Their parents were probably mystified and upset by the reality of Michael's burial. They did not have the benefit of Margaret's experiences at the cemetery and again on the grounds of the hospital. Absent that strange insight, they would not understand why Michael had chosen to have his remains interred in France.

Learning of his marriage to Anna would worsen their sense of confusion and isolation. Even having the benefit of Anna's insight, Margaret could not yet understand why Michael acted as he had. Their exclusion from the happiest occasion of their son's life would baffle and further sadden the elder Jeromes.

How could she explain these things when she could not fully understand them herself? Margaret had no answers to the questions she knew would come.

A sense of inadequacy heightened her edgy mood. She tried to take some measure of comfort from her ignorance regarding Michael's private life. She was his fraternal twin and they had much in common, had once shared something of a spiritual bond. But each had their own unique mind, a private sense of self completely isolated from that of any other person. Clearly, Margaret had been presumptuous and more than a little foolish to believe she could discern her brother's deepest thoughts or feelings.

Obviously Michael had secrets—but so did Margaret—and she could no longer keep an unpleasant truth within herself. She had been terribly jealous of him, had wished for some way to lessen the magnitude of his presence in their lives; had secretly yearned for an opportunity to step away from his shadow. Then, like some fairy tale gone awry, her wish had come true: Michael was suddenly gone. Ironically, his unexpected passing had also extinguished the great light that had made the shadow possible.

If there was any chance for a life with Robert then she must first find a way to lessen the sense of shame that cluttered her emotions. Confession would help, but she could think of no remedy that would completely eradicate the wine-red stain of guilt.

Margaret sighed and forced her mind back to the present.

Her father had telephoned from Calais at noon; he and mother planned to arrive in Paris on the three o'clock train. Even allowing for luggage handling and travel time from the station, they should have been here by now. She had tried to gauge Mike Jerome's disposition, but his voice had sounded cordial and revealed little that might indicate his intentions. She had also spoken with her mother, but gleaned nothing of Emily Jerome's mood from their brief exchange. Margaret felt her insides quiver, but managed to conceal her nervousness.

"The train must be late," she observed.

Beatrice squirmed in her chair. "It would be, today of all days."

The tall, potbellied Comtoise timepiece struck four sonorous tones.

From her seat in the lobby Margaret had a view of Boulevard Raspail and the intersecting Rue de Sevres. When a taxi rolled to a stop near the door, the nervous quiver became an undulating wave. The driver opened the rear door and her father stepped out. He turned, extended his hand inside the automobile, and helped her mother to the sidewalk. Hotel staff immediately attended to luggage.

"They're here," she said.

Seven weeks had passed since Margaret last saw her parents. Emily Jerome, doubly sickened by news of Michael's death and her bout with influenza, looked healthier now. Her color much improved and she appeared fit and energetic. Mike Jerome looked like his old self: tall, ruddy complexioned and broad across the shoulders. There was no trace of the serious illness that had left him weak and bedridden. The name 'Big Mike', a sobriquet used by friends and employees, was clearly appropriate. Both in their early-fifties, her parents were a handsome and distinguished-looking couple. Margaret felt her lips curve into a smile.

They exchanged greetings and hugs inside the foyer. Their pleasant words and wide smiles further eased the fluttering inside Margaret's stomach. She sensed none of the resentment they had expressed upon her hasty departure.

"There is no need to register," Margaret said. "We've already taken care of that."

"How thoughtful," Emily remarked. "Thank you, dear."

"We're on the same floor, just down the hall from each other," Beatrice added.

"Excellent," Big Mike said.

"And you are just in time for afternoon tea," Margaret suggested.

"That is, if you're not too tired."

Emily turned to her husband. "I could do with a cup, dear. How about you?"

He turned to the nearest porter. "Please take our luggage upstairs."

"Would you like them to unpack for you?" Margaret asked.

"That would be nice," her mother replied.

Margaret gave instructions in French and the porters headed for the elevators, each richer by a franc.

"I'm impressed, Maggie," Mike said. "And repentant. Until now, I believed all those French lessons at Stephen's College were a waste of good money."

Margaret felt a warm familiar rush. Michael had often called her 'Mags', but no one dared address her as 'Maggie'. No one, that is, except her father. It was a term that made her feel special. She looked up at him. "Let's have our tea."

Big Mike took his wife's arm in his. "I presume," he said to Margaret as they strolled toward the lounge, "this fine hotel offers liquid refreshments other than tea?"

"Maybe not the brand you're accustomed to, Father. But I could suggest an acceptable substitute."

"Is that so?" he replied. "How intriguing."

A few minutes later, with everyone seated around a table, Mike Jerome sniffed the glass of amber whiskey to which he had added a small amount of water. He took a sip and then nodded appreciatively. He looked at Margaret and raised an eyebrow. "I'm surprised... and curious. How did you come to know so much about whiskey?"

Margaret shrugged. "Oh, one hears things."

"A gentleman friend of hers drinks this brand," Beatrice volunteered, a satisfied smile on her face. "In moderation, of course."

"Is that so?" her father replied. "Now I'm even more curious."

"What gentleman friend?" Emily asked, sipping her tea.

"I thought you wanted to learn more about Michael's situation. Isn't that why you're here?" Margaret answered.

"Of course we want that, my dear," Emily said, patting Margaret gently on the forearm. "Your father and I have hardly spoken of anything else since your letter. We understand what must be done and we will talk about Michael soon enough."

A shadow danced across her mother's face at the mention of Michael's name, a fleeting expression quickly erased by a tiny smile. Margaret realized her mother was still in mourning. They all were, really, but there was a reluctance to discuss the persistent melancholy that clouded their lives. It was a characteristic Margaret understood. The Irish tended to suffer personal grief in silence, so her family saw no need to express aloud the deep sense of loss everyone felt but kept inside.

Emily Jerome continued: "But right now, let's talk about something else. Tell us about your gentleman friend."

Margaret glared at Beatrice. "Perhaps we should discuss your gentleman friend, as well."

Emily eyed her youngest daughter. "Oh? Is this true?"

The rising flush in Beatrice's cheeks answered her mother's question.

"Well now," Mike said to his wife. "It seems to me we have arrived in the nick of time."

"I certainly hope so," her mother remarked. A small twinkle flickered in her eyes, erasing for a moment the sadness that had taken root there.

Margaret found it difficult to conceal her discomfiture. She had not expected the discussion to begin with an explanation of her relationship with Robert. Thanks to Beatrice however, that's exactly where the conversation appeared to be going. She had hoped to introduce the subject gradually but that was no longer an option.

Her mother's face reflected gentle understanding. She looked first at Beatrice then settled on Margaret. "Seriously, I have no concerns regarding either of your behaviors. But, like your father, I too am curious. Who is this young man, Margaret? Tell us, please."

Margaret, seeing no alternative, sighed. "His name is Robert Butler."

"Butler?" Her father's brow wrinkled slightly. "English or Irish?"

"American."

"You know what I mean, Maggie dear. Where did his family come from?"

"Rochester, New York."

Mike Jerome stared at her for a long moment. "I see."

"He is a handsome Irishman, I think," Beatrice piped in, an obvious effort to keep the conversation focused on her older sister.

"Please go on, Margaret," her mother said. She cast a warning look at her husband.

"Robert is a surgeon. We met on the voyage over. He volunteered to serve in the Army, but intends to resume his practice when the war ends. At this moment he is assigned to a hospital at Chateau-Thierry, about sixty miles from here."

"Is the war that near?" Mike Jerome asked.

"Not quite. Hospitals are several miles farther back from the front line."

"That's still close," her father observed.

"An Army surgeon." Emily Jerome remarked. "How interesting. Is there more?"

Margaret, seeing no alternative, began to speak. Once started, she found it easy to continue. Words tumbled from her mouth, almost without effort. She described how they had first met, exchanged letters, and then spent time together this past weekend. Before she knew it, Margaret had completely revealed her feelings for him, not exactly in words, but by her manner and the tone of her voice. Belatedly, she realized her family now knew far more about her feelings for Robert than she had intended to share.

"He sounds like a nice young man," her mother remarked. "When do you suppose we can meet him?"

"I'm not sure. It depends on how many casualties there are."

"Yes, of course."

"While we're on the subject," Margaret began, "I wanted to talk to both of you about what I plan to do."

Emily Jerome raised an eyebrow. "Plan to do about what, my dear?"

"My situation. I've decided to remain in Paris until the war is over."

Margaret had been thinking about staying ever since Robert confessed his feelings for her at the Jardin de Tuileries. His open admission about how he felt had started the process in her mind. That she would even consider such a possibility arose unexpectedly. An earlier discussion with Beatrice, a breakfast conversation about Michael not wanting to live his life as others expected, had triggered a deep self-examination of her own attitudes and expectations. What she discovered had surprised and disappointed her.

Although respectful of tradition, Margaret had always considered herself an independent thinker, one who set her own course and followed where her mind led. What she had recently discovered about herself was something quite different. Her strong opinions regarding social inequality notwithstanding, Margaret realized she was quite conventional. In fact, she and Michael shared a strong sense of obligation. Both did what the family expected, each apparently following a predetermined course much like a planet is slave to the unwavering trajectory dictated by velocity and gravity. It was a difficult fact to acknowledge and a less honest person might have rationalized such acquiescent behavior. Margaret, however, could not. Self-delusion was merely a trick one played on oneself.

"Have you now?" her father asked.

"Yes, I want to spend as much time with Robert as I can."

Now that the idea was out in the open, it didn't seem as outrageous as she had first thought. In fact, doing otherwise made no sense whatsoever.

Her mother said: "You hardly know the gentleman, dear. Have you thought this through?"

"Yes, I have. Perhaps not as completely as you might like, but it's something I feel strongly about."

Margaret met her father's gaze. His silence was puzzling. She had expected much more resistance from him. Instead, he nodded slightly, gave her a tiny smile, and took an easy sip of his whiskey.

After a moment Big Mike broke the silence. "Will you be staying here, in the hotel?"

She tried to conceal her astonishment. Mike Jerome, without quarrel or objection, had accepted her decision. His response was unanticipated and it caught her by surprise.

As she puzzled over her father's reaction, Margaret felt a sense of time gone by. A listless inner clock had tolled a fateful chord—one long, reverberating chime announcing a change of seasons. With it came realization that she was no longer a child, safe and protected and subject to the wishes of her parents. Adolescence, immaturity, and dependence had quietly passed by, much as Michael had slipped away, leaving in its place a solitary soul—herself. At that moment Margaret knew she had come of age—had become a grown woman responsible for her own life. It was an instant of perfect comprehension; a moment of wonder and melancholy beyond anything she had ever experienced.

With what sounded like a new voice, Margaret answered her father's question. "Yes, I suppose so."

"What will you do with your time, Maggie?" he continued. "It may be weeks and weeks between visits. Won't you be bored, doing nothing all day?"

"Not really, Father. Beatrice and I have been spending our days doing volunteer work at the American hospital. I plan to continue."

"This is the first I've heard about that," Emily admitted. "When did this happen and what sort of volunteer work?"

"We've been helping out for two weeks or so. We roll bandages, help clean up after surgeries, and read to wounded soldiers."

"My, my. You are full of surprises, aren't you?"

Margaret wanted to tell her mother the surprises were not over, but held her tongue. There would be time enough for that later.

Emily spoke to her youngest child. "What about you, Beatrice? Do you also have surprises for us?"

Beatrice appeared to be in a state of shock, probably due to Margaret's sudden announcement to remain in Paris, a decision not shared with her sister. "Uh, no, Mother. Not really."

"What about the young man Margaret mentioned earlier?"

"His name is Jack Mayo," Margaret said, smiling sweetly at her sister. "She met him about the same time I met Robert."

"Mayo," her father repeated. "Your great-grandmother was a Mayo. Is he a surgeon too?"

"No," Beatrice answered, regaining her composure. "He delayed his fourth year of college to join the Army. He's serving as a medical orderly. We've exchanged letters, but we haven't spoken since he left for duty at the front."

Emily said: "I take it then you have no plans to remain in Paris... to keep your sister company?"

"No, I suppose not. But I really haven't thought about it."

Beatrice speared Margaret with a glance. "This is the first I've heard about such plans."

Margaret ignored the comment and studied her father. Mike Jerome did not look upset or displeased, but rather someone who had accepted established fact. His reaction aroused her curiosity.

"Father, how do you feel about me staying on for a while?" she asked.

He took another sip of his whiskey before answering. "Well Maggie, it's like this: I feel like a man who has just discovered that his offspring are no longer children but rather adults with minds and plans of their own. That the world is changing, and I am not sure what to make of it. And, with Michael gone and you about to leave, I find myself contemplating a future much different than one I had always imagined."

Margaret felt a warm rush of love for her father. Instinctively she understood what he was experiencing. First, he had lost the only son he would ever have in a European war he did not support. Next, the oldest of his baby girls had magically sped through diapers and dolls and silly school plays. The cuddly daughter of memory had stepped behind a velvet curtain and re-emerged a grown woman. In a flickering moment of inattention, the future became the present. Staring into his gentle blue eyes, Margaret wondered how she would feel when, God willing, the time came to let her own children go.

Big Mike finished his whiskey with a gentlemanly flourish. "And," he said, staring at his empty glass, "I am also thinking I should have another one of these."

Margaret covered her mouth and chuckled softly. As their eyes met, Mike Jerome smiled and uttered a small harrumph.

"I'm glad you two find this so amusing," Emily said. The tone of her voice belied the beginnings of another twinkle at the corner of her eyes. "Perhaps we should all stay in Paris. Make it a family affair."

Mike turned to his wife. "You may remain for as long as you like, my dear. I shall stay a while longer, do what we came here to do, and then go home. Despite persistent rumors, our company will not run itself."

Then his voice changed and his expression became serious. "Maggie, how long do you think it will take to settle our business regarding Michael?"

Margaret sipped her tea, not from thirst but rather to buy time while she formed a careful response. By 'settle our business' Margaret knew her father meant exhuming Michael's casket and re-interring his remains in the family cemetery. The plan, once appropriate and logical, now felt wrong...and disrespectful. Her sense of connection to Michael rose again. Was he pleading from beyond the grave?

No, that wasn't exactly how it felt.

Margaret had attempted to vocalize what she had experienced with such clarity. Turning it over in her mind she had come to believe that what she had felt was *comfort*—a feeling of *rightness*, of *belonging*.

It was difficult for Margaret to accept, but Michael did indeed belong among those with whom he had once shared a unique kinship. The prospect of exhuming his remains from that lovely serene place was abhorrent; an event she could not allow to happen.

Maintaining her composure she said: "I'm not sure. There are some things you should know about Michael before you decide on a course of action."

"If you mean his joining the Army and earning medals, then your mother and I have already discussed that. It hasn't changed our minds. Michael's final resting place belongs near his family, not amongst strangers in a foreign land far from home. I'm surprised you'd even question such a thing."

Margaret expected the firm pronouncement. Still…

"I understand how you feel, believe me, I do. But this is much more complicated than what I wrote about. Beatrice and I have made unexpected discoveries, and a public hotel lounge is not the place to discuss personal family affairs. We need a measure of privacy. I suggest we go upstairs to our suite."

"Privacy? That sounds ominous," Emily said. "Or are you merely being dramatic?" A wary look crept across her face, mixing with that aura of sadness Margaret had noted upon their arrival.

"It is neither…or both. I just think you should hear what else we've discovered about Michael—in private."

"If you're trying to upset us, then you are succeeding." Her mother did not look pleased.

"I'm sorry, Mother. That was never my intent."

Emily Jerome's expression softened. "Of course it wasn't."

All right then," Big Mike said. "I suppose we should do as Maggie suggests. Let's go up to our rooms." He rose to his feet quickly, a gesture hinting of a man having difficulty controlling his patience. "If she believes we need to discuss this further, then let's get on with it."

46

At Margaret's request, hotel staff had arranged their sitting room so that four people could sit on facing sofas separated by a low table that now contained the items Anna had given to her and Beatrice. As they took seats, her parent's attention seemed to focus on the colorful ribbons fixed above the left front pocket of Michael's neatly folded uniform tunic.

"I'll begin by explaining Michael's transition from civilian to a military officer." Margaret quickly related the circumstances of how the American Field Service, a humanitarian endeavor comprised of volunteer civilian ambulance drivers, had transitioned to become a part of the American Expeditionary Forces when the United State entered the war in the spring of 1917.

"Then," she continued, "given his education and responsibilities, the AEF offered Michael a temporary commission, which he accepted, with the understanding he could continue to serve in the same capacity as he had since coming to France. Apparently, Michael was acquainted with many French soldiers—one in particular, a close friend who died—and wished to continue serving with French units."

Margaret paused, realizing the need for a more detailed explanation. "I don't think the word 'acquaintant' is quite accurate. Those French soldiers were much more than that. Michael had shared their experiences and suffered their wounds. Together, they endured

349

horrors I cannot begin to imagine or describe. What I'm trying to say is this: The experience of war had transformed them. They and he became brothers, men who shared a fraternal bond no less compelling than birth or blood."

Mike Jerome grimaced but said nothing.

Trying to describe the unexplainable had caused Margaret's heartbeat to increase. She took a moment to settle herself and then spoke about the three medals along with the significance of each decoration including Michael's rank as a Knight of the Legion of Honor. "They carved those words into the cross on his grave," she said. "I'm told it's customary. You will see it when we visit Suresnes."

As she continued to explain the other two awards, her mother's eyes began to fill once more. Mike Jerome's expression was a kaleidoscope that flickered between sadness, pride, consternation, and bewilderment. Beatrice remained silent, her eyes shifting from one parent to the other as Margaret spoke.

"And now we come to this," Margaret said. She handed each of her parents a copy of the leather-bound book Anna had printed for each of them.

"What do we have here?" her father asked, taking the slim volume.

"This is Michael's journal."

"Michael kept a journal?" Emily Jerome examined the embossed leather front and then opened the book to Michael's photograph. She stared at the likeness of her dead son, gently touching his image with her fingertips. Then she began to read the biography.

Her father did likewise, his brow wrinkled.

"What a wonderful memento," her mother said, not looking up, her voice hardly more than a whisper. "Where did this come from?"

Margaret took a deep breath and let it out slowly. "That is the most difficult part of what I have to tell you. I cannot explain the why of it, but I can tell you what I've been told by others."

Neither of her parents had lifted their eyes from the journals they held. Noting the movement of their eyes across the page, it was clear they were engrossed in reading Michael's words and probably had not heard the answer to her mother's question. Margaret leaned back on the sofa and waited.

After several minutes, Emily looked up. "I would like to read this now if I may. It shouldn't take long. Do you mind?"

"No, of course not. There's no hurry. It will probably help explain things."

Initially, it had taken Margaret less than an hour to read the entire journal. Sitting there watching her parents, Margaret felt a small sense of relief. It was better for them to learn about Anna through Michael's own words rather than from a second-hand telling. His journal did not mention the wedding specifically, only that he had asked Anna to marry him, and her acceptance. At least the subject of love and marriage would not come as a complete surprise.

Nevertheless, learning of their exclusion from Michael's wedding ceremony would deeply sadden both of them. The journal might give them a better insight into how the war might have changed Michael's normally convivial outlook. Margaret *thought* she understood—part of it anyway. But, like her attempted explanation about Michael's sense of brotherhood with French soldiers, it wasn't something she could easily put into words. Instead, what she felt was more like a haunting sense of her brother's discordant state of mind; an emotional stew of love, anger, frustration and guilt—an alchemy of sensations resulting in a mood neither he nor she could clearly explain.

As they continued reading the journal, Margaret tried to judge her parent's reaction by observing their facial expressions. She was marginally successful. Except for an occasional smile, frown or wrinkled brow, her parents gave little clue as to what they might be thinking or how they felt.

Beatrice had taken her book and was likewise occupied, probably more to pass the time than anything else. It was not a bad idea. Margaret picked up her copy from the small table and joined the quiet threesome. She was just beyond the halfway point when her mother interrupted the silence.

"I presume Michael's friend Anna had these books made."

Margaret looked up. Both her parents had finished reading, their eyes fixed on hers. She set her copy aside. "Yes, she did."

"That was a thoughtful gesture. I'm looking forward to meeting her. However, I have a question. What happened to the original, the journal written in Michael's own hand?"

"Anna has it."

Perhaps something in Margaret's tone caused her mother to tense slightly. Emily said, "As Michael's fiancé, shall I presume that Anna intends to keep it?"

"Yes, you may. But Anna was more than Michael's fiancé. They were married on the first day of June. Anna was Michael's wife— now she is Michael's widow."

"*What...?!*" Her father stood abruptly, arms at his side, hands balled into fists, his expression one of helpless exasperation. "Wife? Widow? You can't be serious. Who is this woman?" He stopped and his expression changed, apparently realizing an unpleasant possibility. "Did he *have* to marry her? Is *that* what you're trying to tell us?"

Margaret shook her head. "No, I don't believe that was the case."

"Then how could he have done such a thing without telling us about it?"

"I don't know, Father. I simply don't know." She wrung her

hands, shifted her gaze, and concentrated on her mother's reaction.

Emily's expression reminded Margaret of a department store manikin, its pale, waxen features fixed for all time. Her mother's blue eyes, now glazed, stared into the middle distance halfway between herself and the curtained window opposite. Then Emily shook her head, a mother denying an unpleasant thought about a loved child, but remained silent.

"I am so sorry," Margaret said, reaching out and grasping her mother's hand. "I don't know what to say."

Her father began pacing—quick, agitated strides back and forth across the room. After a moment he stopped, a look of painful empathy on his face. Then he sat and put a muscular arm around his wife. His expression softened to one of gentle compassion.

"I am truly sorry too, Em. And I'm quite certain Michael acted as he did to spite me. I should have paid more attention to what he wanted and preached less about what I thought was right for him. This is not Michael's fault, not entirely—it's mine as well."

Long moments passed in silence. Then Emily turned and gave her husband a sad smile. She freed herself from Margaret's grasp and then patted her husband gently on the knee. "Nonsense," she said. "Michael was a grown man. You read his journal. He fell in love and got married. Not telling us was something he truly regretted. He wrote it so himself. As far as those other things, becoming a soldier in the Army probably made little difference to him. His work did not change so he probably didn't give it much thought."

"And the medals?" Big Mike asked.

"Telling us about how he earned those decorations would have seemed like bragging. He was never a boastful sort."

"True, and it's gracious of you to remind us of that, Em, but I'm not buying it. Our son was angry with me for keeping him on such a tight leash, for not paying more attention to his own interests. My single-minded insistence that he take over the business I started is the cause for his contrariness. That is plain and simple enough for anyone to understand."

"There might be some small truth in what you say, my dear, but I'm comfortable believing as I do about the Army and his medals. Besides, I think Michael had another, far more compelling reason for marrying so quickly."

Margaret responded to her mother's veiled implication. "I don't believe he got Anna pregnant. She would have told Beatrice and me. I'm sure of it. Besides, we saw no evidence of pregnancy."

"That is not what I had in mind."

"Oh? What did you have in mind, Em?"

Emily Jerome opened the journal and turned to a page near the back.

"Listen to this," she said. "It's dated Wednesday, May 8, this year.

The loss of Montdidier to General von Hutier's Eighteenth Army left me with a feeling of impending doom, as though we were about to lose the war. Dread clings to me with stubborn persistence. I have been here too long. This ugly war has robbed me of youthful optimism."

She turned several pages. "This entry is dated a week later, May 14. *The dread I felt last week has become a monotonous melancholy. I should speak to Anna about it but I fear alarming her with what is probably nothing more than a symptom of mental exhaustion."*

She turned another page.

"A week after that, Michael wrote this: *Sometimes God or fate offers a clue regarding future events. More often than not we are too ignorant to understand their significance. Worse yet, we realize what those clues are trying to reveal but deliberately choose to ignore their meaning, hoping to avoid the inevitable. I shall not."*

Emily closed the journal and looked at Margaret. "You said Michael and Anna were married on June the first, did you not?"

"Yes, that's what Anna told me."

"Well, don't you see it?"

"See what? I'm not sure what you're seeing, Mother."

"Did you read his journal?"

"Yes, every word."

"In the passage I just recited, what do you suppose Michael was trying to say?"

As Margaret was considering her answer, Beatrice spoke up. "He was afraid we were going to lose the war. He even admitted such."

Margaret said: "That's what I thought, too."

Emily smiled that sad smile of hers and then shook her head, disappointed by their reply. "Then you missed what was really on his mind."

"What was that, Em?" Mike Jerome's voice was unnaturally soft, almost a murmur.

"I believe Michael knew something awful was going to happen— that he didn't have much time left to live. On June the first, less than two weeks after he wrote that entry, he and Anna were married. He died a few weeks later, on the twenty-fifth."

Mike Jerome sighed. "I understand what you're trying to do, Em. But that doesn't explain why he didn't write and tell us about how he felt or what he planned on doing."

"What would you expect him to say? 'Dear Mother, I think I'm going to die soon, so I'm going to marry the woman I love before that happens. Sorry about the short notice. Love, Michael.'"

"I don't know, Em. I just don't know."

"Then listen to this, please. It takes two weeks for a letter to travel from France to America. How long did it take you to arrange our passage to France?"

"About two weeks the first time, a bit longer this time around."

"So, that's two weeks for Michael's letter to arrive plus two more weeks for us to book passage. Add to that another ten or eleven days for the voyage, plus a few more days to meet Anna's parents. That's two months, under ideal conditions. Michael didn't have that much time and I think he realized that."

Margaret studied each parent. As they spoke she wondered if Emily Jerome, nee Patrick, was creating an illusion to help ease the sorrowful burden now pressing upon her heart. It was certainly understandable. Michael's unexplainable conduct might have been a puzzle, but he was her son—the bearer of both family names—and what her mother put forth as a hidden truth was certainly possible.

Try as she might, Margaret could find no flaw in Emily Jerome's reasoning about the time line. However, it made little difference. Michael was dead. What he may or may not have felt or intended was beyond anyone's ability to prove or disprove. Each of them could make whatever assumptions they chose and each could feel comfortable in the rightness of their inarguable position. It was, she thought, a perversely perfect state of affairs.

"I need some time to think that through," Mike said. "Either way, it's not something we can settle one way or the other."

And that was the crux of it. If it gave Emily Jerome a measure of comfort to believe as she did, then Margaret was prepared to accept it as well. Everyone had suffered enough. Even Michael. It was much easier to retain a pleasant memory rather than admonish each other over actions and events that nobody could completely understand or change.

Mike Jerome said to Margaret: "What do you suppose was the great secret Michael wrote about in his journal?"

"I asked Anna about that. She thinks it was something Michael could have experienced on the battlefield—something he might have done, probably under stress—an event that left him ashamed."

Her father nodded. "That sounds like Michael. Everything he did had to be perfect, or close to it. Unfortunately, war has but one perfection: the flawless ability to inflict pain and death with absolute impartiality."

"No matter," her mother said, not looking up from the closed journal in her hands. "What's done is done." She rubbed her fingers across the fine leather. "This is a lovely memento. I shall cherish it always." Then she looked at Margaret, her eyes glistening. "I must tell Anna how much this means to me. When can we meet?"

Margaret took a deep breath. Somehow, they had crossed a great chasm together and the queasiness she had experienced earlier gradually eased. However, one more significant issue remained: the matter of Michael's final resting place. She hesitated to bring it up now—to add further emotional turmoil to what both Mike and Emily doubtlessly felt. Better to address it now rather than put them through another session like this one.

"We can meet with Anna tomorrow, or the day after if you like. She will adjust her schedule to suit yours."

Big Mike said: "By schedule, I assume she's employed?"

"Yes. Anna is a fully qualified nurse, but doesn't really need to work. She has duties at the American hospital at Neuilly. That's where she first met Michael. It was her idea that Beatrice and I pass the time by volunteering to help with the wounded."

"Perhaps we could meet tomorrow then," her mother said.

"I'll telephone Anna as soon as we're finished here."

"Is there anything else we need to discuss?" her father asked.

"Yes." Margaret met her father's gaze squarely. "There still remains the issue of Michael's Last Will and Testament. We discovered it's a codicil—an amendment—not really a new will. It has three provisions: two regarding disposition of his monthly income and the other his desire for interment among the soldiers with whom he served. I obtained a certified copy from Colonel Andrews." She took the two pages given to her by Michael's commanding officer and handed them to her father. "You should read this. I don't think you will object to how Michael allocated a portion of his income, but his instructions regarding burial are quite clear and explicit."

Big Mike seemed reluctant to take the codicil, as though the act of acceptance would commit him to a course of action he did not wish to take. He sat for a moment, unmoving, big hands resting on his knees. Then he said: "Michael belongs with his own kind. There's nothing more to discuss."

"He *is* with his own kind," Margaret told him.

Her father's eyes flashed. "You mean to tell me he'd rather be buried amongst a bunch of strangers than with his own family?" His complexion began to redden once more. "I refuse to believe that."

"They are not strangers, not to him—they're soldiers, comrades, and friends. And I would not be surprised if Michael thought of them as his brothers."

Mike frowned, confronted with the possibility of an unpleasant truth. There was more, but Margaret had difficulty reading the flurry of emotions in her father's face. Finally, he leaned forward and took the codicil.

Margaret continued. "Michael was of legal age and a commissioned military officer. He filed copies with the AEF judge advocate, the American Embassy, and the French government. I've been told the language provides no opportunity for challenge. Nor are his last wishes ambiguous. Father, it pains me to say this, but we should honor his final request. It is what he wanted, and we should leave him be."

Mike Jerome shook his head. "I cannot accept that. There's

always a way around an obstacle if one looks hard enough. When I read your cable about Michael's burial, I made arrangements to talk with William Sharp, the American Ambassador to France. Lord knows, I've donated enough money to Wilson's Democratic Party to earn a dozen presidential favors. Burying Michael in this country was a huge mistake and I intend to set it right."

An icy stab of apprehension left her breathless. It was a much worse response than she had expected. There was no doubt in her mind that Mike Jerome could exact such a favor; nor was there any doubt such would be granted. The political risk was practically non-existent. No politician would dare oppose such a thing. Returning the body of a decorated American soldier to his family for a hero's burial in their hometown would garner public kudos not criticism. Margaret dreaded challenging her father, but the haunting sense of rightful purpose refused to yield.

Before Margaret could respond, Emily spoke. "Where is this place, the one you mentioned earlier? I mean, where Michael is buried."

Margaret took a deep breath, forcing herself to be calm. "The cemetery is located in Suresnes," Margaret answered, "on a hill called Mount Valerian. It's not far from the hospital where Beatrice and I volunteer."

"How long would it take us to get there?"

"A half hour or so. But it's getting late and you both look tired. Let's plan to go first thing tomorrow morning. Afterwards, we can meet with Anna."

Her mother nodded, and then said, "I would like our first visit to Michael's grave to be private. Do you suppose Anna would take offense?"

"No, of course not."

Her parents rose from their seats, getting to their feet almost simultaneously. They looked much more fatigued than when they had arrived two hours ago. Margaret felt an unutterable rush of sadness, an unwelcome sense of growing older and wiser. She embraced first her mother, then her father.

"I'm sorry about all this, really I am."

"Nonsense, Maggie. You told us what we needed to hear. Never be ashamed of doing what must be done. That sort of courage is what separates the strong from everyone else." He looked at his wife. "Shall we go to our rooms?"

Emily Jerome nodded.

After her parents left, Margaret plopped back onto the sofa and uttered a long sigh. The meeting she had dreaded was behind her but she did not feel any great sense of relief. The worst, she believed, was yet to come. As she sat pondering how to communicate to her father what she had experienced, Beatrice spoke.

"I'm glad that's over with," she said. "I'm worn out."

Margaret turned and stared at her sister. Other than commenting once on Michael's journal, Beatrice had remained unusually quiet since tea in the Lutetia's dining room, leaving Margaret to carry the discussion and answer questions—or make the attempt.

"It's not over with, Beatrice," she replied. "I'm afraid it's just starting."

47

Standing beside Michael's grave and reading his name etched into a white cross was ultimate proof that his presence was gone forever. Never again would they hear his voice or feel the warmth of his touch.

Emily Jerome cried softly into a white silk handkerchief as did Beatrice. Margaret, her eyes near to overflowing, was not surprised by their tears. What did surprise her was Mike Jerome's reaction.

She had never seen her father weep. Yet, on that peaceful hillside, his face a mask of indescribable sorrow, Margaret saw him knuckle away silent tears, a mournful flow that eventually stopped but might never end.

A while later as they made their way toward the waiting carriage, her father finally broke his silence. "This is not what I expected."

"What do you mean?" Margaret asked.

"Well, every grave looks the same. There are no statues or other monuments like in other cemeteries, just all those white crosses. Most of them are new, indistinguishable from one another. It's like the dead belonged to the same family—close relatives who passed away at the same time, the result of some unspeakable tragedy." He paused for a moment. "In a way I suppose that's exactly what happened to them."

"Yes," Emily added, "and it's much more dignified than I imagined."

"That it is," Mike agreed.

He exchanged a long glance with Margaret. Was there something different in his expression? What might her parents have discussed last evening after they had returned to their suite? Given her father's plan to contact Ambassador Sharp, was it possible they were now having second thoughts about removing Michael from this special place?

By the time they arrived at Anna's for tea and lunch, everyone had regained somewhat more control over their emotions.

"I want to thank you for returning Michael's uniform and medals, and especially for what you did with Michael's journal," Emily Jerome said, following introductions. "They are mementos we will always treasure."

"It was my honor to do so," Anna replied.

"Do you think we might discuss the journal? You could help us understand some of what Michael wrote."

"I shall do my best."

Sitting together in Anna's parlor, Margaret listened quietly as her parents and Anna talked their way through Michael's original journal, sometimes page by page, sometimes finding answers to their questions, sometimes not.

The passages that remained unclear, including the thing Michael called his 'great unholy secret', was a topic Anna tried hard to explain. "It was the second wound," she told them. "His behavior changed a short while following that. As we have read, Michael was depressed over the death of his friend Aubray, and he anguished over not attending the funeral. In fact, he expressed guilt for not paying last respects... for abandoning his friend." She shrugged. "Perhaps it was that; perhaps not. It was a thing he would not discuss."

"Whatever it was," Emily Jerome suggested, "no doubt it was an awful experience, one that caused him a great deal of consternation.

Did you notice how his handwriting changed?" Emily remarked. "The entries before February of this year were written in his normal script. However, his handwriting became cramped and less flowing afterwards."

"I noticed that too," Anna said.

"Nevertheless," Emily continued, "I believe whatever happened to him probably wasn't as bad as Michael led himself to believe."

"That makes sense to me," Mike Jerome added. "We will never know what actually caused him such torment but Michael always demanded a great deal from himself. Sometimes he made too much of too little. I have a sense Michael might have done the same with this—secret—if indeed it was."

Emily Jerome nodded silent agreement.

That seemed to settle the issue; and as far as Margaret was concerned, that was fine. She was tired of secrets—including her own. If her parents were satisfied then that was good enough for her.

"Thank you so much for your patience," Emily said to Anna.

"Not at all."

They sat for a moment, then Emily again spoke to Anna. "The cemetery is far lovelier than I had imagined. Margaret told me a little of its history and what Napoleon once planned for it. Can you tell me a little about Michael's funeral service?"

Anna did not respond immediately. Then she looked up from her tea and began to speak

"It was a beautiful ceremony, a dignified funeral procession befitting a Chevalier in the Legion of Honor."

"Please tell us about it," Mike Jerome suggested.

"Of course." Anna set her teacup aside before she spoke again. "On the day we buried Michael, dozens of us gathered at the foot of Mont Valerian—friends, fellow soldiers—even a few of those Michael had rescued from the battlefield. It was early morning and the sky was without clouds.

"First in line was a French soldier leading a black stallion. The horse with no rider pulled a caisson. Strapped to the caisson was Michael's coffin, draped in a French flag. Moving slowly, they led us up the hill. A troop of soldiers and a small brass band followed as did I and his many friends—French and Americans mixed together— they wearing their best uniforms, my family and I in black, all of us on foot.

"At the cemetery soldiers arranged the coffin properly over the grave. Then Bishop Lemieux conducted the Rite of Committal. After prayer, the band played *La Marseillaise* and *Aux Champs*."

"*Aux Champs?*" Emily Jerome asked. "I know the French national anthem but I've never heard of… what was that again? *Aux Champs?*"

"Ah," Anna said. "My apologies. The full name is *Le tambour bat aux champs*—it means 'the drum beats in the field'. It is a mournful song, one played for soldiers who have died on the field of battle."

Drumbeats in the field. The phrase conjured an image of a lone drummer slowly marching between endless rows of white crosses. The vision sent a tremor of sadness through Margaret.

Emily Jerome sat there for a moment, staring at her tea. Then she looked up. "Thank you, Anna. And it is I who should apologize for interrupting. Please go on."

Anna continued. "After the music, six soldiers—three Frenchmen and three Americans—fired rifles over his coffin. Then an American soldier played Taps on a coronet. Finally, a military officer from each of our countries gave me a folded flag. I have both but you may have the one presented by the American."

"Thank you," Emily said. "I would like that."

As Anna continued, Margaret pictured the scene in her mind. It was the first description she had heard of Michael's funeral service. Why she had not asked about it earlier was a mystery to her. Then, as she thought about it, Margaret knew the answer. Until today, until she saw her father's tears, the reality of her brother's death had been a fact she could not fully acknowledge.

"We said a final prayer," Anna concluded, "and then it was done."

Big Mike sipped tea. In his huge hands the delicate cup and saucer looked like toys from a child's play set. He turned to his wife. "It sounds like a grand ceremony, Em. I'm sorry we missed it."

Her mother's lips turned up in a sad, reflective smile and her eyes took on a faraway look.

In her mind, Margaret could see and hear the ancient ceremony: young men in crisp uniforms—French blue and American brown— the clop of hooves on cobblestone, the solemn prayers uttered in Latin, the rifle volley echoing in clear morning air.

After a moment Emily turned to her husband. "So am I."

Her parents continued to stare into each other's eyes, seemingly afraid to say what might be on their minds.

"All the crosses are wooden," Anna told them. "But I have heard that each will be replaced by one of stone after the war. Stone is better, I think."

"Yes," Big Mike agreed. "Stone is much better. We shall have a proper stone marker when Michael is re-settled in the family plot back home. Don't you agree, Em?"

Hearing Mike Jerome's comment caused Anna's eyes to grow wide. She looked at Margaret, a question forming across her face.

Margaret gave Anna a quick shake of her head. *I'll tell you about this later*, she wanted to say. Thankfully, Anna seemed to read her thoughts and remained silent.

"I suppose I do," Emily replied. "Burying Michael among his

own kind would seem proper but the thought of disturbing his grave—removing him from the place he chose to rest—" She stopped and placed a hand on his forearm. "That doesn't sound right, either."

Anna spoke. "If I may…"

Her soft voice captured everyone's attention. "I agree with what you said, Mrs. Jerome. Disturbing Michael's grave might indeed be a sacrilege. I understand the pain in your heart but you must consider Michael's wishes. You should also consider one other thing as well." She paused and focused her eyes on Mike Jerome. "A passage in the bible, one believed written by Solomon, tells us this: 'Where the tree falls, there let it be.' Michael's roots may indeed be in America, but he fell here, among those with whom he served, doing what he chose to do. We should let him be."

"Where the tree falls, there let it be," Emily Jerome repeated softly.

Her father said nothing for a long moment. He set the teacup aside, folded his hands, and stared at the floor, obviously struck by her words. Then he turned to his wife. "Is that what you truly want, Em?"

Emily gave her husband a soft smile. "No, it's not what I want. What I want is our son to be alive—for none of this to have happened. But since it has, and because we can do nothing to change it, then we should at least talk about leaving him undisturbed."

Big Mike seemed at a loss for words.

Grateful for Anna's contribution to the discussion, Margaret sat back and allowed herself a moment of quiet reflection.

In spite of surprising and unexpected events, this sad symphony might well end on a more upbeat note than she had once feared. The threat of her father's influence on Ambassador Sharp seemed less so now. Had the reality of Michael's grave altered her parents' commitment? It seemed an unlikely possibility but the concept of 'likeliness' seemed to matter little.

The unexpected illness of her parents had sent Margaret scurrying off to France on a quest to fulfill what she believed was her brother's last request. Yet, what she had *thought* he wanted was something altogether different from what he truly desired. Had Michael perceived her father's intent to disinter his remains? Had he somehow managed to convey his despair to his twin sister? Still, rather than accomplishing what she had set out to do, the voyage and subsequent revelations about Michael had opened her eyes; had allowed Margaret to view her brother from a unique perspective.

First, the stark reality of his grave had shocked her into accepting the truth of his death. Second, Michael's unexpected marriage and the decision regarding burial in foreign soil among his fellow soldiers had aroused in Margaret an unwavering commitment to follow her own path in life; to go wherever it led.

Mike Jerome rose to his feet. "Thank you for inviting us here, Anna, and also for your wonderful description of our son's burial ceremony. Please understand that we mean you no disrespect, nor do we wish to add to your sorrow. But, truth be told, we need some time among ourselves. What was once so clear to all of us no longer seems to be. Please try to understand how difficult this is for us."

"I *do* understand," Anna said, her eyes moving to each member of the Jerome family. "I cannot imagine how awkward this must be for you."

"Thank you, Anna. We will talk again—soon," Emily said.

As her family prepared to leave, Margaret spoke to Anna. "Perhaps you and I can get together later?"

"Yes, of course," she replied. "I have no plans."

*

Shortly after lunch—a quiet affair in Lutetia's dining room—Margaret excused herself and revisited Anna.

Once again, they sat in the front parlor, across from each other, much as they had earlier in the day.

"As you have no doubt realized," Margaret began, "the purpose of our voyage was to transport Michael's remains back to America and then inter his body in our family's plot. My father sent a cable to that effect."

Anna's expression reflected mild astonishment. "I knew of no such cable."

"I realize that, but Gurney knew of it. With help from his friends my father's cable was conveniently misplaced."

"I am not surprised by this. Gurney was a good friend to Michael."

"Yes, he was. In any case, we believed our brother's casket was in storage, awaiting our arrival. Learning of his actual burial came as a shock. On top of that, visiting his grave at Suresnes affected me in a strange way. The longer I stood there the worse I felt about the prospect of removing his body from that quiet, serene place—of going against his wishes. Beatrice felt the same way. It just seemed wrong. News of your marriage added another layer of emotional confusion.

"I sent a cable to my parents informing them of the situation and suggested we probably had no legal grounds to return Michael's remains to America. I had hoped they would agree. In the meantime, I thought it best to keep all this to ourselves. Beatrice and I never intended to deceive you, Anna. I hope you believe that."

"I believe you," Anna said. "Were I in your place, I would have done the same. However, you must also know that I will do everything in my power to fulfill Michael's wishes."

"I understand."

"What do you think your father will do now?"

Margaret shrugged. "I wish I knew."

48

Arm upraised, ready to knock, Margaret hesitated at the door to her parents' suite. It was late afternoon, a few hours following her visit with Anna. Echoing in her mind were the words spoken by her father during their first meeting: *Never be ashamed of doing what must be done.* She was here now to do exactly that, but not without a deep sense of anxiety.

Margaret rapped lightly on the door and waited.

"Hello, Maggie," her father said. He stepped aside, inviting her in.

She stepped past him and walked into the suite, a near duplicate of the one shared by herself and Beatrice.

"Your mother just woke from a nap. She'll be out in a minute."

Margaret nodded but said nothing.

"It's been quite a day, hasn't it?" A tired smile creased his lips.

"Yes, it has."

"Come sit by the window," he suggested, leading the way. "Would you like something? Tea, perhaps?"

Margaret shook her head. "I'm fine."

He eased his heavy frame into a comfortable chair across from where she now sat. "How was your visit with Anna? I presume she knew nothing of our plans regarding Michael?"

Margaret leaned forward; hands tightly clasped together on her knees, her long fingers crushing a silk handkerchief.

"That's true, and I want to talk more about that," she said, not knowing how else to begin. "The grave, I mean, plus another thing."

His words were exactly what Margaret expected. "There is nothing to talk about regarding Michael's burial. His remains belong in the family plot. Your mother might be having second thoughts but I see no reason to alter what we came here to do."

"I understand how you feel, but you should know why Anna was unaware of the real reason we came to France until today. When I discovered she was Michael's wife, I thought it best to keep quiet on the subject. Naturally, she thought we came here to pay our respects."

"And so we are, but her not knowing our intent doesn't change things."

"I'm afraid it does. I believe Anna will contest your claim; do everything in her power to see that Michael's wishes are not circumvented. You will be up against a determined wife with the financial and political means to explore every aspect of French law. The litigation could take years. And, regardless of political pressure from Ambassador Sharp, you will probably lose."

He stared at her for a moment, perhaps surprised by her response. "I suspect she will, but what about you, Maggie? Will you fight me on this as well?"

Margaret turned and gazed through the curtained window for a moment before speaking. Then, looking directly into his blue eyes, said, "I hate the word 'fight' when it comes to our family. Nevertheless, I do not believe we should desecrate Michael's grave—nor should we disregard his last wish. I feel so strongly about this that I will do everything I can to convince you to change your mind."

Big Mike raised an eyebrow, but remained silent.

"Now, having said that," Margaret continued, "the last thing I want is a public squabble over my brother's remains. I find that prospect ghoulish and repulsive, as would Michael. However, if you insist on doing this, then you will do it without me being part of it."

He sighed, a wistful exhalation. "What's happened to you, Maggie? I thought you were all for this. Why are you now so against me?"

It was a question she had expected, and Margaret wondered if she could explain how it had occurred without sounding like a madwoman.

"I'm not sure I can tell it in a way that makes sense, Father. At first, I felt exactly the same as you. Then, something strange happened. It occurred a few days after you announced your sailing plans. I was alone in the study, thinking about Michael's funeral arrangements, just as you asked me to do. Suddenly, I felt he was trying to communicate something, a final wish I could not quite understand. Then, when you and Mother became ill I believed Michael wanted me to continue what you intended. At least, that's what I thought at the time."

Mike Jerome's expression became unreadable, a look Margaret had never seen. She continued, afraid to stop.

"When Beatrice and I first visited Michael's grave, it happened again, but this time it was different. The atmosphere of sadness was gone. Rather, I felt that Michael was happy to lay beside the soldiers with whom he had served. Later, when I visited the hospital and saw all those wounded men, I felt it once again. Father, I think my original impression was wrong. I don't think Michael wanted me to claim his remains. I think he was telling me he was at peace and that we should leave him buried in the place he wished."

Big Mike turned toward the window and stared through the curtains. His face seemed to lose a bit of color. "I see."

Margaret sensed her father's apparent discomfort so she reached out and touched his forearm causing him to focus on her. "I know that sounds crazy, but I'm trying to explain something that I don't quite understand myself. All I'm asking is for you to think about it some more. To consider what Michael wanted."

Mike Jerome shrugged, his expression reflecting a man uncertain of himself. "You don't sound crazy, Maggie. Not at all. You've given me something to think on, and I will. Your mother will want a say in this as well, so it's not my decision alone." Then he smiled. "Perhaps it never was, not entirely."

Nor was it mine, she wanted to reply, but instead said nothing.

Despite the intense strangeness of her experiences, Margaret never believed she could easily alter her father's intentions. Yet, he seemed touched by her explanation. Did he truly understand or would he ultimately brush it off as a natural reaction to her twin brother's unexpected death? The dead were gone from us, he would probably tell her, and it was up to the living to carry on.

Mike Jerome interrupted her thoughts. "What about that other thing?" he asked.

"What?"

"When you first came in, you said you wanted to talk about Michael, plus another thing. What other thing?"

Her mind refocused. "Oh, that. I wanted to apologize for stealing your steamship tickets. What I did was unconscionable."

He waved a hand dismissively. "You have nothing to be sorry for, Maggie. Yes, I was put off but no longer. Given what you just told me about—your experience—I believe you did what you had to do. In your place, I would have probably done the same thing."

"Maybe so, but exposing Beatrice to danger was never my intention."

"I know that, my dear. So does your mother. Beatrice made her own choice. In any case, the two of you are safe now and that's all that matters."

Margaret nodded but said nothing. Once again, her fingers began to mangle the handkerchief.

Big Mike tilted his head and his eyes narrowed slightly. "Is there something more about this you want to say?"

She had explained what she'd intended, but there was still that one other thing. Margaret felt a lump rising in her chest but she swallowed several times, forcing it down, determined to maintain self-control. How could she possibly articulate what weighed so heavily on her mind? Margaret cherished the close relationship with her father. He was a good and gentle man and she loved him dearly. What would he think of her now?

"Sometimes," he suggested, "the best way to say something difficult is to just come out and say it."

Sound advice, she admitted. So simple. So Irish. And so *difficult*.

"Father, except for this one time, have I ever so thoroughly disobeyed your wishes?"

"No," he answered after a short pause. "Not that I can recall. You have strong opinions about certain things, like that suffrage business for one, but you've always been a good daughter; a bright and wonderful child any father would be proud to call his own."

His tender response worsened Margaret's discomfort. She did not deserve such compliments. She looked at the crushed handkerchief and tried to gather her thoughts. "Not always," she managed to say. "I haven't always deserved your affection."

"Nonsense. I don't believe that for a minute."

"Listen," she began. "It was that awful telegram. When we learned of Michael's death, I refused to believe it. Given how close we were, I should have felt something the moment he died—some inkling of his sudden passing—but I didn't. I was completely oblivious to my brother's passing."

"As was I," her father admitted. "It came as a shock to all of us."

"But I was his *twin*. We always had a sense about one another; we knew when either of us was happy or sad or hurt. Yet, he died... was gone, and I felt nothing."

Her father started to speak but she held up her hand.

"Please let me finish. I was always a bit envious of Michael. He was everyone's favorite, and for good reason. I suppose I resented him for that. Worse still, Michael knew he was the favored child, the heir apparent, but he was always so considerate. I loved him for that, truly I did, but I also disliked him for being the perfect son, for making the difficult appear effortless."

Mike Jerome interrupted. "So you were a bit jealous of your brother. So what? Maybe he was likewise envious of you as well, but for a different reason. Look: I put the entire future of the business in *his* hands, not yours. Was that right of me to do that? I don't know. It was traditional and expected and I never gave it much thought. Now, in hindsight, I'm positive it was a burden he never wanted. If you're looking for the truth, then here it is: I believe the real reason he went off to France was to get away from me, to get away from what I wanted his life to be." He paused for a moment. Then, "None of us is perfect. Everyone has regrets for things done or left undone."

"You could be right about Michael not wanting to follow in your footsteps, but what I'm trying to say is this: When Michael left for France, I saw it as my opportunity to show you that I could do more than supervise your bookkeepers. I wanted to prove I was his equal in other things as well."

"But you were always his equal," Big Mike explained. "I thought you understood that."

"Maybe I did in certain ways, but Michael cast such a long shadow..." She left the sentence incomplete, unsure what to say next.

"He did indeed, Maggie."

"And then came that dreadful day when notice of his death arrived. I should have felt something beforehand, but I didn't. I think my envious feelings might have kept me isolated from him."

Mike took her hands in both of his, completely enveloping them. "You don't have to say anything more. I understand."

"No, I don't think you do; not really."

"Maggie, Maggie. I *do* understand how you feel. Listen to me. In the first place, you are not the blame for any of this. Michael's death was an unspeakable tragedy for all of us. You may be guilty of envy—God knows that's common enough in families—but I could never believe, not for a moment, that you wished ill for Michael."

Margaret's shoulders slumped and she suddenly felt exhausted. That part was certainly true: she had never for an instant wished her brother harm.

"Listen to me," her father said again. He leaned toward her and gently lifted her chin with the crook of his index finger. "Listen to me, now."

She met his blue eyes; an older, wiser version of her own.

He dropped his hand and nodded once, perhaps granting himself permission to say what he truly desired to keep to himself. "I had an older brother back in Ireland. Seamus was bright and cheerful and a natural born leader. In many ways he and your brother were alike. That's why I might have favored him a bit. If so, it was unintentional, truly it was. In any case, I felt the same jealousy toward Seamus that you felt about Michael. Seamus was the pride of our family, an exceptional young man highly regarded by everyone who knew him.

"I was happy as a clam when he left home to join the Fenian Brotherhood. Irish Home Rule was a cause we all believed in, but some of what the Finians did might have gotten out of hand. Like you, I was glad to see him go for the same selfish reasons. I wanted out from under his shadow. I wanted everyone to see me as his equal.

But then the damned English killed him; stood him against a wall at Beggars Bush Barracks and shot him dead with no more concern than they would for a stray dog.

"I blamed myself for my brother's death, just as you have taken blame upon yourself for Michael. I was twelve years old but I was prepared to atone for my envious thoughts. Like Seamus, I would join the Fenians and fight the English. God willing, I would help secure Irish independence or die trying."

"What stopped you?"

He smiled. "Your grandmother. Not long after we buried Seamus my mum sat me down and told me that my brother—her dead son—had spoken to her from somewhere beyond the grave."

Margret shuddered at the instant rising of goosebumps.

"Yes, that sounds daft, but she told me that Seamus was at peace; that he understood my yearning to prove myself; that I was not to blame for his death. Seamus told her that my destiny lay elsewhere, that I was ordained to live a different life in a distant land.

"Yet, despite her words, I have never forgotten how happy I was to see my brother leave home, or how terribly responsible I felt when Seamus died. I have not forgotten it and I never will. Eventually, with your grandmother's help, I was able to make a small peace with myself." He looked away for a moment, then continued. "So, you see, I *do* understand what you felt. But now you must find a way to do as I once did. Forgive yourself. Don't let childish behavior clutter your life."

The shudder that had threatened the foundation of her soul eased. "You never told me about your mum—about her—talk with Seamus."

"There are lots of things you don't know about me and that's the way it should be. We all have our little guilts and secrets. Some we share but most we keep tucked away inside. The point is this: Life is what it is and things happen to us. Some of it we can explain, some we cannot. Sometimes we have a say in the turn of events, but most times we don't. More often than not, life grabs us by the scruff of the neck and we have no choice but to stumble along."

Margaret nodded. "Still…"

"There's no 'still' about it. You're ashamed of your selfish feelings, and that's to be expected. So was I. But shame and blame are not the same." He blinked and then chuckled quietly. "Now you've gone and done it, Maggie. Turned your old man into a blithering poet. And a poor one at that."

She smiled at his unintended rhyme.

A moment later, her smile faded. "I read a story once, about a magical monkey paw. The moral was: Be careful what you wish for. Well, I got my wish but it didn't make me any happier. In fact, there were times when I wanted to die as well, to put an end to my selfish misery."

Her father stood, took Margaret by the shoulders and raised her to her feet. Then he put his huge arms around her and held her close. "You are not selfish and you are *not* going to die," he told her in a quiet voice. "Not yet, anyway. I won't hear of it."

Tension slowly drained from her body, his magnetic presence drawing away some of the self-loathing she had kept locked within herself for so long. She would never be completely free of guilt, that she understood, but she could cope with it now; get on with living her life and doing whatever God had in mind for her. Exhausted by months of pent-up feelings, Margaret clung to her father, gaining strength from his embrace.

Margaret felt a slow, warming rush of well-being, a sense of stability that had vanished upon hearing of her brother's death. The truth in her father's words seemed to form a clod of solid ground beneath her feet. It wasn't much, but it was a beginning. For the time being it would be enough.

Coming to terms with her tarnished self-image would not be easy; but, as had her father, Margaret silently vowed to give it her best.

Somehow, she would find a way to make a small peace with herself.

49

The next morning Margaret and her family again visited Michael's grave and placed a bouquet of flowers at the base of his cross.

Afterwards they visited Gurney Shaw whose medical condition had worsened since partial amputation of his left leg. Without hesitation Gurney explained his reasons for diverting Mike Jerome's cable. His face—even paler complexioned than normal, dark smudges under his eyes—reflected the unmistakable expression of a man who seemed to understand how close he was to death. The meeting visibly shook Mike and Emily as it did Margaret who, for the first time, realized that Gurney might indeed be dying.

Perhaps it was the solemn beauty of the cemetery, or the aftereffect of visiting Gurney Shaw, or the sight of all those mangled young men recuperating in the halls and on the courtyard lawn, but her father seemed much quieter and a great deal more thoughtful. Or so she hoped.

Now, standing on the sidewalk outside the hospital, Mike Jerome hailed a taxi.

"I don't think all of us will fit into one of those little automobiles," Beatrice said. "Perhaps we should wait for a fiacre."

"A what?" her father asked.

"A horse-drawn carriage," Beatrice replied. "We can sit two across, facing each other like we did this morning when we visited the cemetery."

He waved off the taxi but said nothing more.

"Where shall we have lunch?" Beatrice asked.

"Let's find a restaurant other than the Lutetia," Emily suggested.

"I know just the place," Margaret said, remembering her last afternoon with Robert. "It's a pleasant little sidewalk café near the Jardin de Tuileries."

Her father seemed preoccupied, both on the ride to the café and as they were seated.

Finally, over a glass of *vin rouge*, Mike Jerome came out of his reverie. "I like Anna," he said, looking at Margaret. "She impressed me as a fine young lady. Any father would be proud to call her daughter-in-law."

"I'm glad you think so," Margaret replied. "I think she was a great comfort to Michael."

"So she was. And I like Gurney, too. Regardless of what he did about my cable, I wish him no ill. He's suffering enough without my adding to his troubles."

"I believe you would have done the same thing under similar circumstances," Emily said.

"Maybe so, Em. Maybe so."

He took a sip of his wine and then added, "I've been thinking a lot about Michael lately—about why he came over here—and other things. I'm glad he married Anna and found some happiness. Lord knows he deserved it after putting up with my shenanigans."

Emily fixed her husband with a hard stare. "Self-pity was never one of your qualities, my dear. Please don't start now."

He offered a sad, half-smile. "I take your point." A moment later he continued. "You know, the Frenchies aren't a bad sort. They sided with us against the English on the Home Rule question. They even offered refuge to the likes of Dillon and a few others."

"Let's not forget their help at Yorktown, my dear," Emily Jerome added.

"I admit, there's no love lost between the French and English. We Irish have that in common."

"But we are allies now," Margaret added, "America and England and France. Even the Irish are on our side."

"Indeed we are," Mike conceded. "And, given that, I think I understand Michael better now than when he first announced his intention to come over here and lend a hand."

"I'm glad to hear that," Emily said.

He took another sip of wine, set the glass carefully on the table, and then looked directly at his wife. "Em, in the core of your truest heart, do you really believe we should leave things as they are; I mean with Michael's grave being so far from home?"

"I want to say I'm sure, but I can't. However, Michael *was* sure. He was sure enough to make it legal. If we decide to go through with this, then we must first challenge that provision of his will. Anna would certainly fight us and she might well have the stronger case. It could take years to resolve. But let's suppose for a moment that we won in court; then what? Would our family ever feel good about ignoring Michael's last wish on this earth? Could we ever visit his grave and not think about what we did to him? Could we live with that selfish betrayal on our minds?"

Margaret felt a tremor along her spine. She wasn't sure if the reaction was due to her mother's words or what she thought might be coming next.

Her father looked away and his eyes seemed to focus on something in the middle distance. A small frown touched his lips. "I never thought of it as selfishness or betrayal," he said. "But then, I wasn't thinking of Michael. I was thinking of us... me."

"Don't be so hard on yourself," Emily said to him. "All of us wanted the same thing. We never dreamed Michael had formed such strong personal ties over here, like his friendship with that Aubray fellow, the young man with the mustaches. Nor did we know about his marriage to Anna. Each of us based our notion on what we thought was real, but wasn't."

Mike nodded. "Apparently so."

As her parents grew silent, Margaret felt a familiar sensation and the beginnings of an idea. "Listen," she began, the words forming as she spoke, "if we leave Michael undisturbed as he wished, then we could place a special marker beside Grandma and Grandpa Patrick's headstone—one with the same words carved on Michael's cross—as though Michael were there in spirit. He would be here *and* back home— in both places at the same time."

Emily's expression grew thoughtful but she said nothing.

"We could ask Father Hayes to conduct a memorial service," Margaret continued. "Maybe post a notice in the newspaper." She looked at her father. "We could have our own service for Michael— private or public—whichever we decide. How does that sound?"

Emily looked at Margaret. "What kind of a marker?"

"Well," she began. "As I said, we could use the same words carved into his cross, but then add something like 'To the Memory of' above his name, and then finish the inscription with the words 'who rests in France'. That way people would know."

The family owned a number of adjacent gravesites at Mount Olive Cemetery. Setting a stone marker next to his maternal grandparents would give assurance that Michael would always be there in spirit.

Her suggestion wasn't ideal but perfection seldom occurs on this earth. The granite marker—more properly a cenotaph—was an idea that had spontaneously voiced itself in her mind. Was that another message from Michael? Perhaps, but wherever it's origin, the marker would provide a lasting memorial to Michael's memory.

Emily turned toward her husband. "What do you think of that?"

A range of conflicting emotions danced across his face. Finally, he said, "I suppose that would be better than nothing."

Margaret studied her father. He seemed more resigned than convinced. She said, "Are you sure about this, Father?"

He looked at her and shook his head slightly. "No, I am not sure. Not at all. But what Anna said makes sense: *Where the tree falls, there let it be.*"

*

The decision to leave Michael's grave undisturbed lifted a great burden from Margaret's shoulders. However, her parents seemed more resigned to the inevitable rather than satisfied; a mood that probably was the best she could have expected. Anna, of course, was relieved.

The next morning Mike Jerome took Margaret aside after breakfast. "I'd like to have a word with you in private," he said.

Apparently, there was something on her father's mind. Was he having second thoughts about Michael's grave? Had her parents changed their minds?

Please, God—not that.

He steered her toward a quiet corner of the lobby where they sat next to each other in comfortable chairs.

"When you get back home and settled in," he began, "I'd like you to consider helping me out a bit more at the office."

Margaret shifted uneasily in her chair. "Helping out more? In what way?"

"Well," he began, "Maybe you could turn over the bookkeeping to Mrs. Hoffman and spend more time helping me run the place."

For a moment she couldn't find her voice. Then she said, "If you're thinking I could fill Michael's shoes, then you are mistaken. I could never take his place— or yours, for that matter."

"True enough, but you could make a place of your own, couldn't you? Put your own special mark on what I started. Times change and so should the company when it makes sense to do so. God knows, you have the brains for it—and the determination. There's a fire inside you that I chose to ignore, just as I ignored the possibility of Michael wanting a life different from what I had planned. Those were selfish mistakes. I can see that now. Besides, it's something you've always wanted, isn't it?"

Of course it was.

Working side by side with her father would fulfill a long-held but unspoken dream. In fact, it was the primary source of her envy: Michael had gotten what she so desperately wanted. The fact that her wish became possible because Michael was no longer alive quashed her enthusiasm. It would be a dubious achievement, no more satisfying than winning a race because the favorite and faster runner had stumbled before crossing the finish line.

Given all that had occurred, did she still harbor the same passion for the family business? She wasn't sure. And what about Robert? What might he think of all this? If Margaret agreed to take up her father's offer, would she have the energy and commitment to satisfy both passions?

"Well?" he asked.

She reached out and grasped his hand. "This is a sad time for our family. Let's wait until we're home, until Michael's memorial service is behind us. You've put a lot in my mind and I need time to think it over."

He nodded, understanding all that she felt. "Yes, of course. You'll let me know?"

She smiled and squeezed his hand. "When the time comes, I'll let you know," she said.

50

Later that afternoon Margaret stood before her dressing room mirror, tricorn in hand, preparing to meet the rest of the family for tea. She and Beatrice had talked about shopping—browsing lazily underneath the immense glass dome of the Galleries Lafayette—but neither felt comfortable with the idea. Although they had replenished toiletries and cosmetics, the act of shopping seemed disrespectful.

She placed the hat atop her head, fastened it with a long pin and then turned from side to side. Satisfied, she patted her gold unicorn locket and strode into the sitting room. Just then, the telephone rang.

"*Bon jour,*" she said.

"Margaret? Is that you?"

The mechanically distorted but unmistakable voice caused her heart to beat faster. "Robert! What a pleasant surprise. I never expected a telephone call."

"And for good reason. It's usually a futile exercise. I've been trying for hours to get a connection. I was lucky but we may be cut off at any time."

His voice sounded oddly tense, and mildly irritated. Given his previous remark, she attributed his tone to frustration with the French telephone service.

"Well, we're connected now," she said. "How are you?"

"Well enough, I suppose. What about you?"

"I miss you, Robert, but I'm fine otherwise."

"I miss you too, Margaret." A short silence followed. Then he added: "Are you alone?"

What an odd question. "Yes, I am. Beatrice and my parents are downstairs waiting for me. Why do you ask?"

Robert didn't answer immediately. The hiss across the telephone line gave her a feeling of immense distance.

"I have some bad news, Margaret. We lost Jack Mayo."

"Lost him?" She didn't quite understand what he was telling her. Was Jack wandering about, lost in some thicket? What on earth was Robert trying to say? "I don't understand. What happened to Jack?"

"He's dead, Margaret. Jack was killed earlier this morning."

The meaning of Robert's words finally got through. "Dead? Jack is dead?"

"I am sorry to tell you this way, but I had to let you know before tomorrow. That's when Jack planned to meet Beatrice." His voice cracked, and then became firm. "I didn't know what else to do."

Realization struck and her knees suddenly felt weak. She sat heavily on the chair next to the telephone. She opened her mouth, but no words formed.

"Margaret? Are you still there?"

"Yes. Yes, I am." Her mind seemed unable to focus. Did Robert say Jack Mayo was dead? The words cycled through her brain but they lacked meaning. How could Jack be dead? Beatrice got a letter from him today.

"I'm sorry, Margaret. Truly I am."

Nausea fluttered through her stomach. Poor Beatrice... She talked endlessly about Jack's arrival and what they planned to do together; had bought several gifts for him—affectionate tokens she would never give to anyone else. And now...

"Tell me what happened."

An electrical crackle preceded his reply. "Just before dawn the

Germans lobbed artillery shells into Jack's aid station. The barrage killed a dozen men including several medical orderlies and the surgeon in charge. Two orderlies survived. Both are badly wounded."

"And you are positive it's Jack?"

"Yes, I saw his body. There is no doubt."

The telephone hissed and clicked.

"I believe we're losing our connection, Margaret. Please tell Beatrice and your family how sorry I am."

His voice sounded sadly urgent.

"I will, Robert."

Another series of clicks and hums distorted his next words.

"What was that, Robert? I didn't hear what you said."

"...love you, Margaret."

"I love you, too, Robert."

All she heard in reply was the vacant hiss of a lost connection; a long, empty sigh like the immeasurable passing of eternity.

*

Margaret cradled the handset and stared through the lace-curtained window.

Jack Mayo was dead.

The words kept repeating themselves in her mind. It didn't seem real. She tried to picture him but was unable to do so. She concentrated, trying to visualize Beatrice and Jack together, happily strolling the deck of the USS *Mongolia*. Finally, a vague image appeared.

She had no trouble at all picturing Robert's face in her mind, crisp and lifelike.

Margaret had always accepted the possibility that Robert could be at risk. If death could claim her brother Michael, then a similar fate might well befall Robert. Yet, she had never allowed anxiety to fully bloom into despair. But now Jack Mayo was gone, and she could no longer ignore the fear that lurked just beneath the surface of her consciousness. She leaned forward; hands pressed into her abdomen as a cold emptiness formed in the pit of her stomach. Death, it seemed, took great pleasure from haunting the thoughts of those it had yet to claim.

With concerted effort she focused her mind and concentrated on what she must do next.

How and when would she break the news to Beatrice? Should she do it immediately? Perhaps it was better to wait, to tell Beatrice first, when they were alone. Yes, that seemed right. Margaret decided they should have one more pleasant dinner together before telling Beatrice of the latest tragedy to visit their family. Later this evening would be better, when the two of them were alone in their suite. Beatrice could then hear about Jack in private.

She picked up her handbag, composed her features, and then walked toward the door. Until that time came, Margaret would force herself to mask her own fearful emotions.

51

News of Jack's death sent Beatrice into seclusion. For the next three days she remained in their suite, talking little and eating less. When she wasn't sobbing quietly, Beatrice stared out the window, lost in whatever world her profound grief had created. It was heartbreaking for Margaret to watch her sister mourn in silence, but efforts to initiate a two-way conversation proved fruitless.

Margaret stayed close by, as did her parents, usually in the adjoining room. Often peering through the archway between rooms to observe a stone-still Beatrice, the three of them spent long hours quietly talking among themselves, playing cards, or reading. From time to time one of them would step away and spend a quiet hour or so with Beatrice, but there was little real conversation with her.

On the fourth morning following Jack's death Beatrice emerged from her bedroom. "I'd like to join everyone for breakfast," she said.

Beatrice looked pale and eyes were still red-streaked and puffy, but her voice sounded more like her usual self.

It was a positive sign and Margaret smiled. "We missed you."

Beatrice shrugged. "I think you were right, Margaret."

"I was? About what?"

A sad smile touched Beatrice's lips. "Do you remember what you said about sorrow being born in the hasty heart? Well, I was being hasty about my feelings toward Jack."

Margaret clasped her hands behind her, hoping to hide her

growing unease. "Do you really think so?"

"Yes, I do. Jack was a nice young man, but we couldn't possibly have fallen in love so quickly. I understand that now. What we experienced was a romantic infatuation, pleasant in itself, but nothing more."

"Are you certain about that, Beatrice?"

"Absolutely."

Margaret said nothing. Was Beatrice attempting to shield herself from grief?

Beatrice smiled. "I'm starving. Shall we go?"

They met their parents downstairs. Emily and Mike Jerome were clearly relieved to see their youngest daughter in a more normal mood.

After ordering breakfast, Beatrice turned toward her mother and asked, rather casually, "When do you plan on returning home?"

Emily didn't answer immediately. She exchanged quick glances with Margaret and her husband. Then she said: "We have no definite plans." A furrow crossed her brow and she seemed to have something else on her mind. "Well, if you must know, I was hoping for news of a grandchild. If such was going to be, then Anna should know by now."

Margaret said, "Anna wanted a child as well, but there is no possibility of a pregnancy. I'm afraid that time has passed."

"I see," Emily said, apparently resigned to the news. "Then I suppose we can leave anytime." She looked at Beatrice. "Why did you ask?"

Beatrice shrugged. "I just wanted to know."

"Are you going with them?" Margaret asked.

"Yes, I am. I hate deserting you but Anna will be here. You won't be completely alone. Besides, there's no *reason* for me to stay any longer than necessary."

"What about your work at the hospital?" Margaret inquired. "Isn't that important to you?"

Beatrice shook her head. "I never really enjoyed picking up blood-clotted dressings from operating room floors, *or* emptying pus buckets. I thought by helping others I might save Jack from harm. Silly me. There's no need for that now."

"You could still read to them," Margaret persisted. "The men always enjoyed the way you assumed the identity of different characters."

A faint smile quick-stepped across her face. "Yes, that was fun."

"Then why not stay and keep me company?"

Beatrice set her jaw and Margaret realized her sister had made up her mind.

"No, I can't do that anymore. Soldiers will always remind me of Jack, and Paris is too close to the war. I need to get away from here."

Beatrice's neutral tone of voice when speaking about Jack sounded forced and artificial. On the one hand Beatrice claimed their relationship was hardly more than a romantic interlude. On the other she couldn't bear to be reminded of him. Those conflicting views disturbed Margaret, but she had no idea how to address it. Beatrice had wept for three days, obviously heartbroken and deeply affected by the young man's death. Margaret doubted a return to familiar surroundings would suddenly end her sister's mourning for Jack Mayo.

"Are you sure you'll be all right, living over here by yourself?" Emily Jerome asked Margaret.

"Yes, Mother. Please don't worry about me. I'm a grown woman, capable of looking after myself."

"I know that, dear, but I'd feel better if you came home with us. Robert can easily find you when this is all over." She leaned forward. "I worry about you being alone in a foreign land. And with the war so close…"

"I won't be alone, Mother. Anna has plenty of room. She offered to put me up for as long as I like. I've accepted her invitation."

"That was considerate of her," Emily said.

"It's settled then," Big Mike announced. It was the first time he had spoken since they sat down to breakfast. "I mean, our business here is done, is it not?"

Margaret looked at everyone seated around the table. Beatrice turned away, reluctant to meet her gaze. Finally Margaret spoke to her father.

"Yes," she answered. "I suppose it is."

52

"Wake up and piss, the world's on fire," the duty sergeant announced.

A shoulder-shake followed by the familiar litany roused Butler from sleep. He sat up, swiveled himself to a feet-on-the-floor sitting position and fingered grit from his eyes. "What time is it?"

"Twenty-three hundred, Lieutenant. Same as yesterday only different."

"Very funny."

The duty sergeant chuckled.

"What's it like this evening?"

"Not much going on, Lieutenant. It should be a quiet night."

"Okay, thanks."

The sergeant left, closing the door behind him.

Since his initial posting to Chateau-Thierry six weeks ago, the base hospital—its staff, medical equipment and beds—had moved three times, first to Epernay, then to Chalons; each move trailing behind American and French troops as they advanced eastward beyond the Marne. The hospital was now in Bar-le-Duc, a small town straddling the Ornain River. The operating theatre, wards and diagnostic labs had become fully operational earlier that afternoon.

Butler stood and stretched, forcing weariness from his body. The locations changed but the never-ending stream of dead and wounded seldom varied. Neither did the work routine of twelve hours on followed by twelve off. At midnight, less than an hour from now, Butler and two other surgeons would relieve the Woody Peckham trio. Twelve hours later, at noon, Woody's team would relieve Butler. And so it went. If it weren't for Margaret's letters—two, sometimes three in a week, all of which he promptly answered—it would have been easy to fall prey to cynicism and depression.

He yawned, took his toilet kit and headed for the lavatory.

*

Three hours into his unusually quiet shift, Nurse Glover approached Butler's duty station. The other two surgeons were napping, resting atop cots in the adjacent recovery ward. Hearing soft footsteps, he looked up from a copy of *Lancet*, the British medical journal, and recognized the middle-aged ward nurse. A wisp of dark hair dangled from beneath her white cap. When she spoke, her voice was nighttime quiet.

"Pardon me, Doctor Butler, but would you mind lending a hand?"

"Not at all. What can I do for you?"

"Johnny Cruikshank just passed and the orderlies have gone off to have their coffee and a smoke. I'd like him to be ready when they return."

"Of course."

He had been engrossed in *The Repression of War Experience*, a paper describing certain battle-related neuroses. Butler marked his place, set the journal aside and followed her upstairs to Ward B Two kerosene lanterns formed yellow cones of subdued illumination.

Four days ago Private John Philip Cruikshank, age 20, had suffered a bayonet thrust into his abdomen. As so often happened with deep abdominal lesions, bacteria from the grossly unsanitary weapon quickly spread to the peritoneum. Once infected, the grim outcome was a near certainty. An hour earlier Butler had placed a half-grain morphine tablet under the young man's tongue. In the final, agonizing stage of peritonitis, easing Private Cruikshank's pain was all anyone could do.

Butler turned the dead man on his side while Mrs. Glover untied heavy cloth tabs used to hold the nightshirt together along the patient's back. They drew the soiled garment off and tossed it aside for laundering and reuse. Butler kept the body immobile while Nurse Glover pulled the tucked sheet from the mattress top and bottom so that the longer upper portion covered the naked soldier's ash-gray face and neck. Then, working one side at a time, they wrapped him tight, pulling the cotton material snug across Johnny Cruikshank's distended abdomen. They secured the sheet with bandages looped around the body and tied in a knot. All that now showed of Private Cruikshank were his bare ankles and feet, which extended beyond the makeshift shroud.

"He was a tall young fellow, wasn't he?" Butler whispered.

"Yes, he was. And such a nice looking boy, too. His mother will be devastated."

Butler couldn't help thinking about Michael Jerome and how one death had affected a wife, parents, siblings and friends. Their lives would never be the same. Nor would his—Jack's death had left him angry and morbidly depressed, but it would have an even worse effect on the Mayo family. The violent passing of two young men had caused dozens of people to anguish over their loss. The cumulative, heartbreaking result of millions dead was beyond imagination. The whole world must be in mourning.

Nurse Glover removed the linen case from Private Cruikshank's pillow and slipped it over the soldier's exposed feet, tying it snugly with more bandages. Then she stepped back.

"I wish we had more coffins," she whispered. "It doesn't seem right sending him off like this."

Jack Mayo, Rotelli, Hanssen, and the nine other men killed on that unforgettable day six weeks ago had gone to their graves in canvas sacks, still wearing their blood-soaked uniforms, as did the arrogant surgeon who had refused to lower the red Geneva Cross banner fluttering like a beacon above their aid station. How many others had died due to the smug ignorance of incompetent officers? Far too many; numbers that exceeded the AEF's ability to provide the dead with the simple dignity of an unpainted wooden coffin.

Butler did not understand why there weren't more available. The dense summer heat prohibited storing bodies until re-supply, which occurred sporadically. Rather than let them putrefy, those in charge decided to bury the dead immediately, loosely sewing the bodies into gray canvas sacks. It was one more example of the many silent atrocities he once vowed never to accept but now took as commonplace.

"No, it doesn't," he replied. "But we can't let them lay untended in the heat. That would be worse, I think."

"Yes, of course. Anyway, thank you, Doctor. When the orderlies take him outside, I'll come back and straighten things out."

By 'straighten things out' Nurse Glover meant she would quietly strip the bed down to its oilcloth-covered mattress, wipe down everything with a chlorine solution, and then remake it with fresh linen. When the ward's other wounded soldiers awoke, they would see an empty cot where their wounded bedfellow had once laid. That, almost everyone on staff believed, was better than having patients wake up to see one of their own wrapped head to toe in a white sheet; then watch as orderlies removed the body while others prepared the bed for the next patient.

The clean-up Nurse Glover did in the silent stillness of night was a practice deemed best for all concerned.

All, that is, except those who lay awake, smoking in near darkness, their gaunt faces briefly exposed by a tiny orange coal made bright as they dragged on cigarettes.

"You know where to find me if you need help," he murmured.

*

The unconscious man lying on the operating table had a penetrating wound in the long muscle group at the front of his thigh, a common injury resulting from an explosive artillery shell. The X-ray surgeon had marked the exact location with dots of silver nitrate at the twelve and nine o'clock positions. The metal fragment lay at the horizontal and vertical intersection of those two marks.

Using a scalpel like a writing instrument, Butler made a long incision above and below the wound. The flesh sprung apart, revealing red muscle beneath a pale, fatty layer. As he worked deeper into the flesh, excising tissue with scalpel and scissors, warm blood gushed from severed veins. With the help of an assistant who blotted the wound with gauze, Butler located and immediately tied off the larger vessels. He clipped smaller ones with a hemostat. Before long, hemostats dangled from the open wound like so many pairs of manicure scissors.

Probing with his fingers, Butler located the inch-square hunk of shrapnel and worked it loose from between muscle bundles. He probed once more until he located a small piece of cloth, a tatter of the soldier's uniform carried into the wound by the shrapnel. He then began the process of debridement: carefully removing clots and cutting away every fiber of damaged tissue until only healthy muscle remained. Finally, one by one, he tied off the blood vessels held by hemostats. When he finished, what was once a wound measuring a quarter-inch wide and two inches long was four times larger.

After flushing the gaping maw with a chlorine solution, Butler took a half-dozen red rubber tubes from the surgical table, each about the size of a wooden pencil. The tubes were open at one end. The closed end had numerous perforations. He carefully placed all six tubes deep into the incision, leaving the open end protruding. A nurse immediately packed the wound with gauze soaked in the same chlorine solution, leaving the open ends of the red tubes outside the dressing.

His job was finished. Butler stepped back and dictated his treatment to a recording nurse.

"October 10, 1918. 0210 hours. Lemuel Fisk, B Company, Ninth Infantry Regiment. G.S.W. right thigh. Éclat. Rectus femoris. Lodged against anterior surface of vastus intermedius. Myotomy. Shrapnel measuring one inch by one inch by one centimeter removed. Debridement. Wound irrigated with Dakin solution and left open for drainage. Six Carrel-Dakin tubes in posterior wound. Evacuate. Lieutenant Butler. M.O."

As he dictated, another nurse wrapped bandages around the incision, leaving the red tubes exposed. Afterwards, about every couple of hours or so, a nurse would dribble chlorine solution into the open end of each rubber tube. The solution, draining from perforations in the closed end, would keep the deep wound soaked. When the daily cultures were free of bacteria, a surgeon at Meaux or Neuilly would suture the wound. Only then could the soldier begin the process of healing and recuperation.

Butler removed his surgical garb while orderlies carried the patient to the recovery room. As he scrubbed, other orderlies cleared away debris from the just completed surgery. When he returned to the operating table, a nurse helped him into a sterile smock, mask, and rubber gloves. Then he leaned over the next patient who lay ready and waiting on the freshly cleaned table beside a new set of surgical instruments.

He studied the wound. The patient's left leg below the knee was missing. A tourniquet above the knee had stopped the flow of blood. He reached for a scalpel and began to work.

As Butler gradually lost track of passing time, so did the wounded slowly lose their individuality. The soldiers placed on his operating table became an endless procession of arms and legs, chests and backs, heads and faces—lacerated, punctured, fractured and shattered—an overwhelming mass of humanity, all brutally violated beyond anything one could or should lay eyes upon. Bloody towels and dressings littered the floor, cleared away as he worked by equally exhausted orderlies.

After each procedure he removed his blood-spattered outfit, scrubbed, and then donned another sterile mask and gown. As he changed, orderlies removed surgical clutter, scrubbed the table and laid on new sheets before strapping down another man to his table; it was a practiced routine executed with soundless efficiency.

The wounded seemed apprehensive by the sight of so many sharp, bright instruments lining the small table beside them; still, they never quailed in fear. Neither did they mouth a single complaint or curse God's cruel indifference to their unbearable suffering. What always surprised Butler was the fact that most of the wounded soldiers smiled up at him. However, when the anesthetist placed the gauze mask over their nose and mouth, their eyes quickly reflected a mixture of fear and helpless trust. As ether dribbled onto the mask, every man struggled against the icy-sweet vapor, moaning and fighting his restraints until eyelids fluttered and closed. Still, their courage gave him strength, a temporary surge of energy.

But grinding toil quickly wore it away.

Ignoring weariness, he paused infrequently; to empty his bladder, gulp coffee, or swallow a bite or two from a cold sandwich. Fatigue became numbing, creeping inexorably up his legs and back. After the third or fourth operation Butler found it difficult to concentrate. With enormous effort he purged the effect of exhaustion from his mind and concentrated harder on the exposed square of human anatomy before him, focusing on the technical aspects of that particular surgery.

As darkness waned and became morning, he began to question his judgment and doubt his skills. Exhaustion had transformed him into a doddering incompetent. And yet, the eyes of wounded men never wavered in their absolute confidence in his abilities.

How could they trust him when he no longer trusted himself?

A new surgical team arrived at noon to begin their twelve-hour shift. Butler turned his patient over to Woody Peckham.

"Looks like another busy day," Woody observed. "And I had such great plans, too."

"What sort of plans?"

"Nothing that would interest someone who gets leave to visit Paris and then wastes valuable time visiting museums."

Butler smiled. "Sorry about your plans."

"I bet you are. Get out before I have you arrested for impersonating a soldier."

Butler shed his blood-stained garb, gave himself a good wash, and then left the operating room. In the reception area more wounded lay on stretchers; some dazed by morphine, some moaning, others quietly waiting for treatment. Butler eased his way past them, careful not to step too close to anyone.

According to news reports, the Germans and Austrians had written to President Wilson requesting talks that might lead to an armistice. If one could believe rumors then peace was indeed in the making. Butler, however, saw little evidence that might indicate an end to this conflict. In fact, the opposite was clearly obvious. There seemed to be a concerted effort on both sides to inflict as many casualties upon each other as humanly possible in the shortest amount of time.

Outside, a light drizzle fell. As he debated the merits of going to bed immediately or joining his shift for a bite to eat, three more ambulances arrived, clattering to a stop a dozen steps away from where he stood. Orderlies quickly unloaded wounded men and carried them inside. A damp, olive drab blanket covered each man.

A hollow growl rumbled through his stomach.

As he trudged toward the mess hall, the prospect of an armistice and a world at peace seemed distant and remote.

53

"Are you not in pain, *mon ami*?" Anna said in a soft, soothing voice.

Margaret studied Gurney's ashen face. A few hours ago doctors had amputated what remained of his left leg, leaving a heavily bandaged stub an inch or two below the hip socket. A nurse came by to offer morphia, but Gurney had sent her away, saying he needed to remain alert for a little while longer.

He looked at Anna and a weak smile crossed his face. "It seems I'm slowly being whittled away. How fitting."

Anna placed a straw into a glass of water and raised his head. After Gurney took a small sip she eased him back onto the pillow and dabbed his lips with a small white cloth.

"You make jokes, even now?" she chided good-naturedly.

"Why not? Fretting will do no good. I've seen my condition many times in others. So have you. We both know the sepsis has progressed too far. Taking my leg was a futile gesture. My hash is already settled."

It was true, Margaret thought. She retrieved a handkerchief from her purse and lightly dabbed both cheeks. Army doctors held little hope for Gurney's survival. After weeks of little to no improvement, his physical decline had been swift and calamitous. The amputation was a last attempt to grasp at fading hope for his survival. Soon, Gurney Shaw would join the millions who had died before him.

A familiar melancholy arose inside Margaret's chest, a deep ache she'd felt often since learning of Michael's death. So many fine young men had been lost—her brother, then poor Jack Mayo, and now Michael's best friend—all dead or dying. The entire human race had gone berserk, consuming itself like a frenzied horde of starving cannibals.

"There is always hope," Anna offered.

Margaret could not help thinking about Robert. His work in an Evacuation Hospital was certainly less hazardous than duties on the battlefield, but such was no guarantee. The Germans routinely dropped bombs and explosive artillery shells on allied medical facilities, exactly as had happened to Jack.

But Anna was right: One must always have hope.

"Not this time," Gurney rasped.

"You must not give up," Anna told him.

"I seldom do. But a man must also accept reality, no matter how unpleasant. Anyway, I'm glad the three of you are here. There is something I must tell you about Michael and myself. Something I should have told you long before now."

Margaret's fingers tightened into fists. *Please, God. No more secrets.*

With infinite tenderness, Anna blotted perspiration from Gurney's forehead. "Of course, you must. But not now; tomorrow, when you are feeling better."

"Anna, dear. We both know I will not be feeling better. I am a liar and a coward but please allow me one last opportunity to say what I must. What I have waited too long to reveal."

"Dear Gurney. You are sometimes foolish, like now, but you are not a coward."

"Oh, but I am. And my cowardice probably caused Michael's death."

Time seemed to stop abruptly. A heavy, suffocating silence filled the room. Dust motes hung suspended in mid-air, trapped by a golden sunbeam. Margaret realized she had a death grip on her silk handkerchief. She forced herself to relax, taking in measured breaths of air while her mind searched for a response.

But Anna spoke first. "The *Boche* killed Michael, like they have so many others."

"True enough, but listen to me. Michael was a good man, kind and brave, but did you ever wonder why he changed so abruptly... why he seemed to close himself off from everyone, especially me?"

A great, crushing weight seemed to press on Margaret's shoulders. "What do you mean?"

Anna looked at Margaret. "Pay him no mind. It is the drug that speaks."

But Margaret persisted, unable to leave the question unanswered. "Why did he close himself off?" she repeated in a softer tone.

Gurney's eyes seemed to focus on a point in space somewhere between himself and Margaret. "I did something unspeakable, and then I asked Michael to become a part of it. He was horrified and angry and nearly shattered by grief, but he agreed. He agreed because I was his best friend. But the price of keeping such a damnable secret was too steep for him to pay."

"Unspeakable? What are you saying?" Anna asked.

Gurney's eyes moistened. "I killed a man."

Anna seemed to relax. "But every soldier kills, *mon ami*. That is the grim truth of war."

Gurney shook his head, a movement restricted by the flat pillow. "This was not a random killing on the battlefield. Nor was it a matter of survival. No, I committed murder—killed a French soldier—right here in Paris, on the Quai de Passy."

Margaret remembered several odd passages from Michael's

journal—brief entries in which he expressed anguish and anger over an incident he could not reveal. Was Gurney's crime the cause of Michael's grief?

Anna leaned back, her expression quizzical. "This cannot be."

Gurney's eyes refocused. "Sadly, it is."

"This soldier you say you killed," Anna said, her voice hesitant, searching for words. "Who was he? And why would you do such a bad thing?"

"Now we come to the bitter heart of the matter," Gurney replied, hoarsely. "The man I killed was Michael's good friend, a soldier named Aubray."

"I do not understand," Anna said. "You make no sense."

"Please listen," Gurney replied. "Please hear me out. Michael was in the field tending to this officer's wounded men when a German shell landed nearby. They ended up side by side in this very hospital, recuperating. It was here that their friendship began and blossomed."

"When did this occur?" Anna's voice had taken on an edge.

"Last spring," Gurney replied, "in late April."

"I remember," Anna whispered. "That was when I first met Michael. I also remember the man next to him. They seemed to like each other."

Margaret looked at Gurney. "Tell us what happened."

Gurney took several breaths before answering. "You see, I had a lady friend—Lizette. We were… close. Unfortunately, she was also married… to Michael's friend Aubray… to the man I killed."

Margaret felt color rise in her face. She looked from side to side, wanting to be someplace else, anywhere but in this room where death hovered, waiting to claim its next victim. She did not want to hear the sordid details of an illicit affair nor bear witness to a dying man's last confession. Turning, she stole a quick glance at Beatrice, whose wide-eyed expression reflected mild shock but also intense interest.

Gurney's eyes turned to Anna, his sweat-sheened face a silent plea for understanding.

Anna's posture had become rigid. "You kept shameful company with the wife of another soldier...a man who was also Michael's friend? I do not believe it."

"It's true, Anna. But, at the time, I did not know she was married to Michael's friend. She'd used a different last name. Only when confronted by Aubray did I discover that Lizette had not been truthful with me. Nor, I found out later, had she been truthful with several other soldiers."

Anna nodded. "There are such women... and men. War, I think, brings out the best and worst in all of us."

"Perhaps," Gurney admitted. "But that does not excuse my crime."

"Please go on," Margaret said, now more curious than revolted.

She had learned so much about Michael, had gained insights into his character that alternately surprised and disappointed her. Margaret also realized that some of what she had learned about her brother should not have surprised her—it had been there all along but she did not have eyes to see it. Was her blindness a self-inflicted malady?

In hindsight she should have been more perceptive, should have relied less on their imperfect fraternal bond. But concealing a *murder*? How could anyone possibly suspect that Michael would be party to such a thing?

Gurney said: "Margaret, you visited our facility on Rue Raynouard, did you not?"

"Yes, that was where we first met Colonel Andrews and learned Michael was buried at Suresnes."

"Do you remember how the mansion's long back lawn slopes

down toward the Quai de Passy?"

"Yes, of course."

"I worked late that night, making one last check on my ambulances. Our three-day leave was up and my detachment was returning to the field the next morning. Before turning in I decided to take a stroll along the quay. On that particular night however, I had company.

"Aubray saw me leave their apartment earlier that evening. It seems he waited in darkness while I inspected my ambulances. He then followed me down to the quay, keeping to the shadows.

"That's where he confronted me; that's where he told me I had ruined his life. He was a bit drunk and his uniform looked like he'd slept in it. And tears ran down both cheeks as he spoke." Gurney paused, blinked several times, and then continued. "I was shocked by the news. This man was Michael's friend! We'd never actually met, but I knew the name. Michael had spoken kindly of him often. I tried to explain to Aubray that I did not know Lizette was his wife, but he called me a liar. That's when he pointed a pistol at me. He must have had it the entire time, either behind him or at his side. It was dark. I never noticed it until that moment. Then I suppose instinct took over. Everything happened in a blur. I heard a muffled shot and then I was looking down at his body."

"So it was an act to protect yourself from harm, not a murder," Anna said.

"Possibly, up to that point. But what I did next changed everything."

Anna frowned. "You ran away?"

"Yes, but not before I threw the pistol into the Seine and straightened out the man's body."

"Straightened out the body? What are you trying to say," Anna asked.

Gurney's breath caught several times before he was able to continue. "Aubray looked so crumpled, so empty. I had robbed this man of his life, yes; but I also did something almost as bad. I had stolen his dignity, his honor, his self-respect. That's why I could not bear to leave him that way—twisted, arms splayed, his legs folded awkwardly. Lieutenant Aubray deserved better, but all I could do for him then was to rearrange his corpse."

"But why was it necessary to involve our brother Michael?" Margaret asked.

"For selfish reasons, of course. I needed an alibi. French authorities can be forgiving when a husband surrenders to passionate rage and kills his wife's lover. But they have no sympathy for the cad who kills a husband—a decorated soldier, no less.

"Michael knew nothing about Lizette and me. No matter. Fearing the worst, I confessed everything to him. He was thunderstruck by his friend's death, of course; but doubly so by my admission of guilt, and once again by my affair with Lizette. I have never seen such torment in a man; desperate pain that I alone caused. It was then that Michael's entire demeanor changed. Silent tears streamed down his cheeks and his body seemed to shrivel and collapse within itself. And then I made matters even worse. I asked, and he reluctantly agreed, to help me avoid the guillotine.

"When the police investigated, Michael remained true to his word but I cannot imagine what he felt. Nevertheless, he provided me with the alibi I needed; verified my presence at a café, miles away, the two of us enjoying our last evening in Paris before returning to the front. He lied to the police on my behalf; betrayed one friend for the sake of another."

Margaret was finding it difficult to breathe.

"When did this happen?" Anna asked.

"Earlier this year, on the ninth of February, a date I shall never forget."

Anna nodded. "Nearly one year after Michael and I met."

"Yes," Gurney said. "Michael was first wounded in April of '17. He suffered wounds a second time in January of '18."

"He had a visitor then," Anna said, her voice sounding as though it came from far away. "I remember a well-dressed French officer, the same young man who occupied the bed next to Michael when he was first wounded. I was grateful at the time because they laughed a lot, enjoying each other's company. It helped Michael forget his wound for a little while." She turned and stared at Gurney. "Michael proposed to me not long after you killed his friend, yet he never spoke of it."

"How could he?" Gurney replied through teeth clamped shut.

"I was his wife," Anna replied. "I should have known." Then her expression became wary. "If you had indeed murdered his friend, then why were you best man at our wedding. That does not seem appropriate."

"He had no choice," Gurney explained. "If I were not in his wedding, you would have raised a question. Michael had lied on my account once. He did not want to deceive you as well, nor did he want to arouse your curiosity by barring me from your wedding. Rather than lie again, he chose to keep it all inside, and that's why he felt compelled to risk his life."

Another tremor rippled through Margaret's body. "What do you mean?"

"Don't you see? Michael had found and married Anna, a woman he loved. He desperately wanted to live, to spend the rest of his life with her, but he couldn't... not yet." Gurney seemed to have trouble breathing and his body strained against the sheets. He closed his eyes and slowly inhaled several times.

From another part of the ward John McCormack's tenor voice

floated from the golden horn of a Gramophone…

Little girl don't cry
I must say goodbye…

The music triggered a series of revelations inside Margaret's head. One by one they illuminated what she had sensed but not understood until this very moment.

Gurney opened his eyes. He began to speak again, but she already knew what he was going to say.

"Michael had found love with Anna, but he had also betrayed a dear friend, had lied to the police about the circumstances of his death. Although he wanted to live, he also became obsessed with saving as many lives as possible. He refused to leave even a single wounded man on the battlefield, regardless of the danger. Bombs, bullets, gas—none of those dangers mattered. Before I forced him to live with an impossible situation, Michael was brave but never foolhardy. But, probably because of what he did for me, he became a lunatic when it came to rescuing soldiers, taking risks no sane man would consider. I believe Michael was trying to atone for his part in keeping my secret."

"Of course he was," Margaret added.

Michael despised war but his respect for soldiers came through in the many letters he wrote to Margaret and the family. His admiration for their sacrifices was boundless, reenforcing his determination to help those who faced and fought the enemy.

"Yet," Margaret continued, "because of what he had to do for you, he was now an accomplice in the murder of his dear friend. It seems to me that Michael's careless disregard for his own life was his way to lighten the awful burden you placed on his shoulders. Michael thought that if he rescued enough men from the battlefield he might repudiate his betrayal and perhaps save himself from God's judgment. Only then could he earn the right to a happy life with Anna."

"Yes, yes," Gurney wheezed, "That's it exactly. My crime and selfish demand for his loyalty was an unbearable torment that drove him to take such risks."

He paused, gathering waning strength for one last effort, and his eyes locked onto Margaret's.

"And that is the real reason I intercepted your father's cable. You see, the Army will always try to return a soldier's remains back home for burial, particularly when accompanied by next-of-kin. Your father's cable told me he intended to do exactly that. I made it my business to carry out Michael's last request exactly as he wrote in the codicil. After what he did for me, and for what I did to him, I had no other choice."

Gurney shuddered and his body tensed; then he relaxed and his jaw sagged. The long confession seemed to have exhausted him.

Was it possible? Margaret asked herself. Was the unintentional killing of Michael's friend by Gurney Shaw the cause for so much grief? If so—and she had no reason to doubt what she'd been told—then Gurney may indeed have been responsible for Michael's uncharacteristic secrecy, and probably the indirect cause of his death.

And, she admitted reluctantly, if she believed that of Gurney, then she must also acknowledge the unpleasant fact that her brother Michael had been a tormented accomplice in the concealment of murder.

Was she prepared to accept that?

Slowly, like the irresistible pressure of water as one sank to the bottom of a deep pool, all the unforeseen revelations about Michael settled upon her shoulders. With it came sad acceptance of the obvious: no human being could truly fathom the mind of another, no matter how close they might be. In one fleeting moment of ageless wisdom and mental clarity, she also realized that even the noblest soul bore secret dishonesties—faint smudges of petty deceits accumulated over an imperfect lifetime.

It was an unwelcome insight into the human character and a terribly frightening one as well. She now understood that God would measure each soul not only by principles of goodness and grace, sin and shortcoming, but also by the secrets it carried.

"You must rest now," Anna said, gently blotting perspiration from Gurney's bloodless face. "Go to sleep."

"I am so sorry," he rasped, his liquid gaze fixing on each woman as he spoke. "Please forgive me."

"Yes, of course we do," Anna soothed. "But it is better you should rest for a little while."

Gurney closed his eyes and a long tear slid from the corner of one onto the damp pillow.

> *But if fight here we must*
> *Then in God is our trust*
> *So, send me away with a smile....*

Margaret twisted her silk handkerchief as the song ended. Had Michael's unbearably painful inner conflict—agony fed by concealment of a friend's murder—caused her brother's death? If so, then how could she possibly forgive Gurney? Although racked by mental anguish, the answer was clear. Yes, she must. If she could not forgive the soul-damning transgressions of a repentant man dying of his wounds—Michael's best friend—then she would never be able to rise above her own deficiencies.

Despite an earlier silent prayer about not wanting to hear any more secrets, Margaret understood that concealing certain truths—

lying by omission?—was sometimes necessary to preserve an otherwise pleasant memory.

She turned and spoke to Beatrice. "Mother and Father must never hear about this. They—all of us—have suffered enough. Promise me you will remain silent."

Beatrice nodded. "I promise."

Margaret looked at Anna.

"I agree," Anna said. "It is best to keep this among ourselves."

Gurney expelled a long, rattling breath. No more followed. As his lifeless body relaxed, it appeared to sink deeper into the narrow hospital cot.

How odd, Margaret thought, easing her grip on the handkerchief.

Unburdening his conscience had made Gurney's frail body appear heavier, not lighter as one might presume. He had asked and received their forgiveness but perhaps Gurney was still unable to forgive himself, thus choosing to carry the burden of his mortal sin through all eternity.

54

Fernand Raux opened the familiar dog-eared folder—for the last time, he believed—and wondered again about life's random and unpredictable occurrences.

His original theory regarding the murder of Lieutenant Guy Jean Aubray, an idea formed many months ago, had been correct. The unfortunate Lieutenant had met death at the hands of another soldier—a fellow officer posted to the American Ambulance Field Service headquarters located on the hill above the Quai de Passy.

A sad smile touched the corners of his mouth. Sometimes, he reflected, the solution to a crime resulted from an otherwise good man's troubled conscience yearning to free itself from guilt.

Raux shook loose a Gauloises and lit it with a wooden match.

Was Lieutenant Gurney Ambrose Shaw truly a good man? Raux blew smoke toward the ceiling. Except for one deadly response to preserve his own life, the answer seemed to be yes. According to his military record, Lieutenant Shaw had rescued numerous *poilus* at the risk of his own, removing dozens of wounded French soldiers from the battlefield and then driving them to hospitals. The *Croix de Guerre* numbered among his decorations.

Yet, all those selfless accomplishments could not erase the fact that Shaw had been responsible for the death of Lieutenant Aubray. The letter Raux had received that morning—hand written, dated and signed by Shaw weeks ago—left little cause for doubt. The letter

414

describing Aubray's killing matched exactly those details contained in the file. Raux also believed the French officer's death was unintentional—an act of self-defense—an opinion based on his own religious belief. Why would Shaw, a man who had truly gotten away with murder, freely confess to the crime? Telling a deathbed lie made no sense. To Raux, the letter rang true.

Apparently Shaw had written his confession soon after suffering an amputation due to a serious leg wound. According to a hospital nurse, the American knew he was dying and had posted the letter shortly before his death. Ironically, Gurney Shaw's corpse now lay in a grave indistinguishable from that of the man he had killed.

Still, Raux knew this unfortunate case was far from unique. Human history echoed many such instances and the lesson was clear: a single corrupt act, regardless of intent, can destroy a lifetime of good work.

Raux took the letter and placed it inside the folder. Then he took his pen and added the following note to the file: *See enclosed letter. Confessed killer deceased. No further investigation necessary.*

He dated and initialed the note, then closed the file.

One last detail remained: the drafting of a factual but discreetly worded *communiqué* for the local newspapers. Something to the effect that Lieutenant Aubray died as a result of an unfortunate quarrel between himself and Lieutenant Shaw, an American ambulance driver who had confessed to the unintentional crime shortly before succumbing to his own wounds.

Raux would make no mention of Madame Aubray, the faithless wife turned whore, a woman herself murdered. That particular crime remained unsolved but everyone suspected the pimp whom she had stabbed during a previous drunken episode. Obviously resentful of the knife wound, Pacu Mirković—the whoremaster in question—had no doubt taken his revenge and then tossed Madame Aubray's lifeless body into the Seine where policemen discovered it several days later.

Since there were no witnesses or other evidence to prove Mirković's guilt, it would serve no purpose to sully the French officer's reputation by revealing all those sordid details. Let people draw their own conclusions. Raux would not contribute to their prurient speculations. Eventually the criminal Mirković would run afoul of the law and justice would prevail, perhaps not in full, but sufficiently.

Satisfied, he took another puff from his Gauloises and turned toward the window.

It was raining again.

Epilogue

Nice, Côte d'Azur, France
January 1919

Robert and Margaret ambled slowly along the Promenade des Anglais, smiling at each other every now and then, arm in arm under bright sunshine. In the distance, Mont Boron rose gently from the blue sea, its winter-faded green hillside dotted with sparkling pink and white villas overlooking the Bay of Angels. They were among many who comprised the Sunday afternoon crowd strolling along the wide avenue. No one appeared in a hurry and unseasonably mild weather seemed to lift everyone's mood.

Walking toward them Butler saw a gaily-dressed woman snuggled into a long neck fur, chuckling at some witticism uttered by her companion, a rakishly attired gentleman in formal afternoon wear. Another couple followed close behind, also smiling and similarly dressed, the soft trill of their laughter rising and falling as they passed alongside. Almost everyone seemed happy and energetic. That wasn't surprising. The signing of the Armistice eight weeks ago had returned the wealthy to their grand villas, allowing the French Riviera to again become a guiltless playground.

The war's end notwithstanding, the beginning of each New Year also brought with it a sense of optimism—an opportunity to write a new page in the journal of their lives—hopefully one with fewer cross-outs and smudges than those preceding it.

Well-dressed civilians were clearly in the majority so those in comparatively drab military uniforms stood out from the array of smiling faces garbed in fashionable mufti. Butler took special note of the wounded: a one-armed French captain with icy blue eyes; a thin British officer sitting on a stone bench, coughing politely into a pink-stained handkerchief; a blind *poilu* on the arm of a solemn young girl, his cane tucked under his arm like a riding crop; a gray-faced American aviator leaning heavily on wooden crutches as he passed by, his breath coming in short, soft gasps. Butler, also in uniform, met the eyes of each soldier, whether injured or whole. Most acknowledged him with a quick smile or nod; a few stared through him as though he did not exist.

The Great War was over. The living celebrated, the casualties brooded, and the dead lay silent beneath a hundred fallow wheat fields.

He had survived the worst man-man cataclysm in history, emerging unscathed while so many millions had not. God, fate, or good fortune had seen him through, spared him so that he could walk erect beside the woman he loved, to enjoy her company without fear of shot, shell, or marauding aeroplanes.

Butler thought about Jack Mayo, a fine young man who had carried no lucky token. Jack's shattered body lay moldering in a soggy hole near Chery-Chartreuve, his identity scratched into a small wooden shingle. The shabby marker was an excruciating outrage, a constant source of anguish that darkened Butler's mood.

Thankfully, that gross indignity would not continue much longer. There were ambitious plans afoot to exhume soldiers whose graves now filled scores of nameless plots scattered across Flanders and Picardy—to re-inter their remains in permanent locations specifically reserved for war dead, a belated but proper burial ceremony complete with individual headstones. Butler and Margaret would return to France for dedication services. To do otherwise had never occurred to either.

A few minutes before one o'clock they left the promenade, crossed the boulevard, and stepped into the marble-floored lobby of the Hotel Beau-Rivage. Once seated inside the bustling restaurant they ordered *bouillabaisse* and *pissaladiere*—a savory fish stew accompanied by an onion and anchovy pie—along with a bottle of Sancerre from the Loire Valley.

The wine was poured, tasted, and poured again.

Although he gladly accepted his elegant surroundings as real, they nevertheless exuded a bizarre quality, much like an eerily lifelike dream. He recognized the psychological symptoms from his readings and understood that his mind had not wholly caught up with the reality of peacetime. Part of him still wandered grim battlefields littered with the dead, the dying, and the gruesomely injured; another peered into dimly lit hospital tents stacked high with amputated limbs; and still another tended gangrenous wounds reeking with the stench of moldering flesh and rotten cabbages.

He had treated hundreds of wounded men and saved many from death, but that seemed of little consequence now. What troubled him most was the persistent memory of his dismal conduct toward one specific soldier, a man bent backwards in half, his lips forming a silent plea for help as rats gnawed at his insides, a sight so repulsive that Butler had fled the scene in horror. Staring at his wine he knew that singular image—and his cowardly abandonment of a soldier in need—would haunt his memories for as long as he lived.

Self-conscious, he looked up from his wine.

Margaret was studying him, a mixture of love, concern, and empathy swirling through her clear blue eyes. She seemed more at ease now than when they had first met aboard ship. Her smile was quicker, a laugh or chuckle more easily coaxed from her. He hoped he was the cause for a little of her apparently more tranquil mood. Some, he knew, came from the difficult but satisfactory conclusion of the sad duty she had come here to fulfill. Butler had no doubt that Margaret continued to mourn her brother's death. Given the opportunity, he would attempt to ease some of her unspoken pain.

He eyed the engagement ring adorning her left hand. They planned to marry soon after their return to the United States, and then live in St. Louis. Since he was without close personal ties in New York or Cambridge, making his home in the Midwest did not concern him. On the contrary, the prospect of peace—of living a life of quiet normalcy, Margaret by his side—seemed more dreamlike than real. Despite the nagging memory of his wartime failures, Butler considered himself the luckiest man on Earth.

An odd thought popped into his mind. His parents' death aside, the worst and best things that had ever happened to him had occurred during one long agonizing season in an ancient part of the world.

"Are you feeling all right?" she asked.

He smiled. "Yes, just a little bone weary, that's all."

She reached across the table and covered his hand with hers. "Yes, I see that, but what else?"

"I love you."

"And I love you too, Robert. Now please answer my question. What is it that still troubles you?"

He looked away for a moment, his eyes focused somewhere between Margaret and the far wall, searching for words to describe the somber fury he sometimes felt, not only for his shortcomings as a military surgeon, but also for an inept monarchy who had failed to anticipate the consequences of their own witlessness.

That small gaggle of arrogant fools had ignited humanity's most devastating conflict, a war that had consumed millions of lives. It had also compelled Butler to see himself as someone other than a noble healer, condemning him to view the world as it was, not as he hoped it might be. Like a stubborn child, he had been force-fed dose after dose of reality, a bitter medicine that cured him of comfortable ignorance.

The war had also driven him to make cruel choices. Despite his personal belief, Butler had indeed administered a lethal dose of narcotic to a mortally wounded soldier rather than leave him untended to die in agony. How many other surgeons had made similar decisions; how many had likewise broken their sacred oath to 'first do no harm'? Were lofty ideals merely an illusion—a grinning theatrical mask that concealed an ugly truth?

Like the mask, Butler's melancholy introspection had an opposite side.

Along with the subdued rage he harbored for those who had plunged the world into the most catastrophic war in human history, Butler also felt a warm, powerful affection for every soldier who answered the call to duty; for those who served and suffered and died in nameless places far from home; and for those who nursed wounds by day and dreaded the coming of night. Soldiers like those quiet casualties on the Promenade des Anglais—men who had prematurely exchanged youthful dreams for an old man's nightmares: a scarred battalion not unlike those long ranks of gray-bearded Civil War veterans moving slowly down Rochester's main street during that long-ago summer before his life changed forever.

Those two conflicting emotions—anger and affection—vied for supremacy, a psychological conflict that almost always ended in restless stalemate. He searched his brain for the right phrases to answer Margaret's question, but could find none to explain his dilemma. He began to suspect that adequate words did not yet exist in any human-language dictionary. Perhaps they never would.

He was about to confess his inability to articulate those feelings when a nearly forgotten stanza from his favorite hymn resurfaced from deep memory, words he had sung many times as a boy standing between his parents, their voices joined in soaring melody.

Time, like an ever-rolling stream,
Bears all its sons away;
They fly, forgotten, as a dream
Dies at the opening day.

The old hymn filled Butler with a profound sense of destiny, of his generation's special niche in history; a wistfully brief appearance in the still unfolding drama of human existence. Seared by war, they had survived a terrible hour, long moments trembling with medieval barbarism and eye-shattering images; ordeals that forever granted membership into a neglected fraternity of kindred souls.

Butler knew he could never abandon those with whom he had once served, nor could they forsake him, for in so doing each would deny the reality of their shared agonies. Worst of all, denial would forever tarnish the memory of those who lay in sodden graves—good men like Jack Mayo and Rotelli and Hanssen—strangers who became his brothers; men he admired and loved and then buried in a desolate field near Chery-Chartreuve.

He felt tears gathering in his eyes and quickly blinked them away, embarrassed by the sudden clutch of emotion.

He turned and met Margaret's patient gaze.

"I don't want to forget them," he told her. "None of them. Not ever."

Margaret squeezed his hand. The warmth in her blue eyes told him she fully understood what he was unable to form into meaningful words.

"I would be disappointed if you did," she replied.

THE END

CPSIA information can be obtained
at www.ICGtesting.com
Printed in the USA
BVHW031720170123
656451BV00004B/35